Loosely Based

a novel

by Storey Clayton

"Loosely Based," by Storey Clayton. ISBN 1-58939-409-7 (softcover), 1-58939-410-0 (electronic).

Published 2003 by Virtualbookworm.com Publishing Inc., P.O. Box 9949, College Station, TX , 77842, US. ©2003 Storey Clayton. All rights reserved. No part of this publication may be reproduced, stored in a retrieval system, or transmitted in any form or by any means, electronic, mechanical, recording or otherwise, without the prior written permission of Storey Clayton.

Manufactured in the United States of America

For my parents,
who taught me to read
and gave me my voice.

<u>CONTENTS</u>

PROLOGUE

LOGICAL PROOF

Premise One: **Life imitates art.**

Premise Two: **Art imitates life.**

Conclusion: **Life imitates life.**

TOPEKA

Matt Norton had spent the better part of his life in Topeka, Kansas, though he was far from convinced of this. He had found his four years at the local high school to be marked by unending drudgery of a magnitude that could only be trumped by the surrounding state. In both cases, the people were boring. There was less corn in his classroom, though, and this provided a break from the monotony of the rest of Kansas.

His parents had also, for a time, provided a break from Kansan monotony, though that had not been wholly positive. By the time they finally decided to leave each other alone, Matt had learned to ignore the yelling. It too had gained a tedious quality, tempered only by the unpredictability of certain shrieks or bellows. This required turning up the television, which would not uncommonly incur a louder response from his parents. It seemed they got along best when they both weren't getting along with him. He had no siblings with which to share this burden.

This meant that, when the split came, he had to be an equal part of it. Neither of his parents could bring themselves to face a custody battle, so they agreed to haul him back and forth like so many ears of corn. This necessitated that both of them remain in relative proximity to each other, which saved them the game of chicken that would be created by one of them leaving town. So they negotiated schedules and addresses and holidays. They were forced to treat each other rationally, which was a refreshing surprise to all parties. They almost got back together.

Storey Clayton

"They won't even fight over me," Matt told his friend Sam one night after his fourteenth birthday party. The party had been held at Sam's, since Matt's house was in no condition to host anything but a meager truce. "It's like neither of them can deal with having me all the time, so they're fighting over who *doesn't* have me."

Sam had been skeptical about this, but kept it to himself. "Yeah, that sucks," was Sam's stirring rebuttal to Matt's analysis of the situation.

So the split was his fourteenth birthday present, and though there was an attempted overcompensation via material goods, Matt was mostly grateful for being able to listen to the TV again at a reasonable volume. Though now he had two TV's with which to contend, and two of just about everything else. He started calling himself the Double Agent, to amuse himself, and almost let this slip to Sam, who he was sure would have said "Yeah, that's cool." Sam was certainly not much of a break from the cornfed Kansan routine.

After an afternoon of reading through *Calvin and Hobbes* comic books (a complete set after his fourteenth birthday extravaganza), Matt would one-up Calvin's antics by reciting his mundane actions to himself. "The steely Double Agent, though loyal to the Mom Brigade, will now attempt to con a tunafish sandwich from the Dad Crew." Then he'd inch away from his room (Dad's place), slide along the hallway to the kitchen/dining room/living room. His father would look up from his magazine, smile, and ask him if he wanted some PB&J. ("Oh no! A daring attempt at counter-espionage! But our hero will not be thwarted...") After negotiations which often lasted as long as fifteen seconds ("A taxing struggle against the forces of evil"), a tunafish sandwich would be procured and, the day won, the hero would scurry back to his room. "Our Double Agent is victorious again, friends," he would say, almost audibly, to himself. "He will always remain loyal to the Mom Brigade," dramatic pause for effect, timed perfectly, "or *will he*?!"

Needless to say, Matt was always more loyal to the parent that wasn't around. Like any good Double Agent, he was sacrificing present comforts for future goals. The future just kept becoming the present before he could straighten out a plan. After all, it was just a game, and one he had stolen at that.

There wasn't much else he needed to steal. His parents, both being doctors, were good at competing for his attentions through financial means. His Dad, who threw himself into his surgical practice after the divorce, lived humbly but showered Matt with gifts. His Mom, a pediatrician, had more time on her hands, filling the old oversized house with gadgets for his entertainment. It unnerved her that he still took more interest in the television than the computer or stereo, but he spent enough time meandering through all of them to allay her. Neither parent was home much, and they both were pretty sure that stuff would be more fun than they were.

As a result, Matt went through high school fairly lonely. Sam was over a lot of the time, but he seemed more interested in Matt's stuff than he did in Matt. That worked out well, though, since Matt wasn't paying much attention to the stuff anyway. A typical Saturday would consist of Matt flipping channels while Sam played video games on his computer. Occasionally they'd yell at each other from one room to the next. "New high score!" Sam would call, to no immediate response.

After a few minutes Matt would ask "You wanna watch *Simpsons* reruns?"

Amidst the rapid pounding of keys "Naww" would come back from Sam.

With the backdrop of Sam's friendship, which had gone on so long that he didn't know what else to look for in a friend, or even that he could have more than one friend, Matt became accustomed to loneliness. He was brighter than he should have been for the time he spent in front of the tube, as if he were only half-absorbing its endless drone, while the useful half of his brain was coming up with something intriguing. He constantly questioned his life for its lack of intrigue. His parents had managed to convince him that high school would be the dawn of intrigue, but that had turned out as promisingly as most of his parents' promises. The only advantage high school offered was that Social Studies was no longer just about Kansas anymore.

Matt had always known there was something beyond the borders of Kansas, but as yet his only experience with that had been a trip to Kansas City. His parents had so little time off from work, especially coordinated time off, that travel was not an aspect of the Norton lifestyle. But when Matt was twelve, his parents both got some vacation time in late August to go to Kansas City and watch the Royals play the New York Yankees.

7

Storey Clayton

The entire trip had seemed so exotic that Matt could barely sit still for a week before the trip. Between his antsiness and his parents' continual distraction, none of them realized prior to their arrival at Kauffman Stadium that there was a baseball strike, let alone that this meant the cancellation of their travel plans. The trip ended up amounting to aimless wandering through downtown Kansas City, culminating in the inevitable fight between his parents. As Matt recalled, it had been primarily about parking.

Suddenly, however, the non-Kansas landscape had opened up to him in sophomore History. It wasn't even called Social Studies. Sure, he'd been raised more on TV than corn, but that carried with it a level of surreality that made his life bearable. Most of what he watched were cartoons, even into high school, and those were no more about real places outside of Kansas than the *Wizard of Oz*. When he delved into shows with human actors, or ventured to the Topeka movie theater, usually with one or the other parent, they always hit him like cartoons. The actions of the people depicted were equally sensible, and their reactions just as exaggerated. The lives lived by television people were exciting, which made them worth watching, but impossible to relate to. James Bond was just Calvin daydreaming. Jerry Seinfeld was merely a witty Homer Simpson. The cast of *Friends* was about as aware of their surroundings as Coyote was, five feet deep into a lofty airwalk. All of them entertained, but only because of how much more fun they had than Matt.

Mr. Riordan, Matt's sophomore American History teacher, was not entertaining. The class text, however, was just as exciting as television, but carried with it a gravity absent in cartoons. There was no denying the reality of the stories told therein. From the Underground Railroad to Pearl Harbor, people had lived and died and been *interesting*. Even more to the point, they had existed in a strange netherworld between Kansas and surreality that must have been the rest of the country. The country! Prior to this year, there had only been a flag and a pledge and the game of baseball. And corn.

Sophomore year became Matt's own American Revolution. Punctuated by Sam's family abruptly moving to Philadelphia in December, Matt acquired a renewed awareness of everything, but especially the United States. His friend's move was confirmation of what he had always known: Kansas is the epicenter of nothing. What he now knew to back this up was that there were places outside of Kansas. Geography, like a bridge to salvation, extended its welcome and Matt was ready to walk.

"Mom, can we move?"

"What's wrong, hon? Don't you like the stuff I give you?"

"No, it's not that. It's, well, I've been reading about history. There's a whole country out there beyond this state. Beyond Topeka. Why don't we ever go there?"

"You know I have to work. I work hard so you, so *we* can have all these things. Do you know how hard I have to work?"

"Mom, I'm not, no, you're missing the point. It's just, I want to see America."

"Kansas is the *heart* of America. I grew up here. You grew up here. What's wrong with Kansas?"

"Well, it's no Philadelphia."

"Oh, I see. This is about your friend moving, isn't it? What was his name, Dan? Sam? Something like that. I get him mixed up with all my patients. I still don't know why the MacDonalds went to Dr. Levine. It's like they didn't trust me. And now you don't trust me either; you want to go to Philadelphia with the MacDonalds. I know it's hard, Matty, but there'll be other friends."

Matt winced every time his Mom called him Matty. "I don't have other friends." This was purely for dramatic effect, and had nothing to do with his point.

"Would you like to call him? Would that make you feel better?"

"Um."

"Here, we'll dial information right now. Philadelphia?"

This was a tough one for Matt. Thinking over it, he couldn't remember ever just talking to Sam. This was a burden greater than staying in Kansas. Phone calls had always been practical five-second planning sessions; the idea of a conversation on a phone was impalpable. "Never mind. I want to *see* Philadelphia, Mom. I want to see Independence Hall."

"Independence indeed. You'll have plenty of that soon enough. For now, you can go look it up on the computer. While you live under this roof, you can be happy with Kansas."

Matt fared no better with his father. Both of his parents seemed to be too mired in human geography to look to the greater landscape with anything but scorn. Their understanding was microscopic, a vision that had been passed on to their son until

Storey Clayton

Mr. Riordan distributed copies of a history text to his eager tenth graders. Matt would remember the day as prison inmates recall a jailbreak. Now he had an outside world to contend with, and he was just realizing the nature of the prison to which he'd been confined.

Matt was not exactly remembering that day while he was confined to another space, just thirty-three months later. While not precisely a prison, his movements were certainly constricted therein, much to his consternation. Honda Civics were not designed to accommodate vast spans of physical human interaction within. Sitting and driving were what the Honda engineers had had in mind; Matt had quite another thing on his brain.

The girl was Catherine "Catie" Hanson, and though she spelled it with a C, she pronounced it with a K, so as to avoid the feline association. She signed her name with a heart capping her i and the flourish from the e doubling back to cross the t. She was on the Topeka High varsity soccer team. When Matt was a senior at the outset of their relationship, Catie was over two years his junior.

"You never take me anywhere romantic. You ever notice that? We're supposed to be looking out on a beautiful view, gently holding hands as the moon rises. We always end up back here. Haven't we spent *enough* time in school?"

Catie, in Matt's opinion, had an unnerving way of ignoring what she was doing, or at least of talking through it. He stopped moving his hands, which were under her shirt. "We aren't *in* school."

Catie rolled her eyes. "Oh Matthew." (Not as bad as "Matty", granted, but she sounded a bit motherly with this utterance.) "Don't quibble. And don't stop doing *that* either." He slowly obliged. "All I'm saying is, I wouldn't mind something different."

"Well, you'll be rid of me soon enough." This was not how he'd planned the evening at all. "Or you could just come visit me in college..." This was an idea he'd been pitching to her for the better part of a month.

"I'm not having this conversation with you, Matt. It's not my fault that Washburn isn't good enough for you. The *least* you could do is go to KU or K-State. What's so great about Harrison again?"

It's not in fucking Kansas, Matt thought, but he knew that

10

would come off sounding like he didn't want to be near her. A more subtle approach, perhaps: "It's in Pennsylvania. It's, as you say so much, *dif*ferent."

"Right. I guess they didn't have any openings at Moon State University. My bad."

He sighed. "Are you even en*joy*ing yourself?"

"It's my last night with you, babe. Do I have a choice?"

"Christ," he said, disengaging from her and turning to face the window. In their initial hurry, they were still in the front seat and Matt banged his elbow against the steering wheel as he turned. His move was the picture of awkwardness. His elbow smarted as Catie touched it.

"You okay?"

"After a comment like that? What am I to you, tax-deductible?"

"Hon*ey*..." He had never had the guts to tell her that he hated these conjugal sounding endearments. Matt. Plain old, one syllable, short and sweet. Was that so hard? "Don't be like that. It *is* your last night here. I want it to be special."

This couldn't help but perk his ears up, though he suspected they had differing views on what would make a special close to their relationship. But he was determined to pout. "Well act like it."

There was a suspended moment, and then she reached for his jeans zipper. He was still in a bad mood, though; this hardly made up for her earlier remark. He sighed in frustration, which Catie mistook for anticipation, and as she moved in, he opened the door. The interior lights flashed on to the tune of warning beeps; apparently the key was still in the ignition. "No. You can't just do that. It's not that easy. *I'm* not that easy. For Christ's sake, you tell *me* about *ro*mance."

He stepped into the warm night air, which was probably muggy but felt like a cool wind after fighting for oxygen in the Civic. He ducked his head to look back into the car, and it seemed like Catie was waiting it out. He wanted her to cry, but he knew better. He had never seen her cry. The closest he'd come was before they started dating, after she'd been blindsided in a soccer game and rolled her head into a bench. Even then, she'd looked more annoyed than sad. At this moment, contemplating her seeming heartlessness, he felt sure that what he'd taken for a tear at the time was simply well-placed sweat.

Storey Clayton

He was disappointed that, in the intervening time, he hadn't seen her sweat nearly as much as he would have preferred. The fact that she put a lot more effort into soccer than their relationship had dogged him for the whole six months, from their first date in mid-February to his Senior Prom to this last night before he fled Kansas (finally) for the hills of rural Pennsylvania. Kansas City had given him a bad taste for cities, not to mention that American History classes always gave them such a shameful aura. Good red-blooded Americans worked hard on the farm, while the nefarious squatters lazed in the cities, or worse yet, plotted the downfall of the agricultural economy. Such filth and squalor radiated from tales of the Industrial Revolution, not to mention Mr. Riordan's editorial commentary, that urbanity seemed something *worse* than Kansas, if that were possible. There may be something to *do* there, but nothing good.

So he'd turned his back on the Kansas public schools, along with exotic-sounding dens like Chicago and even old Philadelphia, with its Independence Hall. Instead, it would be Harrison College in Fifeburg, Pennsylvania. What could be more American than a college named for the ninth President in a town named for the sounds of the Revolutionary War? His Dad had been proud, even after he'd noted with some disdain that there was no such animal as a preMed major at Harrison. His Mom had never heard of Harrison, but the trusty Double Agent had assured himself that she had also never heard of William Henry Harrison or a drum and fife corps, and probably would place Pennsylvania somewhere west of what, Orion...?

He was searching the sky again, at once looking for and refusing to admit that he was looking for a shooting star. No problem seeing stars in Kansas, where there was barely enough artificial light to see the ground beneath one, flat as it may be. Catie was flat in all ways not topographical--she was unexcited about Harrison and had gone cold at nights ever since his decision to attend had been sealed.

He heard the car door slam. "Do you remember when we met?" It was halfway between bellowing and beseeching, as if she were forcing him to care, please.

"Um." This was really difficult. Did she mean when he'd first *noticed* her, or when they'd actually spoken? Or when she'd noticed him? Three things virtually unrelated indeed.

"The soccer game," she led him on, walking slowly over

12

towards him and nodding leftward across the parking lot, though he resisted looking her way. As if he needed to be reminded which way the field was; did he ever *not* think about her soccer games? "The game I sat out with my hamstring? The game I came up and sat with you? How I had to practically kick you before you'd say hel*lo*?" Her voice would raise with each inquiry, or maybe she was just getting closer. He felt like a freight train was closing in, derailed and whistling. "The first time we *ever spoke to each other*? The day it all started?!!"

She was sixteen and naive. "It all started" when he was her age and would stand behind the bleachers so she wouldn't see him at her JV soccer tryouts. She'd been at the school at least four days. He'd planned a meeting between them for fifteen months before she made it happen. The day it all *start*ed? Who was she kidding? She was probably about to say it had been a surreptitious bumping in the hall when the planets had aligned and the fates had smiled. "Yeah," he whispered. It was about two-thirds true, he figured. He was mostly thinking about that day, the day he'd spent three hours talking at Sam about the freshman girl with the half-and-half hair. (He *still* didn't know whether to call it brown or blonde.) But he could remember the day Catie meant too. He was lying because he didn't remember anything substantive *about* that day. He waited for her to expound.

"Oh yeah? What'd I say to you?"

"Hello."

She snorted. Okay, he is sort of right. "And...?"

"And," he repeated, not comprehending, transparently stalling. "How are you?"

"Oh Matthew." She looked the way his mother had looked the day he informed her that he had less interest in being a doctor than delivering mail. "And here I was, thinking you liked me."

He walked to the edge of the parking lot, about five paces from where they'd been standing next to each other, but not touching. There were some scraggly weeds growing between the asphalt and the chain-link fence beyond which was the practice field, followed in the distance by the all-purpose sports "stadium". He tore at a clump of weeds, picking up some leaves, then tearing at them delicately. He focused on each leaf, looking to shred it as thinly as possible before discarding the natural confetti, fluttering to the pavement. This pattern repeated several times as he spoke softly. "Can I tell you something?" Now or never, he thought, his

13

hands gently ripping.

She sighed audibly, shrugged invisibly, walked towards the chain-link, plopped herself against it with a rattle, and slid down to settle her seat in the weeds. She was diagonal from him, and would spend the next few minutes unsuccessfully trying to make eye-contact with him. This was as close to assent as he was going to receive.

"First Monday of school." He sounded like a reporter, telegraphing the details of a very vital description to his home office. The voice was even, definite. There were pauses where the "stop"s should have been, defining each fact for absorption. "Your first Monday of school. Here. Ever. There was a freshman team. You were better than that. You walked by a dorky-looking junior. He was waiting for the bus. You were going to the JV tryouts. He stopped waiting for the bus." It felt cinematic in his memory, like a dream where one could see oneself stepping off the ledge and falling to one's death.

"He followed you, keeping you just in sight, but he knew where you were going. You had checkered black soccer shorts on. You carried black-and-white cleats in your left hand. Your white shoes were untied, dragging the laces in the dirt. They were already dirty. Your hair was in a ponytail, tied with a purple scrunchie." (He had spent weeks repeating that word, he loved its sound and was thrilled by the very thought of her putting up her hair. She seemed surprised, though he didn't see this surprise, that he knew the word in the first place.) "You were wearing a faded T-shirt, white letters that had disappeared on a green background. Some logo too, for a rental car company. You walked at a perfect pace. Purposeful. Ready." This last part was more opinion than fact, but seemed equally part of the cinema in his head, playing itself out against a shredding backdrop of chlorophyll. Just one of many screens conquered.

"Your hair was exactly brown and blonde. Both at once. Half and half. Your legs were muscular, developed, shaped. You were thin. Your other features were, uh, rounded. Your eyes could not be seen by your follower. He stopped, behind the bleachers, and watched your tryouts."

She was sure he was done, but had no idea what to say.

"You high-fived a friend with short black hair as you hit the practice field. You went up to the coach and gave him your name. You laughed at something he said. You turned around, looked at the field, talked to your friend. You ran to the soccer balls, which were wrapped in a net. You tried to remove one, but were told not to. You started stretching, first your arms, then your legs. You touched your toes. Your friend came up, said something to you, and you stopped. Then you picked up your cleats and ran back to the buildings."

He was right, or must have been, since she couldn't remember that much. The physical description was weak and he saw her every day anyway. She was more impressed by everything else, since her only recollection of the day was being disappointed that the first day was only for signing up. It was already a week into school, after all.

"Every day, for two seasons, I watched you practice. I watched you play every game. I missed the days when it rained and you practiced indoors, since I would've been seen. Two seasons," he repeated. "You had to get hurt to see me." On this comment he looked up, trying to maximize his impact.

She had known he had been one of the regulars at her games, which was more noticeable when she was on JV than this past year on varsity. She figured he'd been a brother of one of her teammates; he was one of maybe a half-dozen guys at every game. It wasn't until her hamstringed game when her friend Jessica (the one with the short black hair), then the manager of the varsity team, had noticed Matt. *This* she remembered.

"Um, C-dog?"

"J'?"

"Don't look now, but, shit, I told you not to look."

"I don't even *know* where I'm looking."

"Seven o'clock, since you're fuckin' scanning the crowd... No, no the *other* seven o'clock. From where we're *fac*ing."

"The one by himself?"

"Yes..."

"He's not hot, what's wrong with you?"

"Maybe if you'd let me finish a sentence."

"Okay, *what*?"

"He's staring!"

"Well I can see *that*."

"Do you see wh*ere* he's staring?"

"Yeah, at you."

"If by 'you', you mean *you*."

"What?"

15

"You, sister. It's some C-dog lovin' that he wants."

"He's just here for the game. We *were* staring at him."

"Is that what you think?"

"No, I'm *ly*ing."

"Well turn around anytime. He'll be lookin' right back atchya."

"Bullshit."

"Try."

She did. And Jessica was right. And kept being right. She had to go say hello. He looked older, after all, and she had gotten a reputation on her team for only seeing boys the same age. Was that the reputation anyone wanted? Even if he wasn't hot, maybe he was *fun*.

He was about as much fun as a dead turtle. But she'd never flirted with a dead turtle before, and there was something strangely fun about *that*.

The rest, as they say, should have been history. It wasn't until Valentine's Day when he finally asked her out. Well, it wasn't that simple either. She actually went through two boyfriends, one of whom was *young*er, in the meantime. On Valentine's Day, the freshman, who was still not over her, dropped a crude and hopeless note in her locker "from a not-so-secret admirer". At lunch, which she routinely ate with her friend Matt, who was almost learning how to flirt, she confronted him with it.

"You wrote this, didn't you?"

"What's that?"

"Your handwriting!"

He read the sloppy script, blanched, and turned, crimsony-pink, towards her. "N-no."

"Bullshit. This is you. You want me. I've known all along." Triumphantly, she sat up and slurped milk from the carton. Then she wrapped her legs around his under the table. She looked impatient.

"Even *if* I want--" he started.

"I knew it!" she jumped up, banged her knee against the bottom of the table, and sat back down. "I. Knew. It. What are you doing Friday?"

"Don't you... *what*?!"

She looked nervously at him, for a couple friends were walking over to the table with trays. "I asked what you're doing

16

Friday. You *heard* me."

"Watching your game."

She'd forgotten about that. Friday was such a good default. Then she got a devious grin on her face. "If that's what you want to call it..." Her friends sat down, with greetings, and the typical bemused look at Matt.

"How are ya?"

"Great. Matt here just asked me out. After the game Friday. On Valentine's Day, he does this. Isn't he *sweet*?" The swooning around the table turned Matt's startled and long-standing distant dream into an obligation. He'd never seen anything change so fast in his life. Catie would always remember it as the longest courtship she ever wanted to endure. The idea that it had been, from his perspective, over a year *long*er, was incomprehensible.

But she met his gaze, and verified that it was true. Good God.

Her mental focus swung back to the patch of undergrowth between the fence and the parking lot. There were actually crickets chirping in the background, creating an air of a stereotypical night on the prairie. Matt had finally curbed his assault on the weeds, was staring at her while she contemplated their past. "Catie," he intoned, not quite in her direction.

"C'mere." She motioned him over, extending her arm and taking his head and shoulders into her lap. She started stroking his short brown hair, looking more at the high school's brick facade than at him. "What am I gonna do with you, babe?"

Not much after tonight, Matt knew, but he kept it to himself. "I've got some ideas..." he trailed off as they began to kiss.

ROAD TRIP

T wo days later, her words were ringing in his ears. He had bid his father goodbye, still unable to forgive him for withholding his Chevy Suburban on his last date with Catie, his last night in town. It was his mother's Honda Civic that they packed all his stuff into once he brought it home, at 2:30 in the morning, but this was forgivable on his last night as a child. His mother was still awake, unable to sleep before the next day's journey, so they packed haphazard boxes into the car in the middle of the night. To get it over with. They wanted to leave early the next day.

"You look tired, Matty."

"Mmmf."

"How's Catherine?"

"Fine."

"Everything okay with you two?"

There isn't any *us two*, his mind screamed. "Sure."

"Can you help me with this box? I think it's your monitor."

"Yup."

"Careful not to drop it, Matt. No, don't put it there, we can't stack anything on top of it if you do that. Here, let me..."

He walked away from the back of the Civic. Were all women like his mother? Or just the ones that he liked? He couldn't remember running anything, and now he was running away from everything.

By 4:00, they had collapsed, leaving a particularly weighty box of books in the driveway, assured that anyone who could haul it off and had the inclination would not be out there before 8:00.

Matt's Dad stopped by at 7:30, late for work, hugging his son in a curt goodbye. Matt could barely say anything, walking him back out to his still-idling Suburban in the driveway. "Make sure to call," he was telling his son, as if he would be home when the phone rang, or any other time.

"Right."

"And keep up the studies. Take a science class, too." He smiled quirkily. "It's in your genes."

Another quick hug, and Alexander Norton, M.D. was in the vehicle Matt had wanted to be in just hours before. It would be a better machine for transport of all his possessions to college too, but that was far from Matt's mind. He turned around, tripped over the box of books in the driveway, and sprawled out on the pale cement. He caught himself on a hand and an elbow, preventing much damage, and then decided to lie there, surprised and winded, for a moment. No rush to get up. "Damn," he whispered to himself, but it was more for the benefit of the blasted Civic than his offending driveway. Two more days to live in that car.

Missouri, Illinois, Indiana, Ohio. The states were surprisingly little better than Kansas as they flew by his window, and in each of their parking lots, he saw small cars but could only envision his last night with Catie. He was unable to sleep well, though still hopelessly deprived after the night of goodbyes in Topeka. He would doze in the passenger seat, waking as the sun hit his eyes, then seeing his mother steadily humming to classical music on the radio as she drove eleven and a half miles an hour over the speed limit. She was a meticulous person, and hearing once that cops only pulled over highway drivers if they were doing twelve over or more, she had trained herself to plateau at eleven-point-five. Margin of error was not part of her conception of radar guns, nor of her own precision, which now was as reliable as cruise-control. She'd never received a ticket.

When Matt drove, he was slower, usually creeping about five over the limit, and often dipping well below it. There was a lot on his mind and his mother kept trying to extract his feelings, like wisdom teeth, from his unwilling mouth. "Do you miss Catherine?" was a classic query as to his morose demeanor.

As if that were relevant. Did *she* miss *him*? Had she ever? And why was his Mom so acutely aware of Catie's importance in his life? And why had she purchased a freaking Honda *Civic*? "A little."

"Are you excited about school?" Mom was as subtle as a tank brigade, creeping toward an anthill in the vain hope that the ants would suspect nothing.

Matt couldn't imagine being excited about much at this point. "I guess." If he weren't, he'd risk her turning that car around in the direction of KU and a preMed program when she started driving again. "Yeah, I mean, uh-huh."

"That doesn't *sound* like the Matt who jumped up and down when he was accepted to Harrison."

The Matt who'd been accepted had a girlfriend, and occasional access to a Suburban. This Matt was bereft of both. "We've been driving a long time."

"Do you want to switch?"

"Let's get something to eat. Okay?"

They pulled into a McDonald's just outside of Columbus. These restaurants, like most everything he'd seen since crossing through Kansas City (again), were eerily similar to what he'd grown up with his whole life. He walked in, was confronted by the same menu, the same happy meal toys, the same mildly annoyed workers who were younger than he was. He had never had a fast-food job.

"It's all the same," he muttered to himself, stepping up to order chicken nuggets. "Just like Kansas."

The girl behind the counter was a not unattractive redhead, her face almost obscured by freckles. She had a purple McD visor and a perky way of shifting back and forth behind the counter, as though she desperately had to go to the bathroom but was holding it for just one more customer. "Welcome to McDonald's, may I help you?" But she'd been paying attention, too (it *was* a boy her age and she was bored out of her visor-blocked mind), so she added "First time in Ohio?"

Time stopped.

Matt flushed, turned away slowly, watching people and food flash from the corner of his consciousness. He saw a kid, half his age, push open a Thank You flap and dump the trash from his tray within. The flap swung back so slowly he thought he had time to jump through it himself. The cup and straw slid belatedly from the tray, followed even more deliberately by the crumpled napkin, and then finally the sheet of paper which advertised McDonald's in bright loud colors. The whole scene took an hour to unfold, another twenty minutes to wrap up. Then he was just facing Thank

You again. He heard only one thing, a voice barely higher and angrier than the question he'd just ducked.

"I'm not having my first time in the back of a Honda Civic!"

The voice had been sitting in the back of his mind for thirty-six of the longest hours he had known. Ringing, echoing, spinning, swirling, washing away his fairy-tale high-school romance and leaving him on the rocks of 18-year-old virginity. College-bound and undone.

No insult sounds so bad as the second time it's said. Or implied, or alluded to, or just barely hinted at. The first time stings, but the second time is seeing the blood gushing from the wound. One *felt* before, but now one has to *see*. The pain is in the witnessing. As his head mechanically reversed, his eyes refocusing, his mind was still reeling from the pain he'd had on the tip of his mind for a day and a half. He couldn't hear her say "Um, um, excuse me, uh, can I, y'know, *help* you?"

He heard her say "I'm not having my first time in the back of a Honda Civic!"

To which he replied "Chicken."

While she was reacting with "Uh, okay, well, would you like a sandwich or nuggets?" he looked away from her eyes (too blue), drooping towards anything he could cling to. The natural inclination went a little south and he focused on the nametag. There was a little yellow happy-face, which seemed easier to make eye-contact with than those blue discs, and then a faded pink heart of equal size, and then **KATHY** in black block letters. Just as he'd read it, the name vanished, then reappeared, vanished again. His focus was ebbing, flowing, ebbing, flowing, rhythmically keeping time with KATHY. (Honda-*da*-da-*da* Civic-*ic*-ic-*ic* flowed through his ears to match.)

"Kathy?" it was a thought that somehow emerged from his mouth.

She rolled her eyes. She wished that she'd not paid attention to his stupid Kansas comment. "Ah, you can, uh, read. That's what the nametag says, huh?" He wasn't paying attention. She stopped shifting, which broke his focus. "Sir?!" she just about yelled, even though he'd just caught his own attention.

Sheepish, blatantly red-faced, and bewildered, Matt looked behind him for someone old enough to fit the inquiry. But the line behind him did not exist; the restaurant was virtually empty. He looked back. "Oh God, I'm, I, uh, sor--"

"Matthew, haven't you *ord*ered yet? C'mon, it's getting late and we have to hit the road! I'm not having this trip take us another day. I have work to get back to and, well, what's *tak*ing you so long?" His mother's voice, in this tone, was nothing like Catie's. Or Kathy's. He was back.

"Chicken nuggets," he whispered, staring at the words on the backlit menu as though he needed to read them to pronounce it right. "Ten. Coke. Large. Here." He extended an arm with a crumpled five at the end. He hated wallets and carried all his cash in his right jeans pocket, from where he'd just retrieved the bill. His hand waited for the change, and he refused to look where he would have seen that his hand was almost touching Kathy's nametag, which of course was pinned just above her left breast.

She slid out from under the hand after plucking its five, setting it atop the register and slinking off to get the Coke. The creeps that came off the highway! This kid made her yearn for truckers.

"Thirty-six cents is your change, and, uh, well, have a day." She pushed Matt's hand away as she put three coins into it, and immediately he snapped it back into his pocket. Finally looking down from the menu, he nodded to Kathy rather professionally and grabbed his tray. As he was walking off to find his mother, who had finished eating and would tell him to take his food to-go, Kathy told a co-worker "Let's hope it's his *last* time in Ohio."

"Ohio's a big place," replied her colleague.

On the road again, Matt's mother sped towards Pennsylvania. In the passenger seat, Matt chewed like a person learning how to eat for the first time, taking care with each bite to not risk his tongue, or cheek, or too much of any given chicken nugget. "Matty, what's wrong?"

No matter how far forward he leaned in his seat, he remained the same distance from the infernal back seat of the car, where he had *not* had his first time with Catie Hanson. That was just for starters, a cube off the old iceberg. He looked out the window, noticing a Ryder truck falling behind them on the right. Hadn't Ryder trucks been *yellow*? He could have sworn that a yellow Ryder truck was responsible for the Oklahoma City bombing. Maybe it was a different Ryder. "Nothin'."

Matt sighed. "Look, dear, I know college can be a daunting experience. I know what it's like to be nervous. Especially if you're going this far from home." She had to drop that in there, didn't she? But how many Ryder truck companies could there *be*? "Did I ever tell you about my first time in college?"

It had to be the same co-, *what* did she just say?! "Noooo," he moaned, trailing off as another round of Catie's shrill echo filled his perception. He was overflowing with rejection, hearing nothing but his demise, as his mother described the scene.

"Well, let me tell you the story now. Are you *sure* I didn't, well it doesn't matter. I was your age, not surprisingly. I still had that dreadful name Lutz at the time, which hadn't made grade school easier, let me tell you." Miriam Dawn Lutz had taken the name Norton at marriage (who wouldn't?) and dropped both the Lutz and the Norton at divorce. She tried to go by "Dr. Dawn" nowadays, but her older kids still clung to "Dr. Norton". At least she was a pediatrician and didn't keep patients for life. "Anyway, I had gotten a Presidential scholarship at KU. You could've done the same, you know, if you'd tried. Well, if you'd applied, y'know. I still don't know why your father didn't make you apply to, well, never mind. You always did want to leave ever since that friend of yours left."

The remaining nuggets were growing cold, just like his ex-girlfriend.

"So I walked into the dorm and this girl I was supposed to room with had her hair all up in curlers. It was the first day of school! I thought I was there to learn, but I guess most people were just there to find a husband. I promptly told her that I was there to study, but my name was Miriam, and how did she do? And she did just fine and told me she was looking for her ticket out of learning as fast as she knew how. She had one thing right: she was fast." Miriam caught herself going twelve and a half over at the thought of it. "It's no wonder I didn't tell you about this before, I guess. Anyway, after my parents left, grandma and grandpa, this girl just went on about how quickly she was going to find herself a smart, capable man to take her away. This was the last thing I'd had on my mind. I mean can you *imag*ine? Going to school to find a man?"

Had he been listening, Matt might have pointed out that he could only imagine going to school to be*come* a man. Not that his imagination had proved terribly realistic at the last school he'd attended.

"Rose. That was her name. So Rose leaves that night and comes back at two in the morning from this freshman thing. I think it was a frat party. And she walks in the door, without knocking, and this guy is following her around like the drunk he is. 'Get up, Miriam!' she calls to me, as if I weren't already awake. The nerve she had! 'I'm done looking, Miriam. Alex here is going to be a *doc*tor. A doctor! Whoo!' Well I'd had enough at that point. I told her who was going to *need* a doctor if she kept up her racket. Can you blame me? I mean, two in the morning. The first night of college!"

Matt's mother's thoughts trailed off rapidly after this comment, as she simultaneously noticed that they were out of gas and her son had not been paying much attention. Just as well, she thought. She remembered a time when she'd enjoyed telling that story, getting to know Alex as Rose's boy, eventually stealing him away as her final act of revenge on the hated roommate. Then falling in love, almost an afterthought, and marrying, and what a sweet story it had been at one time. How coyly she had dropped in his last name to the story as she was mentioning her first time with him. Of *course* she hadn't told this story to Matt! Sometimes it seemed that he'd been around long enough to hear everything at some point. And now he wasn't even listening.

"Welcome to Pennsylvania," she exhaled slowly, scanning the road for a gas station sign.

Catching the sign out of the corner of his eye, and hearing the shell of his mother's voice in tandem, Matt felt pretty sure he'd be more welcome anywhere that wasn't a blue Honda Civic.

FIRST SEMESTER

ONE

William Henry Harrison College is situated in the picturesque village of Fifeburg, Pennsylvania, population 7,600. About halfway between Pittsburgh and Philadelphia, Fifeburg was founded by a zealous Revolutionary War vet, Albert Eaton, whose job during the war had been to play in a drum and fife corps. He had never fired a gun and all his friends had been Tories, but he was a loyal Revolutionary during the last month of the war. He had signed up twenty-two days before Yorktown, when it appeared imminent that the damn Yankees might win it after all.

Having properly hedged his bets and emerging successful for it, he took his family and a handful of friends (mostly Tory activists who feared for their lives) to the frontier of western Pennsylvania to start Fifeburg. He was the town's first mayor, and insisted on building five war memorials to the brave Revolutionaries who had died in the struggle for independence. One of them was a mock bell, made of wood, whose size rivaled the cracked version down the road in Philadelphia. This was carved with all the names of the Declaration of Independence signers, and sat beneath a delicate gazebo in the town square. Between paying for the construction of these various memorials and the hired men to defend against the threat of Indian attack, Fifeburg had little money to build an infrastructure, and languished even after Eaton's death.

Fifeburg played little role in America's early years until it gradually became a haven for abolitionists in the 1850's. The reputation the town had for gallant displays of liberty made it a natural choice for the headquarters of several abolitionist movements. Rallies were frequently held on the town square, where the great wooden bell made a fabulous prop. "And by the very names of liberty inscribed on this bell..." and so on. Frederick Douglass even came to speak there, and one man by the name of Ed Crabtree was so moved by Douglass' words that he joined the U.S. Army the next day.

His commander was a southern slave-owner named Mahorn who certainly dampened Crabtree's enthusiasm for joining the Army. Mahorn was a bitter, aging soul whose only joy came from ragging on young recruits and old colleagues. His favorite colleague to bash was William Henry Harrison, with whom he'd served during the Indian Wars. "Tip this, Tip that," he'd say. "Well fuck Old Tip, he only used this Army to get to Washington! And fuck Tyler too!"

It was only natural for Crabtree to assume that if *Mahorn* hated Harrison, he must have been a pretty good guy.

In 1861, a week before the declaration of hostilities between the states, Pvt. Edward Crabtree was inadvertently stabbed in the knee with a bayonet during a drill. He returned to Fifeburg unable to walk properly and without a job. It was a shame; he'd wanted a chance to shoot at old Sgt. Mahorn.

Alone, lame, and unskilled, Crabtree had few options available to him in the lowly climes of rural Pennsylvania. There was going to be a war, which would take at least a week, and then there would be even more competent young men returning home, just as he had. Often injured, perhaps, and unskilled. They would need training. They would need a college.

Crabtree had never been terribly well educated, but that didn't stop him from opening the doors of William Henry Harrison College in 1862, built on grants from several newly dissolved abolitionist groups that appeared to have little remaining purpose. They invested in the College on the condition that anyone who had been part of an abolitionist group prior to the war be admitted free of charge. They too were relatively unskilled. Former members of abolitionist groups everywhere enrolled forthwith.

The school flourished, as many young men attempting to quietly avoid the war took a new interest in higher education. The standards remained lax and the teachers relaxed, and classes often became forums for discussion of American politics. "They put the 'liberal' in a liberal education," wrote one critical columnist for the *Fifeburg Almanac*. The criticism, much like "Yankee Doodle Dandy" during the Revolution, became an unofficial motto for the College.

In fact, WHHC was so successful that Ed Crabtree, the College President, never bothered to look up the details on the life and presidency of its namesake. It wasn't until just before his death of pneumonia in 1875 that a forlorn American History grad came to see him. "Oh Mr. Crabtree, what a terrible fate to befall you, just as your most honorable predecessor."

Crabtree had coughed profusely before sputtering. "What predecessor? I founded the College!"

"Alas, in the name of our ninth President, who fell to this same disease after a solitary month in office."

"Is that so?" Crabtree asked, and then died.

One-hundred and twenty-five years later, a blue Honda Civic drove into Fifeburg. It parked, without hesitation, in a lot next to the campus, whereon the old hospital had been. In fact, the parking space was neatly placed exactly where Edward Crabtree's deathbed had lain. Dusk was settling over the town, and the lights in the parking lot were flickering on and off, sensitive to the failing and reappearing light.

"All right, get your things, let's get this over with."

"Huh?"

"I said to get your things. We don't have much time. Take the heavy stuff first."

"What are you *talk*ing about?"

"We're here and we're late. I've got to start heading back home. So you grab that big box and I'll take your backpack. C'mon!" Miriam stepped out of the car and left Matt to let his head settle into the dashboard. He was fairly sure his dorm was on the other end of campus. A frequent visitor to the Harrison College website, Matt had memorized the small school's geography. The parking lot was on the far west, while the Tyler dormitory fronted the eastern edge of campus.

Sighing, he exited the car, slammed the door, and confronted the box with his monitor in it. He was fairly reliant on his computer, and facing a year without television (his parents had refused to allow him to bring one; the first stand they had taken in unison in his recent memory) would make him all the more so. This box made him question his devotion to screens. He was convinced that it had been specifically engineered to be unwieldy, as though hundreds of scientists had gathered in a secret underground lab, carefully conducting psychological surveys of how to break people simply by making them carry a heavy burden. Eventually, after months of struggling, they must have perfected the shape, size, and weight of a computer monitor box! They had pride in their work, whose success was strewn across the twisted backs and shattered mentalities of long-time box-carriers.

"You sure we shouldn't, y'know, get the *key* first or something?"

"Dorms," his Mom spouted, quoting a brochure she'd been mailed, "will be open and unlocked during the duration of Orientation Week." Anticipating the next protest, she added "And I have your room number right here. Tyler 401." 401! Oh, the humanity! There were no elevators on campus. In fact, the entire ville of Fifeburg probably lacked the lifting devices.

"Well, I know, but--"

"Matt, en*ough*. Let's *go*!"

They went. Matt grabbed the carrying flaps on each end of the box (indeed, a concession the lab engineers begrudgingly must have made to the computer company's public relations department) and lifted. Balancing the box on his knee, he tried to shift the weight but realized that he already *had* control of the only carrying flaps amidst the vast expanse of cardboard. His instincts had told him that there must be a more stable way of carrying this thing. His instincts, if he pressed them, probably wouldn't recommend him breaking his spine either.

The trek across campus was slow going. Matt's mother, a hurried woman in the first place, was practically sprinting ahead of him. Meanwhile, he was sweating profusely as he laboriously hauled the infernal box first across asphalt, then cement, and now the unfortunate brick path that cut through the campus's lush lawns. The bricks were ill-kempt and uneven, threatening a perilous trip at any moment. At least the monitor would break his fall before breaking apart. "Maybe," his mother ventured during one of his brief pauses, setting the monitor down, panting, and wiping the sweat from his dripping forehead, "you'll app*rec*iate having these things more now." Going this far from home for college had definitely been a sound idea.

As they left the main path cutting through campus, forking onto an even less even brick path which led to Tyler, Matt began to perceive chanting in the background. He had begun to carry the box by holding its underside, since his hands were turning red-purple and felt raw enough to shed what little skin seemed to be left. While this method spared his aching hands, it made the box heavier and managed to render him blind. The latter of these facts became more frustrating as he distinctly verified the chanting.

He saw cardboard, and the logo indicating which end was supposed to be up. He couldn't read "THIS END UP" because it was upside-down. He heard "Harr-i-son, Harr-i-son, Harr-i-son!" with rising crescendo. He was immediately reminded of one of the few books that he had both read and remembered, *The Lord of the Flies*. Piggy was about to get slaughtered.

Slaughter would be a nice change of pace, Matt thought. He set the box down and was greeted by his mother's rolling eyes. He was relieved to see they weren't, for once, rolling at him. "Who *are* these people?" she asked, indicating the hitherto unseen throng of older college kids. They all wore insipid yellow T-shirts. In loud red letters across the front of each shirt "MAKE **EVERY MONTH** COUNT!" greeted Matt's eyes. He noticed the back of one, "HARISON ORIENTATION 2000". Weren't there two R's in Harrison? There was no spelling in their endless chanting. ("Kill the pig!" Matt mused.)

A short, somewhat rounded girl ran up from the crowd to greet Miriam, and then Matt. "Hi!" she screamed. "Welcome to Harrison! My name is Lily!" She positively beamed at the two of them, Miriam giving her a mystified glance and Matt just tired and growing confused. "We're very very *ve*ry happy to see you!" Miriam didn't doubt this. She saw a lot of suffering individuals under the age of 20, but had no idea what she would have prescribed for this malady. Matt had not been a hyperactive child, but this level of enthusiasm was still beyond any reasonable pale. "You need help with that?"

Matt quickly checked to see if the monitor box she was referring to was in fact taller than she was. Lily won the contest by at least an inch, he estimated. "I think, uh, I've got it?"

"Oh, I didn't mean *I* would help you!" she laughed, forcedly, making each "ha" distinct and deliberate. "Hey guys, it's another froshie! What's your name again?"

Matt was too ashamed, but Miriam told her "Matthew."

"Hey guys! Let's say hi to froshie Matthew!" It was a code. On an implied 3-count, the entire world seemed to erupt into song. Discordant, abrasive, and obscenely loud, but song nonetheless.

"Harrison is the place to be! Harrison is for you and me! Just ask us and you will see! Harrison is the place to be! Now we say hello to you, Froshie! Harr-i-son! Hey Matth-ew! Harr-i-son! Hey Matth-ew! Harr-i-son!"

Crimson-faced and sweating uncontrollably, Matt tried to pick up the box again. He wondered absently why it sounded like they were greeting Matthew Harrison, and what *would* they have done if his name hadn't been two syllables? Much of the chanting dissipated, though a few die-hards persisted.

"Need some help, um, Matthew?" a tall strapping guy, who must have been a senior, asked him. Miriam, observing the scene, had to ask herself why her son didn't look like *that*. Probably because Alex didn't.

"I'm *fine*," Matt insisted, and barreled up the steps into the Zachary Tyler Dormitory, whose name was obscured by a large red-on-yellow sign with the now familiar call to value *every month*. Miriam followed behind, smiling briefly at the guy.

"It's been a long day." Then, addressing the collective, "Thanks for the, well, y'know, welcome."

Ah, four flights of stairs. Rome rose and fell on those stairs, centuries passing with small victories and crushing setbacks, and the impending atmosphere of being sacked. World history had never measured up to American for Matt.

Atop the final flight, like a specter of Attila the Hun, stood a kid who looked even dorkier than Matt perceived himself. Unlike Matt, he wore glasses, hanging precariously on a short nose and giving him the classic owlish appearance, offset only by his curious childish grin and a T-shirt which proudly rooted for the Harrison Bell-Ringers. Similar to Matt, he had short brown hair and the build of a couch potato. He backed off the top step as Miriam approached, slowly guiding Matt up to the final landing. Holding open the fire door so they could enter, the kid stepped aside and with surprising authority asked, "What room do you seek?"

Matt wanted to collapse on the floor, burrowing into the carpet and resting for a decade or two. Sweet oxygen. When he felt he had enough of a reserve to speak, "oh-one" emerged.

The kid's goofy grin got that much goofier. "Well then you

must be Matthew!" He extended a hand, received the limp purple excuse for one that was offered back. "I'm David Benowski," pausing to let this sink in, "your roommate."

"I'm Matt," he sighed back.

"So it would seem," David returned, now with an edge of sly tacked on to the initial goofy.

Miriam looked expectantly at Matt. "What do you s*ayyy*?" she inquired, in the way she had extracted "thank you"s from him when she was still married.

"Nicetomeetyou," he blurted, ashamed at his mother's perception of him, but far too drained to resist.

"Charmed, I'm sure," David winked and withdrew immediately to the nearest door, which was wide open. "Right this way, my loyal comrade!" This habit he had of looking twelve and speaking thirty was certainly disquieting.

Matt had seen televisions larger than Room 401. On his left was a bunkbed whose top bunk must have been about a foot below the ceiling. Straight ahead was the room's lone window, about four feet by four feet square. Immediately he thought he was in prison, and began searching for the sink, toilet, and chained-to-the-wall bench. Finding none of these, he saw two sparse desks, some random shelving, and a closet that would make an uncomfortably small home for a family of moths. Miriam came in behind him, ducking instinctually though this was (barely) unnecessary. She was an inch shorter than her son, but always felt her advanced age should physically manifest itself somehow.

"A little grim," she commented, "but hey, it's college!"

"It's not so bad," David shrugged at them. "You'll get used to it. I have, er, taken the *liberty*" the emphasis made it sound as though he were about to invoke the Constitution and other fundamental documents protecting his rights, "of claiming the bottom bunk. I'm rather, um, *warm* when I sleep and I don't think I could handle the top bunk's higher climes." A pause, shifty at the lack of immediate response. "I hate to mention it, but I was here first."

Mother and son looked at each other, the former accusing of the son's tardiness, the latter beseeching for salvation from this pushy roommate. Silence was all that could settle the issue.

David coughed. "Right then, so I guess that's *that*. Maybe, if it bothers you, we can switch at semester or something. Hm." He looked around the walls, in Matt's opinion as though he were hoping that they would move farther apart if he stared long enough, or could merely *find* the button that expanded the room. "Oh! Before I forget! Here." He handed a small package to Matt, clearly the precise size of a compact disc case. "A little something of a greeting gift. Something close to my heart, and soon to yours too, I hope." He pushed his sliding glasses back on his insubstantial nose and smiled awkwardly, on one side of his mouth, but not the other.

"Oh, uh, thanks. Sure." Matt absently took the package and put it directly on the top bunk, which he exaggeratedly stretched to reach, even though the bunk wasn't *that* far away. "I guess I should get my other stuff." He said it with the luster of a man addressing his firing squad who, despite careful planning, had forgotten to bring bullets. "I guess you guys should get your bullets" would have sounded perhaps a smidgen more enthusiastic.

Miriam nodded and the two left before David could begin to offer help. It was clear that he would be more hindrance than assistance; Matt would probably have to help David take his backpack to classes. It wasn't really that Matt was better built than David, far more of this came from a general sense of David's physical motivations. Had he ever tried to carry anything? Matt could envision a cartoon feature in which David struggled to lift a feather, taking several heaves and eventually creating an ocean of sweat in which he would summarily drown.

Miriam knew that things would progress more quickly if Matt were in higher spirits. "He seemed like a very nice boy, dontchya think?"

The last episode he'd seen of the *Conan O'Brien* show came to mind and Matt took considerable restraint to avoid blurting "a very nice boy... for me to poop on!" Instead, he placated with "I've met worse, I'm sure." He couldn't think of any off-hand, but they had to be out there. At least he wasn't a jock. Though he imagined that Harrison was not known for its jocks--the Bell-Ringers were in fact compelling arguments for a Division IV in collegiate athletics. If David had been a jock, though, at least the heaviest boxes remaining in the Civic would not be his responsibility.

They proceeded to the car in silence, both too occupied in different forthcoming futures to sustain a common-ground conversation.

It was long after nightfall by the time everything had been hauled from the small blue vehicle to the smaller dorm room that was to be Matt's new home. The boxes became progressively lighter as Matt became progressively more light-headed, entering depths of weariness he had never known. Every time they passed through the path leading up to Tyler, the flock of yellow-shirted Orientation helpers greeted Matt, assured each time that this was a new "froshie". Their zeal was not limited by the awareness most of them steadily acquired that this was actually someone they had seen before, perhaps multiple times. If anything, they became more ardent in their welcome, as though they secretly feared that Matt and his beleaguered mother kept returning because their prior greeting had been insufficient.

By the fifth and final trip, however, the throng had thinned to a paltry three people (it was getting awfully late), of whom Lily, the original greeter, was one. She was about to sound the alarm, but (finally) recognized Matt and simply said "Hi Matthew" instead. Matt was sorely tempted to dump his box of sheets and towels on the girl, 'neath which he was positive she'd be crushed and eternally silenced.

Instead, he said "Heyya" and kept on walking.

Upstairs, David was at his desk, which already held his laptop computer, fully operational. His left hand was where it had been the last three times Matt had visited 401, covering a rash of acne on his chin and left cheek. Matt hadn't noticed this, but Miriam, who took an interest in behaviors of this age group, had. "You know," she started. David didn't turn around. "David." He looked up as though shot. "You, uh, your acne problem is probably primarily due to your repeated placement of your hand on your face." She was trying to sound clinical, as she always did when delivering a diagnosis. "If you kept your hands off your face, it might go away."

David had gradually turned pink during the utterance of the unrequested prescription and now looked out the window, perhaps for a second opinion. He had developed the habit of covering his pimples in order to hide them from the world, which had the added side benefit of giving him a thoughtful and scholarly air. Where was Rodin when he needed him, anyway? And who *was* this woman to see through his hand?

"Uhhhh."

As he was deciding which box to unpack first, Matt's face

slowly broke out into a shit-eating grin. He always knew his mother was good for something. Cutting this guy down a couple notches might knock him off his high horse, bring him to a level where he could tell him what was up. Nothing like embarrassment for leveling the playing field.

"Just a suggestion." Miriam considered the matter closed; she rarely got a response from her patients beyond a quick obligatory nod. Enforcement of her suggestions was the job of *parents*. She just gave them the tools to use at their own discretion. "Well, Matty, it's late."

"Yeah, there's a Dorm Meeting in four minutes!" David had been searching for a response and a subject change equally. This worked nicely, he thought.

"Uh-huh," Miriam again looked at this boy who was to share college with her son quizzically. She doubted that Matt would have the same hard time *she'd* had in school with the freshman roommate--she couldn't imagine this David character bringing *anyone* home for the night. Ever. "So, I should probably get going." She expected this to be difficult. She expected Matt to break down, to see tears in her son's eyes, to be party to a five-minute embrace wherein he would try to prevent her leaving. She'd already prepared the line "I've spent one first night in college already" as a response to her expectation that he'd beg her not to leave.

"Okay. Bye Mom." He looked up from the box he was opening, meeting her eyes and then returning to the box. "Have a safe trip back."

"Do I get a *hug*?" Matt had hoped to avoid this in front of David, but his mother sounded slighted.

He went over, hugged Miriam, and she hit him with "I love you."

He'd heard it before, but it was not a big thing in their family, especially after it became two families. His primary association with the phrase was a rough moment in April when he'd tried the line on Catie. He had not precisely appreciated her laughter which followed. Then he got a lecture about what that word meant, about her being 16 and him being 18, and he couldn't remember saying it since. "Uh. You... too," trickled from his mouth. He barely heard him say it himself, though he'd said it as loudly as he dared.

When the embracees separated, Miriam found herself tearful,

at least half of which had to be because of her son's lack of affection. She saw so much of Alex in him; she'd always tried to separate the two, but he'd grown to look just like him. After all, Alex had only been a year older than Matthew, a lonely sophomore, when Rose Panini had hauled him into her room. She blinked, felt a tear fall, and turned. "Have fun son don't forget to call I'll miss you." It was a running stream of words, receding in volume as she fled the room, taking the same approach she recommended for ripping off band-aids in one fell swoop. On "you" she was on the stairs, descending clamorously to keep herself from running back to hug her son forever. Why was that so *hard*? It wasn't until her hand hit the handle of the Honda Civic's door that she realized, *I am alone*. Sitting in the driver's seat, bawling, she saw her recent years as a Nicotine-patch-style step-down process, leaving Alex, but spending time with a smaller version of him, gradually less time as he grew older, and finally no time as of now. She had never smoked, but she was pretty sure she wanted a cigarette.

Back in 401, David was reassembling his pride while Matt was disassembling his boxes. Finally he decided to ask the question he would have liked to hear had someone else been there after his mother had just left him. "You okay?"

That was rich. "*Fine*," Matt insisted, and he was. Of the three partings he'd undergone in the past three days, only one had been taxing. He was still paying half his thoughts to that, even this minute. The thought that, with each passing moment, the Civic was receding from physical proximity was his only source of reassurance.

"All right, all right, just making sure." David's thoughts were still with his parents, who were together and had left him simultaneously. He had never been away from home longer than twenty-four hours. And while he did relish some time with people his age, to try to make friends and spread his ideas, the comfort of doting parents would be greatly missed. How could others deny this reality? "So, uh, about thirty seconds till Dorm Meeting. We're supposed to go together."

Matt rolled his eyes and turned to face his roommate. "Where do you find out all this shit?"

David was not accustomed to swearing. "Uhhhh. I was here earlier, you know. The R.A. down the hall told me. Resident Advisor, that is."

So David *did* think he was stupid, Matt concluded. "I *know* what an R.A. is." Standing, something occurred to him, along with the realization that he probably shouldn't try standing on his sore legs for the next half-century. "Just because I'm from Kansas doesn't mean I was born yesterday."

"Oh, Kansas, huh? I'm from Pittsburgh. Hey, wait up! You don't even know where the meeting is!"

But outside in the hall, there were scores of boys filing in the same general direction, all moving slowly and almost dazedly, bumping into each other and muttering hellos and small complaints. There was thunder coming from the stairs, as the crowd of teens proceeded down the stairs, hitting a landing, and down the stairs again. Though his mind was still occupied by one Catie Hanson, her smile, her laugh, her rude dismissal of his mother's vehicle, the birthmark just above her right hip, he was beginning to realize he was not in Kansas anymore. After all, he *was* rooming with the Cowardly Lion.

Until that day, Matt had never seen the purpose of staircase railings. He clutched the railing all the way down, both for support and as a bulwark against the masses of stampeding youth. Crowds had not been a big part of his experience. The last similar setting had been, what, elementary school recess? Even then, the classes had been small and the playground unfilled.

On the ground floor of Tyler was a large common room, filled with ratty couches and a slanted ping-pong table all perched on stained wall-to-wall carpeting. The carpeting had once been gray, which still showed through in patches. At one of the narrow ends of the rectangular room was a white marker-board. Five yellow-shirts stood astride this board, watching the students fill in. In the crowd, Matt had successfully ditched David and ended up pressed against a window, standing, as more boys filed in behind him.

David walked in, scanned the crowd, found Matt (he was too squeezed to duck), and made a big show of "excuse me, pardon me" on his way over. Just as he reached Matt, the boys were asked to sit on the floor, and the presentation began. It was surprisingly dark outside, revealing through the windows that Harrison was still on the eastern edge of Fifeburg, as it had been almost 140 years prior. Bald florescent bulbs shined down on the boys.

"On behalf of Harrison Orientation 2000, I welcome you all to Harrison College!" The guy, who Matt was awfully sure had been the one to offer help with the monitor box earlier that evening, paused, seemingly waiting for applause or cheers. Hearing none, he continued. "You will spend the best four years of your life here." Matt had been told this by every one of his high school teachers, many of his classmates, countless television sources, and himself. "As you do, we'd like to remind you to make *every month count*!!" He was delivering the canned material like a State of the Union address, expecting partisan Senators to stand up and offer countless ovations. Matt found himself waiting for the latest report on the budget.

"My name is Bill Dean. I'm the R.A. on Tyler 4th, all the way upstairs. This is Mack, the R.A. on Tyler 3rd, Phil on Tyler 2nd, and Samrat on Tyler Ground." They all smiled and nodded, in turn. "We'll be having individual Hall Meetings directly after this," this brought the first audible response, as groans erupted from the crowd, "but I'd first like to introduce our Director of Campus Living, Mrs. Helga Feirstone, to say a few words to you about *the rules*."

Mrs. Helga Feirstone looked positively bizarre in a yellow Orientation T-shirt. She had to be sixty, and probably had not worn a T-shirt, other than during past Freshman Orientations, since she had been fifteen. Maybe it was just the contrast between her and all of her twenty-year-old counterparts that made the yellow so odd.

"Good evening, gentlemen," she began. "And again, welcome to Harrison. We are a 138-year-old university" (just older than you!, Matt thought in Mrs. Feirstone's direction) "with a proud tradition. We are sure that you will do this university proud." A knowing pause. "But I fear that some among you are *not* here to do this school proud! Some are here, just having rid yourselves of parents, to do *whatever you like*. And while we are a *lib-er-al*" (she enunciated dramatically, almost disdainfully) "institution, do not let that go to your head! I suggest you familiarize yourself with the laws of the great state of Pennsylvania. Many of you are from elsewhere, and the laws of your home state shall not be upheld. The drinking age here is *twen-ty-one*" (more pained enunciation) "and shall be strictly enforced. Illicit substances, such as cocaine, heroin, and *mar-i-jua-na*, are utterly illegal. This too shall be strictly enforced. Are there any *quesi*ons?"

A kid with shoulder-length black hair shot his hand into the air. He didn't wait to be recognized. "Yeah! What about sex?!" The predictable laughter ensued from the crowd.

Mrs. Feirstone adopted a cryptic smile. "You are not original, young sir. We get that question *ev-e-ry* year." A pause. "Sexual intercourse is legal in the state of Pennsylvania." Laughter here was interspersed with all the claps and cheers that Matt's R.A. had been expecting. Mrs. Feirstone bowed her head, as if she were about to lose her composure. "But be forewarned, you horny gentlemen, that you'd best use protection to guard your wild oats. Some of them may just get *sewn*, if you catch my drift. We don't think you'll like any *sur-pri-ses*, of the venereal kind, or the, shall we say, *cry-ing* kind. Harrison will not take responsibility for your mistakes, or accidents. Are there any *other* questions?"

Everyone's question had been answered, really, though this prompted another slew of painful recollections from Matt. He always was just that close to living in the moment, getting beyond his last night in Topeka, but the world would not let him forget his virginity, his rejection. His mother's Civic.

"Seeing none, I will dismiss you," people jumped up, "*but* remember!," people paused in seeming midair, "you are not only here to have fun, but also to *learrrrrn*!" And the boys dispersed, leaping over the din of Matt's R.A. again yelling about the individual Hall Meetings. David looked at Matt mischievously.

"We *are* here to learn, huh?"

Matt saw right through him. "Like *you're* ever gonna get any."

"And you are?" David fired back.

This hit a nerve. "Fuck off," he said and took off again.

He ran for his room, realizing as he went that this was not a refuge from the person he ran from. But he had nowhere else to go, and there was the exhaustion again, bowling him over and making him stop on a railing. He continued, running until he was ready to collapse in a heap on the top step, as he had hours earlier. He felt the rushing of water behind his eyes, and was flooded by the vision of Catie and his mother and the lovely white Suburban and Catie's lovely white skin, how the two were inextricably bound beyond his reach, how he saw his roommate in himself and a life of solitary hiding behind one's pimples.

He ran into his room, crying, not thinking to close, let alone lock, the door behind him. He tumbled into the bed before him, sobbing, crying for himself and his lost energy, his lost love (could he call it that?), his lost hope, himself, lost.

I am being childish, he thought, and young and immature and stupid. *And* I don't care.

"Matthew?" the annoying superior voice sounded in the doorway. For the love of God!

"Matt," he insisted into the pillow.

"Huh?"

With effort, he turned his head to the wall, allowing his mouth to separate from the cloth below. "It's fucking *Matt*, all right? Not Matty or Matthew or Matthias. Just Matt." He returned to the pillow, where the tears had not stopped.

"Okay, let's start again then. Matt?"

"What?" his tongue felt cloth again.

"I--I'm sorry. I think we got off to a bad start back there. We have a year together, and I want it to be a beneficial one. Mutually beneficial. For both of us. Can, can, well, could you stop crying?"

Matt looked up, miserable, seeing the sodden world through layers of filmy water. "Who says I'm *cry*ing?" He knew he sounded like a four-year-old.

"Okay, okay. What's wrong? And don't tell me 'nothing' because this doesn't, well, look like nothing."

He sounded so damned parental. He was *his age*! "I miss Catie," he sobbed.

"That's not your mother's name, is it?"

He shot him a venomous glance, slowly heaving up the last of his snuffles. "My girlfri, well, shit, my ex-girlfriend."

"Junior?" David queried.

"Sophomore," Matt admitted sheepishly. He was trying to suppress the next wave of drops.

David nodded, as though seeing it all on a screen hidden within his broad-lensed glasses. Shortly, his attention returned to Matt. "Are you, uh, well, going to keep crying?"

"What the hell do you care?" Matt was defensive again at the description of this shameful act.

"Well, uh, you're on my bed. And, I think," he scratched the back of his neck carefully, "I think my sheets are getting soggy."

Matt pitifully attempted to wipe off David's pillow and sheets with a wet hand, then stood up. "Sorry," he muttered. "Y'know what, I'm really just," heave "just tired. It's not a big deal. It's n-n-n-nothing."

"Sure," David said, going to his pillow, and holding it up to the light to inspect the damage. His parents *had* warned him about people not up to his standard of cleanliness. Or maturity, for that matter. But was this the start to the best four years of his life? Only one way to find out. "Speaking of your bed vs. my bed," he segued, "have you opened the package sitting on *your* bed?"

Matt let go a great whirling sigh, finally drying out, and attacked his tear-stained cheeks with his palms. Then, he aggressively grabbed for the wrapped CD case. "Should I?" he asked, contemplating it, stalling for composure.

"You may already have a copy," David pre-empted, "I'd almost be surprised if you didn't. But this is the *remastered* copy, special limited edition. For better sound quality. You do listen to music, don't you?"

This question could mean anything. He hoped it had nothing to do with his mother's classical music, though that was unlikely to be in need of *"remastering"*. They were hardly uncovering Bach's basement tapes from cathedral wine cellars in Europe. He had a few soundtracks, himself, and a couple of random other CD's, mostly recently released, that he'd been given, but truly preferred seeing a new TV show to listening to an oft-heard disc. There was something about the repetition of collecting favorite music that eluded his understanding. He had to avoid the radio for much the same reason. "Sometimes," he said truthfully.

"Well, I listen to this CD all the time. It's my religion, my Bible, my alpha and omega, my, well, just open the thing already! This will change your life, if it hasn't already."

Skeptically, but thankful for something other than Catie to anticipate, Matt pulled the wrapping apart to reveal four men in rather shoddy animal suits. In rainbow lettering beneath them, **MAGICAL MYSTERY TOUR** was proudly displayed. "O-kayyy," he slowly exhaled.

David set his pillow down and leapt off the bed, narrowly missing the bottom of the top bunk. "Okay?! Have you *heard* it?!"

"No," Matt admitted, trying to discern the starry yellow lettering at the top of the disc case. "Who is this?"

"The Beatles!" David screamed, at least uttering a name Matt had heard of before. Though his first thought, admittedly, was of Volkswagen *Beetles*. He had spent altogether too much time wondering exactly what size car *would* have sufficed for Catie.

"Right, I've heard of them," he said, trying to sound nonchalant, ahead of the game. That was always tough enough with shaky post-crying voice.

David rolled his eyes. "You're screwing around with me."

"No, I really have heard of them. They do, uh, what's it called. Well *you* know. What's that song about needing help?"

"You mean *Help!*?" For a second, David had thought this kid had a wry sense of humor. Now he was merely convinced that Kansas was the missing second moon, orbiting Earth once every 10,000 years. "Where do you *come from*? Don't you know *any*thing? The Beatles are only the biggest band, let's see, *ev-er*!"

"In yo-*ur* opinion." Matt snuffled, wiped his nose.

David wrestled the disc from Matt's inattentive hands and approached his laptop. "Well, then, let's get *your* opinion, shall we?"

Tiredly, Matt nodded, and began his first ascent of many to the top bunk. Maybe he could just fall asleep. He was getting the idea that there'd be plenty of opportunities to hear this music, and he was none too eager to start *anything* right now. The mattress looked like it had been through Sherman's visit to Atlanta, but he slid on top of it (flopping not permitted by the low ceiling), and settled in, hearing the sound of a bus coming from the laptop's weak speakers just before slipping into unconsciousness.

TWO

H ours later and hundreds of miles west, Antigone Edgewood was storming down I-65 from Chicago, south towards Indianapolis. She drove an aging green Volvo station wagon with one broken brake-light and Illinois license plate "NTGONE". It was 2:47 in the morning, or so the clock on her cell phone told her. She had a very important coin to flip in Indianapolis. She was not calm, but talking to herself helped.

"Allll right. Okay. Here we are." The cell phone rang. "There it goes again. Sorry, punkass, Antigone is not here to take your call. Antigone is not here to take your *fist*. Antigone is *never coming back*, so you can shove it! That's *right* you're hanging up the phone. You don't have a cell phone. As long as you're calling, you're not chasing me. Yet."

She was good at talking. She was not always positive that she was equally good at thinking. If she were, how did this happen? How had she stayed seven months, eighteen days, and twelve and a half hours with Rick Spiers? The drugs weren't so bad, but whenever he went to the alcohol, there would always be trouble. But he had so much *potential*. She could save him, right? That's what he had always told her. And she had been believing, at least until July. Something about the heat changed Rick. Or so it seemed.

"You're not going to find me. You're not going to see me again." If she said it enough, it had to be true. She had a nasty habit of making things she said enough come true for other people. In addition to serving as a useful hobby, this made her a great professional telemarketer. She set sales records wherever she

went, and never had to worry about finding work. It was *avoid*ing
things that gave her trouble. And saying things to guys like Rick
Spiers, just waiting for them to become true. "You're not going to
hit me" had debuted on July sixth, but she was still waiting for
that one to sell.

She stopped addressing the phantom Rick, who she was very
nearly sure was not on the road yet (he could always be stopping
periodically to call from payphones, but no, that's paranoia), and
turned to herself. "Honey, you've got to get yourself cleaned up.
You've got to get some food in that belly. You've got to take a
nice long break from running. Maybe get a room. No, that would
be pushing it. He'll find you in a room, he can sense you. He's
intuitive. That's why you fucking liked him, isn't it? 'How bad
could he *be* if he under*stands* so well?' All right, hon, lay off.
We're getting away. We're on the road. The road."

As if to respond, two cars travelling north passed by, their
headlights shining brightly, then fading behind her and leaving her
to face the long straight interstate. "You are doing the right thing.
Rick's not gonna change. You can't let other people do the
changing, cuz they're never gonna. Never until you change. Here I
am, ma, look at me, I'm changing. I'm getting the fuck outta
Dodge."

Her breathing was gradually becoming normalized, but her
foot was glued to the floor, where the gas pedal prompted her car
to stay around 90 miles per hour. She was good with cops. She
was good in any situation she could talk herself out of, that she
felt she had control. Why did this never apply to guys like Rick?
Where did they get all that power? Admittedly she was never
trying to *save* cops, let alone long-distance phone service
customers, but why did offering salvation mean weakness? Was
that what Jesus was getting at?

"Oh Buddha," she prayed, "let me find someone worth
saving." She couldn't help but feel that this, in itself, implied
something contradictory, but maybe the old man wouldn't notice.
After all, he liked paradoxes. Her life had always struck her as a
koan, anyway, which had first drawn her to Buddhism. It was her
devout experience that karma was a living daily reality that had
led her towards Hinduism. And who didn't like a walk in the
woods, talking to the woods instead of herself? Wicca worked
well with the parts of Christianity she liked. She would have loved
John Lennon if he'd advocated *all* religions instead of none. As it

was, she had to live for the day. Especially now.

"How random is a coin toss? Nothing's random; I'm being silly again. Should I do two out of three? Does it work if I don't have a quarter? I'm sure I can find a quarter. Maybe I should call Ashley and Betsy first. No, that's crazy. They won't be up, they'll be mad, and they won't think it's urgent if I have to call. Shit. Twenty-five cents to destiny. Do I even have their phone numbers? I might have left them. That would be just perfect. Tomorrow Rick's gonna go through my fucking phone book, number by number, and raise hell. Would Ashley or Betsy be more likely to tell? That's silly too, they're friends. They wouldn't rat on me unless someone paid them enough. I can outbid whoever would pay."

Ashley lived in St. Louis and Betsy lived in Philadelphia. St. Louis was closer, which was good in the short-term, but bad in the long-term. Philadelphia had the opposite characteristics, being farther. They were both good friends, though her best friend was an artist in Taos, New Mexico. She was not going to Taos. Taos did not need telemarketers, and she'd promised herself to never waitress again, even for a day. So it was her next-best friends, both from Amherst, where she'd been a drama major before dropping out after sophomore year. She'd stayed close in the ensuing six years, living on the cell phone and trying to explain herself and her unending changes. Ashley and Betsy didn't understand, but they would always help. That was all she needed right now.

Indianapolis, where I-70 collided with I-65. West was St. Louis, east was Philly. In the center would be a much-needed stop at an all-night diner. And a meeting with destiny, in the form of George Washington or an eagle.

"Maybe I should let someone else flip the coin. I've never been much good with responsibility. I think if I flip it, it'll land in my coffee and then I'll take that to mean that I should go back to Chicago." The very word brought shivers to her spine. Chicago had been the worst mistake yet, and not just because of Rick. Rick was intuitive, but he was too close to his hometown to pick up on the malignant undercurrent of America's third largest city. There was a weighty hostility in the air that had always perturbed Antigone, and on the nights when Rick drank, she saw it (and often felt it) manifested in Rick himself. "I am not going back to Chicago. I should make a list of changes. Not writing in the car.

But number one is no more Chicago. God. Number two is no more tattoos." She refused to let herself lift her own ratty T-shirt, which would reveal an inscription dedicating her stomach to Rick. This would certainly make it a challenge to find a better boyfriend. "Number three," she sighed, facing the enormity of possible number threes. "Let's stop telling people that I used to be called Emily. Emily was a kid. I may act like it, but I'm not a kid. Emily's history." Seven years ago, as her nineteenth birthday present to herself, she'd gone to the courthouse with all proper documents and changed her name to Antigone. "Legal civil disobedience," she'd joked, accompanied by her best friend Rachel. "You should become Ophelia and then we could have a travelling troupe." Rachel liked her name, though, and more importantly, had no interest in drowning herself. Which had made her wonder if Em wanted to die for her brother's memory. Did Em *have* a brother?

"Number four," she said, swerving to miss a rabbit running across the road, then quickly righting the car. "Not get killed. That's not a change, but it's sure as hell a good idea." The lights of Indianapolis were just barely visible on the horizon. "Number five," she sighed. "Get some coffee before I break number four." She accelerated to 95, feeling the Volvo start to shake to mimic her own unsteady hands.

"No I don't want to go to the Motor Speedway," she yelled minutes later at the highway exit signs. "I want to go to breakfast." After considerable searching, she rolled into a downtown parking lot under a fading sign that said **Albert's All-Night Cafe**. "Albert was probably forty-two owners ago," Antigone mused, "and curses this place every time he sees it for it still being open." She scanned the locals through the window-walls which separated the Cafe interior from the August night. "That one's going to ogle me. Baldy on the left there. Best to sit at the counter, close to the action. The help is always better than the customers at this hour anyway." In this particular case, by "the customers" she meant, "the bald man who I've predicted will ogle me, and that infatuated couple in the corner who I'd rather not recognize right now". The place was all but empty, and the cook and the waitress were chatting between the grill and the register.

She walked in, pressing both hands on the glass door, ducking at the sound of chimes spurred by her own movement. "Mornin'," she muttered at the counter, taking the middle seat.

"Coffee-black. You got egg sandwiches?"

"Yes ma'am."

"You got bacon?"

"Yes ma'am." The waitress's eyes receded into her head, getting a good look at whatever is behind one's eyes.

"You got sourdough?" The waitress shook her head. "Damn! I was on such a roll." The waitress smiled faintly in the same way that she humored the 65-year-old grizzled drunks that would be dining there come sunup. "Alright, egg and bacon on wheat, if you please."

"Here's your black coffee, miss. Or ma'am?"

"Miss." Always miss, she was getting pretty sure, at this rate. "I'm having the worst fucking day of my life, too, while we're at it."

"Anything we can do?" She said this and turned away, handing the ticket to the cook, who began by cracking eggs. He turned around and looked at Antigone, who was awfully pretty for half past three. Maybe *too* pretty, indeed, but she was dressed better than that.

Antigone looked right at the waitress, insisting on her eye-contact, a good way of talking to people. "You got a quarter?" She received a look from the waitress that made her say "No, I'm not bumming *change*, I'm making a decision."

"What kind of decision, miss? Is it men?" She *had* said something about "worst fucking day," so it had to be men, she was sure.

Before she could answer, the cook stepped in, "You know if you ask me," he smiled, "coins are a bit too, well, *arbitrary*." He checked to make sure she caught his drift--one never knew with the half-wits that rolled into this dump. Pretty and sharper than average, for this place, which was saying nothing. He turned back to the eggs. "I always was partial to rock-paper-scissors."

She hadn't thought of that. "Good call," she said earnestly. "But I don't really have a side I want to defend. And no opponent. And, wait a minute. Hang on. When you're done, could you do me a favor?"

He'd been waiting to hear those words, even though he knew much better.

"Order up!" he called, wiping his hands on his apron and approaching the counter directly, leaving the waitress out of her normal role of taking the plate from grillside to counter. "Yes?"

Loosely Based

"You too, please." She nodded to the waitress. "Okay, best two outta three. I have to figure out which city is who."

"You leavin' town?" the cook blurted.

"Just got here and I'm not staying," she admitted, but was not to be distracted. "All right now, you're Philadelphia, and you're St. Louis. Go for it."

"You want us to decide where you're *going*?" asked St. Louis the waitress.

Antigone guzzled coffee, bit half a sandwich half in one bite. Through the combined mouthful, "Sure. Why not?"

Philadelphia the cook shrugged. "Okay, le's do it, then. Two outta three?" he confirmed. "We'll go one, two, shoot, 'kay? Not one, two, *three*, shoot, but *one, two, shoot*. Ready?"

The waitress's pupils again sought comfort in the nether regions of her head. "I haven't done this since grade school." Which must have been, Antigone quickly reasoned, during the sixties? Maybe the seventies. Her worn hands stretched out, fist on palm, to meet their much darker partners, younger and twice as large. Antigone could hardly watch, knowing that she had to keep her mind blank; any will-power of her own would taint the results. She figured the stubbornness of St. Louis was a roughly fair match for the enthusiasm of Philadelphia.

She closed one eye and wincingly witnessed a paper-rock, scissors-paper decision in favor of Philly. She was fairly sure that the waitress still perceived a one, two, *three*, shoot reality which left her with rock the first time around, but her heart hadn't been in it to protest. "More coffee, Miss Philly?" she asked after it was over. Antigone nodded vigorously through her sandwich. "You ever *been* to Philadelphia?"

Antigone had to think on this, which she did by looking at the ceiling and bugging her eyes out. A boyfriend who'd been kinder than Rick had described this as her "fish looking out of water" look. This took a minute. "Uhhhh. No, I don't s'pose I have," she concluded. "Maybe I went through it once. But I haven't been properly introduced."

"You got friends there? Family?" The cook had returned to the grill, which he was diligently scraping with a spatula.

"Brotherly love!" They hadn't heard from the bald guy on the left yet. He had heard from them. Three pairs of eyes wheeled.

"What?" Antigone asked, dreading initiating a conversation.

"City of brotherly love," he slurred. "You're talking about

Philadelphia. That's its nickname."

"Well see if you can come up with the Pennsylvania state *bird*," Antigone muttered under her breath. Louder, "And do you love your brothers?" That should keep him guessing.

"Huh?"

"Do," she articulated slowly, as though he had misheard, not misunderstood. "you love your bro-thers?"

He scratched his head, possibly excavating for hair. "Lady," he finally slurred, "this is Indianapolis."

That seemed conclusive enough, a fitting curtain for her stay here at Albert's, but she definitely was a last cup away from drivability. *Philadelphia*? That was going to be a haul. She would have to crash between here and there, but let her put some miles on first. Rick would not go looking for her in Ohio, would he? Which was interrupted neatly by the cook, "You never told us what was wrong. Just said you was leaving."

"Oh. That's very astute." She winked at him. "I don't suppose it matters much. Just a tattoo I shouldn't have gotten, really." My story, she suddenly realized, is rather unoriginal. What killed her about her youth was that she'd lived it. She'd failed to elevate her youth to the level of behavior of those wise beyond their years. There was nothing new under the sun and, oh God, she even was beginning to *think* in cliches. It was bad enough that she behaved in them. The tattoo was Rick's idea, of course, but still. "I'm going to come back as a fruit fly," she said aloud. "Check please." The last of her coffee was lukewarm in her mouth, downright cold in her throat.

"You take care," the cook looked her in the eye as the waitress silently rang up the check. "Don't let anyone give you no trouble out there. Have a safe trip." He smiled.

"Thanks," she said, dropping a five on the counter. "If Philly works out, I'll come back and tip *you* some day." She laughed and fled, making sure to orchestrate a perfect exit. A heartbreaking finale. That made her night. A little confidence boost never hurt anyone. And where were her keys?

She turned around, seeing them in her mind before she witnessed them on the counter. Sighing, realizing that it really was becoming her worst fucking night, she re-entered. "How was Philadelphia?" asked the waitress snidely.

"Brotherly love!" bellowed the bald customer.

"Forget something?" the cook smiled playfully.

She grabbed her keys and ran out silently into the night. August's warmth enveloped her, and she could hear the gentle hum of whizzing cars on the freeway in the distance. "This is it. It's just me, future fruit fly, at your service. Onward we go. Siddhartha help me." She unlocked her car, got in, and prayed that it would start. On the lookout for anything that could possibly go wrong, she was warming to the idea that something had to go right. "But I have to make it go right. 'Be the change you want to see in the world,'" she quoted. This deserved another. "'Instant karma's gonna get you.'" She turned the ignition, revved the engine, reached for the radio dial, thought better of it, was overcome by curiosity, flipped it, realized it was set to a Chicago station, turned it to the nearest break in the static, and found only a commercial. "Maybe the *next* song will be 'Instant Karma'." The next song was "Under My Thumb", a Rick favorite. Touché.

She drove back to I-65 south, shortly thereafter exiting to I-70 east. "The change has come indeed," she intoned, switching the radio off.

"What I need," she reminded herself some time later, "is some good karma." She vaguely remembered a sign denoting arrival in Ohio, and about a thousand headlights since. Where did all these people come from at this time? Hers was supposed to be a solitary flight. "There's no sense in waiting for things to turn around without pushing them yourself. Let's get cranking. Time to push. I need to be on the lookout for some good karma making opportunities. You're not gonna make a fruit fly outta me. Yet."

A bug smashed into her windshield, splattering its remains in a concentrated area which, upon examination, was just out of the wipers' range. As the lights of cross-traffic vehicles passed by, they expanded in the translucent guts of the deceased insect. "It is ti-ime," she sang softly to herself, tunelessly, "for some go-od karma. Let's go kar-ma, let's go kar-ma!" She scanned the horizon, a steady line of trees, highway, trees. Trees, highway, trees. Trees, truck, highway, trees. Trees, broken-down vehicle, highway, trees.

Broken-down vehicle?

"It's going the wrong way. Damn. This night just keeps getting worse. Maybe I can, well, shoot, when's the next exit? If it's a mile or two, I can, hell, if it's five miles, I'd better go back there. There's probably nobody in it or some murderer, but I can try. I don't have a choice right now. What's gonna go wrong, are things gonna get *worse*?" She chuckled at the elusive idea. "Maybe it's Rick's car. He flew to Columbus and is coming back for me." A sign indicating Columbus's distance flew by, followed shortly by an exit sign. "Let's turn around and pray, shall we?" She did so, slowing her way up the off-ramp, across the overpass, back down onto the other side of the highway. "I-70 West," she read the sign. "Maybe this takes me to St. Louis after all."

She slowed to a moderated speed of 65 as she sought the broken-down vehicle she'd briefly spotted from the eastbound side. Seeing a dark splotch up ahead, she slowed, starting to drive into the shoulder, pulling up behind what appeared to be a very small car. She was fortunate to have seen it from the road. Guided, perhaps. "Well what have we here? You'd think these well-built economical Japanese cars never broke down. What was I thinking? They probably don't. This person's probably just tired. For Christ's sake, Antigone, it's almost dawn. It's like stopping at a rest area so you don't kill yourself with tired driving." She paused, wondering why she hadn't followed suit. "Or maybe it's a trap. There's a thousand ways this ends badly. Walk away." She had pulled the parking brake and was stepping out of her car. "Walk a-way." It didn't *feel* wrong. It felt, sorta, neutral? She was next to dark roadside woods in the middle of a very unfamiliar state. "Antigone Edgewood. Walk out of this situation now." She was running on fumes, and certainly not taking orders. She walked over to the car, hearing the soft crunch of shoulder gravel under her, and peered in, seeing nothing, half expecting something to jump out from the woods and consume her.

She ran back to her car, half fear, half the self-told excuse that she'd forgotten her flashlight. She got in the car, sat down, but didn't close the door. The glove-box was hanging open. This was creepy. There was a flashlight in the middle of it, small, innocent, waiting.

Like her, in this car.

"Who am I kidding?" She saw "ICK" protruding from her half-bare belly. "I'm not innocent and I certainly should stop being scared." She bravely, trying to laugh, stepped up, slammed the Volvo's car door, turned on the weak little flashlight, marched up to the small car, and in a cavalier manner knocked on the driver's side window.   Seeing movement inside, towards the back, she jumped a mile high, almost landing in the road behind her. "That," she said, regaining balance as a truck blew its horn at her, "would have been very bad. Fitting," she admitted, "but very bad still."

Nothing brings a person to their senses like almost getting run over by a honking semi.

Before she could act with her newly-acquired bearings in order, the back door of the car opened, and a haggard older woman poked her head out. "What on Earth is going on?"

She was certainly awake, shaken up, but not articulate quite. "Well, I, uh, y'know, um, y'see, do you need--"

"Are you here to rape and kill me?" the older woman asked baldly, cutting her babble. Antigone stepped forward, now just a foot from the car. "Oh," the woman blinked. "You're female. Couldn't quite see in the, do you have a cell phone?"

"Help," Antigone managed. "Do you need help?"

"You just heard me ask for it, didn't you? Thank you very much."

"Right, well. I can offer you a cell phone, sure. Are you lost, though? Is there something, uh, I could do?"

The woman was not in the mood for nonsense. She stepped up out of the car, squarely, shorter than Antigone, and had clearly just been sleeping awkwardly in the back seat of her Honda Civic. "Cell. Phone. All the help I need. Thanks again."

"Right." Antigone trudged back to her car, feeling strangely little better for the good karma she must have been earning. Looking back at the license plate, trying to determine what state was low on compassion, she saw this woman was from Kansas. Figures. But then she realized, just after looking away, that "KANSAS" was at quite a down-sloping angle, towards the woods.

"Lady!" she called, not looking up, but not opening her car either.

"My *na-ame* is Miriam!"

"It's not just the tire, is it?"

"What part of 'cell phone' don't you understand? I'm tired, I've just spent the night in my car, and I want to call triple-A and get out of this god-forsaken state. Why do you offer me *help* if you just ask *questions*?!"

"Do you have a spare?" Antigone proved Miriam's point.

"Would I be sleeping here, dealing with you, if I had a spare? I'm sorry. I'm just really tired and this has been a rough night and I would like to use a phone. That would be great. Thank you so much." She was trying not to talk incessantly, incoherently, and was starting to be pretty sure that this woman was about to rob her. Any minute, she'd see the man come out of the passenger seat, ready to steal, and maybe rape and kill for good measure.

Antigone opened her door again, fumbled around for the phone on her seat, and found it one and a half seconds before it rang. "Shiiiit!" she yelled, fearing that she'd answered it. "Oh crap. Uh, Miriam?!" Stepping out of the car again, to be heard. "Mir-i-am?! My cell phone's, uh, broken."

Oh God, here it came. This was the story. There was always a story. Whenever she read the paper about god-awful men in Kansas City or other urban areas, they always started the con with a story. It was really believable too, and everything sounded great until wham!, down came the tire-iron, or the knife, or out came the gun, and you always ended up stripped and bleeding in a cornfield somewhere. They hooked you with the story. Then came the kill. But she couldn't drive away on a flat, and where would she run? She'd always thought people were so *stupid* to get into these situations...

"Oh yeah? Broken?" she called meekly. Hadn't she heard it ringing just a second ago? Focus was sliding out from under her. Time to withdraw.

"Think, Antigone, think," she muttered under her breath. "This is a golden platter-served opportunity. Not time to fuck up. You get demoted to ant for stunts like this. But what am I gonna do, have her talk to Rick?" Speaking of spare tires... no time for mental tangents, though. Spare tires! She'd have to be careful on the way to Philly, but this was the opportunity she'd begged for.

"Miriam?!" Looking at the Civic, she saw no Miriam. She walked up, knocked on the driver's window. It wasn't exactly cold; what was she doing back inside?

Can I afford to open it a crack?, Miriam wondered behind her locked car door. She yelled through the window instead. "What?!"

"You can have my spare!"

Still trying to hook, knowing that she'd lost credibility, trying to restore it with generosity. She shook her head. "I'd just like a phone if that's okay."

"I can't use the phone. But you can *have* my spare tire! C'mon, I'll help you put it on." That would be necessary, if this were a sincere offer, because Miriam didn't know how to change a tire herself. But she wasn't biting.

"I'll just wait for someone with a phone."

The sun started to crack the horizon behind Antigone. "You don't trust me, do you?" She was getting hoarse yelling through the window. "I'll just leave the tire with you then. Shit."

Muttering all the way back, "You try to do something nice for people and they just flip you off. Nothing but the finger, all day long." More than anything, she was personally insulted that she hadn't been able to talk her way into this person's trust. Granted she had more impact with males, but generally she could get people to buy anything. Then again, they usually weren't bidding just before dawn on I-70. This somehow seemed to be little consolation.

She opened the trunk, hauled out the spare, slammed it back down amidst a flutter of dust. Coughing, she rolled the tire along the shoulder gravel, towards its new home on the back right wheel of a blue Honda Civic. Leaning it against the side of the car, she slapped the Civic's back windshield twice, waved at the car in general, and trudged finally back to the Volvo. She was ready to collapse. Just as she opened the door, for the last time, Miriam poked her head out of the car again, leaving her door open a crack.

"Uh, well, I didn't get your name, but uh, you know what? I don't know how to change a tire." A nervous laugh, just sounding inane. "Really. Do you think you could, uh, do it? I'd appreciate it a lot." She had no earthly idea whether to trust this bizarre blonde with the tire. Did people just forfeit their spare tires? This was more trap-like than ever, but the girl *was* about to drive off. Or was this just the perfect timing in her act? Sleep had not been restful on the roadside, and it was really time to either move on with life, or move on with the potential nightmare scene. As consciousness wobbled, Miriam distanced herself slightly from herself, and almost stopped taking an interest in what happened, as long as whatever it was happened *soon.*

Antigone, meanwhile, looked skyward with bugged eyes, the fish searching beyond water. "I better get to be a mammal of some kind for this. Or at least a reptile." She shrugged, wandered over to the Civic again, this time just leaving her damn door open. "You got a tire iron?"

Flinching at the mention of her expected murder weapon, Miriam almost fell out of the Civic. Getting herself together, she went to the trunk. Then she turned. "You're not going to kill me, are you?" She figured it couldn't hurt to ask, maybe gauge a reaction.

"I will if you don't hurry," Antigone sighed. "What kinda question is that? Do I look like I could kill you? Like I would want to?" She wrenched the tire iron from Miriam's hand and went to work.

Seeking evidence, Miriam found only traces of a tattoo on the girl's stomach. And her hair was awfully unkempt, but she was sure hers was about the same. Fair enough. "No. But you never know."

That was certainly true, Antigone thought. Truest comment of the night. "Damn straight," she had to concur.

It was becoming fully light by the time Antigone had finished changing the tire in the lingering uneasy silence. Her fingers felt weak and frail, and her whole soul seemed poised on the brink of implosion. The work gave her an outlet of mental energy, a depository for stress, but this drainage also took its toll. By the time she'd screwed the last nut, she could barely stand up. "Can I keep the old tire as a souvenir?"

"Uh, sure. Good night." This seemed a bit hasty, and at the Civic door, Miriam turned again. "Thanks a whole lot for this. I'm sorry about, well, being snippy. Is there anything I can, I mean, do you want some compensation?" This would break the cardinal rule of good karma and so Antigone vehemently shook her head. "Well okay, if you're sure." Ducking into the car, and then popping back out, "I didn't even get your name, did I?"

Antigone sighed. A really good test for new rule number three. It would be so easy to clunk out her old nondescript name in this situation, and be forgotten by morning. To end this dialogue with this silly ungrateful woman. To sleep, perchance to dream. "Antigone," she called.

The girl was certifiable. Perhaps a certified mechanic, too, but certifiable. Time to go. Miriam slammed the door without another word, started the car, and tore out of the gravel. She parted with a honk, Antigone not knowing if it was a parting farewell or a warning to any semis that might be in her future lane.

This was the last thing Antigone would think about for a while. She closed the door she'd deliberately left open, opened the back door, pushed some of her ramshackly laid out clothes into a more comfortable pillow-sized heap, closed the door behind her, and collapsed. She didn't even lock her Volvo before she fell asleep.

THREE

D aylight streamed through the open window of Tyler 401, waking its inhabitants almost simultaneously. Neither Matt nor David had thought to pull down the shade before sleeping. Matt had been trying not to look like he was failing asleep and David had never lived in a room with natural light before. His own room at home was in the basement of his parents' house, and everything was nice and artificial.

The sun had just risen in the east, and was now commanding the two young men to rise to face it. Clearly, either Matt or David would have to take this outside. As it turned out, they both did.

"Morning, roomie," David called loudly enough to wake Matt, but he was already. "How'd ya sleep?"

Matt looked around. Where *was* he? What was this *voice*? Who left the window open? "Uhh. I dunno."

David bounced out of bed, becoming resigned to rising early. "You don't know how you slept?"

Matt's recognition was awakening, though he was not. This was college, right? "Uhh. Sure."

David gave up. "So, how'd you like the album?"

What album?

"You fell asleep while I was playing it, I think." David had walked to the right side of the room, opposite the beds, so he could look at his roommate while he spoke to him. An even more than expectedly blank look was plastered to this still prostrate kid. "The disc. You know. Magical Mystery Tour. The *Beat*les." Blankness abounded. "Do you remember last night?"

Matt closed his eyes. It was like having a hangover that

55

talked. He remembered only strands of the previous night, most of which were manifesting themselves as he tried to move. *That* muscle had certainly been pulled, *this* one would rather not move for the next month. And when was the last time he'd *eaten*? "Did we eat last night?" Part of him was fairly sure he was addressing his central nervous system when actually talking to David.

David laughed uncomfortably. "I did, after the Tour ended. There was a bag of chips left over from the Hall Meeting. Which we missed."

Matt tried to suppress memories of Mrs. Helga Feirstone, and then her mention of sex, and then Catie, and then everything flooded back into the limelight of consciousness. Sobbing like a baby in front of, in front of, he looked across the room, David Benowski! "Christ," he couldn't help but utter.

"Huh?"

"Breakfast."

"Okay."

"Let's go." An odd thing to say, since he hadn't moved. He shook a foot. "You first."

"No."

No? A sigh. His mother had trained him well: do things like ripping off band-aids. "All right. Getting up." He rose all at once, was beaten back down by the ceiling. "Owwwww."

"You okay?"

"No."

"Still hungry?"

Cradling his head still, Matt jumped off the bed, nearly hitting his head again on the floor as he landed. Catching himself with his hands, he sprung back up and opened the door. "We are switching beds at semester," he informed David, "or I'm moving out."

They walked to breakfast in silence, purposefully, their shoes brushing the dew off the top of the grass and feeling the surging energy of not only a new day, but a new set of four years. Life had new perspective, and as Matt walked across his new campus, he felt the rush he'd been expecting after crossing the border into Missouri, or at the very least into Pennsylvania. Finally, he was on his way.

The dining hall, located in the student center, was closed. In fact, the student center was closed and would be for another twelve minutes. It was 6:48.

"So," David wheedled, leaning against a glass door with "Tippecanoe Student Union Building" plastered on it. "you've still never heard the Tour?"

Matt shrugged, coming back from his cross-lawn high. "In my sleep."

"That doesn't count."

"Guess not."

"Well, tonight then."

"I can't wait." A deep-fat fryer of sarcasm, with words held captive in metal mesh, then dumped into the vat to simmer and pop. This was becoming Matt's style, especially when dealing with someone who certainly seemed less mature than college.

6:52.

"Do you think the food'll be good?"

At least he wasn't talking about the CD! "Nope."

"Really? I hear they spend a lot of money on the dining facilities."

"I think they spend a lot on *every*thing." Matt's father had really impressed this idea upon him.

"Makes sense." A pause, as if the conversation would take wing and fly on its own after enough encouragement. Finding himself wrong, David began again. "Did, did your high school have good food?"

"Nope."

"Your mom?"

Matt looked down from his examination of the student center, generally called "T-SUB" by the locals. "She doesn't cook."

David blinked. "The microwave?"

"What about it?"

"Does it have good food?"

What kind of a question was that? "Nope."

David concluded that Matt did not believe in good food. Or good music, apparently, but that may have just been a lack of exposure. Kids really did come to college without much experience! A seeming non sequitir, "Do you have a guideline for life?"

"What?"

6:57.

"A guideline, you know, a way of well, leading your life."

Trying to drive larger vehicles in the future was about all

Matt could think of on the spot. He hadn't been expecting this kind of serious question from David and had been caught briefly unaware. The normal defenses weren't quite up with such an inquiry. "Not... really. I dunno."

"You're not religious, I take it?"

"Nope."

"You believe in anything?"

This kid was either really aggressive or just stupid. "What do you mean by *that*?"

"You have faith in anything? You know, trust. Parents? Friends? Your girlfriend?"

Did wounds create the urge for people to distribute salt? If no one ever got hurt, the sea would probably be fresh water. "Trust," Matt repeated.

"Exactly." David smiled, thinking Matt was getting something.

"Oh look, it's time to go in!" Matt pulled on the door, but even though the clock visible through the glass said 7:01, the door remained locked.

David chuckled. "Maybe you believe in *time*." He thought. "You look like you trust it enough." He was thinking to say "too much", but would let Matt figure that out himself.

Matt was motioning to a janitor on the other side of the door. "Hmmm?"

"*Time*. You believe in time?"

Matt turned around when he was sure that the door was soon to be opened. "The past," he said authoritatively. "I believe in history."

"Now we're getting somewhere!" David had almost assuredly not meant to say that aloud. "History."

The door hit Matt in the back, almost sending him into David. The moment was lost and they both wandered into T-SUB, nodding their appreciation at the janitor. Matt remembered his hunger and David was dealing with this new aspect of Matt, much like discovering a fourth dimension and reexamining the contents of a previously three-dimensional world. Hadn't "they" theorized that time was the fourth dimension?

T-SUB's interior was uninspired, or maybe it was just the early morning light. There was a large portrait of William Henry Harrison himself on one wall near the stairs, which was behind a large plexiglass sheet so as not to be vandalized. This was only moderately functional, as several etched names could be seen carved into the plexiglass at a certain angle or under certain light. The stairs went down into the basement of T-SUB, where the dining hall was, presumably so they could capture unwitting freshmen (did everyone use that insipid term "froshies"?) there and whisk them into the next day's meal before they'd met enough friends to notice their absence. At least such legends had been the lore at Topeka High School, and only made more sense given a basement cafeteria. Taped to one of the poles near the stairs was a large sign that said **FOOD** with an arrow pointing downwards.

"History," David nodded as they passed the portrait of William Henry Harrison. "There's a lot of history here. That's probably why you came, huh?"

"I came here," Matt maintained his acidic tone as he dropped off the final step, "to eat." With that he walked off in the direction of the grill. "Maybe," he told himself when out of earshot, "we'll have Benowski Sandwiches for lunch." His eyes were so focused on the grill he'd spotted as he walked through the empty cafeteria that he didn't notice that it wasn't actually empty. He almost plowed into someone who was just as intently focused on reaching a salad bar filled with, from the looks of it, tiny bite-size boxes of cereal.

"Uh, sorry," said the guy as he brushed against Matt. "You might wanna watch where you're going."

Matt looked up and kept looking up. He was confronted with someone a foot taller and proportionally much wider than himself. "Right," he delivered promptly. He'd been good at handling bullies since middle school. You agree with everything they say, wait till they turn around, and run like hell.

Were there bullies in college? How could there not be?

They were both standing there, perhaps rueful at their focus on their respective destinations. "What floor you on?"

"Tyler fourth."

"Hey! Me too, man. I'm Oliver Joseph. I don't remember seeing you at the hall meeting."

David had caught up, and was suddenly *there* next to Matt. "We missed it."

"Hey Joaquin! These are the guys that ditched the hall meeting!" His voice positively filled the cafeteria. Joaquin was nowhere to be found. "Bill missed you guys. I think you were the only two." There was suspicion in his voice that unnerved Matt.

"I was awfully tired," Matt mentioned.

"Whatever. Hey, you mind if we sit with you guys? Gonna be hallmates and all."

Matt had been hoping that there might not be an "us guys", that he might get a moment away from the ubiquitous David Benowski. "Sure."

"Great. Lemme get some cereal."

When Matt found the table, which happened to be the only one occupied in the sea of tables and chairs that filled the basement, he noted that Oliver's face was obscured by the wall of cereal he had amassed on (and around) his tray. An army of milk cartons was preparing a Viking-style assault on the cereal wall. Just visible beyond the milk army was a set of stacked arms with the top of a head centered squarely in their midst.

"Hey Joaquin. These are the guys that missed the hall meeting. Matt and Dave, I think."

"Flgorp" was audible from Joaquin's mouth, buried in his arms.

"Joaquin's tired," said a voice from behind the cereal boxes. "Some asshole woke us up this morning."

"Woke *you* up this morning," this correction was worth Joaquin raising his head to facilitate audibility. "*You*'re the asshole that woke *me* up this morning."

"What happened?" David asked.

"Some asshole, as I said, next door, was causing a ruckus. I think he threw something at the wall. Hit it pretty hard. Woke me up."

"It was the ceiling," Joaquin chimed in. Suddenly Oliver's hand was visible, dismantling the top of the wall, revealing his face. The sound of more cereal pouring could be heard, but was not yet within sight. "Because you woke up on top bunk, but I didn't wake up till you *jumped* down."

"So now you're not so tired, gettin' riled up, huh?" Joaquin replied to this accusation with renewed facial burial.

"You live in 403, don't you?" David was about to give the game up, Matt despaired.

"Why you say that?" Oliver queried through a mouthful of cereal.

"Oh. I read the names on the door. Trying to learn everyone, y'know."

"Since you missed the hall meeting."

"Exactly."

"Good idea. So which one's Matt and Dave?"

"I'm David. That's Matt."

"Great. Are either of your mothers dead?"

Joaquin groaned again. "What?" asked Matt, speaking for the first time since sitting down and still mostly in awe of what looked like four columns against seven rows of cereal. The diversity of brands was admirable, but maybe they only stocked thirty at a time in the salad bar.

"Just checking. They aren't, are they? 'Cause that's my one rule. No busting on the dead."

David ran a fork through his eggs. "Busting?"

Joaquin looked up. "Just lie. Trust me, say both parents are dead. And your children to come, just in case."

"Mine aren't dead, just divorced." Matt took a swig of coffee. Nope, still couldn't stomach the taste. "Can I have a milk, Oliver? Got enough?"

A protective hand blocked the path towards the milk army. "Well shit, man, everyone's mom's di*vorced*. Get your own milk. Can't you see I'm eating cereal?"

"Mine aren't," insisted David.

"No, I can't *see* the cereal," Matt backed his chair out from under the table. At least it wasn't an attached bench like at Topeka High. Wood chairs, wood tables! This was why there was no tuition at a public high school. Or maybe it was just that there were trees in Pennsylvania from which to extract wood. Corn stalks made lousy furniture.

"A smartass. Nobody likes a smartass, Matt."

"Mine aren't divorced."

"Do you want a cookie?"

"No," said David, turning back to his eggs quietly. "I just wanted you to know."

"*Your mom* wanted me to know!"

Joaquin groaned again, retreating from slumber once more. "It doesn't even make sense. It's such a stretch most of the time."

"Your mom stretched most of the time!"

David spit out part of his egg laughing. Joaquin rolled his tired eyes. "Oh sure, laugh now. One out of twenty are actually good. But you'll get tired of it real quick."

"Your mom *didn't* get tired of it real quick! In fact, she thought a lot more than one out of twenty were actually good!"

Matt returned with three cartons of milk and confusion as to why his roommate was choking. A modicum of hope, granted, but mostly confusion. "Here" he set two milks next to the army. "Reinforcements. What's wrong with *him*?"

"What did I tell you about smartasses?" But there was a grin through Oliver's tough demeanor. "He thinks I'm funny." David's breathing was almost normalized, and he began panting a little. "You sound like your mom!"

David kept panting, and Matt looked over the cereal wall. "You played football in high school, didn't you?"

Oliver gulped more cereal. "You kidding? I don't run."

"But I bet you hit."

"No." Oliver looked away, eating more cereal. "But I'm gonna lose some weight, if that's where you're going, smartass."

Did this guy actually think that *he*, Matt, was one to crack jokes about others' weight? Between the three of them that were awake, they could start a chapter of Jenny Craig! "Good for you."

Oliver couldn't tell if he was serious or not, but this Matt character didn't seem to be serious much of the time. "Hey, I don't see you eating cereal, smartass. You could drop a few pounds yourself."

"No, I mean it, good for you."

"Oh."

There was silence, and another row of cereal boxes began to fall. "Say, Oliver? You ever hear *Magical Mystery Tour*?"

"Sure. Saw the movie too. Trippy shit."

"Do you know the *real meaning* behind it?"

"Yeah. Do drugs. That's it. That's all the sixties were about."

"No, I mean the *real* meaning. I mean, yeah, there's drug stuff too, but the *real*ly good stuff. The *meaning*." If he said that word enough, maybe it would *mean* more.

"Uh. Is there one?"

David beamed. "Is there? Is there ever! Let me tell you about *meaning*!"

"Your mom told me about meaning," Oliver interjected, but his expression looked interested.

"The Tour," David announced, "is a Metaphor for Life."

"Yeah?"

"I dare say," David was almost breathless, about to display the map with the most treasure-laden X on the planet. "*The* Metaphor for Life."

"Hm," Oliver said through more cereal. He was really putting those flakes away.

"Each song," David continued, enraptured, "is a symbol, no, a guidebook for a phase of life. Eleven tracks, eleven life stages. Eleven ways of living. Perfectly timed, in perfect accordance with reality." It was fascinating to see this kid aglow.

"Your mom," muttered Oliver through his mouthfuls, "was perfectly timed." He said it softly, perhaps actually thinking about David's words. Matt was laughing to himself and wondering if Joaquin's haircut was more attractive than his own. Though Catie had always liked his hair, before that night...

David was hurt. "If you keep cracking those jokes," he said, "I'll keep the secrets of life to myself."

"Okay, kid, okay. Just razzing ya. Can't help it. Like your mom, I can't help it."

David nodded through a dubious look. "Right, so like I was saying, the key to life. Stage by stage." He had become disinterested in food. "You want to head back to Tyler and give it a listen?"

"Gimme a minute. Cereal calls." If it were a long-distance call, it would break his bank. Fortunately, there was very little distance indeed between him and the remaining boxes. "Gimme a preview."

"'Magical Mystery Tour'," David said, "the first song, the first stage. The introduction. Just as we are introduced to life, the song introduces us with simple words and repetition. Roll up, roll up--"

"Do you *rehearse* this?" Matt had to know.

"No, I, I just st*udy* it. Roll up, roll up--"

"Drug reference!" shouted Oliver, and some milk splattered on David's cheek. "Rolling papers! Roll up a joint!"

David bent his head down as if mentioning marijuana were as illegal as distributing it. "Right, sure, that's one way of looking at it. You can say the whole album," he was snarling now, after remembering the cafeteria was devoid of listeners, "is just a bunch of high musicians getting high and singing about it." A pause. "Hell, you can say *life* is just people getting high and talking about it! But *that*... would miss the point."

"Your mom didn't miss the point."

David got up, picked up his tray, and stormed away from the table. Dropping it on the now stationary conveyor belt, he came back to collect his roommate as he would a backpack. "Coming Matt?"

"Um. In a while. You go on ahead."

"You're done eating."

"I, uh, yeah."

"So, what're you gonna wait for?"

"Maybe I feel like it."

"Okay." And he was gone.

Joaquin looked up, as though startled. "Oliver go? Oh."

"Just my crazy roommate."

"I'm not going anywhere," Oliver chewed, "until I finish this meal."

Making silent eye-contact, Joaquin and Matt stood up, Matt grabbed his tray, and they both left Oliver amongst the ruins of his breakfast.

When they were on the steps between the basement and the ground floor of T-SUB, judging themselves to be halfway between their roommates, Joaquin finally seemed passably awake. "I'm sorry. I'm really bad with names. What's yours again? If I had to guess, I'd say it's 'Your Mom'."

"Matt."

They shook hands, awkwardly, on the steps. "Joaquin."

"I remember."

William Henry gazed from over Joaquin's shoulder, looking ready to extend his own hand through the etchings of "98 RULZ".

"Oh."

"I hate my roommate."

"Me too. I mean, my roommate. You understand."

"Yeah. I'm not a huge fan of your roommate either."

Joaquin laughed. "He's a huge fan of your mom, apparently."

"All our moms."

"Right."

"Where you from?"

"Taos, New Mexico. You?"

"Topeka, Kansas. Wow, New Mexico's even farther west than Kansas!"

"Harrison tries to draw from all fifty, every year. That's what the Orientation folks told me."

They were at the doors exiting T-SUB again, and Matt could barely see David's silhouette against the rising sunlight in the distance. He thought David was kicking at the grass, but it could merely have been the way he walked normally. "Why'd you come here?"

"My roommate woke me up. He said someone next door--"

"No. Harrison."

"Oh. My sister liked it."

"Your sister?"

"Yeah. She's a senior here."

"Cool."

"She thinks so."

They paused, looking at the grass, Matt shading his eyes against the sun, making sure that David was well ahead of them, out of earshot. "She's not an Orientation uh, person, is she?"

"No."

"Is she up?"

Joaquin checked his watch, revealing 7:47. "I don't think she's flown in yet."

"Oh."

"Hey, I'm going to get some more sleep, dude. Maybe I can sleep through the Orientation activities."

"Activities?"

"You didn't know? Didn't you read through the packet they sent home?"

Which home had they sent it to? "Uh, packet? No. I guess not."

"Mandatory. But I don't think we're graded. Show us the campus, get people to meet people, you know. Bill told us all about it last night."

"Bill."

"Our R.A.. He's a cool guy. A little uptight, but I guess they pay him to be."

The sun seemed to be ascending awfully quickly. "Yeah."

"Well, I'll see you around, Matt. What room did you say you were in?"

"401. Next door. Get some sleep."

Joaquin had been walking away slowly and now he jogged off, anticipating renewed rest with every step. Toni, his sister, had advised against every Orientation activity there was. She had helped him lobby their parents that he not even attend the Orientation days, but the elder Garcias had flatly refused. "Not everyone's an art major, Antonia," they had reminded her. "Some students actually study things and like to meet other people." This information hadn't surprised Toni quite as much as they'd expected, but almost. Joaquin was already meeting people left and right, he realized, and the studying would come soon enough. For now, he was sure the inside of his eyelids would provide plenty of scintillating facts.

Up four flights of stairs, down two doors, a right turn, and he leapt into bed. The room was still dark and comforting, a little unfamiliar, awfully small, far too humid, but he was utterly exhausted. No rush for anything. Right now, it was still summer. Still warm, and there was time to rest...

Horns blasted through the walls, shoving him into consciousness. *"Roll up roll up for the Magical Mystery Tour, step right this way!"*

It was going to be a long morning.

FOUR

They let her into the room. It was a stereotype incarnate. Dark walls, blinds on one side, closed. A square table in the center, metal. A lamp hanging down, lit. Two chairs, one nearer and empty. An armed guard in the back-right corner, by the window. A mirror on the left wall. A tape-recorder.

"Hello. Have a seat." The man in the chair, fortyish, blunt, trying to be friendly but he'd forgotten how.

"Hi."

"You don't want to have a seat?"

She sat, almost dropping immediately from her position. The door closed behind her.

"You've refused counsel?"

"Not refused. I can't afford it."

"One may be provided for you, free of charge."

"I don't like lawyers."

"You seem awfully young to have an opinion on lawyers."

"My parents don't like lawyers."

"Where are your parents?"

"I don't want them here."

"Where are they?"

"At work."

"Why don't you want them here?"

"You're going to ask me questions."

"You don't like your parents, do you?"

"I didn't say that."

"Do they know you're here?"

"Kinda."

"All right then. Shall we begin?"

"I guess."

The man reached for the tape-recorder. "I'm on your side. I'm Joe and this is Mitch, and we're here to ask you a few questions today. As you know. I'm going to turn this on for everyone's protection." He did so. "State your name for the tape."

"Catie."

"Your full name."

"Catie Hanson."

"Your full official name. Your *legal* name."

"Catherine Ramona Hanson."

"All right, then Catherine,"

"*Catie.*"

"Katie."

"Yeah?"

"Okay, Katie, state the date for the tape."

"I don't know what day it is. School's out."

"It's December 22nd, Katie."

"December 22nd."

"The year, too."

"December 22nd, 2000."

"And who is present in the room?"

"You. And me. And that guy."

"Mitch."

"Yeah, with the gun. Mitch."

"And who am I?"

"Joe?"

"Officer Joe Ewing, examiner."

"Right."

"Okay, Katie, how did you know Matthew Norton?"

"I dated him."

"Was he your steady boyfriend?"

"I dunno how steady he was. Do you mean was he stable?"

"Was he your, uh, regular boyfriend?"

"He was my boyfriend for a while, yeah."

"How long?"

"I dunno. Six months."

"Oh, I'm sorry I didn't ask earlier, do you want anything? Cup of coffee?"

"You got any smokes?"

"Are you of age?"

"You asked if I wanted anything. I'm not buying them from you."

"Well, uh."

"It's legal for a two-year-old to smoke in Kansas. It's not legal to *buy*. Are you selling?"

"I guess you don't need a lawyer."

"Excuse me?"

"Here."

"Thank you." She lit up. "Can I use the recorder as an ashtray?"

"I will take this opportunity to remind you that you're in a police station, Katie! Not to mention on tape with an officer of the law."

"I don't have to be here." She stood up.

"That's true, that's true, you don't." He looked at a notepad he'd brought from under the table as she slowly resumed her seat. "Six months, you said?"

"Something like that."

"Were you sleeping with him?"

"Excuse me?"

"Did you and Matthew Norton have sexual intercourse?"

"No."

"I can give you immunity for being under age, if that's what you're worried about."

"No. We weren't fucking."

"Why not?"

"What kind of a question is that? Would my lawyer object to a question like that?"

"You've watched too many courtroom dramas, Katie."

"I didn't want to fuck him. Would you?"

"I don't even know him. That's why I'm asking you these questions, Katie. Was he ugly?"

"Ugly? No, that's not it. He's just not the kind you sleep with, that's all."

"Are you a virgin?"

"How is this relevant?"

"So you're not."

"No, I am!"

"So that's why you didn't sleep with Mr. Norton."

"You make him sound like a spy."

"Was he a spy?"

"Of course not. He was a dork."

"A dork?"

"Yes, a dork. I was two years younger than him. He wanted me to sleep with him. He said he loved me."

"Did he love you?"

"How the hell should I know?"

"You dated him for six months."

"That doesn't tell me a thing about love, now does it?"

"I'm asking the questions, if you don't mind."

She put her cigarette out on the table. "He wanted me to sleep with him as his going-away present."

"Going away to..."

"College."

"Ah. Did you?"

"I already *told* you I didn't."

"Why didn't you?"

"Are you deaf? I didn't want him to be my first time. He just wasn't *that* guy, you know?"

"Did you tell him that?"

"No."

"What did you tell him?"

"I made up some excuse. I think it was being outdoors."

"Outdoors?"

"Well, I, now I remember, I saw this cricket and it freaked me out. Did you know crickets are actual insects? They look freaking scary. Like cockroaches. I flipped out."

"You were going to do it outdoors?"

"Not really. We were, you know, I don't see how any of this is relevant."

"That's for me to see. You could have a lawyer here if you wanted."

"That's going to keep coming back up, isn't it?"

"Quite possibly. Now then, you were outside?"

"I don't remember. I flipped out, then we went in the car. I made something up about his car."

"What was his car?"

"Well it wasn't his car. It was his mom's. A Honda Civic."

"A Civic? Are you sure?"

"Yeah. It was his mom's. Sometimes he'd drive his dad's Suburban."

"They're divorced."

"Yeah."

"A Suburban? He drove that often?"

"Not really. Once in a while."

"Maybe he just didn't drive it much around you."

"No, I think he drove it around me as much as he could."

"Hm."

"You got another cigarette?"

He slid a pack at her across the table, coming from the same mysterious location as the notepad.

"Thanks."

"Yeah. You ever see him drive anything else?"

"Like what?"

"I dunno. An Oldsmobile?"

"A *what*?"

"An Oldsmobile."

"You've got to be joking."

"Okay, I guess that's a 'no'."

"Good guess."

"How'd you meet Matthew?"

"Soccer game."

"Yours or his?"

"You don't know much about this kid, do you?"

"Why do you say that?"

"It's obvious is all. My soccer game."

"He saw you there?"

"You could say that."

"Was he stalking you?"

"You might call it that."

"Would you call it that?"

"No. We have... fans."

"Who want to sleep with you."

"You're really focused on sex, aren't you?"

"People do things for sex. I see a lot of crimes for sex. I need to understand the motivations of people to know why they commit crimes."

"Motivations, huh?"

"Yes, I'm trying to establish Mr. Norton's motivations."

"He liked soccer. He liked *me*."

"Does he still like you?"

"How the hell should I know?"

"When did you last talk to him?"

71

"A few weeks ago."

"In person?"

"No, on I.M."

"'I.M.'?"

"Instant Messenger."

"I see."

"It's a computer program that lets you chat."

"Oh! Chat! I see. Did you do that regularly?"

"Every now and then."

"What did he say?"

"You want a transcript?"

"Interesting details."

"There weren't any. He's fine, his friends are fine, his classes are fine."

"Sounds like my children."

"What?"

"Nothing. Everything's just fine, huh?"

"Yeah, I guess so. Or it was."

"Were you proud of him?"

"Proud?"

"Yeah."

"He was older, I guess, so that was something. I mean, a lot of boys like me. I don't really need to, well, I dunno. I mean I like the kid, don't get me wrong. *Proud* doesn't really say what I'd say though."

"What would you say?"

"Well. I wish he'd stayed with me in college."

"Oh yeah?"

"That'd make me proud. To have a college boyfriend."

"Is *that* why you didn't sleep with him?"

"No! Jesus! What's with all the sex?"

"Just motivations."

"I'm starting to wonder about *your* motivations."

"So why did he break up with you?"

"He didn't. We were thinking about staying through in college, but he was going to Harrison."

"Right, Harrison."

"Well I can't stay with someone long-distance!"

"You wanted him to go to, uh, what's the local school?"

"Washburn. You're from out of town?"

"I'm asking the questions, as you may recall. Washburn."

"Or the state schools, those would have been fine. Something in Kansas. Exactly what I wanted was exactly what he didn't want."

"He wanted to get away?"

"You could say that."

"Did he have, uh, enemies?"

"Lord no."

"That was emphatic."

"Yeah, it's just absurd. Matt? Enemies? It's like a soccer field having enemies. He just sat there and got walked on, y'know? He couldn't have had enemies."

"What about other boys who liked you?"

"I wouldn't call that an enemy. And no one liked me *that* much. Except Matt. But he got me."

"Any former friends?"

"Of mine?"

"Of Matt's."

"I'm not convinced Matt had friends. Except for my friends, y'know. We'd hang out, all of us, sometimes."

"What did you do?"

"What do you mean?"

"Describe hanging out with Matt and your friends."

"We'd just do shit, y'know, like the movies or cards or something. Bowling once, I think. Nothing special."

"Drinking?"

"I don't know if Matt was exactly a drinker."

"Really? He did other stuff?"

"Other stuff?"

"Like what you're doing. Smoking."

"Lord no. I smoke sometimes. Matt never smoked."

"Did he know you smoked?"

"I didn't then, really."

"You sure Matt never smoked?"

"Positive."

"Would you bet money on that?"

"Millions."

"Interesting."

"Is it?"

"Did Matt buy you lots of gifts?"

"Once or twice."

"Lots?"

"I wouldn't call it lots. He was infatuated. He was a good guy. He got me flowers and a few little things."

"Little things?"

"Yeah, nothing big."

"Nothing... costly?"

"No, I don't think so. Matt's parents are kinda rich, but they mostly got him things. Not much cash. He always wanted to show me in, uh, other ways."

"Oh?"

"I don't think he valued gifts much. They never really got him excited, so he figured they wouldn't do much for me."

"You talked about this?"

"Once or twice."

"And he didn't get excited because he was so rich?"

"His parents were."

"How rich?"

"I don't know. Doctors."

"But Matt didn't have much cash?"

"Enough. Not tons."

"Not tons. Hm. What about his college friends? You said you talked to him recently."

"IMed him."

"Right. Chat. Uh, what were his friends like?"

"I never met them. I haven't seen Matt since August."

"Well what kind of crowd did he seem to be running in?"

"Dorks, mostly."

"Dorks?"

"Harrison's full of 'em. He hated his roommate. He was always playing this CD over and over and talking about how it was the key to life. Funny shit, really."

"Which CD?"

"I dunno. Some Beatles CD, I think."

"Beatles. A bit old, isn't it?"

"The roommate's a weird kid. You should be talking to him."

"I intend to."

"Good for you. Anything else?"

"You know, Katie, your contempt will not stand up in court."

"We're not in court, are we?"

"You could be soon."

"Well maybe I should get a lawyer."

"Katie, there is one more very important thing."

"Shoot."

"What was Matt's involvement with drugs?"

"Drugs?"

"Illegal drugs."

"You're asking me what Matt's involvement was with *drugs*?"

"That's correct. Marijuana, narcotics, anything like that."

"Are you sure we're talking about the same Matt Norton here?"

FIVE

R ain had covered much of the day's Orientation activities, leaving the freshman-drenched campus cooped up and cranky. Eager yellow-shirts had barely noticed the onrushing clouds and consequential downpours, but rational people had stepped in and informed them that already disinterested "froshies" were not up to enduring the moisture. It seemed novel to the volunteers that disoriented freshmen were likely to stay that way under rainfall.

Joaquin had finally hoped to acquire some blissful rest after two renditions of David's "Tour" from next-door, but by that time, the rain on the roof had obliterated any opportunity for sleep. Matt, after being given a chance to "savor" the experience of the CD (which was, after all, his own as a gift from David) without interruption, was to receive an indoctrination lecture from Mr. Benowski later that evening.

Meanwhile, both David and Matt had people to call back home. For David, it was a long and benign chat with the parents. For Matt, it was time to confront Catie.

For David, said confrontation meant a monologue, which he had to admit he was paying a good bit of attention to.

"Well, you know, not so bad. I mean, really, I could do much worse.

"Yeah, I guess you could say that.

"What?

"Yeah, I think it's *prob*ably better than a Kansas school. I don't know. It's too early to tell! The only thing is these Orientation volunteers. They're like rabid dogs. Nipping at our heels all the time, threatening us with hydrophobia.

"Hydrophobia. It's when you're scared of water. Yeah, if you get rabies you get that. That's not really the point, but...

"I just know. I don't know how I know. Some TV show, I think. Anyway, I was *say*ing that they're really a pain in the rear. Too happy somehow.

"I am not morose! I'm just glad to be away from Kansas, but, what?

"No, not *every*thing I thought. Gimme some time! Classes don't start for a long time yet. How are yours going?

"Yeah, Miller's a weirdo, but I wouldn't worry about it much. Just don't talk too much in class and he won't think you're a problem. That was my solution anyway.

"Okay, so talk in class *some*. Just don't over-do it.

"Really?

"I miss you too, Catie. More than you know.

"Not enough to transfer. But I do miss you. I wish things had turned out...

"No, it was my fault. I should've gotten the Suburban.

"The Suburban. Something other than the Civic. Oh, never mind.

"Dinner? Well, I guess you're an hour earlier. Or something.

"School tomorrow, right.

"We don't start till, I dunno. A week?

"Say hi to him? Are you nuts?

"Well, no, I *like* him, but well, he has this thing. About music.

"A specific kind, look, I'll tell you later, okay?

"I miss you.

"A lot. You too.

"Bye."

"Your girlfriend?"

"Ex."

"Right, sorry. Didn't sound like an ex."

"You were listening?

"A little."

"Well she says to say hi to you."

"Well hi to her right back."

"She's off the phone."

"I can see that." Heavy rainy silence. "Said she was a sophomore?"

"Starting junior."

"You love her?"

"What?"

"All you need is love."

"Oh Christ, don't go starting with that again."

"I haven't *even* started yet. You haven't gotten the real meat of the meaning yet! That'll come in a few minutes. Give it time to sink in. But my question was if you loved her."

Matt was trying hard to give this guy a chance. The disc hadn't been nearly as bad as he'd expected, though parts of it were a tad repetitious and some just didn't make sense. Eggmen? Walrus? Goo goo g'what? But the secret to appeasing David seemed to be putting up with his "Tour" and trying to meet him on reasonable ground elsewhere. He just had this habit of souring said ground with his own *forward*ness. It was like negotiating with a well-meaning Mack truck. But he had a year to spend, seemingly more if it was going to keep raining, and it wasn't going to be well-spent looking down on him and waiting to steal his first girlfriend away.

That would be too long a wait anyway. Oh, he couldn't help it. Speaking of girlfriends though, "Love? I don't know what love is."

"Really?"

"Do you?"

"I didn't say that. I just asked if you really didn't know."

"Is love following someone wherever they go, looking at them from afar, and then finally being bowled over by who they really are?" Well *that* was more open than he'd meant to be, but hey, it was hypothetical. Right? "Being so bowled over that you can't speak, or sit still, or form a complete sentence without thinking of their words, their ideas?"

"Wow. That'd be cool."

"Would it?" Ah, a chance to distance it from himself. "I don't know." And then, because it was on his mind all the time, "Maybe love is sex."

David actually snickered. Matt had not known till that moment in time what a snicker was.

"What? What's wrong with that?"

"Are we..." he was on the verge of another snicker. "Animals?"

"You haven't had sex, have you?" Need to keep him in his

place, especially if he was going to *snicker*.

"Well, *no*, but I can't imagine it'd be much different than..."

Okay, it was definitely too early to think about his roommate masturbating! "There's another *person* there! There's another, another an*atomy*!"

"The *feeling*'s the same." He said the word with a bit too much feeling.

"Not if you're in love."

"Ah, so you have to be in love *before* sex, is that what you're saying? Then the sex has nothing to do with it!" This guy was certainly too sharp for his own good.

"Okay, maybe."

"So love isn't sex."

"What do *you* think love is, since that's all *you* need?"

David had been waiting for this. The whole conversation might just have been a smokescreen for getting this opportunity. "I think love is writing a girl's name onto an overpass."

"*What*? Are you on *crack*?"

"You heard me."

He had indeed. "Hence the question."

"Seriously. Think what that means. A highway is forever. They never repaint graffiti, not for years anyway. And who's going to paint over the name of your girl? Your love? Your gang, sure, but only a real asshole is going to cross out *John Loves Mary*. Or *John Hearts Mary*, that's a real killer. With the heart just barely burgeoning over the J and the M?"

Burgeoning? "You show love in *spray-paint*?"

"Tell me if a girl, if, what's-her-name?"

"Catie."

"If Katie wrote *Katie Hearts Matt* with a big red heart just dipping into the K and the M..."

"The K?"

"Tell me you wouldn't fall over with joy."

"Well..."

"That's love." He smiled with Cheshire satisfaction.

"Huh." It was a full-fledged word, occupying the space of sentences.

After a time, "Well?"

"I think I'd like it better if the heart were through the E and the M. You know? Cuz otherwise the heart is basically just behind her name and not mine, and then what good is that? Because if I already love her, there's no need to see the heart behind *her*; it should be linking us equally, with her expressing love for me."

"You really think so?" David had not been expecting much analysis.

"Yup. I really do."

"Fair enough. I guess that works too. The point is, a highway is forever."

This didn't ring quite true. "Unless there's an earthquake."

"How many earthquakes do you get in Pennsylvania? Or in Kansas, for that matter?"

Yeah, well, Matt had only seen them on TV anyway. "Not a lot," he had to grant.

"You know the other things highways are good for?"

Getting him to this blasted room under the rain with this funky roommate was high on Matt's list. "Travel?"

David shook his head and reacquired the burgeoning grin. "Buses."

"Right. Travel."

"What *kind* of travel?"

Matt shrugged and, as his shoulders fell back to normal position, he realized his fatal error. He'd opened the door to a Benowski Beatles segue.

"Magical Mystery Tour travel!" There was no going back now. It was raining and he wasn't tired and, having missed the hall meeting, they didn't know anyone on the hall. Except the R.A. and Oliver (shudder on two counts), plus Joaquin, who was not precisely enamored with the stream of various noises coming through the wall. And he *was* the *slight*est bit curious about his roommate's crackpot theories.

"Okay, Davey. Gimme the overview."

Davey? "Do you want me to call you Matty?"

"My mother calls me Matty."

"What? Oh, for a second, I thought you were Oliver."

They laughed over this. A good sign for both, more relief for David and vague hope for Matt. Then it was Tour Time again.

"Okay, I'll give you the basic Tour." This did not go over as well as David's prior laugh-inducing success. He moved quickly along. "Eleven tracks, eleven life stages. Eleven guides to what life is all about."

"Mm."

"Exhibit number one, 'Magical Mystery Tour'. Title track.

Title? We are named at birth. We are introduced at birth, to the world. We are invited to, as the Beatles say, 'step right this way'. To be born, to live, to grow, to learn to *walk*. Everything is rosy at life's beginning. 'They've got everything you need. Satisfaction guaranteed.' Not, as some would say, petty drug references.

"What you *really* need to know at birth, you don't learn till death, which is 'All You Need is Love'. It takes a lifetime of living before you realize that, or at least for most people. By that time, too, all you get is love, if you've done right and get to Heaven."

"The Beatles believed in Heaven?" It was Matt's first interruption. He had to admit that the explanation of the title track seemed to make sense.

"Of course! Track two, 'The Fool on the Hill'. Do you know who the fool *is*?"

"Uh." He had honestly thought of David while hearing the song.

"Jesus Christ!"

Matt interpreted this as an interjection. After a pause, which David spent thinking that his revelation was merely hitting Matt like a ton of bricks, Matt had to say "I'm sorry I don't get everything you say. Will you *tell* me?"

He *had* to have heard him. The rain was awfully loud though. "Jesus Christ!"

"I guess not."

"You don't see it? You don't see the references laden in the song? Okay, you've only heard it once, but listen! 'He never listens to them, he knows that they're the fools, they don't like him.' It's Biblical! The whole song is about a guy rejected by his society, cast out as a fool, with a veritable thorny crown! Yet he's *not* the fool! The fool is the only one who *knows*."

"Oh, like, you really *mean* Jesus Christ."

"Well what else would those words mean? You're nuts! It's all in the words. 'The eyes in his head see the world spinning round.' The eyes of God, in the incarnation of man." He was sounding like a fire-and-brimstone preacher, gaining eloquence and vocabulary as he warmed to his favorite subject.

"Wait a second. How is *Jesus Christ* a phase of life?"

"Religion. Second stage. After you're born and introduced, you get baptized. You learn about God. You think about God. If you know what's right."

"Huh."

"At least, that was the sixties. The Tour may have aged a little. It's a mix, you must remember, of what is and what should be. Not the most perfect consistency. A lot of both. Which is important in life."

"Right."

"Here the Beatles recom*mend* more than they ob*serve*, perhaps."

"The Beatles were religious?"

"They had to be. It's all over their lyrics."

"So are walruses!"

"Well, one walrus. And is that the right plural of *walrus*?"

"Who cares? What else would it be?"

"Well it ends in 'u-s'."

"So?"

"It should have a plural of 'i' in that case, right? Walri."

"Wal*ri*?!"

"Yeah, I think that's gotta be right. Walri. Anyway, about the Walri. Phase six, 'I am the Walrus'. Everyone thinks this is John Lennon going crazy or Paul being dead or who knows what. It's nonsensical, says everyone."

Matt was nodding vaguely. "Call me Everyone."

"You know what else is nonsensical?" It was a rhetorical question, but Matt had a lot of disparate answers chomping at the bit. "A *mid-life crisis*! Eleven stages, and number six has five before it and five after. It's in the middle of the album, in the middle of everything, when someone one day wakes up and realizes that everything is half-over. Their youth is behind them. They have seen their parents go in 'Your Mother Should Know', realizing their own mortality! They have been stressed to the hilt as they reach full adulthood in 'Blue Jay Way'! They have only the slow descent of age ahead. And what happens? As they go crazy, the world strikes back at them. 'Man you been a naughty boy, you let your face grow long.' 'You let your knickers down.' It's non-stop condemnation as they go crazy, often letting their knickers down by sleeping around. Finding a new identity! Becoming the walrus, from a sea of eggmen, asserting individuality against the grain of faceless masses of normal married men! It's the quintessential mid-life chaos, complete with consequences in 'Hello Goodbye'!"

Matt was sure that David was about to hyperventilate. His

speech had taken on an almost auctioneer-like quality, as though he were surprised himself at how it all fit together, but it would fall apart should he not say it all in a certain allotted time. "It *is* crazy," was all Matt could think of to share the air with David's labored breathing.

"Of course it's crazy! *Life* is crazy! Life is a non-stop bus ride, spinning out of control. It's nuts."

"Yeah. So, if there's finding religion and getting stressed, haven't we skipped most of our real youth? I mean, where's high school? Where's college? Where's the senior prom and graduation?"

David, recovering from the excitement of pre-living his mid-life crisis, regained the Cheshire look one more time. "*That*," he drew out his words, "is stage three."

"Song?"

"The most enigmatic song on the whole album. Provides very few clues, and almost no guidelines. It is chaotic, it is strange, it is impossible. 'Flying' is stage three, and there are no words. Only a bizarre progression of music."

"So why are you so sure that's high school and college?"

"Didn't you hear what I just said?"

SIX

A ntigone was dreaming about being in St. Louis and hanging out with Ashley when an air-raid warning foretold doom for Missouri's largest city. Panic overtook the place where Antigone's subconscious imagined Ashley might live, then was suddenly transported to the Gateway Arch as it crumbled in the wake of the deafening noise. It wasn't even the planes that did it, it was the mere *siren*. The place would be leveled only because of its anticipatory harbinger.

And then she woke up, abruptly, to find that she was in Philadelphia, in a place where her conscious perceived that Betsy *did* live, and the place was remarkably resilient in the face of an air-raid siren. Instinctively, she looked to the window for planes, or perhaps a crumbling, well, the Liberty Bell already *was* cracked, wasn't it? But there was only the faint rising light of dawn, in which buildings beyond could begin to be discerned. Not distinctly yet, but seemingly becoming more obvious with every second. So why the air-raid?

She shifted uncomfortably on the couch, sat up, feeling her hair fall across her back in reassuring strands. She was debating whether to stand up when the alarm silenced, without so much as an all-clear signal. There was a great thumping sound in the next room, and then a bedraggled and groggy figure replaced the door between Antigone and the source of the siren. "Do you have a security system, Bets?"

Betsy was not ready for dialogue. She coughed loudly, shuffled about a foot forward, and shifted her face vaguely in the couch's direction. "Gmrmng."

"Uh, morning. Betsy, is there a security system in this place? Are we being intruded?"

Painfully slowly, Betsy shuffled across the carpeting, pausing at the wall between the bathroom door and the kitchen counter. She turned back towards the couch, as though Antigone would assist the decision. Then she leaned away from the bathroom and her shuffling made noise as carpet gave way to linoleum. A cavernous yawn, and then "I hope not" emerged from the back throes of her throat's oxygen-grab.

"Well that's reassuring. Bets, are you all right? Is that your a*larm*? And why do you have it set for *now*? Isn't it about three hours too early to be *breath*ing?"

Betsy was smacking her lips against each other. Then, without having to pay much attention, or even particularly observe her own actions, she opened the refrigerator, removed a plastic bottle, proceeded to the coffee maker, dumped the water in, and turned it on. The actual instant coffee had already been dispensed, and soon noises emanated from the machine. Antigone wrested herself from the couch in just enough time to read "Water Joe" on the label. This was impossible. Though she had still not heard much in the way of English from her hostess, she had to wonder, "Why do you keep water in old plastic bottles?"

Betsy blinked and turned from the fridge to the sink, where she apparently began to examine the drain meticulously. Her entire head was engulfed by the sink. Then, she fumbled with her right hand, maladroitly given her physical position, until it found the **C**, and this she pulled violently toward her. A torrent of water spilled onto her short cropped hair and the head below. After a full minute, she moved her hand, which had not left the **C**, back into its prior position, grabbed the hand towel from a rack beneath the sink, and gradually dried while lifting her head from the sink. She looked much wetter, but only marginally more awake.

Water dripped to the linoleum. The silence was distressing, bordering on inhuman in the face of a clearly active person. "*Betsy*! Are you a*live* in there?!"

Betsy blinked again, seemed to recall her coffee, and without checking the status of the dripping brown fluid, grabbed a mug from the countertop, pulled out the pot, replaced it immediately with the mug, heard the sound of dripping soon ensue, and waited impatiently for the mug to fill. This break from her automatic movements provided her finally sufficient disruption. Her head swiveled towards Antigone, this time clearly addressing her eyes. "You want to buy a car?"

"Excuse me?"

"A car." Her head swiveled back to the coffee maker, where she reversed her previous switch and took the mug, in one fluid motion, from the base of dripping to the crest of her lips. "A reliable car."

"I *have* a car." Antigone was wondering if she was missing a joke. "And good morning to you too."

"Too bad." Betsy was taking staccato sips. "You were my last hope."

"Does this mean you're awake now?"

Betsy looked into her mug, swilled the remaining coffee around by rocking said mug, and flatly drained the remaining fluid in a long gulp. "Getting there." She wheeled towards the coffee maker, which had finished dripping and now waited dispassionately for Betsy's renewed assault.

"Did you brew that with..."

"Caffeinated water, that's right."

"I was afraid of that."

"Why?" She was starting on her second mug, leaning against the countertop and crossing her ankles.

"Isn't that, well, dis*gust*ing?"

"Not once you're used to it." A gulp. "Nothing is, really."

Antigone winced and looked away, as if shielding herself from the coffee's fallout. "So I can stay here?"

"For a while. Till I start dating again."

Betsy was between girlfriends at the moment. "Gee, thanks."

"No, you know, it'd just look weird. Sure you don't want that car?"

"What kind of car is it?" Not that Antigone was interested, but she may as well sound interested in as much of Betsy's ideas as possible.

"'86 Oldsmobile. They could land aircraft on it."

"Do I look like a pimp to you?"

"Well, you don't have any *other* job, do you?" It was time for cup number three. Antigone had rarely seen high school classmates drink alcohol this quickly.

"Oh, I'd be a world-class pimp. Start by whoring my*self* out. To guys like Rick."

"You haven't told me *that* full story yet."

"Indeed."

"So are you looking?" Betsy's eyes were starting to bulge out of her head. The coffee was likely displacing them directly. Was there room for anything else inside her small frame at this point?

"For a job? Or a boyfriend?" Antigone really wasn't sure.

"Why not a girlfriend?" Betsy jokingly lifted her leg to meet Antigone's. "Best way to get over a guy..."

"Oh baby." Antigone was sardonic. "I don't think I could date anyone for a while. But I am looking for a job."

"Waitressing? I know this guy..."

"Might as well be a pimp. No, I think I'll be telemarketing, like I've done for the last bazillion years."

"*Tele*marketing? Waste of your pretty features, girl." Betsy looked sincerely disappointed.

"Hey, I'll ride my voice any day. Besides, I look awfully sexy with a headset."

Betsy laughed at this. "'Sthat what Rick said?"

Antigone frowned. "Can we not use that word?"

"Fine, is that what Rick *spoke*?"

"Bitch. You know what I meant."

"Yes I did. Shit, Tig, you've got his name on your *stomach*! It's not like I brought him up first. What time is it?"

"Time for you to leave?"

"Kicking me outta my own house now?"

"No, just guessing from your morning routine. Where are you working, anyway?"

"Hell. Masquerading as Starbucks."

"Where's that?"

"By the school, towards the city, but not all the way downtown. Corner of Fire and Brimstone."

"Cute."

Betsy flipped her head back, only just displacing a few strands of hair. Playfully to Antigone, "I try."

Then she bolted for the bathroom. Antigone sighed, hearing the noise of a shower beginning. She imagined the water temperature to be hovering around 40 degrees Fahrenheit, knowing Betsy's apparent morning practices. Betsy had been a heavy sleeper in college, but this was new territory altogether. At least she was self-disciplined. Hopefully she would be less so about finding a new girlfriend.

Discipline. She looked at the coffee maker, a half-full pot

still simmering. "*Betsy!*" No response. "*Betsy! Can I have some of your coffee*?!*" The bellowing was met only with the sound of cascading water. "Hmm..." now to herself. "Maybe there's some discipline in that mud."

Finding a mug was difficult (it would appear that Betsy had been living alone for a while, a probable good sign), but the fourth cupboard revealed a series of plastic glasses, and that would have to do. "I wonder just how bad this is." She poured some, cautiously. She sipped, too quickly, swore, and set the glass down hard, spilling more of the coffee on her hand. The burns burned. She picked the coffee back up, sipped again, and discovered that the coffee didn't taste like anything. In fact, nothing would taste like anything for about a day. "Well done," she congratulated herself on the self-inflicted numbing.

The shower stopped, revealing Betsy in a towel over her hair, but nothing else. "Oh yeah," she said absently. "You're here." And slowly took the towel down to cover herself as she ran to her room. "Don't drink my coffee!" she yelled from the bedroom.

"*What?*"

Betsy popped out of her room, half-dressed. "Don't drink my coffee. I don't want to have to drink the weak Starbucks crap all day." She popped back in.

"You drink this *all day*?" Antigone started pouring her glass back into the pot, looking for a paper towel to absorb the spilt coffee simultaneously. When empty, she hid the glass in the trash bag.

"Yeah," said Betsy, dressed and leaving her room permanently. "How else would I make it through?"

"Lord knows." Antigone was beginning to wonder.

Betsy held a large thermos which she now unscrewed, dumping the remainder of the pot into it, and rescrewed. "Ah, survival. Well, I'm off. Don't burn the place down. And, uh, do you need the car?"

"I *have* a car."

"Damn. You remembered. See you tonight!" The door slammed.

And it occurred to Antigone that she had no understanding of Philadelphia, and almost less of her friend Betsy.

Antigone spent too much of the day watching TV and lazing around Betsy's apartment. She hadn't lazed in a long while, and it was good to feel relaxation without the pure apprehension that living with Rick had always consisted of. She could laze then, but at any moment Rick might come back with demands or expectations, most of which were small and spontaneous at the outset of their living together, becoming gradually overwhelming and grating as time tread onward. He had been intuitive all right, just enough to know what buttons to push in order to yield results.

She was trying to put Rick out of her mind, but everything on the screen in front of her was trying to put guys *in* her mind. If these commercials weren't busy making her feel inferior, leaving her in the lonely desolation of possible boyfriendlessness, they were trying to put *her* in *guys'* minds. Not that that had ever seemed much of a challenge. And then there were the shows, most of which were about amnesia, or *menage a trois* involving two siblings and the mailman, and the people who love all three. No wonder the commercials seemed like the main event. At least those had some small figment of realism, putting the target audience down for their vast absences and cravings. She could not recall any sexual cravings for relatives or postal workers. And she could recall everything. This left her apparently distinct from the stars of the afternoon.

"Oh Buddha," she told the screen at one point, "can I be a lifeform that doesn't have sex next time? Even if that means a regression. You know, I think amoeba would be some sort of improvement. At least a little. They just divide, and I bet they're not as obsessed with that as we are with sex. So, no fucking please. For a whole lifetime. That'd be a relief."

The phone rang.

This device, in Betsy's place, seemed to emit the same noise as the alarm clock. Turning from the commercial she was observing, Antigone mused at a product called Fire Alarm Fone, not available in stores, $19.95 plus shipping and handling, Massachusetts residents add 6% sales tax. The ad could even have a firetruck and an overfed dalmatian, with a smiling fireman saying that it's the next-best thing to being sprayed by a fire hose. For the unaware world of those like Betsy, it would probably be an appealing idea to get soaked every time someone wanted to communicate. After all, then one would be prepared for it, especially if one had a towel...

The phone rang.

Was she supposed to *get* the phone here? It was an awkward contemplation. She was a friend, she'd be able to explain a few things about Besty's whereabouts (not *too* many, though), and it was an easy explanation of why she was there. Not that she wanted to go into why. But if she didn't, there was the whole jealous interested party issue that Betsy'd alluded to. Which frankly didn't make any sense, because surely lesbians still had female roommates, right? Perhaps not. She hadn't lived with any lesbians, had she? So she could just go into talking about having a boyfriend who was a bit too violent, overbearing, and might even stalk her... Good God! Might even stalk her! This could be Rick, calling right now, having tracked down the phone numbers of all her friends...

The phone rang.

Well, hang on a minute, she'd found her address book, when she finally called Betsy upon reaching Philadelphia, so Rick didn't have that. He'd just call her cell phone over and over till she had to get a new one, or change the number somehow. She'd given him the slip, right? Pretty definitely. Meanwhile, she better get this phone in case it were important for Betsy. Did Betsy have an answering machine? She knew so little about this person's daily habits, and here she was about to find out more...

She jumped to her feet, ditching the pillow which had been clutched on her lap, and ran for the phone. It rang halfway, its fourth ring, and she gasped a breathless "Hello" into the receiver.

"Hello ma'am, how are you today?" *It's not Rick!*

"Um. I'm alright. How're you?"

"Just great. I'm calling you today to tell you about a special offer from your friends at Working Without Wires."

"Working Without... Wires?"

"Yes, it's the latest in cellular technology! Do you have a cell phone, ma'am?"

"Miss."

"My humblest apologies. Do you have a cell phone, miss?"

"Yes, no. Maybe. I'm not sure. Yes, but I can't use it. Shouldn't."

"You shouldn't indeed. Because whatever plan you were on, Working Without Wires can give you an infinitely better one! Guaranteed! Now, how much are you paying for cell phone service right now?"

"Are you local?"

"We have both national and local plans available, depending upon your situation."

"No, no, are *you* local?"

"I'm not sure I understand. Working Without Wires is a global company, ready for the demands of the 21st century."

"You're not listening to me. You're a human being, right?"

His demeanor changed; suddenly he had lost control of the sale. "Of course."

"Where are you sitting?"

"Philadelphia. But I hardly see how this is--"

"So you *are* local! Great. Can I have your address?"

"Look, miss, I apologize for disturbing you. I assure you that Working Without Wires has no interest in causing any unwanted intrusion. You don't have to take anything out on us."

"No, look, you don't understand. I'm just getting this for my own information."

"Why?"

"I need a job."

"A job?"

"Yes. I'm sure Working Without Wires is hiring."

"Well, actually--"

"So, please give me your address."

"You could be bluffing. Who wants to work in telemarketing?"

"You do. Or if you don't, I'll take your job. Now if you don't give me the address, I'll just look it up in the phone book." This *was* a bluff--where did Betsy keep her phone book? Given her organization style, it could be nestled behind the caffeinated water! "Unless your company is so fly-by-night that you're less than a year old, in which case I'll have to spend seventy-five cents on information." Nicely saved, if she did think so herself.

"Okay, you win. But do you want that cell phone?"

"Lemme think about it. Lemme talk to your boss first. Maybe I can get a free one when I'm working in the cubicle next to you. What's the address?"

He gave it to her.

"Beautiful. And what did you say your name was?"

"I didn't."

"You have to, by solicitation laws." There was a syrupy texture to her voice.

"Brett."

She hung up, smiled at herself, checked a mirror, felt in her pocket for the extra key that Betsy had given her, and made sure

91

to lock the door behind her. "Thank you Buddha, thank you Jesus," she told her station wagon. She drove aimlessly until she found a gas station, at which she filled up and purchased a map of metro Philly. Then she climbed back in her Volvo and got on the freeway. She cruised beneath several overpasses, searching carefully for the proper exit. After nine miles, she was where she wanted to be, just short of Jersey, and exited before crossing the Delaware. A few turns, busy with traffic, led her to the home of Working Without Wires. She had only pennies for the meter, but this seemed like good luck. Sticking them in the machine failed to remove the **VIOLATION**, but it did convey the aura of a wishing well, which seemed positive.

Given the size of the building, she had not expected an elaborate lobby with hanging banners displaying the slogans of "a new kind of WWW". This resembled corporate headquarters more than a phone bank. Maybe it was both, and this really was a fly-by-night. She could see herself getting paid in penny-a-share stock-options, and making two dollars an hour otherwise. At least the place could afford air-conditioning, and honestly, too much air-conditioning.

"Hi," she smiled at the receptionist, who seemed to be in the process of being eaten by her desk. It was lined with marble (or at least the appearance of marble), circular in shape, and ringed her completely. She barely protruded from it, a mere head with the opportunity to cry for help before the desk finally swallowed.

"How may I help you?"

"Can I see the telemarketing manager?"

"Is there a problem?"

"No, I'm here to inquire about employment."

"Well, Mr. Tucker handles telemarketing. But I don't think you can see him right now. If you'd like an application, I'm sure Mr. Tucker will get back to you within the week."

She laid her hand face-up on the desk. "I'll take an application, but I'd really prefer to see Mr. Tucker."

"Well, I'm sorry, I--" she wheeled, literally, in her wheeled chair, to address the sound of the elevator from the right side of the lobby. The elevator opened, to reveal a harried looking man in a formal shirt with the sleeves rolled up. He was no older than thirty. "Mr. Tucker."

"Hey, Maggie, any calls?"

"Well, this woman here would like to see you, I guess."

92

"Oh *really*?" He had reached the desk with swift paces and now lifted his elbow from it to shake hands. "Do I know you?"

"Not yet. Antigone Edgewood."

He tried to smile. "Is that some sort of riddle?"

"It's my name." She said it simply, without irony or malice or iciness or any other tone one might say that phrase with.

"Ah. Martin Tucker, at your service. What can I do for *you*?"

"Give me a job." At this, she smiled.

Martin Tucker smiled too, a little less innocently. "Well, you've got your application already, I can see. But I'll save you some ink. We're not hiring."

"Telemarketers are *always* hiring," she said confidently.

"Know the business?"

"Worked in it forever. Trust me, I could replace a third of your employees. What's your payroll?"

"That's a little forward, Miss, Missus, uh, may I call you Antigone?"

"Please do. Anyway, I talked to Brett not so long ago. I could replace him." She was trying not to flirt, trying to be firm. If she flirted, this particular guy would stop taking her seriously, or wouldn't start if she was having less of an impact than she thought. Besides, how would flirting be a good start to her campaign to come back as a sexless species?

"Brett's one of our best. I take it he didn't have much impact on you."

"Give me a phone. And a number. What's your average sales percentage? Five? Seven?"

"Shouldn't you be able to sell *me* before you sell someone else?" He was accustomed to this line of argumentation.

Antigone's smile broadened, for she was accustomed to this too. "You're intelligent. And jaded by a career in sales and management. *They* are stupid. I don't sell you. Brett didn't sell me. But *I*," here she paused, wanting Martin Tucker to think about her, even if she wasn't quite flirting, "I sell *them*."

The receptionist, who had not received any phone calls in this time, was taken aback.

Martin Tucker was not accustomed to this argument. She might just be arrogant enough to be good. But then why would she be looking for a job? Especially if she knew the business? "Let me get a rap sheet, and you can read off of that. I'll give you five numbers, and if you sell someone, I'll think about it."

"Thank you. Very much. But don't bother with the rap sheet."

Oh boy, a maverick. "Look, uh, Antigone, we do have our rules here at Working Without Wires."

"You also have customers, am I wrong? And less than you'd like?"

"Well, doesn't everyone?"

"Five numbers. Where's the headset?" Why could she never be this strong *outside* of business?

"Follow me."

Had either of them turned to see the receptionist as they rounded the corner of the lobby, they would have seen eyes rolling so far back in their head that the pupils actually disappeared.

The phone bank was smaller than any Antigone had seen in years, and while it covered a fairly large expanse on the ground floor, it seemed that only about fifteen people were actually working there, spread out so their voices didn't carry into other conversations. Or to make it look like the company wasn't about to go under before it got off the ground. "This it?"

"I told you we're not hiring. Now this is my desk, over here, and let me get you a sheet to take down their information if you do happen to make a sale." He opened a drawer. "And here's the rap sheet, just in case. To refer to."

She took both from him, looked at the latter, crumpled it, and aimed for a nearby wastebasket. "The numbers?"

He moved the mouse on his desk, waking the computer, and looked for something to print out. Thinking better of it, he wrote down five numbers from the screen on a scrap of paper. "You this aggressive with customers?"

"Some. The ones that want aggressive."

"Okay. I wish you luck. I'll, of course, be, uh, listening in. Here's the headset, and, well, you say you know what to do. Heaven forbid a rap sheet get between you and your calling."

"No kidding. Um, what are we selling again?"

Martin Tucker looked on the verge of finally throwing this tough nuisance out of his establishment, but was just too curious to see how it would turn out. Instead, he put a wide hand to his frustrated forehead. "Cell phones. With advanced technology. The details of which are on a crumpled piece of paper over there."

"Great." She read off the number to herself, dialing, taking a free seat that was available in front of her. Martin had his head set on. Antigone donned hers at the last second, just as the ringing began.

"Hello?"

"Hi! I'm with Working Without Wires, and I'm calling to make your life easier."

"Well, thank you, but..."

"Don't hang up!"

"Why not?"

"Because you're on a very short list of people we're calling today. Your number was randomly selected to see how you would react to new changes in the technological research regarding cellular telephones."

"Huh?"

"You *are* interested in new technology, aren't you?"

"Well, yes, but I don't know, if, well..."

"Great. How would you like a chance to try out some new technology? Do you have a cell phone?"

"No, but I..."

"Do your friends have cell phones?"

"Well some of them do, I suppose. They seem to be much busier than I am."

"Don't you think it would impress them if you, even though you aren't busy, had better cell phone technology than they even *knew existed*? Had a plan that they needed, and you didn't, but you still *had it*?"

"But I don't *need* it!"

"Exactly."

"Oh."

Antigone sold six telephones in the five calls. One person wasn't interested and another wasn't home, but the final person she called bought a phone for his wife and one for his daughter as well as himself. Martin Tucker attempted to get her to sign a contract whereby she agreed to be salaried, not commissioned, but she was far shrewder than that. "What would motivate me *then*?" she asked playfully, feeling more free to flirt now that she had earned his respect.

"I'm not convinced you run on motivation."

"What's *that* supposed to mean?" She stood up, searching around the room. "Hey Brett!" she yelled. Disgruntled employees looked up from their calls, and Brett, not on the phone, paid the most attention, walking towards the desk. "How much you make

Brett?"

"Huh?"

Turning to Martin Tucker, "I want however much he makes."

The addressed shook his head. "If you keep selling at that rate, you'll be making as much as *I* make." He stood up. "Let me get a contract from Maggie."

SEVEN

M att and Joaquin shared English 101, a class for which they had mutual contempt. At Harrison, this introductory course was one of the very few required for all students. "We want to make sure you all have a fundamental understanding of the language which provides the basis of our communication here at college," their professor had read from the syllabus.

"Wasn't that what our SAT's were for?" Joaquin was prompted to mutter at Matt.

To make matters more remedial, most of the class seemed focused on grammar rather than literature. The little literature which adorned the syllabus looked like a review of high school, replete with Shakespeare and Steinbeck and then more deconstruction of sentences. Those who sought a challenge in coming to college were swiftly reminded, as far as Matt could tell, that one of the greatest challenges to the human mind is avoiding insanity in the face of mountainous busywork.

They were walking to Tyler, or T-SUB, from class. "Wanna go to T-SUB?"

"To what?"

Joaquin smiled. "T-SUB. Tippecanoe Student Union Building. You haven't heard that yet?"

"Wasn't it you who told me to avoid the Orientation activities?"

"All right. Well, I'm hungry."

"Then we'll go."

They went. Passing so many people, Matt had spent much of

his time resisting the conviction that people he knew filled the throngs crossing the Harrison campus. Admittedly many of the people he saw would never have been found at Topeka High, but so many more looked like carbon copies of acquaintances and classmates from his Kansan days. It was like God (or whatever) had run out of molds and was just recycling the same ones, putting new minds in the same basic bodies. The one he feared seeing most was his own.

"You ever read *The Grapes of Wrath*?"

"No."

"Don't bother. Six-hundred pages about dust."

"Dust?"

"Yup. That's it. The best chapter's about a turtle crossing a road, because at least it's a break from the dust."

"Nothing to interpret?"

"Well, I bet my roommate would find something in it. A metaphor for life, perhaps."

"What a nutcase."

"Yeah. I bet he's glad we have English 101. I think he'd be really good at English."

"Why's that?"

"All bullshit. Just interpreting whatever you want to see in something. At least with History, you've got facts. Something that has a basis. Something that's *ground*ed. English is just *how does it make you feel*? If you want your life to be guided by a crack-smoking interpretation of some CD, then go for it. Or dust."

"It's not *all* bull, is it?"

"Close enough. Just let David get ahold of it. He'd tell you the dust is, I don't know, the reason we get up in the morning. The grand motivator."

"He'd be right if he were talking about Steinbeck, from what you say. At least it's better than pointing out subjects and predicates all day long."

"At least the rules there are consistent."

A third voice, female, broke the conversation. "Joaquin!"

Joaquin looked up, scanning a horizon packed with people. Matt watched as he was tackled from behind by a darker-haired, darker-skin copy of Catie. She wrestled him almost to the ground before Joaquin finally dislodged himself from her grasp. "Jesus!"

"Hey Quino, how's it going?"

"Quino?" Matt interjected, noting that he would have to use

that at some point in the future.

"Jesus, Toni. There are subtler ways of making yourself known."

"Hey! I gave you warning..."

Joaquin rubbed his neck. "Or something. Anyway, Toni, this is my friend Matt. Matt, my sister Toni."

Matt could not, off hand, remember the last time he'd been introduced to anybody as "my friend". This would have captured more of his attention had he not been trying to confront the clone of his ex-girlfriend. "Uh, h-hi."

"Nice to meet you, Matt." She shook his hand vigorously, seeming shaking out excess energy from tackling her brother. "Good to see that my kid brother's making friends." She rubbed Joaquin's hair, which had little effect on its status. "C'mon, Quino, you gotta see my new stuff."

"We were gonna eat."

"Eat later." To Matt, "You like art?"

Did Matt have an opinion on art? He wasn't sure. It probably leaned too far towards interpretation, like English. At the same time, he was ready to interpret most of what this girl left up for interpreting. "Oh, yeah."

"Great. Two to one. Let's go." She grabbed her brother from behind again, steering him by the shoulders into a turn that would lead off-campus to her studio apartment. She liked to call it that because it was more studio than apartment. Then again, she often thought, the world was her studio.

"I've been working a lot with Rachel back home. She's such an inspiration to me, Quino."

"I know. I was there two weeks ago, you know."

"Well, I'm just saying. My style's changed a bit. I'm doing smaller stuff now. Back to nature. Still life with life. People are out. Bugs are in."

"Bugs?"

"They're beautiful creatures, you know."

"*Bugs?*"

"You'll have to see." They crossed the street from campus to off, entered a building that was probably not up to fire code, and walked up two flights of cement stairs. Toni's place was just under the roof, which was designed to reject snow, so that her ceiling was sloped. True artists, she had always maintained, work under difficult conditions with diverse perspectives. Besides, where she came from, there *weren't* any slanted roofs in the first place. "My humble abode," she welcomed.

The place was a mess. It carried a musty smell of absence and maybe even decay. Light streamed through two squares that were somewhere between windows and skylights, which probably amounted to the same thing given this sort of building structure. There were no curtains in the way of either light source. A bare bulb could be seen down the hallway, illuminating what seemed to be the only vaguely clean room in the apartment. And that only looked clean because it was *empty*. The white walls threw the glare back at the bulb, and the whole room just sat there glowing from the interaction.

"Nice place," Matt mumbled.

"I make due," Toni returned, somewhat melodramatically. "Studio's this way."

But Joaquin was ten paces ahead, and already searching the glowing room for new material. He found a case that was about as large as he was. "They let you take this on the *plane*?"

"It's not a bomb." She grinned. "*The* bomb, but not *a* bomb."

"Uh-huh." He opened the case, and began to pull the sheets of textured paper from within. They were enormous, and Toni fussed over him pulling them out without doing damage or risking rips. It seemed to Joaquin that he was lifting a solid mass of paper that was about a foot thick, there were so many drawings. "Any trees left back home?"

"Oh shush. Quantity creates quality. It's the artist's motto."

"I thought 'bugs' was the artist's motto. Or maybe 'do whatever Rachel does'."

"Oh shush. Here, give me that." Joaquin surrendered control of the case and its contents to his sister, who painstakingly carried them to an easel in the room's best lit corner. "You ready?" She asked, holding the art-side of the works against a wall, revealing only blankness. Joaquin shrugged and Matt nodded. The latter was still spending more time looking at Toni than her textured paper.

Toni lifted a sheet onto the large easel, where it barely fit. She had to hold it as well to make sure it didn't fall. Once Matt looked away from Toni, he became even more transfixed by her art. It wasn't necessarily that good, or even compelling, but it did present him with a larger-than-life cricket. About eight-hundred times larger than life, he estimated. Just slightly larger than the cricket which had been on his back a few days earlier.

"Well?" She deemed there to be insufficient spouting of immediate praise from her critics.

"What *is* that?" Joaquin scrunched his face up.

Before she could respond, Matt took care of it. "A cricket."

"I'm impressed," Toni admitted. "What do you think?"

"It's *ac*curate," Matt ventured.

"A *cricket*?!" Joaquin's face was still scrunched.

"I'm drawing crickets now, mostly. Some other bugs, too, but crickets are so perfect." She was going unappreciated again. "Think about it! Most people only *hear* crickets. Crickets are not a being, they're a *sound*. The *look* of crickets is a summer night, a picnic, making out with your lover on a park bench. But it's not what they really are. They actually ex*ist*. They won't ever let you get a look at them, but if you do, if you *could*, you'd see this. And this." She added to the easel. "And this. And this."

But Matt had seen a cricket, one that had been climbing on him, and unfortunately Catie had seen a cricket too, and he'd earnestly hoped never to see one again. She was screaming bloody murder into the August air. He could hear it now, and looking at Toni didn't help matters. Once she'd been calmed, he suggested they go back in the car, away from chain link and tall grass and *crickets*. Then he'd suggested sex. She'd suggested that she was not having her first time in the back of a Honda Civic.

"I call it the *Looking at Noise* series."

"You've gotta stop spending so much time with Rachel."

"Thanks for the support, bro. What do you think, Matt?"

"Um."

"If you don't like it, say so." Then more softly, "I can take it."

"No!" he shouted, his emotion likely of myriad sources. "I mean, um. They're very good. Very very good. Yeah."

"You're not just *say*ing that?"

"I, I had a bad experience with crickets is all. But these are very... lifelike."

"You *what*? What, did a cricket *bite* you or something?" She knew full well that crickets didn't bite. This kid was going a long way to make it seem like he liked her drawings.

I wish it had bitten me, he thought. There was no way to explain, and he realized he sounded like an idiot saying he'd had a bad experience with crickets. Really, who saw crickcts? Toni had a very good point there. If this were a TV show, he'd have something extremely witty to say. Or they'd cut to commercial. Or he'd say something painfully witty, and then they'd roll the credits. The bare bulb shone twice, through each of Toni's eyes as she waited for conversation to proceed as normal. "Uh. Bugs. I don't really like, bugs," he said lamely. "They're like spiders." A nervous laugh. "Who likes spiders?"

"That's actually the next series," Toni admitted in an even split between triumphant and disappointed. The tension of those two emotions played off of every syllable. "A whole set of spiders and their webs, and the occasional fly."

Matt just stood there, not reacting. He actually had nothing against spiders, especially compared to the average person one encountered. And he was not making a terribly favorable impression on Toni. But what business did he have taking an interest in other girls anyway? Clearly Catie was too much on his mind. But wasn't that why Toni looked so appealing? He had a sudden urge, just barely suppressed, to ask Toni if she played soccer.

"So, lunch?" Joaquin perceived the emerging discord between his friend and sister. And the less time he could spend facing his sister's new affection for insects and arachnids, the better. There had been a time when she painted vibrant watercolors and vaunted herself as the next Georgia O'Keeffe. Georgia O'Keeffe would likely have been dismayed to see so much use of gray pencil. Where was this *bug* stuff coming from? Though it possibly had originality behind it. But wasn't *bad art* original? No one famous had ever produced bad art, had they? Well, did "modern" art count? And why was no one reacting to his question? "Anyone else hungry?"

Toni was trying valiantly to conceal her disappointment. "Well, I guess you can see the spider series later. When Matt's not around, since he doesn't like it."

"I didn't say--"

"Don't worry about it. Do you mind if I, uh, don't tag along? You want to call any roommates instead?"

Joaquin and Matt looked at each other, in a habit they'd developed at the mention of their living companions. "That won't be necessary, sis."

She smiled. "Bad matches?"

"Not *bad*, necessarily," Matt was becoming a stuck record for minimizing the poorness of all he saw. "Just, *dif*ferent? Y'see, he's got this *thing* about Magical Mystery Tour."

"Thing?"

Matt sighed. "I guess it's an obsession. He has this theory that the whole world revolves around those eleven songs. Or that those eleven songs make the world revolve. Or something... revolutionary."

"Sounds interesting!"

"It isn't," Joaquin notified her. "He's almost as bad as my roommate. All your mom, all the time."

"Sounds like Oedipus."

"More like Oliver. And he never says *his mom*."

"He wouldn't."

"Speaking of Mom, what does *she* think about your drawings?"

Toni sighed and shuffled them out of the apartment. "You don't expect our *pare*nts to under*stand*, do you?"

No more than Joaquin expected himself to understand, he figured.

EIGHT

T hey let the two of them into the room. He was her doctor. She was his lawyer. He was twice her age. She was just out of law school. He was surprised to see that there actually were rooms that looked like this, and men with guns in them as well! She was surprised he'd finally asked her to something, even if serving as his lawyer officially didn't quite *seem* like a date. There was nothing romantic about the man they shook hands with.

"Joe Ewing. I see you've brought your, uh, friend?"

"Lawyer."

"Oh really? Very well, then. Now you know, this is still an *investigation*. Not a deposition. So your lawyer can provide you, as they say, counsel, but no objections will be heard."

"Is that the law?"

"Under circumstances like these, yes."

"What really *are* the circumstances right now, Mr. Ewing?"

"Call me Joe. And I'll ask the questions, okay?"

"Sure. You sure she can't object?"

"She can advise you whether or not to cooperate. She can observe the proceedings. She's not here to really play a role, just for your protection."

He wasn't sure what kind of protection this really would be, in that case. She was becoming more sure it was a date, in a really bizarre unfortunate kind of way.

"Uh, okay."

"State your name for the tape."

"Dr. Norton."

104

"Your full name."

"Dr. Alexander Maxwell Norton, M.D."

"And who is in the room today?"

"You. Joe. Ewing. And this is my lawyer, Tammy Rittenbauer. And there's a man with a gun over there."

"Mitch."

"Sure, Mitch."

"Alright, Dr. Norton, is there anything we can get for you?"

"Glass of water would be fine. Would you like anything, Tammy?"

"Let the record show that Miss Rickenbacker declined."

"*Rittenbauer*. Why does the record care?"

"Just having a little fun. Mitch, a glass of water for Dr. Norton? Thanks so much." The door closed. "State the date for the tape."

"December 22nd, 2000."

"Now then, how do you know Matthew Norton?"

"He's my son."

"Is he a good son?"

"Of course."

"Do you have any other children?"

"No."

"Are you married?"

"No."

"Why did you divorce your wife?"

"It was a no-fault divorce."

"That wasn't my question. Why?"

"It wasn't working out."

"That's very nondescript. Are there details of the divorce you don't want us to know about?"

"Half the country gets a divorce, okay? You do the math."

"You were seeing someone else?"

"No!" Mitch returned, setting the water down hard on the desk as an exclamation point to his comment.

"Then she was?"

"I don't think she had time. I didn't have time. We just didn't have time for the marriage."

"Did you have time for your *son*?"

"Of course."

"How well do you know your son?"

"Very well. We're quite close."

"Do you talk to him often?"

"Often enough."

"Once a week?"

"If I get the chance."

"How often do you not get the chance?"

"Not, often. I don't know. Once in a while. We're close, all right? He's a good kid."

"Calm down, Mr. Norton."

"*Doctor.*"

"Right. Now then, how do you think the divorce affected Matthew?"

"Affected?"

"Did he become angry? Hostile? Reserved? Vindictive? Many children, for example, enter *therapy* for a time after their parents get divorced."

"No therapy."

"Any signs whatsoever that he knew you were divorced?"

"He once said, I think he told me one time that he was glad we were done arguing."

"You and he?"

"No, my ex-wife and I."

"It was a rough marriage?"

"It ended."

"So you say. Indeed. Tell me, was Matthew a *happy* child?"

"Aren't all children?"

"In my learned experience, no, Dr. Norton. But Matthew was?"

"Sure. Why wouldn't he be? I gave him everything a kid could want. He always preferred the TV, but there were games and sports and,"

"Friends?"

"Some friends. One in particular, who ended up moving. But yeah, lots of friends."

"Tell me about his girlfriend."

"He would have had to tell me about her."

"He didn't? But you were close?"

"Who talks about dating with their kids? Whose kids *let* them talk about dating with them?"

"Was she a bad influence on Matthew?"

"A bad influence?"

"Into drugs, drinking, motorcycle gangs?"

"I don't think so."

"You don't know?"

"I can't be sure. But Matthew would have told me about something like that."

"Would he?"

"I think so." He was quiet and reached for a glass of water. He looked over at Tammy, who was studying the narrow window and barely paying attention.

"You *think* so? A lot of circumstantial evidence, Dr. Norton?"

"Look, my son's a good kid. I've told you that. Nobody tells everything to their father. Did he tell me 'fine' too much? Sure. Doesn't every kid? Absolutely. If Matt was running with the wrong kids, I would've known about it. Hell, if he was doing that, he wouldn't be going to Harrison would he?"

"Tell me about Harrison."

"It's a good school. An old school. Not much of a science program, but nothing's perfect."

"Matthew liked science?"

"Unfortunately not."

"What about Matthew's friends at Harrison?"

"He had 'em."

"Sure. But who *were* they?"

"Well I never *met* them. They were his kind of people."

"And what exactly *was his* kind of people?!"

"You know, smart. A little... weird."

"Weird how?"

"I don't know, strange. Probably not very *pop*ular."

"And why weren't they popular?"

"Because they were smart, probably. And strange."

"Are you avoiding telling me something? We're only trying to do the best for your son. I can understand evading us if you thought we would harm you, but only the truth will help your son."

"Is that a threat?"

"Dr. Norton, how can the truth be a threat?"

"I'm not hiding anything. What would I be hiding?"

"Your son's connection to drugs."

"Drugs?!"

"Yes, drugs. You've heard of them?"

"I am a medical doctor, Mr. Ewing, or whoever you are, and

I would recognize the consequences of my son being *on drugs*! I've never *heard* of such a thing!"

"How often did you see your son?"

"Before school? Three days out of seven."

"Were you working during most of that time?"

"Some."

"Would you say most?"

"It's hard to say."

"Isn't it possible that you would not have *noticed* if your son had a drug addiction?"

"No."

"What about selling drugs, not necessarily an addiction?"

"Selling?"

"Very rarely are those who sell using. That's why they can sell so effectively. We usually round up the ones that use *and* sell. They're not very... *aware* of their situation."

"Matt was aware. He got good grades and went to Harrison."

"So you say, so you say. But why is he in so much trouble there?"

"Trouble?"

"This investigation, for example. He got into this mess in Pennsylvania. You can't justify everything with Harrison, because it was Harrison that contributed to the trouble, right?"

"Then why are you spending so much time questioning *me*?"

"You don't really know anything about his life at Harrison, do you? Or maybe you do, and you're trying to get yourself off the hook?"

"I love my son!"

"Enough to lie to us?"

"Excuse me, isn't that inappropriate?" Tammy Rittenbauer's voice had not been registered on the tape prior.

"I'm here to determine what is and is not inappropriate."

"Well I think that's inappropriate. Alex, honey, don't answer that one."

Honey? All three of the men in the room were a little surprised by that.

"I'm not lying," Alex muttered through clenched teeth. "I *am* going though."

"We can call you back anytime? You're not fleeing the investigation?"

He stood up. "No, I'm calmly walking away. This is

insulting. C'mon, Tammy."

"Let the record state that Dr. Norton and his *lawyer* are leaving the examining room."

NINE

T he door slammed. David only mildly looked up. Two weeks into living with this character and progress seemed remarkably slow. And meeting other people was even more difficult. Not that either of the inhabitants of 401 had exerted any particular effort in the direction of others. Weren't people supposed to come to *you* in college? With a "small" college still maintaining hundreds of people in each grade level, wouldn't that yield endless throngs of eager fellow friends? But they still ate in the cafeteria with the two kids from next door, and occasionally Bill, who was concerned about them as their R.A..

"Don't you four ever, uh, branch out?" he'd asked at one dinner.

"Your mom branched out," Oliver replied, munching through his evening bowls of cereal. "With *every*one," he added. Bill had promptly dropped the matter.

That had been two nights previously. Now, the door had just slammed and Matt was angrily boarding the second bunk of their bed. He seemed to be fighting the rungs as he climbed to the top, making his journey difficult.

"Hey," David ventured.

"How much longer till this fucking album's over?" He (at last!) flopped on the bed, remembering to slink more than really flop, lest his ceiling attack.

"This is track ten," David sighed.

"How does it feel to be one of the beautiful people?" the Beatles asked.

"How can you listen to it over and over again like this?" This was far from the first time he'd thrown this confounded query out.

"How can you not? You still don't know what track 'Baby You're a Rich Man' is!"

"I don't even know what *'phase of life'* it is. What an ignorant bastard I am."

"You should like this one. It's dripping with all the irony you attempt so often. This phase is where people get rich when they're too old to enjoy it. Classic scenario. We spend our lives working for cash, not love, and then we end up with all this cash when it's too late to enjoy anything. We've traveled everywhere, we've seen all sorts of things, and now finally we're one of the beautiful people. But we're *not* beautiful because we're crusty and old and have used up all our life. We're just *seen* as beautiful because baby, we're a rich man."

"That's very clever," Matt mumbled into his pillow. "But who's this *we*?"

David put his pimpled chin back into its handheld position, inflaming the rash unknowingly. "'We' in the eyes of the Beatles, y'know. It's sup*pos*ed to be universal."

"You could *ask* why I'm in a bad mood."

"What would the point in that be? It's probably because of that stupid girl."

"Not *ev*erything's about Catie, y'know."

"Coulda fooled me."

"Shut up. Call me when you fall in love. Then we'll see how you like it. It's easy for you... you're just in love with a fucking compact disc!"

"So what is it then?"

"My English class. Got a B-minus on my first response paper."

"Ouch."

"Tell me about it. I'll bet you're good at English."

"Yeah..."

"I was too, once. But they didn't like my *interpretation* of this stupid poem. How the hell am *I* supposed to know what this guy was thinking? If he wanted to be clear, he could've written a newspaper article. There shouldn't be a *wrong* interpretation of a fucking poem!"

"That's why you got a B-minus? You were wrong?"

"Well... mostly I didn't go line-by-line enough. But I don't think she liked what I *did* say."

"Line-by-line." David exposed his teeth. "Here." He clicked on two leftward pointing arrows on his computer screen. The music was interrupted, then began again, wordlessly.

"Oh Christ." Matt burrowed under his pillow, covering his ears.

"Listen!" David stood up, as though to project to his feathered audience.

"*How does it feel to be one of the beautiful people?*" the Beatles inquired. David leaned down to click the two parallel vertical lines, stopping the noise.

"The classic 'how does it feel?' question, usually indicating some bitterness or sarcasm. A pointed question of a rhetorical nature. You know how it feels, but you ask anyway. And you know that it feels less than it should, that it's disappointing. The reasons why will become apparent in later lines." Click.

"*Now that you know who you are, what do you want to be?*"

Click. "The assumption is that knowing who you are means having the ability to do what you want. Money is the driving force in society. Without money, you are nameless. Faceless. Nothing. Certainly not beautiful. But money is self-determination, is power, is the hope for a future. What do you want to be when you grow up? A common question which we confront our children with daily, till they grow old from hearing it so much. Here, we hear the question late in life, on the verge of death, for only in wealth do we have power to control our situation. Only *now* can we become what we *want*. And what we want, of course, was always money in the first place." Click.

"*And have you traveled very far? Far as the eye can see.*"

Click. "How much of your life have you come through to get to this point? The question reaffirms what we have already learned about the entire disc, that it carries one from birth till death, and this is nearing the end. We have come along way on our Tour, to get here, and it has taken an immense amount of travel to acquire the wealth that makes one a rich man. And yet, here we are. One could read that this travel has included many misdeeds associated with acquiring wealth in society, but that is not textually evident, yet." Click.

"*How does it feel to be one of the beautiful people? How often have you been there? Often enough to know.*"

Click. "Here, the song becomes more complex. The 'there' referred to is the being called a beautiful person in the first place.

How often has this question arisen? How often has your beauty been recognized? The question is more of an issue of how does one know when one's reached the top? How do you know you've made it? What's the indicator? Apparently, in this instance, it's hearing the question of what it feels like to be moneyed enough. When enough people recognize you for your influence, then you know you've made it. Making it is about perception, perhaps more than reality. Then again, money is more perception than reality in the first place, as may be a secondary meaning of the line." Click.

"What did you see when you were there? Nothing that doesn't show."

Click. "Here the perceptions from the above line become more clear, almost overstated. All that glitters is gold in the world of the rich and influential. The signs of wealth can be seen, and in fact can't be missed, because those who are wealthy *flaunt*. The flaunting helps the perception, and indeed be*comes* the perception. There is nothing to be seen beyond the perception, which is why there's nothing that doesn't show. Everything that can be flaunted will be, and there's nothing more to the reality of money." Click.

"Baby you're a rich man. Baby you're a rich man. Baby you're a rich man too."

Click. "Here we must pay close attention, as the call goes out to everyone who has finally reached the plateau of being called a rich man. But the third line adds the word 'too', indicating that this is a much more common occurrence than anyone wants to recognize. Everyone becomes a rich man eventually! Or perhaps more likely, it's not that special or great to be a rich man. And secretly, being a rich man turns you back into a baby, not only with the lines of potential and 'what do you want to be' seen earlier, but also because you're spoiled, and want to be more spoiled." Click.

"You keep all your money in a big brown bag inside a zoo. What a thing to do!"

Click. "The eccentricities of the rich are one of the great indicators of *being* rich in the first place. Wealth brings the power to be arbitrary, to exert random power and do random things. This randomness often involves the use of the money in the first place. Putting money in a bag in the zoo! That *is* crazy, so you must be rich. But another level shows the selfishness of wealth. The zoo gets the money, not other people, not friends, not the protagonist of the song who is singing at the rich man admonishingly in the

113

first place. The money is not shared, not benefiting anyone, it randomly goes to the giraffes, but not for their use. First, they *couldn't* use it! They're giraffes! But second, they aren't even given it directly, for it is obscured by the big brown bag of secrecy, of hoarding. The zoo is just a holding pen, locking the animals away from money. Is the zoo also a metaphor for those kept *without* money? Probably. It's a prison to be poor." Click.

"Baby you're a rich man. Baby you're a rich man. Baby you're a rich man too. How does it feel to be one of the beautiful people?"

Click. "Everywhere one goes, one finds people who acclaim the wealth that a wealthy person has. The wealth is revered, and reaffirmed. You're a rich man, how does it feel? This is the burning question that everyone wants to know, and the wealthy hear it early and often, almost unendingly. Thus, it is the chorus." Click.

"Tuned to a natural E, happy to be that way."

Click. "Here we see the embracing of otherwise tedious life habits that the rich come to enjoy. They have become tuned to a natural fee: be it dues to a country club or membership in some exclusive group, or even a higher tax bracket, the rich have attuned their lifestyle to pay something extra for what they have. Perhaps the double meaning here is that this extra something is actually the expense of the real values in their life; their real moral fiber is forfeit in the face of all that money. But does this give them pause? Remorse? No, rather they are, as they declare, happy to be that way. Even though they are bound to extra burdens the poor do *not* experience, they are pleased to undergo anything for the advanced benefits that wealth has brought." Click.

"Now that you've found another key, what are you going to play?"

Click. "The final line before a renewal of the chorus brings all sorts of additional meaning to bear on the song. The additional key is most obviously money that has been acquired to the aging but newly wealthy personage being addressed. But also possible is a lead-in to the final track, the upcoming 'All You Need is Love', in which *love* is the *real* key, the actual unlocker of great potential. Either way, the question remains open to the future, what comes next? What will you spend your money on, most obviously? What little time one has left in which to spend the cash! How little one can actually en*joy* it! Yet you may play away your final years in some modicum of hope, now that your lifelong cash quest is over. Or, rather, possibly, where will your love take you in the final phase? Because while money you may have, love is all you need." Click.

"*Baby you're a rich man. Baby you're a rich man. Baby you're a rich man too. You keep all your money in a big brown bag inside a zoo. What a thing to do! Baby, baby you're a rich man. Baby you're a rich man. Baby you're a rich man too. Oh, baby you're a rich man. Baby you're a rich man. Baby you're a rich man too...*"

Click. "A telling song, a pivotal portent to a future which became even more moneygrubbing than the Beatles ever dreamed. Perhaps the most important testimony to the Beatles' vision is their ability to predict the importance that, in this case, money would have in society. While money was still vital in their time, it has become more so, and with the increase of programs like Social Security, the trend of people slaving their lives away to come into wealth too late to enjoy it has only increased. To ignore such a message from the Beatles would be to miss out on the tenth phase of life. Does that help anything, Matt? See, there's a point to all this! The Tour is life, but it also has practical applications beyond life. Like paper-writing. Right? Matt? Is that *snor*ing, Matt?" A pause. "He wouldn't have appreciated it anyway."

TEN

S he was beaming, and with reason. After counting on at least a week's worth of moping around, she'd had initiative fall into her lap, and it paid off in its usual fashion. Maybe this was the reward for saving that ungrateful woman on the wrong side of I-70. Maybe she should just keep seeking every possible outlet for good karma and see where it went. Maybe Betsy was just good luck. She fumbled for the keys, all jangles until the door opened in front of her, uncommanded.

"Where the *hellll* have you been?" Betsy rolled the l's like a motor starting up, trying to rev itself into internal combustion. Was she drunk?

The wave of her confidence from the job interview was receding, but still rolling through her mentality. "Out," she smiled. "Doing something with myself. *Being*," she stuck her happy face in Betsy's beaded eyes, "a pro*duct*ive member of society."

Betsy was terse. "Hookers in this town usually wait till its dark, dear."

"Not that kind of product." She laughed, knowing this was just Betsy's sense of humor. A sure indicator that somehow she'd woken up over the course of a work day in the process of coffee dispensation. "Cell phones," she decided to communicate.

Betsy was trying to relax, which seemed to be a pitched struggle for her soul. Antigone felt she could make out the wills battling just beneath her skin. "Well that's noble."

"Better than prostitution," given the subject matter of the albeit light-hearted discussion, it seemed a good time to close the door. "Probably the karmic equivalent of schlepping coffee."

116

"People *need* coffee."

"*You* need coffee."

Betsy cocked her head. "Good idea."

As she ambled over to the counter to comply with the suggestion, Antigone flopped on the couch. "What's new with you?"

"Nothing," with her focus clearly on the forthcoming brew. And then, on the fly, "Oh, do you remember Rachel? From school?"

Do I re*member* my best friend? "Uh, yeah."

"She called."

"Here? You two still in touch?"

"She wasn't calling *me*. You want a cup?"

"No thanks. Who was she calling?"

"Rick called her."

"Rick... who?" The alarm was rising, but without reason, right?

Betsy rolled her eyes. "Check your torso, dear."

"Shit. How did he get her num, oh shit."

"Yeah." She sipped.

"Got anything stronger than coffee?"

"You haven't had this stuff."

"You know what I *mean*."

"There might be some beer in the fridge? I think I'm fresh outta vodka. My ex was partial to screwdrivers and it kinda turned me off to the stuff. Haven't been able to look at orange juice since." More sips.

"So what did she *say*?"

"Rache? Not much. Was worried about you, checking around, blah blah, talked to Ash, blah blah, very relieved that you weren't dead in a gutter, jail, or what have you." The final swig. "I told her not to count her chickens on *that* quite yet, before you turned up again."

"I'll leave a note next time, mom."

Betsy stood up, in search of more hot liquid. "You might wanna call her." She opened the fridge. "Mmm... Bud Light."

"There's more fortitude in tap water," Antigone sighed. "Where's the number?"

"The fridge... or wait, no. The wall? I guess I wrote it on, oh, my hand. Hmmm... is that a 3 or a 5?"

Antigone got up to check. "I think it's a 2."

"Really? Well, give 'em all a try. How many numbers can there *be* in New Mexico, anyway?"

"Did she *really* say that Rick called?"

"No, she just wanted to tell me about her alien abduction." She lingered on the open fridge door, reached for a Bud Light, and poured some into her half-full coffee cup. "Is it *really* that weird that Rick would be looking for you? He's on your stomach permanently; why wouldn't he want to join the rest of you?"

"Can we get off my stomach please?" Antigone had forgotten the number and didn't want to ask for it again.

"But it's such a *cute* stomach," Betsy insisted, then sipped. She'd expected it to be putrid, but this was off the charts. She grimaced and tilted the cup.

"Don't you have to go the bathroom a lot?" Antigone had noticed what was keeping Betsy from talking.

"All the time. Right now in fact." She slammed the cup down and shuffled into said section of her apartment.

Through the half-closed door, "Number again?"

"Oh, just call information if you need it ex*act*ly. Taos, New Mexico, number of Rachel."

"Funny." Then, into the phone, "Taos, New Mexico. Number of Rachel Wu. Yes, W, U." Antigone noted with some small irony that she was writing it on her hand. "Thank you very much. It was a 2, Betsy!" She heard a flush in response.

"Hello?"

"Hi Rachel, it's Antigone."

"Oh thank God. Does Betsy know where you are?"

"Physically. It's so good to hear your voice, Rache."

"You too, Em, uh, Antigone. So Betsy told you about Rick?"

"Yeah."

"You wanna tell me the full story?"

"Not really. But inquiring minds keep wanting to know. He hit me."

"Oh God."

"Actually, he'd been hitting me for a while. I finally got up my courage."

"Oh, I'm so sorry."

"Me too. Anyway, what'd he say to you?"

"Just looking for you. Sounded upset. Said you'd left without saying where you were going or when you'd be back or why you'd gone or anything. No note, so he assumed you'd be back.

He was worried. In contact with the police and all."

"The police?"

"He didn't think you'd left *him*. I think he was thinking more that you'd left for a quart of *milk*."

A quart of milk might make a more suitable boyfriend. "With all my clothes?!"

"Well, *I* didn't know your clothes were gone. Maybe he didn't notice? Or maybe he didn't *want* to. How bright is this guy?"

"Well, he was very int*ui*tive..."

"He knew the right places to hit you?"

Rachel knew the right places to hit her, apparently. "Look, that didn't start till... oh God, I've been an idiot. Look, you didn't tell him anything?"

"I didn't *know* anything. Far be it from you to come *here* in your hour of need."

"It's far away. And it's a place he knew to look, evidently. And now I've got a job here."

"More phones?"

"Selling them too, now."

"Well that was fast. Rick made it sound like you just left."

"How long did you talk to him?"

"Long enough to convince him that I was on his side. Which, y'know, you *might* have left for a grocery run and never come back. I didn't know *not* to be on his side just then, did I?"

"Look, I'm *sor*ry. Okay? You make it sound like this hurt you more than it hurt me."

"No, I. Sorry."

There is a sound which telephone connections make when there is no dialogue. Both Antigone and Rachel had enough time to study this sound, though Antigone was more focused on her own jumbled reality, and crashing from her sense of accomplishment at getting a job to disappointing her friends and the cold remembrance of Rick. Rachel, meanwhile, was likening this interim sound to other background noises. Mostly crickets.

"So, what have *you* been up to?"

"You know. The usual. Painting. Sketching. Living the life."

"How far did you get on the God Project?"

"Oh, that. I've kind of moved beyond. Y'know, there's a god in everything, at least a little. Nature. That's what it's about."

Antigone was sincerely let down. "Aw, really? The God

Project was my favorite of your ideas. Trying to draw images of the all-powerful? That's what it's all about."

"If you think about it, insects are pretty powerful. Strongest of the species, really."

"*Insects?*"

"Crickets, grasshoppers. Roaches. You know how long they've been around compared to us?"

"Not as long as God."

"Maybe not. But more readily available to model than God. Hard to put God in a jar and observe for a few hours."

"I guess so."

"You still got that apprentice?"

"Naw. She went back to school. Actually, right by you. At Harrison."

"Is that somewhere rural?"

"I think so. Fifeburg. Wherever that is. She'll be back in summer, I hope."

"Hm."

"Look, I'm just glad you're safe. I really should get going right now, but we can talk more about, things, later. A week or so. Or call me from your phone job. Maybe I'll buy one from you."

"Okay." Antigone sighed loudly, drawing static into the conversation. "Um, so, if Rick calls, you still haven't heard from me and you're worried."

"You got it. Take care, you."

"You too. G'night." Antigone hung up and leaned against the wall.

Betsy was drinking a beer on the couch. "How is Rachel? Hell, how are *you*? You can't get away from your stomach forever, y'know."

Antigone began sliding down the wall she leaned on. "Fine. *Fine*. What do you want to know?"

"D'you love him?" It was impossible to tell if the question had been phrased in the past tense (absent an 'id') or the present tense (absent an 'o').

"I don't know what love is, Bets."

"Sounds like a 'no' in my book."

"You the expert?"

"I didn't say that. But after Amber, y'know, it's hard to say that you can't know if you're in love."

"Well, I didn't know *Amber*." Her head was in her hands,

120

diminishing audibility, but also the feeling of shame.

"Yes you did. You were in Chemistry with her."

"You fell in love with *her*?" A vague recollection of one of the more obese and quiet Amherst kids she could conjure.

Betsy finished her beer. She then stretched out on the couch, leaning her head down lower than her feet. "Sometimes I think you don't remember college at all. It's like you left, so you weren't there in the first place. It hurts me."

"No, it's just. Well, gee."

"I suspect," Betsy was familiar with Amber's critics, "you're still confusing lust and love. A common mistake, symptom of about, oh, 98% of Americans today."

"Intuition is not an element of *lust*."

"Was intuition an element of Rick?"

"The main thing that attracted me to him. The thing I loved, if it was love. I don't know. He made me happy. Isn't that what men are supposed to do? Okay, you know what I mean. *Others*. Regardless, I thought he *could* have been the one. Or *a* one."

"Like the steak sauce?"

"No, like a *possible* one. One that could work out okay. That could father your two point five kids."

"Sounds like he'd do better as steak sauce. Unless you want child abuse."

"It's so easy for you to make fun, isn't it?"

"As long as you're seeing men, I don't think *you'll* be *having* much fun. Not a lot of lesbians hit, you know. Unless you ask them to." The blood was definitely flooding her head.

"It wasn't just the hitting. I don't know. He just turned ugly. Or maybe he was from the start, but he was good at hiding it, y'know? He *cared* more about hiding it."

"He wasn't on the Antigone Abdomen of Fame yet."

"Fuck you."

"Is that a request? I do conversions."

Antigone got up to go to her room, planning the door-slam already, but her room was the couch that Betsy now lopsidedly filled. She sighed in frustration and sat down again, slowly. She assumed the lotus position carefully, pulling her right ankle over her left knee, and then edging her left ankle up over right knee to match. The tension always strained her right shin, but she winced and tried to look contented.

"All right, all right, I'll leave you alone. I just figured that

Storey Clayton

you could use some distractions. Something to cheer you up. Breakups suck. I say, bounce high on the rebound. I can't find you a guy, though, so, hell! But maybe I'm just lonely." The premeditative silence was awfully loud. "Let's see what's on TV."

"Oum," said Antigone.

ELEVEN

M att and Joaquin were at Toni's place, sitting in the kitchen. Toni was glancing at her latest work, her first attempt at a praying mantis. Joaquin was glancing at a newspaper. Matt was glancing at Toni. In between glances, they sporadically spoke.

This had gradually become a routine, hanging out at Toni's place. It was far enough from campus that David and Oliver didn't try to follow, but close enough that it wasn't a strain to get there. Joaquin had always been close to his sister (followed her to college, didn't he?), but didn't share her fondness for Harrison particularly. Matt had plenty of fondness for Joaquin's sister, though he knew somewhere that it was just his emotions for Catie projected on an older and thus even more alluring screen. Most of the things that actually distinguished Toni herself from Catie were somewhat bothersome to Matt, though she wasn't quite so aggressive. Which had its downside, because if anything were ever going to happen, it would have to be Toni's doing. The relationship with Catie had left him even less likely to take initiative, for so many reasons.

Matt, at this particular moment, was wondering whether Toni had had her first time in the back of a Honda Civic. They *were* popular vehicles, and Toni had the appearance of a popular girl...

"Hate crime in Carlisle," Joaquin mentioned, pronouncing the "s" so it sounded like "Carlizzle".

"Carlisle," his sister replied parentally, properly. "The s is silent."

"Whatever. The thing is it was a hate crime. Buncha white

kids beat up this black kid who got better grades than they did. Said he must've cheated. What is *wrong* with people?"

"Lots of things," Toni answered.

"Was that over at Dickinson?" Matt had considered Dickinson as well as Harrison.

"No, I think it was a high school. Yeah, sixteen year olds. Sixteen! What was I doing at sixteen, Toni?"

"I dunno. Wetting your bed?" The praying mantis looked much more like a wounded grasshopper, didn't it?

Matt laughed, a little forcedly, and Joaquin sighed. "Better than what *they're* doing, if I was." He kept reading. Matt really wanted to know what kind of bug was depicted in this latest drawing, but he was pretty sure that Toni'd be insulted if he asked. "I think hate crimes might be the worst possible things," Joaquin commented, folding the paper and setting it in front of him on the kitchen table. "The worst crime, without justification."

"Not murder?" Matt actually turned away from Toni and her drawing, wanting to judge the sincerity of his friend.

"Well murder can be a hate crime. But there can be justification for murder, and never for a hate crime."

"Justification?"

"Okay, like in war. That's a justified killing. Then we've got coercion. Someone walks up to you and says 'kill this man, or we blow up your family'. Better, 'kill this man, or we blow up the world'. Then you're justified in killing. You're saving lives! Like in self-defense, another time. It's you or them. Pick you."

"Okay, maybe. But back to war. How is war not a hate crime?"

"Well, it depends on the war, I guess. If you're a Nazi, there's no difference. But Americans..."

"Just loved the Iraqis?" Matt, getting excited, pulled his feet onto his chair and sat on them, bouncing higher above the kitchen table at the debate.

"They didn't *hate* them." Joaquin scratched the back of his neck.

"Did you *see* any soldier interviews? Look, I'm not saying it wasn't justified, but I'm trying to say that it can be justified to have a hate crime. Saddam Hussein is no friend of mine, don't get me wrong. But people hated him, hated his army. Now you can say war isn't a crime, but you've already lumped it in. And who decides what a war is? What a crime is? What about *war crimes*?"

"Look, the *reason* for war isn't the hate. It's, well, oil, or national security or something. The *rea*son for a hate crime is just the hate."

"Oh? You don't think these white kids in Carlisle had other reasons of their own?"

"Like what?"

"I dunno. They probably took the guy's wallet. They could call the whole thing a robbery. Greed isn't hate, is it?"

"Oh c'mon."

"I'm just saying,"

"Rape." The word thundered softly from Toni's mouth, as she had been standing unbeknownst at the table. Setting the picture down atop the newspaper, she repeated, "Rape." The word jarred the two arguing boys into attempting eye-contact with her, which she denied. Matt's eyes wandered to the, the, deformed cricket? That couldn't be it. "There's your unjustifiable worst crime."

"Huh," her brother sounded a bit trivial in the wake of her new tone.

"Think about it! How many times you hear someone say 'if you don't *rape* this girl, I'll kill you and your family'. Doesn't happen. Rape in self-defense? Gimme a break. The best attempt at a justification you'll ever get out of some raping bastard is 'she was *asking* for it'. If she was *asking* for it, asshole, it wasn't rape!" Her voice slammed the last syllable of every sentence, but especially that one. "If she was *asking for it*, would she come forward, in front of everyone she knows, and say 'I'm weak, I'm a victim, I had no control'?! Idiots!"

It was not time for Matt or Joaquin to speak, in their estimation.

Toni renewed, more quietly, one might say a dull roar. "Rape, that's the worst crime. Murder at least leaves you *dead*. You don't think when you're dead. You don't have to live with yourself, day in, day out, wondering what you did wrong, when you're dead. Compared to rape, it must be very comforting."

Matt couldn't ask, he wanted to so badly, but he just couldn't. Besides, he thought he knew the answer anyway. Could someone who had never experienced it give such a speech? Maybe a fine actress, but not a live person. And why would she care so much otherwise? How would she know to? But then again, well, it couldn't be asked.

Toni's face seemed to focus, as if admonishing thoughts for their existence, as though trying to pull her car through a snowstorm without windshield wipers. Contortion, confusion, and then a slow brightening emerged. A blank sort of calm. "Soooo," she hung on to the 'o' wistfully, as long as she could, till it evaporated in her emptied exhaling lungs. "Whaddya think of my new creation?"

More questions Matt couldn't ask. And how could she shift gears that quickly? He couldn't. Joaquin supplied a question, "You mean the, uh, the bug?"

"Yeah, it's not very good, I know, don't worry about it, you don't have to say you like it, it's okay, I'll do better on it next time, and it's a praying mantis, but I know it's not a very good one, so don't worry about it, it's okay."

"Jeez, Tone! I was just *check*ing! One minute it's the worst thing in the world and the rape crisis hotline, then it's back to artsy fartsy land. I can't always keep up... just *chill*!"

So Joaquin hadn't been so affected, Matt figured. If there was a deeper personal level, Joaquin either didn't know or didn't care. How could he *not* care? He didn't know.

Toni smiled so weakly, it was almost a frown. "I don't like to think about it, bro."

"All right, so art discussion?"

"Whatever you want."

"I think you need to get away from bugs," Joaquin said evenly, frankly.

"Aw, you two aren't that bad." Finally one could tell that her facial expression really *was* a smile. It was like deciphering the mantis on the table.

"No, I mean, drawing them." Joaquin looked very seriously at his sister, who did not reciprocate as such. "I *thought* you knew what I, oh, whatever. What happened to color stuff? You got a thing against color? Is it not trendy enough in art schools? That Rachel chick telling you color is evil or something?"

"It's just... back to basics." Matt was getting the feeling he was spying on a family conversation, and he folded his arms on the table, leaning his chin gently atop them, doing nothing to minimize the fly-on-the-wall sensation.

"Basics? Why don't you try some traditional themes?"

"Nature's very traditional."

"Not traditional *art*, Tone, traditional *cult*ure. *Our* culture."

Matt sunk his chin deeper into his arms. "Something Mom could be proud of."

"So you don't like labels when we're getting beat up, but if we're making art, that's fine?"

"Huh?"

"'Our culture.' You make it sound like we're aliens. Space aliens. Y'know, your friend's right here. He doesn't look Hispanic to me. Maybe you should only have *friends* that are *our* culture." Matt's chin had hit the table. There was no more burrowing that could be done, and any sudden movements would call even more attention. "It's all bullshit."

"Antonia Garcia!" Joaquin couldn't think of anything else to say.

"You sound like Mom. Get a life."

Joaquin still couldn't think of anything else to say. The look of abject shock on his face was best served wordless anyway.

"Oh, c'mon, this can't surprise you that much. Listen, you wanna start living in the past? Because that's all it is, y'know. Just living as if our ancestors are all that matters. Not us, just them. The dead are doing the living. Well, guess what, Quino? We're descended from a rape. No, not Mom and Papa, maybe not even their folks. But somewhere, down the chain, we've evolved from rapes. Lots of them. Everyone has." The anger was coming back, triggered by the word. "That's how humans grew up a lot of the time, on forced sex. And kids were born, and they were forced to have sex, and this is our ancestry. But you don't tell me to paint rapes, do you?"

Joaquin shook his head, taking his sister more seriously this time. Matt imagined Toni trying to paint a rape and ending up just hurling fifty gallons of crimson paint at a canvas, one after the other, till she couldn't leave her room for all the paint cans in her way.

"And not just rapes, Quino. Murders and hate crimes and stealing galore. Violence. That's how people survived for centuries. You want me to celebrate *that*? Heritage is just a pretty name for bias and hatred, bro. Just a way of dressing it up nice to go to the prom, or the art gallery as you want. Well I don't want to be Mom and I don't want to be the rapes of the past. I want to be *me*. I'm going to live in the future, not some sinful past."

This had to be the work of that Sociology class, Joaquin realized. He was liking Harrison less every day. "You given this speech to Mom?"

"Hey, you could start by talking to *them* about hate crimes. Why do you think there *are* hate crimes? Is it because people don't think about culture and just live in the future? No, it's because people are buried in the past, and buried in *culture*. Hate crimes. Are. The result. Of *culture*." She strung the words out with punctuating pauses, as though building to the discussion's closing crescendo.

"*Disrespect* for culture."

"Same difference," Toni said, and picked up her mantis drawing, ripped it cleanly in half, and carried it to the trash bag under the sink.

Joaquin's long-time ally had sold out. "This school's changed you."

"If you're lucky," she turned on a dime from the kitchen sink, "it'll change you too."

"God I hope not. Are you really rejecting our culture? Sitting here, in front of me, in your kitchen, telling me that you're not Hispanic?"

"You heard me." The anger had never really receded. This *had* to be the anger talking. Didn't it?

"*This*," he said pointedly, standing and hunching up his shoulders "is a hate crime. Sister, you're committing a hate crime on me. On Mom. On all of *us*." He stormed out.

"Quino? Quiiino? *Qui*no? I guess he's gone... Moron."

At this, Matt, who had been trying to will himself to sleep, or perhaps into a smaller size, or maybe just a nice convenient coma, lifted his eyebrows. His eyes had spots in front of them, and soon had Toni in front of them as well.

"You didn't go with him? Whose side are you on, anyway?"

Matt hadn't talked much to Toni, especially without the presence of her brother. Had he ever been in this situation? It was awfully unpredictable. Then again, apparently Joaquin was too. "Side?"

"It's me or him, ain't it?" She gave the matter-of-fact look he remembered plastered to Catie's face whenever she felt total control over a situation. It was a very familiar look.

"Well, uh."

"Put it this way. You got a culture?" The anger had been all for Joaquin, evidently.

Matt thought about this. He pulled his arms from the table

and they literally squelched in rising, for they had been pressed so heavily into the wood that it created a slightly adhesive effect. There was deep redness on both arms. He was not focused on this so much as how best to answer a question that had never been put to him before. Why had it never been put to him? Then he started laughing. "Are you kidding? A culture? I'm from *Kansas*!"

TWELVE

They let her into the room. She was trying not to shake, trying to show some fortitude. Physiologically, there was no reason for her to be feeling this way. It was all in her head. But one doesn't leave a message like that on the office answering machine, does one? And why hadn't Matt called her? They still got one phone call, right? She had so many questions and she had been hauled into this overlit room to give answers? She didn't *have* any answers. Without being asked, she stumbled into the chair, silent save for the skidding of its legs.

"Hello, Mrs. Norton."

"My n-name is Dr. Dawn," it wasn't trembling it was just, well, wasn't it a little chilly in this room?

"Ah yes," Joe Ewing flipped through a sea of paper and saw next to nothing. "I should've figured you'd return to your maiden name after the divorce. Lutz... Dr. Lutz. Yet you're still listed as Norton in the phone book? Your practice?"

"*Dawn.* Miriam Dawn. Some patients remember me by my married name."

"Well yes of course, they would, wouldn't they? Now where does this 'Dawn' come from?"

"It's my new last name."

"New? Have you remarried?"

"Well, no, I, it's, y'see, my middle name, really. But I don't really like 'Lutz'."

"I see. Highly irregular. Suit yourself. You, uh, decided against a lawyer?"

"One will be provided for me, right? I know my rights."

Ewing couldn't help but crack a smile. "Well, you see, Dr. Nor, uh, *Dawn*, as you say, you're not really the acc*used* as such in this matter."

"So?"

"So technically you do not have the right to a lawyer provided by the state. If you really *want*, I suppose we could charge you with something. A misdemeanor, perhaps. Shoplifting? Disturbance of the peace?"

"*What*?"

"A joke, doctor, only a joke. I find that the atmosphere of this room is a little lighter with some humor. So then, no legal counsel."

"Just like that?"

"Well, if you in*sist*, you can go find one and come back. But that might take days, and this investigation really is on a tight schedule. I was hoping to leave Topeka by tomorrow at the *late*st. Home for Christmas and all that. You were called earlier, weren't you?"

"One of your guys left a message. He said nothing about lawyers."

"Oh, I guess that must have been Mitch. I don't think I'd do that." He turned to Mitch. "Remember that, next time, Mitch? When we go back to Philly." Mitch was silent. "Now then. I think you'll find it best for your son if this investigation goes as smoothly as possible."

"Okay. Fine. Whatever's best for Matt."

"Good. I'm going to turn this on. You want anything to drink?"

"Uh, a Diet Coke?"

"Mitch would be delighted to get you a Diet Coke." As Ewing pressed **REC** on the tape recorder, Mitch exited, looking like he would be delighted to shoot someone. "Could you state your name for the tape?"

"Miriam Dawn. Dr. Miriam Dawn."

"Is that really your full name?"

"Technically, it's Miriam Dawn Lutz. And I used to be Miriam Dawn Lutz Norton. Happy?"

"And the date?"

"December 23rd."

"The year?"

"Two-thousand."

"And who is in the room today?"

"Looks like you and me. What *is* your name anyway?"

"I'm Officer Joe Ewing of the Philadelphia PD. My assistant Mitch and a Diet Coke will be arriving shortly." They did.

"Thanks."

"Now Dr. Dawn, or Dawn-Lutz, or Lutz-Norton, what is your relation to Matt Norton?"

"I already told you he's my son."

"Not on the tape. Okay, your son. Your only son?"

"Yes."

"When did you last talk to him?"

"Sometime last week, I think."

"He hasn't called you from prison?"

"No."

"But you knew he was in prison?"

"Yes."

"How?"

"Mitch called me the other day."

"I see. We hate to bear bad news. Tell me, what did Mitch say?"

"Nothing. Just that he was jailed and I'd have to come 'round to answer some questions."

"So nothing about *why* he was arrested."

"That's right."

"Doctor, I'm going to ask you to make a guess."

"A guess?"

"Why do *you* think your son is imprisoned right now?"

"How should I know? I just told you I don't--"

"Now, now, Doctor, that's why this is a guess. An *educ*ated guess, hopefully. Why's your son in prison?"

"I don't know. A mistake."

"Come now. Even if it's a mistake, it has a *state*d purpose, right? What do you think the *charges* are?"

"I don't know. Shoplifting. Disturbance of the peace."

"Tell me, Doctor, would we conduct an investigation of this magnitude over a disturbance of the peace?"

"I guess not..."

"Would we be holding your son over *Christmas* without bail for a disturbance of the peace?"

"You mean he's still *in* there?"

"Educated guesses, if you please, Doctor. Yes, he's still in there. He's going to stay in there until we get some answers!"

"I give up. Underage drinking?"

"Doctor, you seem to be missing the felonies. With. Out. Bail."

"Well he didn't kill anybody."

"You know that for sure?"

"Have you talked to Matt?"

"Young people are very good at lying, Doctor. I shouldn't think that I would need to tell you that."

"Not Matt. You can always tell exactly what he's thinking. He's *too* straightforward."

"Or maybe he just gives that appearance? As a way of convincing his mother he's innocent of all sorts of crimes?"

"Well it's not murder. It's nothing violent. It can't be. It has to be, I don't know, are there any non-violent felonies? What is there? Drug dealing? Is that a felony?"

"A-ha! So you *do* know why you're son's in. That wasn't so hard, was it? Now, when did your son first get into drugs?"

"Excuse me?"

"Well, you just told me. I have it on tape. Would you like the playback? You said 'drug dealing'. You asked if that's a felony. Well it is, Doctor, and that's why your little Matthew is in so much trouble."

"Look, I never said he *was* dealing, I just was guessing. You *told* me to guess!"

"So I did. To see what it would reveal."

"Well I would've come up with it *eventually*. This hardly seems fair."

"Fair enough, when we're trying to extract the facts from a protective mother. I'm just doing my job here. Don't kill the messenger. Now, you were about to tell me when Matt got into drugs."

"He *didn't*!"

"You're not under oath, Doctor, so we can't try you for perjury. But I remind you that your *cooperation* is *essential* to the chances of Matt coming home for next Christmas. Do I make myself clear?"

"I *am* cooperating! I don't think Matt ever had a *beer*! Do you hear me? I only guessed underage drinking because I figured that's something they do in college!!"

"Did *you* do that in college?"

"I don't see how that question is relevant."

"Heredity, perhaps? Did you?"

"Sure, some. Everybody did. I'll bet you did."

"Did you do drugs in college, Doctor?"

"Oh yeah, meth looked real appealing from the medical textbooks. No, *Officer*, I did not do drugs in college. Or ever."

"So Matt's liking for them was independent of your influence?"

"Did Matt *say* he did drugs?"

"Matt didn't tell us much of anything, really. But I'll take care of the questions, if you don't mind. Now then, you seem adamant that your son is not a druggie. Why?"

"Well look at me! And you talked to Alex, I'm sure. We're not drug types. Our son is not a drug dealer! We're middle class! We're respectable. Matt didn't need the money. We *gave* him money. He had a nice girlfriend, and friends, and was well-adjusted, and healthy. He was too *healthy* to be into drugs. And where would he get them? Officer, I don't need to tell *you* that middle class youth, the offspring of *doc*tors, would not be dealing drugs!"

"We have stacks of criminal records that might beg to differ with you, I'm afraid. Granted, we're worse at catching the middle class in the act, but well, we caught Matt, didn't we? Now you mention this girlfriend. How would you describe her?"

"Like I said, a very nice girl. Sporty."

"Sporty. How do you mean that exactly?"

"Well, she was athletic. Very healthy. A good influence on Matt, I think."

"A *good* influence?"

"Absolutely."

"I suppose you'll tell me that your ex-*hus*band was a *bad* influence."

"Alex? Why would he be a bad influence?"

"You divorced him, didn't you?"

"That just means he was a bad influence on *me*. I don't think he's evil or anything. I did love him once, you know."

"That's very touching. What happened? He kick you around?"

"No! He just, we just, things happen. We fought. He didn't like the way I did things."

"But he never took that out on you?"

134

"Not like that."

"Did he take it out on Matt?"

"Do you *always* assume the worst about people?"

"In my profession, it pays. In most professions, I would imagine it would. Don't you ever assume the worst possible disease and work backwards, Doctor?"

"I don't tell kids with colds they have cancer."

"A kid with a cold might be coming home for Christmas, Doctor. So no abuse of Matt or you?"

"Never. Not physical. Yelling. Is that abuse these days? I can never keep up."

"Enough for a divorce, apparently."

"Divorce is not a crime, y'know."

"True. But drug dealing is. And I'm trying to determine how your son is charged with so many counts of drug possession, drug dealing, and grand theft auto if--"

"*Grand theft auto*?!"

"Well, that's not really what we're investigating. But yes, there is an associated stolen vehicle. That's really rather common in these cases. Dealers rarely work out of their own cars, at least not when doing big deals. Matt often used your car?"

"Not for *drug dealing*. He took Catherine out in it."

"His girlfriend? The 'good' influence?"

"That's the one."

"And he used your ex-husband's Suburban from time to time?"

"You should've asked him that. I think so."

"Your ex-husband wasn't the most *cooperative* person we've ever encountered."

"I'm not sure I blame him. This is all a little surreal."

"Surreal?"

"It's like walking into an alien abduction. All the faces and all the people seem somewhat real, but deep down, they're not human--"

"Doctor."

"No, really, it's like someone bumped me over the head and now I'm about to be examined in all the wrong places. I feel violated--"

"Doctor, *really*!"

"This is a violative investigation. You have taken my son, or someone you *think* is my son. I mean, who knows who you think

135

my son is!"

"Doctor, I must ask you to cooperate with the questioning without making random speeches."

"Do you have children?"

"Yes. Three."

"Are any of them *drug dealers*?"

"No. I don't know. Maybe. I don't see them that often. And if an officer of the law walked into a room like this and told me one had been arrested for dealing, I wouldn't carry on about aliens. I'd cooperate, and tell them how it's possible that they got involved in drugs. Because *I* know what a widespread problem it is with our youth. I may not see my kids, but at least I *know* what kids are doing! At least I'm not in denial!"

"This seems awfully combative if you're on my side."

"You're the one calling me an alien."

"The exp*erience* is alien."

"Well, maybe your son is alien to you too, Doctor. It's a shame you couldn't help him." Ewing started stacking cluttered (and mostly blank) papers on his desk.

"Was this at a frat party?"

"Was *what* at a frat party?"

"The... incident. The arrest."

"No, it wasn't even at school. But why do you ask? Was your son in a frat?"

"No, no, but he did go to one, I think."

"Oh?"

"Well, I kept encouraging him to have a little fun. He didn't seem to get out much. And I thought he should. I mean, that's half of college. So, I, well, I thought he should go to a frat party. Just one, y'know, to see how he liked it."

"*You* encouraged *your son* to go to a *frat party*?"

"Well kinda. And I just hate to think that he met someone or got mixed up in something like this because of me."

"Well, that's at least a new angle, Doctor. Maybe it will help your son."

"Don't you have any more questions?"

"No, not really. You've convinced me that you don't have much to say." He stood up, waiting for Miriam to join him. "Have you ever been in jail, Doctor?"

"Of course not!"

"Well, I figured. Matt's about to spend his first Christmas in jail, and I'm surprised that you're not out there with him."

"I only heard about this two days ago and I have so many appointments, and the holiday, and--"

"I'm just saying, Doctor. It's very curious."

Miriam finally stood up. "I in*tend* to visit. I just need to clear my schedule. It's a long ways, you know. I drove there once already."

"Some mothers," he selected his words carefully, as he meant them to close the interrogation, "would drive to the end of the earth to comfort their son. Some mothers," even more carefully "are *close* to their son."

"But--"

"Good day, Doctor."

"But, but--"

"Mitch?"

THIRTEEN

I t was the first night in October, but Matt would've bet money that it was the last. He had a sense of foreboding that he could easily associate with Halloween, with the prowling night and its wayward spooks. Leaves had already begun to flee the trees, and a large branch, now barren, swung between a lamppost outside and his dorm window, leaving a continual silhouette against the cloth shade. The outlines of this haunting shadow were just visible in the descending night, as darkness fell a hair earlier on this eastern side of the building.

"Are you coming?" he asked David, putting his jean jacket on and facing the door.

"Where you going again?"

"Frat party. Sigma sigma sigma. Wine, women, and song." He glanced over to see if David were actually considering it. "Probably not *your* songs, though, Dave."

Had he ever asked him to call him Dave? What an aggravating little habit. There had been so few ways around their growing hostility, and now it looked like staying out of each other's way provided the best course. He was leaving voluntarily now, so why miss the chance? And if he ever needed him to fall asleep, he only needed to tell him about a song on the Tour. "Naw, you go on ahead. Someone should be here if the cops come."

"The cops?"

"You know, break up the party. Isn't that what the Fifeburg Police do? When they're not arresting donuts, anyway."

"Oh, right. I thought you meant, never mind. Have a good night, David."

The door closed behind him, not quite slamming, but they must have left the window open again given the closure's pace. He knocked next door. "Guys?"

"Yeah, coming, coming." The voice was Oliver's, a little excited. The door swung wide. "Okay! So glad you guys are coming along for the ride. Gonna be great."

"Yeah, great." Joaquin sounded like he'd just been run over by a highway.

Oliver's hair was slicked back in a manner that utterly transformed his appearance. Suddenly he was bordering on kempt. Joaquin, meanwhile, was hiding under a Los Angeles Dodgers baseball cap. The brim was so low over his face that Matt feared he'd be obliged to give directions all night. "A little to the left," Matt imagined. "No! Your other left... okay, that was a person, but they're all right..."

"Would you turn that around, Garcia?" Oliver, since rushing this fraternity, had developed a penchant for last names. "Seriously, you are Uncool, live and in person, like that."

"What do you care if I'm uncool?" Joaquin's voice was something like a whine mixed with growling.

"You're my *room*mate. I'm showing you off to the boys. Free booze, my friends, comes at a price. Just turn it around, okay?" Joaquin failed to comply, and Oliver shrugged, entered the doorway, and stopped cold. "Norton, what the hell are you wearing?"

"What, this?" Matt had first checked to make sure that Joaquin had not capped his own head as well. He now held out his shirt, his own great second-guess of his appearance, which was actually button-down.

"Well, you could work on that too, but what's *around* that? Does this look like the eighties to you?"

"Well, no, uh."

"Hey, Garcia, look here. Have you seen one of these since maybe '87?"

"Well, I saw him wear it yesterday."

"Well shit. That's impressive. Hey, if you've got the guts, Norton, you're just tagging along. We've got the anti-homeboy here and eighties-dork-man to go with. I bet the ladies will just eat this up." Oliver was like water. If he wasn't getting anywhere with his original path, he'd slide into least resistance and find some other way to soak you. But he refused to be deterred tonight. "No point in asking if we're ready, cuz you guys never will be. Hey, is your uh, Benowski, coming along?"

"Nope."

"Shucks, there goes our chance at the Three Stooges. Oh well. Two Stooges is plenty. Onward, men!" He ushered, virtually carted Joaquin out, locking the door with a flourish and depositing the keys in his ample jeans pocket. "You guys pumped?"

They began down the hall, drifting down the stairs like each step had something special to offer, to be contemplated, to savor. Oliver was bounding ahead of them, doling out questions and instructions without awaiting reply or even acknowledgement. Already, he was planning introductions of his freaky hallmates. What had begun as an innocent way of urging them to meet more people had rapidly evolved into exploitation central. If this didn't attract peoples' attention at the party, very little would.

What had really surprised him, he thought as he reached the ground floor and could barely hear the gradual stepping above, was Norton's eagerness to embrace this offer. "I'd just been thinking how much I needed to meet new people," he'd told Oliver the day before.

"You being a smartass again?"

"No, I'm completely serious. I mean, I know like six people on campus."

"Any females?"

"Just one."

"So you *should* come along!"

"Oliver, you don't have to convince me! I *want* to go."

"Seriously?"

"Seriously."

"Well your mom wanted to go, so I'm not surprised."

"Actually, she kinda did." Norton was grinning like he'd set this up. Never trust a smartass.

"Huh?"

"No, really. She thought I should go to a frat party. She said it was a 'rite of college' or something."

"Your *mom*?"

"Believe it or not."

"Well shit."

But now Oliver had ruefully seen what Norton thought passed for party attire. Instead of bringing another possible recruit to his secret society, he was bringing the sideshow. But it was

140

tough to charge admission to see guests, so there seemed very little profitable in even that. Except the attention. He'd have to make sure to dissociate himself from any actual friendship with the two. Which wouldn't really be far from the truth, would it?

Clomp, clomp, clomp. They practically fell off the bottom step, resignedly. "Is it a long walk, Liver?" Joaquin groaned, and Matt laughed.

"Please don't call me that, Garcia. It's just about four blocks from here."

"That should be your frat name. Liver. Or Chopped Liver. That'd be great."

"Look, it's bad enough as it is." This was a sore spot. Outsiders never *understood* the beauty of fraternity nicknames. His own was "MamaBoy", a direct descendant of his own words.

"No, seriously. And then you'd have a ready joke every time. 'And so I says to the bartender I says what am I, Chopped Liver? And he says yes, yes you are!' That'd be a show-stopper." Joaquin was livening to the topic, animated hands flying before him.

"Listen, Garcia, I'm being kind enough to invite you *as my guest* to this function..."

"I thought you said that all roomies have to come tonight. A rule. That's what this party is for, you told me."

"That doesn't mean you're not my guest."

"Whatever you say, Liver."

Matt still wasn't sure how Joaquin was walking. This was something that would be a good use of time in a math class: calculate the angle of vision he was working under. He could probably see his feet, and maybe even his ankles. But what good was that for avoiding obstacles? At least he was blocking his face from the brunt of the wind that was sweeping through the deserted twilight streets of Fifeburg. They crossed two blocks and it was suddenly the furthest from campus that Matt had been since driving to Harrison weeks earlier.

They all had their own thoughts to keep them company on the short walk. Neither Matt nor Joaquin was exactly looking forward to the upcoming experience, but both had an inkling that this would be a positive venture in the long run. Not unlike a dental visit, without the anticipation of direct pain. There would be some nervous tension, some difficult moments, some squirming, but in the long run, they would feel better as a result, they figured. Meanwhile Oliver was trying to find some way of spinning this to his advantage. If only the Norton kid weren't dressed like such a nerd! He wasn't so bad most of the time, and him being a smartass would work well with his frat brothers, and they could all make fun of his sullen roommate. But in those clothes, well, this would be a challenge.

The house greeted them before they came upon the house. Before Joaquin even saw it, in fact, but that was not necessarily saying anything. "What's up, Mama-B!" yelled someone from the darkening lawn in front of a ramshackle house with a porch, three floors, and a wide-spanning balcony. The lawn was in poor condition, with more dirt than grass, in wide unruly swaths.

"Yo Corndog, how's it going?"

"Who are these kids?"

"This one's my roomie, Joaquin Garcia, and over here is Matt Norton from next door."

"An extra? Thought we were just s'posed to bring the roommates."

"He tagged along for fun." They finally made it to the lawn itself, and Oliver greeted "Corndog" in a rather elaborate fashion, involving slapping of hands and fists and elbows.

"Well we've got fun! What's up, boys? Ready to par-ty?"

"What's your real name?" the LA Dodgers hat appeared to ask.

Corndog frowned. "Uh, just call me Corndog. Corn's cool for short, if you want."

Oliver elbowed Corndog in the stomach. "'Sall he ever eats. Seriously. Morning noon and night."

This, Matt mused to himself, begged the question of how Oliver had ducked the name of a brand of cereal, but perhaps *Honey Bunches of Oats* was too long an appellation. *Lucky*? *Frosted*? *Corn Flakes* might provide a conflict of interests with this fellow here.

Matt shook Corndog's hand, in a style to the latter's displeasure. "Sorry, I don't know all the secret handshakes."

"Nothing *se*cret! Just well, it's what's *cool*. Never mind..." Corndog trailed off, unsure of his audience. "Shall we hit the keg?"

"Your mom hit the keg! And you know what happened then..."

"That's my Mama-Boy!" He threw an arm over Oliver's expansive shoulders and the two traipsed into the house, greeted by sporadic yells and flesh.

Matt looked at LA. "Can you *see* anything?"

"Too much," the hat replied. Matt hadn't really looked around, but now he saw an expanse of humanity milling on the lawn, many smoking, all looking mortifyingly cool. Three sigmas decked the top of the porch, proud black against the flaking white paint of the large house. Without warning, a beat began to emerge from within, giving rise to cheers and preliminary movement from the crowd.

"You wanna go in?"

"I could use a beer, I guess."

They intrepidly braved the slightly confused eyes of their peers as they approached the cracking wood porch, the open entryway, the filth of the interior. Everywhere there was loud conversation, laughter, and the emerging beat of dance music growing in volume and proximity. Its rhythm rose and fell against the rustling of wind in the fallen leaves, now whisked away and replaced by dirty walls and more loud people.

There was a straight hall, narrow enough before the clumps of people, yelling and howling to express themselves, entered the mix. As Joaquin and Matt made their way to the backyard, they found themselves apologizing constantly in their unending displacement of foreign figures. They received little acknowledgement in return beyond disgruntled gasps and disgusted glares.

"Hey man, it's not eighties night!" yelled one in sunglasses, to a resulting bevy of tipsy giggles around him.

The backyard was equally crowded, but more regimented in the line of people awaiting inebriation. An almost tidy double-file line that snaked back up toward the back door from two kegs in the center of the yard, it was headed by two harried guys without shirts, who were pouring hand over fist into nondescript red cups. "Make sure you have your cup! Everyone *must* have a cup," one of them shouted in the midst of serving, "one at a time, folks!"

Cups were handed to them from an apparent apparition, someone who disappeared into the line as soon as they felt cups in their hands. A scrawled paper sign was taped to each keg, with black marker scrawl saying "21 to drink". Spilled beer streamed down the sides of the keg, blurring some of the letters. About every fourth person who made the kegs, Matt noticed, would be greeted with a laugh and violent head-shaking. When he and

Joaquin, silent betwixt the cacophony, finally reached the head of the line, Matt had to ask.

"These signs, they aren't for real, are they?"

"*What*??!"

"The *signs*!" Matt pointed exaggeratedly.

The expected laugh and head-shaking ensued. "No! For *cops*! Are you a cop?"

Matt was a bit concerned to think that cops would filter in plain clothes amongst this scene. "No way!"

The shirtless guy smiled winningly and handed him his cup back, full.

Matt had consumed alcohol before, mostly with Sam before he moved. Early in high school, they made a habit of raiding the refrigerator of one or the other of Matt's parents (who never seemed to be home), which almost invariably yielded light beer. Neither of them had the guts to admit that it tasted only slightly better than apple juice left to age on the counter for a half-century. And the intoxication was appealing, if slightly disappointing. They would run around the house and then get awfully tired. Matt was unsure what all the fuss was about, and had only twice had beers alone after Sam had moved.

The idea of alcohol with Catie just scared him. He didn't know why.

He sipped, found that beer had not drastically improved in taste since his last encounter, and looked for Joaquin. Sure enough, the white-on-blue LA was found atop a red cup, creating an oddly patriotic image that looked altogether inhuman, especially in the artificial lights mounted on the back porch. The cup descended, attached to a hand, and LA spoke. "This," the hat said slowly, "sucks."

Matt was unsure whether Joaquin meant the beer, the party, the situation they were in, or Harrison College. "No kidding," he replied.

They stood there. There was no sign of Oliver, or the mysterious "Corndog". This would be so much worse if he were the only one, Matt realized. "Could you hold this?" Joaquin asked over the din, extending the red cup, now half-full.

"Uh, sure, where you going?"

"Bathroom."

"Good *luck*." And he watched Joaquin bump his way back into the house, looking much more personable from behind. He resolved not to imagine how things could worsen, lest reality feel the need to comply.

The noise and swarms of people were disorienting. That couldn't be a third of a beer. People all around him had so much to say, so much fun to be had, so many laughs to share. There was movement and life and vibrance in all their bodies. This was *college*! This was *youth*! Why wasn't his excitement for it, his appetite building? He'd finally fled Kansas, finally escaped the dreary monochrome cornfields for, for, for this? For clouds of cigarette smoke rising above a din of horny false impressions? His entrance had not been the grandest, but even now, standing in his jean jacket, button down, and dingy corduroys, who would want to talk to him? And what was Catie doing right now? She was evasive on the topic of another boyfriend, though he'd been somewhat evasive in inquiring. Maybe next time he should just come straight out and ask. He looked skyward, finding the bulk of the moon accounted for. The same moon, he knew, that Catie could see from Kansas. Always the same moon, no matter how many miles separated them. As long as it was night at the same time, he could look, and she could look, and they would share an experience, miles apart, that somehow broke the barriers between them. If only the moon reflected! If only he could make eye-contact with her now, and see that another pair of eyes would not dart around hers, as he so surely feared...

"Sorry," he muttered, an involuntary response to being bumped from behind, watching small sloshes of beer escape their cylindrical captors.

"No, no, *I'm* sorry," the voice was almost squeaky. Matt expected dogs to come running at the sound of those words. He turned slightly to face a girl who, in the half-light, was awfully attractive, especially in one rather visible region.

"You okay?"

"I'm *fine*." She giggled. "I'm Jessie. Who's the beer for?" All her sentences rose at the end, like questions, even when they weren't questions. She looked expectantly, then turned her empty palms up to demonstrate the obvious need.

"Uh, well, um, you, right?" Matt tripped over the words as he extended his right arm, offering what he was pretty sure was *his* original beer, not Joaquin's.

"Why thank you! What's your name?"

"I'm Matt."

"Well that's a nice name. And what are you doing here, *Matt*?" Her tongue was trying to play with the word, but there wasn't much to work with.

"Oh, you know, *liv*ing it up!" he faked a smile, very badly.

She giggled loudly and reminded him of everything different he'd liked about Catie. Why did she haunt his thoughts like this? If he hadn't looked up at the moon, but then that was absurd. It wasn't the moon that reminded him of Catie, it was females. Any females. Look at Toni, for God's sake. She was as carbon a copy as he could envision of his ex-girlfriend, and even then he couldn't find enough desire to take action! Had he been spoiled by wanting and then receiving? The fulfillment of his only memorable love left him bereft of future potential. He was nonplussed. And ignoring this mouse of a girl, despite her unreasonably large endowment, which she was not exactly hiding.

"So, uh, come here often?" he regretted it as soon as he'd said it, but most of his conventional wisdom came from television.

The girl's lips formed into a pout, and Matt imagined that the word *often* might be just outside her vocabulary. "Haven't you seen me here before? Do *you* come here often?"

Relaxing a bit, Matt leaned back. "Oh. No. Actually it's my first time here, I,"

"You mean you're not *pledging*?"

"Well, um, I don't think so, exactly, what is--"

"Eee!" That was it. She had actually *shrieked* as she walked away. It sounded a bit more like the hiccup of a piccolo, but the result was the same. He was rid of her, at least, though he was taken aback by her blatant shallowness. One moment he'd been getting the visual tour, and the next, there wasn't even a hand left to talk to. Just as well. And where was Joaquin? It was time to leave.

The wind rustled again, and just before going inside to seek his neighbor, Matt noticed Jessie's arm protrude out of the crowd to point in his general direction. He wasn't sure if the accompanying whistle was from the soundtrack within or the pointer without.

FOURTEEN

"So what's 'Brett' short for, anyway?" After working (Without Wires) for weeks, Antigone had finally cornered her cagey co-worker into a friendly dinner. Explicitly not a date. Merely a shared dinner hour for Antigone to find out how much fate was operating on the afternoon that Brett had called her. Since that afternoon, she had started making enough to pay Betsy a reasonable portion of the rent, afford gas on her lengthy commute, and even catch the attention (and envy) of all her co-workers, except Brett. Brett was just cold with her. She had called her shot to him and nailed it, not only diverting his sale on her, but taking the honor of top seller from him, as she'd predicted. Not quite his job, but what his job there had become. But he'd found that trying to avoid some sort of encounter with this woman was hopeless, as she bothered him overtly about it daily. There was finally no purpose in resisting her pitch.

"Nothing. Just Brett." He stabbed some lettuce and coughed slightly.

"Really? Not Brettino or Bretholemew or Brettany? It sounds so short and choppy as-is. Brett. Must be short for *some*thing."

"Just Brett," he repeated, elbows on the table and salad half-eaten.

"Huh." Her salad was already gone, and she bobbed in her chair waiting for the main course. She had taken to partaking in Betsy's morning caffeinated-water coffee, which kept her hyper and energetic for much of the day. She wished she could sleep in, but with Betsy's air-raid wake-up, there was no way she could return to sleep after six on any given morning. So she wasted half

147

her artificial energy bouncing around the apartment as the morning wore on, since she didn't go to work till noon. The (early) dinner break was actually in the midst of work; they would return to proffer cell phones during everyone *else*'s dinner. As Martin had told them a week earlier, at least they knew that people were *home* then.

"What's Antigone long for? Not your *real* name, is it?"

Antigone relished this challenge, which all new friends would confront sooner or later. Sooner for Brett. Was he really a *friend*? She hauled out her purse, fishing for her driver's license. "Here."

The legality of **Antigone Edgewood** was not what Brett noticed first. "Illinois?"

"Yeah. Just moved. That's why I needed the job when you called."

Brett grimaced at the reminder of that call. In retrospect, even if he made peace with this woman over this makeshift dinner, he should have hung up on her. He thought often about what it would take for him to hang up on a customer. Several of them campaigned for it, so annoyed that they insisted on turning the tables and *actually* annoying him. He always tried valiantly to work with someone's difficulties, turning them to his side, or at least showing how painfully reasonable a company Working Without Wires was. There was always the odd person that, if Brett survived enough testing, would give in and at least take a free month trial or something. A reward for his sincerity. "Yeah. What part of Illinois?"

"Chicago."

"I have an aunt in Springfield. Why'd you leave?"

The waitress stepped in, "Are you done, sir?" She had picked up Antigone's shining plate without asking. This delay gave Antigone time to think about the response. For all her practice at explaining her name or her life history, fleeing an abusive relationship just didn't have a witty rejoinder. There was no way to deal with the innocent (and perfectly reasonable) question without hauling herself in front of oncoming emotional rush-hour traffic. At the same time, she was obsessed with not lying, especially in more personal encounters, for she was sure that deception would always provide disastrous karmic results.

"Yeah, thanks," he told the waitress. Then he looked expectantly at Antigone.

"I, uh, you know, needed a change."

"From what? Chicago's a great city."

This guy *would* think Chicago was great. "Well, really, it was, um, y'know, myboyfriendandIsplitup." The words cascaded in a steady stream that she was soon hoping he wouldn't hear properly, would ask for clarification, and she could say that it was an ancient Mongolian word meaning *the need for change.*

"Oh yeah?" Brett's eyebrows raised. Damn, he'd heard just fine.

"Yeah. So I got a change of scenery." She noticed that she had dropped her napkin on the floor.

"Apparently." She could see the wheels turning in his head. "You always this good at selling?"

"Yeah. Just comes naturally, I guess." Something different to discuss! She barreled through the conversational emergency exit door. "I mean, it's one of those things. Had a lemonade stand when I was nine and just flashed everyone a cute smile and they came running. Ever since, I've been perfecting ways to read people, to get into their head and look around, see what they want. It works well in a business standpoint. Need *some* way to make money, right?"

Brett was drumming fingers on the table, either impatient or engrossed. "So it's just a way to make money?"

"Unfortunately, I think so. Not like I'm on a moral crusade for cell phone use. Quite the opposite, really." Her tone shifted, and she looked down. Why did she always have the desire to spill her guts to everyone who talked to her for five minutes? "Do you ever have any, well, *qualms* about what we do?"

"What *we* do?"

"Telemarketing."

"*Oh*, oh. That. Well, no, not really. You mean what, bothering people during dinner?"

"No. I mean, well, just blindly selling. Being mercenaries to the consumer world. How many people you think actually need what we sell them? How many people you think end up looking at their cell phone with regret a month after we call them, getting yelled at by their family as they pay the bills and don't go to the latest movie as a result?"

"Oh, poor little Joey doesn't get to go to the moo-vie! I mean, the market will solve, right?" Antigone rolled her eyes and fidgeted. "Seriously. This is the *economy*. The lifeblood of

America. We run it, we make it happen, we support ourselves and that supports the nation. If we weren't working hard, then the whole country would suffer. We suffer enough for those that don't work hard, so we have to take their money to make sure they don't have the power in this country."

The waitress brought their food, fish and chips for Antigone, spaghetti with meatballs for Brett. "That's cold."

"What, the fish? Oh, you mean my attitude? Are you some closet socialist or something? Shouldn't you be out protesting instead of selling cell phones?"

"Look, I'm just saying that, well, hey. I agree with you about a lot of people. Most of them are stupid. We couldn't sell if they were sharp, or clear-headed or whatever. But is that any reason to take advantage of them? To play off their insecurities? I get sick nights staying up thinking about this sometimes. Don't you ever wonder what we're doing to people?"

Brett twirled his fork. "I thought this was a friendly lunch. Now you're trying to drive me off my job for real? Haven't you done enough damage to my career?"

Antigone was defensive at this. "No, I'm just trying to talk to you. It's not like I can talk to Martin about this, and most of the other folks in there are kids. If you want to talk about the weather..." She prodded her fish, as though expecting them to ask for a glass of water.

"Kids are often socialists."

"That's not the point. I just don't expect them to, well, *worry* about this. I mean, I didn't when I was twenty. What did you worry about when you were twenty?"

"Getting laid," Brett answered definitively, through a meatball.

"There you go. That's *certainly* not worrying about what you're doing to other people, is it?"

"Okay. Here's my answer. If you're dumb enough to buy, then I deserve to sell. I don't worry about that. Maybe if all of America were starving like a third world country, I'd worry. But we aren't. We're just fine." He smiled smugly, downed some Coke, and leaned back in his chair. "Why can't you talk to Martin about it?"

"He'd fire me!" This was not the real reason, exactly, but it sounded reasonable.

"You underestimate him. He's all touchy-feely like you are.

He gave *you* a job, didn't he?"

Antigone brushed her hair away from her face. "I don't know much about him." Ah, a good lead. Show misunderstanding, and then nothing's suspect! "I mean, does he have a family?"

"I think he's divorced with a kid or something. Yeah, I saw a picture once. Arthur, after his middle name. He's real concerned about that baby."

"Concerned?"

"Well he gets to see it about twice a month between his job and the custody agreement. I dunno, this was a while back. I think this is why he's all soft, though."

Martin Arthur Tucker. He *was* soft. He was big and lovable and Antigone deeply wished she didn't find him so attractive. And knowing that he had a child who he loved didn't help anything, though it certainly explained a few things. Why he worked so hard. Why he seemed so selfless. Why he had such a good sense of people's most important values and worries. This wasn't just intuition, this wasn't how Rick had appeared, for Rick's intuition had always had such a selfish bent to it. But maybe that was just retrospect. She had no interest in returning to that branch of Memory Lane. "Mmmhmm."

"Talk to him about this. Leave me alone. I don't need your moralizing."

Antigone frequently found her mind to be like a rusty standard automobile transmission. Shifting gears was almost impossible sometimes. This was useful for focusing on making a sale or understanding someone's perspective, but it made dealing with bad thoughts a nightmare. There was something so compelling about all the haunting mistakes of her past, and it took more concentration than she could usually muster to pull the stick back under her control. And even if she *could* shift, the transmission would often pop back of its own accord, spinning the car out of her grasp. "Yeah..."

"You agree? There's a switch." He was really putting away those meatballs.

"I, uh." She looked down at her meal, now truly growing cold and almost untouched. This was getting unappetizing, and she was not in a mode to think about food. She looked up. "Do you think I'm attractive?" Brett stumbled around for words, or maybe oxygen, and found only the half-chewed food in his mouth. He was making a mess of himself, and barely speaking. "No, no,

I'm not asking you for *you*. I couldn't care less what you think. I mean, not that either. Okay, all I'm saying is I'm not *interes*ted. I just want, y'know, an objective opinion."

His napkin went to his mouth and came back with substantial chunks of spaghetti, carefully covered from Antigone's view. He sighed heavily, doing a mental checkup on his air intake procedure. Finding only slight splutters, he'd regained all the composure he didn't appear to have. "For someone who's *not* interested," he took a long draught of Coke, wanting her to think on those words, most especially the *not*, "you're certainly taking an interest in my opinions. Quite an interest."

"Hey, you're a guy, right?"

A little too reminiscent of her first inquiry as to whether he was a person, on a phone weeks earlier. He simply nodded, doing his best to look skeptical.

"Well, I like guys. Not you. But some guys. And it can't hurt to know what a guy thinks, right?"

"I'm just a random sampling?" Now his display of skepticism was authentic.

"You got it." She was almost hungry again, but instead grabbed her glass, took two ice cubes into her mouth and started crunching away.

"That long since you talked to a guy?"

"A reliable one."

"I'm re*lia*ble now?"

"Close enough." She shrugged quirkily right before pulverizing another cube between her teeth.

Brett leaned back again in his chair, pretending that this was the first time he was physically sizing her up. "You're not bad..."

"*Not bad*?!" People at other tables took an instant interest in their own.

He chuckled toothily. "You sure that if I say you're attractive you won't *jump* me?"

Antigone was deadpan. "Promise."

"I find you very *physically* attractive. The mentality needs some serious work." He finished his Coke and stood up. "We're late." Antigone had no watch to verify this claim against. They were, in fact, still rather early.

"Well I'll be later." She gloomily returned her attention to dinner.

"I *drove* you here."

"It's walking distance."

"All right..." He pushed his chair in.

"Oh, and you can leave your share of the check on the table. This isn't a date, remember?"

"How could I *forget*?" He pulled out his wallet, dropped some bills, and walked off. "See you back at work." Walking away, he grumpily wondered if it would have killed her to at least *try* to jump him.

FIFTEEN

IHateMMTDoU2: hey you
PhunkeeGrrl06: hey! what's up?
IHateMMTDoU2: not much
IHateMMTDoU2: you?
PhunkeeGrrl06: not a lot. just got back from practice.
PhunkeeGrrl06: all hot & sweaty. ;-)
IHateMMTDoU2: how'd it go?
PhunkeeGrrl06: same old, same old.
IHateMMTDoU2: how's topeka?
PhunkeeGrrl06: hasn't changed much. you know how it is. you coming back?
IHateMMTDoU2: eventually
IHateMMTDoU2: you know, in december for break
PhunkeeGrrl06: right.
PhunkeeGrrl06: how are you?
IHateMMTDoU2: fine
PhunkeeGrrl06: really?
IHateMMTDoU2: close enough
IHateMMTDoU2: you don't think i sound fine?
PhunkeeGrrl06: I didn't say that.
PhunkeeGrrl06: just, your roommate & all. last time I talked to you...
IHateMMTDoU2: yeah
IHateMMTDoU2: sorry about that
PhunkeeGrrl06: no prob.
IHateMMTDoU2: he's crazy
PhunkeeGrrl06: so you say.

PhunkeeGrrl06: so, classes? stuff in general? should I be looking forward to college?

IHateMMTDoU2: i do say

IHateMMTDoU2: well that depends on how much you like highschool

PhunkeeGrrl06: & if I call it hell on earth?

IHateMMTDoU2: then you might like college

IHateMMTDoU2: :)

PhunkeeGrrl06: naw, it's not that bad.

PhunkeeGrrl06: i like kansas.

PhunkeeGrrl06: unlike SOME people.

IHateMMTDoU2: yeah

IHateMMTDoU2: well i miss YOU

PhunkeeGrrl06: that's sweet.

IHateMMTDoU2: no, i really do

PhunkeeGrrl06: no, I know you do. I was being sincere.

IHateMMTDoU2: oh

IHateMMTDoU2: hard to tell over im :)

PhunkeeGrrl06: yup.

PhunkeeGrrl06: ;-)

IHateMMTDoU2: how's the team?

PhunkeeGrrl06: ok. we're about 500 this year.

IHateMMTDoU2: not bad.

PhunkeeGrrl06: I guess...

PhunkeeGrrl06: could be better.

IHateMMTDoU2: still got number 6?

PhunkeeGrrl06: you see my sn hasn't changed.

PhunkeeGrrl06: do you still hate MMT?

IHateMMTDoU2: with a passion

IHateMMTDoU2: :)

IHateMMTDoU2: he told me all about how your mother should know is about losing parents

PhunkeeGrrl06: your mother should know?

IHateMMTDoU2: yeah

IHateMMTDoU2: it's a song on mmt

IHateMMTDoU2: said that eventually you start to take an interest in parents just when they're about to die

IHateMMTDoU2: and you finally want to know what they know

IHateMMTDoU2: but then it's too late

PhunkeeGrrl06: doesn't sound THAT crazy.

155

PhunkeeGrrl06: does it?
IHateMMTDoU2: he's nuts
IHateMMTDoU2: you haven't heard the song
PhunkeeGrrl06: I think I should meet this kid.
IHateMMTDoU2: the song has nothing to do with that
IHateMMTDoU2: just says your mother should know a lot
IHateMMTDoU2: why? are you coming to visit?
PhunkeeGrrl06: no.
PhunkeeGrrl06: but it would be interesting.
PhunkeeGrrl06: I think I'll like college.
IHateMMTDoU2: you should come here
PhunkeeGrrl06: you like Harrison that much?
IHateMMTDoU2: no
IHateMMTDoU2: but i like you that much
PhunkeeGrrl06: lol
PhunkeeGrrl06: so cute.
IHateMMTDoU2: what's lol mean?
PhunkeeGrrl06: laughing out loud.
PhunkeeGrrl06: hahahaha
PhunkeeGrrl06: that would also work.
IHateMMTDoU2: i see
IHateMMTDoU2: hey, i have to ask you a question
PhunkeeGrrl06: shoot.
IHateMMTDoU2: but its an important question
IHateMMTDoU2: maybe i shouldn't ask
IHateMMTDoU2: don't get upset
IHateMMTDoU2: ok?
PhunkeeGrrl06: god, what is it?
IHateMMTDoU2: well
PhunkeeGrrl06: you can't do that! spit it out already!
PhunkeeGrrl06: c'mon....
PhunkeeGrrl06: I'm wait-ing...
IHateMMTDoU2: are you seeing anyone?
IHateMMTDoU2: just curious
PhunkeeGrrl06: not seriously.
IHateMMTDoU2: not
IHateMMTDoU2: seriously
IHateMMTDoU2: what does that mean?
PhunkeeGrrl06: yeah.
PhunkeeGrrl06: not seriously.
PhunkeeGrrl06: are you seeing anyone?

IHateMMTDoU2: no
PhunkeeGrrl06: look, Matt, it's nothing serious.
PhunkeeGrrl06: like I just said.
PhunkeeGrrl06: ok? :-)
PhunkeeGrrl06: I mean, we broke up.
PhunkeeGrrl06: you're in PENNSYLVANIA!
IHateMMTDoU2: i know
IHateMMTDoU2: i know
IHateMMTDoU2: sorry i asked
PhunkeeGrrl06: I still miss you.
IHateMMTDoU2: yeah
PhunkeeGrrl06: I do.
IHateMMTDoU2: yeah
PhunkeeGrrl06: look, I'm sorry, but I have to go.
PhunkeeGrrl06: my parents are yelling at me.
PhunkeeGrrl06: gotta get off the phone line.
IHateMMTDoU2: ok
IHateMMTDoU2: bye
PhunkeeGrrl06: Matt, are you mad at me?
PhunkeeGrrl06: Matt?
IHateMMTDoU2: no
IHateMMTDoU2: miss you
PhunkeeGrrl06: bye.

Matt watched PhunkeeGrrl06 change to *PhunkeeGrrl06*, then disappear after a door-closing sound. He looked at the list of names, now looking much emptier. Then he double-clicked on IHateMMTDoU2.

    IHateMMTDoU2: you're an idiot
    IHateMMTDoU2: you're an idiot
    IHateMMTDoU2: a big idiot
    IHateMMTDoU2: a big idiot
    IHateMMTDoU2: get over her!
    IHateMMTDoU2: get over her!
    IHateMMTDoU2: i give up
    IHateMMTDoU2: i give up

SIXTEEN

H e was back in the home office, and he was having the roommate drive in from Pittsburgh. The day after Christmas was always a great relief. He remembered when he was younger and it was the ultimate let-down, but now that he no longer anticipated but dreaded Christmas, it was a great burden lifted to have the presents reasonably successful and reasonably assembled and the kids reasonably quieted down.

Mitch was being unreasonable and was trying to get a day off work. He had already given him two days that everyone took, but he didn't want any comparisons to Scrooge, so he took Mitch's gun, which he swore to himself was his only usefulness and waited for this kid to arrive.

There was a knock on the door. Who knocked these days? He went up to get it. The person at the door was much shorter than he'd expected.

"Hello?"

"Yeah, I'm here for the interview."

"The *job* interview?" Was this kid old enough to work legally in Pennsylvania?

"The police interview. The, well, interrogation, perhaps."

"Ah, right. That's here." He felt the need to be paternalistic. "I'm Officer Joe Ewing. And you are the roommate?"

"I have my own identity, independent of Matt. David Benowski." He grabbed Ewing's hand. "You can get me an orange juice."

"An... *orange* juice?"

"Don't I get whatever I want when I'm talking to you? I

don't smoke and coffee's disgusting."

"Whatever you want? This isn't your *last meal*."

"It could be."

"Excuse me?"

"There's buses outside on the street, right? Mack trucks not far? You don't need to tell me that the leading unnatural cause of death in this country is the automobile. I have to drive back to Pittsburgh!" He tried to slide by Ewing through the doorway, but he wasn't particularly adept at sliding. "Uh, can I come in?"

Ewing backed off and scratched his hair.

"Whoa! See, here's a gun threatening me already. This could be a short interview." He sat down. "Yeah, I could definitely use an orange juice."

He had left the gun on the desk, as he wasn't accustomed to carrying it on his person. He reached back, grabbed it, and walked out to the secretary. "Wait here," his voice trailed back to David. Then, forward, "Rita, is there any way you can get an orange juice?"

"Is this a stickup?" Her eyes were all for his left hand.

"Oh, sorry." He pocketed the gun, where it didn't quite fit. "No, it's just a request."

"I see. I'll get back to you."

He looked around the half-staffed station, sighed, and trucked back into his office, smiling perfunctorily at his name in gold plate on the glass door, whose blinds were never up. Chief Investigator, he mused, might be in need of replacing with Orange Juice Dispenser.

He slammed the door, took a seat at the desk, threw his feet on the table, and pressed **REC** on the tape-recorder.

"Okay, David, state your name for the tape."

"What tape?"

"This tape," he pointed.

"You mean *this* tape?" David removed the tape from his pocket and held it up in plain view of Ewing.

Ewing took his feet down and carefully examined the recorder. Not moving his head and only averting his eyes towards David, "Yes, that tape."

David threw it onto the desk. Ewing put it where it belonged. "Just seeing how sharp an observer you are."

"I'll do the investigating, if you don't mind."

"Wouldn't be here if I couldn't *learn* something." As if to

159

illustrate, he overtly visually scanned the room.

"Compulsion of the law not enough? Or protecting your roommate?"

"Yeah, I care deeply about protecting Matt."

"That sounded sarcastic."

"Your observation skills are improving, sir. As we speak!"

"Would it be that troubling for you to at least carry the *illusion* of respect?" He had to be careful with this guy. He'd underestimated him at first, sure, but *look* at him! But after that last comment, he might prove to be the key witness in the case. He clearly wasn't losing sleep over his roommate's arrest; Ewing wouldn't be surprised if he were actually celebrating the occurrence. Finally, he'd found someone close enough to Matt who was willing to speak against him.

"Maybe. How's that orange juice coming?"

"It'll be in in a minute. Now then." He pressed **REC** again, now with something to record. "State your name for the tape."

"David Abraham Benowski."

"And the date?"

"26th of December, year 2000."

"And who is in the room?"

"You and me, baby."

"Who am I?"

"Joe Ewing, according to you."

"Great. Now then, David, how did you meet Matthew Norton?"

"He was my roommate."

"*Was*?"

"Got a letter the other day that he wasn't coming back. Trouble with the law."

"Right. Okay. That's us. So when was he your roommate?"

"Last semester. First semester of freshman year."

"And how did he seem to you?"

"How did he *seem*?"

"Yeah, you know. Distinguishing attributes. Characteristics. Habits."

"Nondescript."

"Nondescript? If he were in a police lineup, how would you pick him out?"

"He'd be the one that was asleep."

"Asleep?"

"Or the one that groaned when I said something about 'Magical Mystery Tour'."

"*Magical Mystery Tour*? That's about *drugs*, isn't it?"

"Not really. It's actually the eleven-step guide to life."

"Eleven steps?"

"I'm talking about the whole CD, not just the title track."

"Ah. But doesn't it usually have a link to drugs? Many drug references? You say your roommate liked this CD?"

"No, he hated it. I worship it."

"I... see."

"Anyway, I don't think you'd say that Matt and I had much to talk about. Nothing really in common, per se."

"Right, right. So you'd be willing to testify against him in court? Even though you haven't brought a lawyer?"

"Where would I get a lawyer? Besides, I can take you on. I'm probably going to law school myself eventually."

"All right. But you didn't answer the question."

"Testify? I mean, if I knew something about what he's done. The most criminal thing I saw Matt ever do was swear."

"Really?"

"Really."

"What about underage drinking?"

"Well, I *heard* about that, but I don't think I ever actually saw it. I mean, who drinks in their room? He went to a frat party or something."

"And you didn't go with him?"

"Nope."

"What about drugs?"

"What about them?"

"Did Matt ever use them?"

"*Matt*? Absolutely not. I think it had something to do with his parents being doctors."

"Right, I've talked to them already. They both seemed to deny the drug angle. All right, David, but what about *deal*ing drugs?"

"*Matt*?"

"That's who we're talking about."

"That's ridiculous."

"Did you know of anyone doing drugs at Harrison?"

"If I did, it's a crime that I didn't report them."

"Won't prosecute. Scout's honor."

161

"Oh, that's worth a lot."

"No, seriously. You can have a copy of this tape when you leave. It says very clearly, that I will not prosecute you for not previously reporting drug crimes, *if* you comply now."

"Yes, people do drugs at Harrison."

"And where do they get them?"

"From certain people. I don't know who they are."

"You don't do drugs?"

"Of course not."

"But you've seen *some* people..."

"Yes."

"But not Matt..."

"No."

"Hm. Now then David, where were you on the night of December 19th?"

"In my room."

"Did you see Matt that night?"

"Yeah."

"When did you last see him?"

"I dunno. Dinnertime."

"You had dinner together?"

"No. Some guys on the hall were getting a pizza and I chipped in and asked Matt if he wanted any. He said no, he had somewhere to be."

"Did he say *where* he had to be?"

"No."

"Was anyone else going with him?"

"I don't think so. Maybe some guys."

"Some guys?"

"No, I don't have any vague clue who they were. Don't bother asking that one."

"Could you *try* to remember?"

Rita walked in with a carton of orange juice. Banging it on the desk, "*Here*," and she walked out, slamming the door so the blinds rattled against the glass.

"Do you need a cup?"

"No, this'll do just fine." David beamed, unscrewed the plastic cap on the carton, poked a hole in the freshness seal, and drank for a while. "Ahhh. Now, where were we?"

"No idea who these people were that were going with Matt?"

"As I said before, Officer, I can't guarantee you that *anyone* was going with Matt. I don't even know *where* Matt was going. I don't even remember the pizza, to be perfectly honest."

"This was a week ago?"

"Well, that's true, but we were all cramming for finals around then. Not much room in the brain for anything else, really."

"Finals week? And yet Matt left during this time?"

"Absolutely. I mean, you found him here in Philadelphia, right?"

"Right."

"And that's not where Harrison is, is it?"

"Okay, David, I'll do the questioning, please."

"Hey, just saying, connect the dots."

"Thank you, that's extremely helpful. Now David..."

"Was I alarmed when Matt didn't come back?"

"Excuse me?"

"That's your next question. Was I alarmed when Matt didn't come back? And the answer is, no, not terribly, because I didn't really feel like he was my responsibility."

"Ah, uh, okay. Did Matt often not come back?"

"Whaddya mean?"

"Did he stay out nights? At a girlfriend's place or something?"

David chuckled. "Er, no. I don't think he'd ever stayed out. I'm not convinced that Matt knew any girls."

"Any?"

"Well, there was his friend's sister."

"His friend?"

"Yeah, the guy next door. Joaquin. I'm sure you've talked to him."

"Well, no, actually..."

"Joaquin Garcia. Lived in Tyler 403. He and Matt were tight. Even when they were fighting. And Joaquin had some big fights with his sister."

"Were they about Matt?"

"I don't think so. From what I could tell, Matt stayed out of them."

"Is Joaquin around right now?"

"How should I know? It's winter break!"

"Okay, is he from around here?"

"No."

"Hm. Well, did *he* go with Matt this night?"

"Uh. Well, he *might*'ve."

"He might have?"

"I really don't remember."

"It was a *week ago*."

"I don't recall."

"You don't recall?"

"I had finals, and was eating pizza. And not precisely, Officer, in the habit of tracking my roommate's every move, let alone the moves made by a friend of his!"

"Well all right. But Joaquin *could* have gone with Matt."

"Anything's possible."

"Was it *likely*?"

"I couldn't comment on the likelihood, as my memory here is unreliable."

"I see."

"Talk to Joaquin."

"I will."

"Did Joaquin do drugs?"

"I don't think so."

"You don't know?"

"Like I said, he was Matt's friend, not mine."

"Do *you* have many friends at Harrison?"

"I can't see how that's relevant."

"Sounds like a 'no'."

"I'm just fine at Harrison."

"Now, back to girls, you're sure Matt wasn't seeing anyone? Sleeping with anyone?"

"Sure. He was too obsessed with this chick from back home."

"This chick?"

"This girl Katie. Talked to her all the time. Talked a*bout* her more."

"Right. I talked to her first, actually. That was Matt's attempt at a phone call."

"Attempt?"

"Yeah, he didn't get through on his one phone call. But he called an ex-girlfriend in Topeka, Kansas from jail in Philadelphia before either of his parents or you or a friend at Harrison. Do you find that odd?"

"Not at all. He was obsessed with her. Like I said."

"Was he close to his parents?"

"I wouldn't say that." Another long swig of orange juice was drained.

"Neither would I. So what did he say about this girl in Topeka?"

"All kinds of stuff. Mostly that he was pretty sure he loved her, I think, though that changed every day. And that he was pretty sure she didn't love him. And how much that sucked. Can hardly blame the guy. But I kept trying to turn his mind to other stuff, mostly my guide to life and all. He wasn't exactly, uh, *recept*ive."

"Did you ever fight with Matt?"

"Not directly. We *avoid*ed."

"I see. Now then, why do you think Matt would deal drugs? Did he have money?"

"First of all, I never said Matt would deal drugs. Quite the opposite."

"But hypothetically. Did he need money?"

"No, his parents were quite well-off. Never seen someone bring so much stuff to school."

"But he might have done it to get girls?"

"Not likely. I don't think this Katie chick was exactly into the druggie type."

"Maybe he wanted to make Katie jealous?"

"Hm."

"Is that possible?"

"Doubtful. I mean, don't you think that's pretty twisted logic, sir? I'm going to make my ex-girlfriend jealous by getting girls by dealing *drugs*? From a thousand miles away? I mean, I don't think there was any way he could have convinced her that he was getting girls. And if there was, I mean, he could have just *said* he was getting girls. Why actually get them?"

"Because they're girls!"

"But, see, you're not understanding. He didn't *want* other girls. He wanted the one he'd had."

"You make her sound like a dead puppy."

"Whatever works. Kids get obsessed with dead puppies, right?"

"They also get obsessed with *addictions*."

"I guess you could call it an addiction."

"So he had an addictive personality?"

"Well, with Katie."

"Did you see any other manifestations of addiction?"

"Sleep?"

"Well that's hardly unusual among your age group, is it?"

"Hard to tell, sir."

Ewing stood up and sighed, putting his hands on his hips and looking out his window at the rather dreary view it afforded of a small run-down section of Philly. "Is there anything else I should know?"

"I don't know. Is there?"

"David, stop playing games! Please! This is a very important case for the health and safety of the people of Philadelphia. Now I don't think you're pro*tec*ting your roommate, exactly, but I want to make sure that we have the whole truth in front of us! Did he ever mention drugs? Talk about drugs? Stolen vehicles? Philadelphia? Anything?!"

"I really doubt it."

"And this 'Magical Mystery Tour' thing. You sure that was you and not him?"

"I couldn't mistake a thing like that."

"You sure?"

"Are you asking for me to discuss my feelings on the CD, linking it to the Beatles' subtle metaphor for the eleven stages of life, in progressive succession?"

"No, I'm just, *ver*ifying."

"Rest assured, Officer."

"Okay."

"And talk to Joaquin."

"Okay."

"And thanks for the orange juice." He stood, carton in hand, and made for the door.

Rita glared at him as he left the station.

SEVENTEEN

M att was in Toni's kitchen, perusing her much improved renditions of praying mantises. Joaquin had not come along on this visit. The siblings were fighting again and besides, Joaquin had to study for their upcoming English 101 midterm. It was almost entirely on *The Grapes of Wrath*, so Matt did not have to study, and had promised to help Joaquin cram later. At this moment, Joaquin was wading through the second chapter, having followed Matt's initial advice on writing off the book until the midterm study guide had been distributed.

"That one's especially lifelike, I think," Matt commented. "The shadows are really great. But you do lose something with these smaller sketches, coming back from the big paper."

"Yeah, well, I just didn't want everything to be such a big production. That's probably Rachel's biggest problem. Everything for her has to be larger than life. It's the *praying mantis that ate New Mexico* every time. Gets old."

"You miss her, though?"

"She's sharp. Freaking brilliant. She's gonna own a gallery someday and I'll be lucky I knew her when. She'll hang my pictures because we're friends, and they'll only sell with her seal of approval."

"Oh c'mon. You're good."

"Listen. Did you know anything about art before you met me?"

"Hey, what about the common person?"

"The common person," she sighed, getting up and moving for the fridge, "has nothing to do with art. Are you kidding? Have

167

you ever seen *modern* art? I mean, there's all the evidence you need. People pay ten bucks a ticket to get into MoMA in New York and stare at a glass of water and call it sophisticated."

"Moma?"

"Museum of Modern Art. And it's not even a metaphor. You know what this ten-foot tall photo of a glass of water is called?" Matt shook his head, but Toni couldn't see him and wasn't waiting for an answer. "*Glass of Water*. That's the name. No fooling. Trust me, the common people wouldn't allow for that. Art is about as far from the common people as you can get."

"Is that why you're in it?"

She pulled two Pepsi cans from the fridge, closed it, and faced him across the counter. "You're swift."

"You've got a theory for everything, don't you?"

"Makes you say that?" She threw a can at him, which he fumbled before gaining control of. He tapped it for about thirty seconds before opening.

"Just do. Race, money, art, the whole bag."

"Is that why you hang out with me?"

He smiled back. "You're funny."

"Not swift?"

"If all I needed were theories, I wouldn't need you. I'd stick with my roommate. You wanna hear the *real* meaning of 'Strawberry Fields Forever'?"

"Why not?"

"Memory loss."

"Huh?"

"Well, being the eighth stage of eleven, it's when people are starting to get older. They start to lose a grasp of their minds, and as a result, nothing is real. It's also, slightly, about confronting your own mortality. When you lose memory, you start to realize that everything's impermanent. So you're confronting the same thought over and over again, just having your short-term memory, which is something like a strawberry field. Everything looks the same and the strawberry field really ends up being a graveyard."

"Huh?"

"It made more sense when he explained it. Not much, mind you. Not much at all, but I guess he at least had a fluid way of looking at the lyrics." He slurped. "He's a nutcase."

"Yeah. So all the confusion in the song is evidence of losing one's mind?"

"Memory."

"Same difference. What about 'nothing to get hung about'?"

"No longer fearing death, because it's inevitable."

"Wouldn't that be nothing to get *hanged* about?" She frowned over the lip of her Pepsi.

"I think he allows the Beatles some poetic license."

"That's hardly precise."

"Neither are some of your drawings."

"So?"

"Well, isn't it the same effort? I mean, clearly yours is *good* and his isn't, but it's basically trying to redefine the world that we see, right? I mean, you see a bug and he hears some songs, and it's just a way of explaining what you've got, right?"

"Yeah, except drawing insects isn't prototypical serial killer behavior."

"What?"

"Think about it, Matt. You better watch yourself. This guy's the next big candidate for committing some old-fashioned rural Pennsylvania murders."

"What are you talking about?"

"Oh, please. All the high-profile murderers. They've all got a little pet obsession that drives them to their crimes. The guy who shot John Lennon, speaking of Beatles, had like 96 copies of *The Catcher in the Rye*, including one with him when he did the deed. Murderers kill based on geography, on timetables, on whatever you want. Hell, Charles Manson blamed it all on 'Helter Skelter'. Is *that* on Magical Mystery Tour?"

"No, I don't think so."

"Well, still, it's Beatles. I can see it now, eleven killings, starting with his roommate. Then he'd go into hiding somewhere outside of Fifeburg, and strike carefully at a series of victims, one for each song. At each scene, he'd leave a pertinent lyric to claim responsibility. Nothing to get *hung* about. The Magical Mystery Tour is *dying* to take you away. All you need is *love*."

"You're giving me chills."

"Well the guy creeps me out, and hearing you and Quino talk about him just makes it worse. The guy's a loner, he's got glasses and is shy, and he has one thing in the world he cares about, and he presses it on everyone. And that makes him more of a loner. Eventually he's gonna snap. I'm just saying to sleep with one eye open."

"Usually I sleep soundly when he's talking about the album."

"Well that's even worse. Oooh! That'd be a great angle. He could do the killings while explaining song interpretations, in order. He'd kill you while explaining the first track, kill Quino while explaining the second track... Every time, he'd lull victims to sleep with a simple diatribe on the song, and then they'd be sunk. Maybe he could even kill them with the CD *itself*. Do you think it's sharp enough?"

"Hang on. If David became a serial killer on this theme, don't you think people would get suspicious every time someone tried to explain the Tour to them?"

"Hmmmm. Well, maybe. But couldn't he start talking about the murders and then say he had a theory on song number four?"

"I think after three murders, that would get very eerie. Hell, I'm spooked *now*, talking to *you* about it."

There was a glow in Toni's eyes that Matt had never seen before, and the light fading fast in the late autumn sky outside was not reassuring. Given the skylights and Toni's affection for natural light in great quantities, the approach of dusk resembled an interior fade to black.

"There's nothing to fear, Matthew." Her voice took on a deliberately creepy tone. "It's just your friendly roommate, David. David is harmless. He's never *mentioned* killing, has he?"

"Well, now that you mention it..."

"*Yes*, Matthew?" The creepiness could stop any time. Just any time. Whenever Toni wanted, that would be fine with Matthew.

"Well, I didn't think much of it at the time, but..."

"*Yes*sss?"

"In 'Penny Lane', he talked about how he always used to mistake the line 'the barber shaves another customer' for 'the barber *shoots* another customer'."

Toni was breathless, leaning halfway over the table, her Pepsi can discarded, her eyes glowing sharply with fascination. "*Another* customer," she whispered.

"In fact, h-he said it was a *deliberate*, uh, confusion by the Beatles. H-he said that they w-w*ant*ed people to think it said sh-shoots, not sh-sh-shaves."

"Indeed. Another customer shot. A *serial* killing. Matt, your roommate is just *wait*ing for the right moment."

"But why? Doesn't he need a mo-motive?"

"Not as a serial killer. The songs, the CD, is motive enough."

"Not David."

"Yes." She drew back to her chair, noticing the full darkness that had now overtaken her apartment. She had tortured the boy long enough. She got up and switched on the overhead lights, flooding the kitchen area with an artificiality that matched the awkward eerieness that so perturbed Matt. "No, you're probably right. I mean, what are the *odds* that any one person is a killer?"

Matt was not reassured. The nervous tension in the fading daylight and Toni's gaspy warnings did not easily recede. "Well, it's not just *any one* person."

"Still." She looked at him wryly. "Oh, c'mon, you didn't actually *fall* for that crap, did you? Look, I was just having a little fun. Throwing a conspiracy theory atchya to go with the others."

"Maybe you *thought* that's what you were doing..."

"Look, David couldn't hurt a fly. Could he?"

"We*llll*..." Matt let his head fall towards the table resignedly. "Look, I don't know if I can face him again. You've put all these thoughts in my head."

"What? All it takes is five minutes of me talking out of my ass to get you losing sleep?" Toni was tempted to shut the lights off again, just to see his reaction.

Now Matt was just embarrassed. "It was all the, the, *dra*ma," he said weakly.

She shut the lights off and Matt jumped, his chair moving and scuttling audibly across the floor. She flashed the lights back on. "Now there's some drama. C'mon, Matt, it's getting late."

"You wanna get some food?" He stood up.

"No. You should go home. Isn't my brother waiting for you or something?"

"You two are speaking again?"

"Kinda. I can't stay mad at him for too long."

"Are you mad at me?"

"No, I'm just, confused. Amused maybe. I wonder if I was like that as a freshman?"

"Like that?"

"Impressionable. *That* impressionable."

"Oh."

"Anyway, I should do another drawing. I think I'm going to have to let this mantis go pretty soon before it dies."

"Dies?"

"It's looking pretty sickly. I don't think they do too well after a week in a jar."

"Sickly?"

"It's turning green." Toni couldn't help but laugh.

"Green?"

"They're already green, Matt. A little joke. So I'll see you around?"

"Yeah." Matt, captive of his myriad thoughts, made his way to the door, almost tripping over various elements of the apartment's clutter. He let the door close softly against his back, facing the ill-lit hallway, and then the even less lit stairway. By the time he made the dark street, his mind was ajar with thoughts of David's analysis of "Penny Lane", primarily, and how that related to Toni's jesting analysis of David.

He had said it was one of their more complex songs and temptingly contradictory on the entire Tour, as Matt could recall. For, after memory loss in "Strawberry Fields", they came back with a hearty air of nostalgia in "Penny Lane". But in the latter, the nostalgia is wrapped in a field of aging eccentricities. People become eccentric and downright funky with age, and this leads to bankers never wearing raincoats in bad weather, firemen running about with alarm, and nurses never knowing whether they're acting or not. Amidst this backdrop is the nefarious barber, who seems innocent enough, showing pictures of heads. But is he shaving or shooting? Does he keep heads trimmed, or does he trim them from bodies? It's left ambiguous.

And now David was ostensibly fitting the profile of the very barber he explained earlier, even though he was well younger than the ninth stage of life. If only Matt had paid more attention to the *details*! He would from now on, lest he already be in danger. Presumably he would not be too late, but it would not altogether shock Matt to arrive to a missing roommate and a deceased hallmate. It was cold and he hugged his jacket to himself in the windswept air of oncoming winter.

Sure, Toni had been joking, or having a little fun, or being condescending or whatever. But wasn't there some truth in every lie? Wasn't there a possible reason for this mild suggestion? Didn't warnings often come in dubious packaging? The entirety of literature prior to medieval times was seemingly devoted to prophecies considered suspect and thus ignored. Toni had her theories, but she also had insights, and this was remarkably moving for someone who had never really met David. David was obsessive, dangerous, and altogether not to be trusted. But more than previously, he would have to be *watch*ed. He would have to be monitored. His guide to life could all too easily become a guide to *death*.

Matt, fumbling with his keys in order to find the building key for Tyler Hall, resolved not to die.

EIGHTEEN

O ctober, November. They were blurs in Antigone's life, normally hotbeds of intensity, but this year they somehow just faded by. A campaign came and went and Antigone laughed at a time when she had cared about politics, but not even the drama of a recount could prompt her to get caught up in this year's debacle and she'd even forgotten to vote for the Socialist candidate, whoever that was these days. She remembered her father telling her she'd become more interested in politics and more conservative as time passed, and this thought prompted near hysterics. Personally, she went to and from work and yearned for Martin Arthur Tucker, sympathizing with her roommate's loneliness but refusing to alleviate it directly. She gradually became sure which would be less tenable: getting booted by her roommate's inevitable reversal (Betsy still insisted that she would not maintain a female roommate if she established a successful relationship) or continuing to live with this incorrigible flirt without giving in to curiosity.

During idle time at work, mostly when dealing with particular dull targets of the Working Without Wires network's expansion, she would slyly steal peeks at her boss and draw hearts on scrap paper in front of her. It was a bad habit from high school that she'd been unable to break, when she would sketch JES and EEE in the same heart, but so often she'd have to stick with two letters and it resulted in JS sharing a heart with EE. She thought this looked slightly more professional, since her full three initials always struck her as more of a cry for help than a personal label. When working in Chicago, she'd had little time to unite RTS and

AEE, the latter part of which she now usually replaced with her full name since she liked it better than Eve or Edgewood. RTS shared a heart with Antigone only once that she could remember before he had taken her to dinner, a terrible movie, and her front porch. She had been prompted to theorize, later, when the spiral notebook sheet with a heart, RTS, and her name had been left defaced on the fridge as her only departing clue, that she should monitor movie quality of first dates as an omen. Not that this held up with anyone else, but it was worth applying to future situations.

She couldn't help but think that if MAT (it looked so, so *solid* sharing a heart with her name) took her to a horrible movie, she'd be willing to overlook that.

Brett was refusing to speak to her for a reason he wouldn't explain and she didn't care enough to explore. About a week after their lunch together, he'd started taking a stolid attitude toward her, she ignored him for a day, and thereafter, she barely got an invisible nod from him. The only major impact this had was that she took great pains to hide her scrap paper from him, since those who ignored as a change of policy were always looking for ways of speaking to the rest of the public. Fortunately it was fairly standard procedure at Working Without Wires for female employees to flirt with the boss, so this looked no more suspicious to Brett than any of her other (probably more aberrant) behavior. Unfortunately, though, this meant she didn't stand out. And did he appear to be taking any more interest in her? There was no telling. The divorce rumor had gone unconfirmed, but she never saw a wedding ring on him.

Most of her trains of thought these days were leading back to this man. Which kept her mind off Rick, which was good. Every few nights, she would toss and turn and see fleeting visions of him and wake up alarmed by how drawn to him she was. After one of these nights, she expressed a concern to Betsy that he was a closet voodoo master, hiding in Chicago and putting himself into her thoughts and dressing up her impressions of him, all with the use of a doll of her and the belongings she'd had to leave behind. Betsy, as usual at that time of day, had been irrelevant.

"Oh, that's right, he's from the Caribbean, right?"

"No, that's Martin who's Haitian!"

"Why would *Martin* be wanting you to think better of *Rick*?"

"No, no. Even poor white trash can do voodoo. That's why he'd be a *closet* voodoo master."

"You've never described Rick as poor white trash."

"He made me get a tattoo, didn't he?"

"Are there trailers in Chicago?"

Truth was, it didn't take voodoo to let Rick infiltrate her thoughts and she knew that far too well. She'd often been accused of living in the past, and had sniped back that she tried to live in a world that transcended time. And we knew more about the past than the future, right? Those who know too much about the future are probably lying, or even scarier than *she* wanted to deal with. And living in the present is admirable, but awfully tiresome when one works in telemarketing and spends a vast amount of time in a nondescript room on the phone to gullible idiots. At least Martin was in the present during these times, but night was almost all Rick's, and in dream after dream after dream she took him back, forgave everything, and once again wore tops that exposed her navel.

"Nothing gets you over the last one like the next one," Betsy had advised when she was in a particularly generous mood one evening.

Antigone, however, was in an especially bad mood, "Is that why you've had *so many* girlfriends since you fell in love in college?"

Betsy mistook the emphasis for straight sarcasm, "But I've had sixteen since school!"

Antigone snickered wickedly, "Exactly. You over her yet?"

She had become more peaceful now, meditating after work, wondering where Betsy was, on a day somewhere between early and mid December. She was trying so hard to clear her mind, but it always seemed easier to have one thing to focus on rather than none. Even something simple. Remarkably, it was often whatever Betsy was doing, for the conjoined focus made her feel more connected to her friend, and more understanding of the general human condition. She would focus on a book (just the object, not the contents), or a coffee mug, or the couch, and this brought a more filled peace than total mind clearance.

Betsy was absent, now, and she had nothing to contemplate.

Her mind, she had discovered through thorough introspection, was a temple to the spirit of stream-of-consciousness. This made contemplation of nothing a dangerous proposition. For it never ever not even once when she was tired or stoned actually meant *nothing*. She sheepishly admitted to herself that throughout learning to meditate, she had never emptied her mind. The closest she'd come was thinking hard on the *idea* of nothing: either the word itself and its syllabic undulations, or the absence of things in an empty room. But her nature abhorred a vacuum, and try as she might to preserve the void, this would always spill into an empty room she'd seen once, or the word *some*thing, and she'd be lost. And then it was just sitting and breathing intently while she felt an unending wave of regret, apprehension, guilt, and desire. So much for enlightenment.

At this particular juncture, with no object of Betsy's attention to garner her own, she was drawn to the door. Breathe in, breathe out. Focus on the door. Breathe in, breathe out. The door. In, out, door. In, out, door. No, no, not leaving. Just the door. In, out, door, in, out, door.

After five minutes of such intense scrutiny, the door cracked under the pressure and opened. Betsy and a strange woman replaced the door, and Antigone's thoughts went haywire. There was a little too much to concentrate on.

"Who's that?"

"Um."

"Is that your roommate? What's she doing on the floor?"

"Uh, she's not staying long, she's just, uh."

"It's okay. I have two female roommates. Don't worry about it. I'm not accusing you of anything."

"Uh, I mean, you're not?"

"Of course not. Beats living with *guys*, doesn't it? Hey you, I'm Alberta!" She looked, at Antigone's first post-meditative glance, just barely more interesting than the Canadian prairie province. Profoundly younger, however, than that possible namesake. What was 20 subtracted from the age of Canada?

"I'm Antigone," she said, content to remain on the floor.

"Oh. Okay. Don't get up. I don't mean to disturb you. Is it, uh, okay, if we stick around?"

"You might want to close the door."

"Oh, right, getting the place cold?"

Antigone shrugged, which she always found a fitting gesture from the lotus position.

Betsy was in the kitchen, doing the one thing that Antigone was convinced she'd mastered in said arena. "Coffee?"

Alberta closed the door. "Oh, me? Well, no thank you."

"Beer?"

"Maybe later."

"Car?"

"Huh?"

"You need a car?"

"We drove over here in mine. Don't you remember?"

"Didn't you say that was your *mom*'s car?"

"Well, she might give it to me." Antigone rolled her eyes and formulated the first draft script of her robbing-the-schoolyard speech for Betsy on the door.

"What if *I* gave you a car?"

"A car? Well, we just met."

"It barely runs, if that makes you feel better."

Alberta frowned obviously, showing that it didn't. "Well, mine, my mom's, maybe mine, runs fine."

"Hm. Well, oh well. Don't worry. I'm just trying to get rid of it, really."

"Is it insured?"

"Not legal otherwise." She was sipping her work in the kitchen, not emerging, as Alberta was still leaning against the outside of the counter.

"Well just leave the keys in the car."

"No one will take it."

"*Some*one will take it." She paused. "Take it to a bad neighborhood."

Betsy smiled all too cutely and looked up from her brewing. "You saying there's *good* neighborhoods in Philly?"

Alberta laughed all too eagerly and Betsy tipped her head back and turned away, confident in her appeal. Antigone wondered what Betsy would tell her if she brought home some college guy. Was she out of college? As if to confirm, proving the power of thoughts formed by the meditating, Alberta, added "Well, none around UPenn, that's for sure. I don't get out too much."

"Just to Starbucks?"

Alberta giggled and blushed. The door was no longer tall enough to hold Antigone's budding script.

NINETEEN

D ecember had descended and Matt had yet to be brutally murdered by his roommate. In fact, there hadn't been a murder in Fifeburg since 1993, and the last serial killing of Fifeburg residents had probably been when two brothers from the town were killed within a week of each other in World War One. To Matt's relief but slight disbelief, David had not broken this streak, and after a time, he had become more mellow around David. They were not, however, precisely getting along.

David was mellower and more likely to get along with almost everyone these days. After he had first experimented with marijuana in early November, he'd made a habit of becoming rather sociable. Initially he'd been convinced to try it by Oliver on a bet that the latter had made with Joaquin. Joaquin had lost big-time, mostly on Oliver's persuasive invocation of the drug references in "Magical Mystery Tour".

"How do you know what you're missing if you don't try it?"

"Does the same logic hold for murder?" This query had given a nerve-wracking jolt to Matt, who was also present at the encounter.

"If the Beatles were *singing* about murder, don't you think you'd try it?"

"Maybe." This response, though fairly plainly (somewhat) facetious, had given a nerve-wracking earthquake to Matt.

"Well there you go. See my point?"

"I suppose. One hit can't hurt, can it?" Matt's parents had told him at length that one hit *could* hurt, very badly. From a purely medical standpoint, they argued, it had been proven that even the most limited experimentation with marijuana could cause brain damage and maybe even cancer. They had never backed up these opinions, though Matt was not one to question his doctoral ancestors on questions of medicine. Had he pressed his mother at the right time, he would have found that she primarily blamed marijuana for her judgments about Alex during a substantial portion of their college romance.

The One-Hit Hurt theory was sufficient to keep Matt in the observer role as Oliver lit up a joint and passed it over to David. After convincing those present that he was about to die of asphyxiation, David finally came up from the haze and stared straight in front of him while dryly inquiring, "Choking smokers, don't you think the joker laughs at you?" Then he himself laughed for the following twelve minutes solid. Matt could not ever remember witnessing such authentic joviality from his roommate, and secretly hoped it would be accompanied by some limited brain damage.

Thereafter, Oliver and David made a tradition of smoking up at least weekly and, at David's insistence, listening to his favorite album as well. Though his understanding of the Beatles' use of drugs deepened, David's primary interpretations of the Tour's songs altered very little. Only "Flying", which he'd always attributed to the higher education phase of life, took much more shape, having no words to interpret in the first place. "So *this* is where you're supposed to discover drugs," he told Oliver after the song ended one evening.

"I started in third grade, man. Where you been?"

David paused, wonderingly. "Pittsburgh," was his final conclusion, to riotous laughter from Oliver and eventually himself.

Joaquin told Matt he'd tried smoking up once back home, but didn't think it was much to get excited about. "Nothing really happened," he admitted. "I think getting drunk's better."

"Your sister tried it?"

"I dunno. Never asked her. She's not much for putting things in her mouth."

"No kidding. Does she ever eat with *you*?"

Joaquin had shifted uneasily in his desk. Their English 101 professor was notoriously late. "Heh. What do you mean?"

"She never eats. I swear, asking her if she wants to eat is like asking if you can kill and eat *her*."

"Oh, uh, really?"

"Don't tell me you haven't noticed this."

"Well she is kinda thin..."

"She's about to disappear!"

"What do you want me to tell you? That she has anorexia or something?"

"Well *does* she?"

"You ever met anyone that thin who didn't?"

Matt, not for the first time in a discussion about Toni, thought of Catie. "Yeah, I think so."

"You think? Guess again, big guy. Whoever that was had an eating disorder too."

"No way!"

"Way. But you didn't hear it from me."

"Like I'm going to tell Catie..."

"No, I mean about Toni."

"About who?"

"Now you're talking."

The professor entered and started talking about word economy and the avoidance of run-on sentences.

Soon after this discussion, classes ended and finals were about to start and Matt found himself with his first chance to catch a breath all semester. Somehow the months had been hijacked by an undying chain of events, none of which stood out in particular, but all of which jumbled in unison to create a picture of profound change. Change? Was he really any different a person? Maybe it was just upheaval more than change. Like tilling the soil, creating a vast disruption in the earth's surface, but eventually leaving the farmer with the exact same stuff. Maybe more productive, but still just dirt.

Matt was tired of being dirt, and was fairly sure that Catie would be tired of him upon his return too. He needed some *event*, some major happening that marked some sort of coming of age. How he wished he'd been able to move on from his Kansas-era desire! But tied to it though he was, it was time to have Pennsylvanian proof of his own advancement. A 4.0 was nearly out of the question, and wouldn't really mark much of an improvement from his high school dork persona. A brush with death would be at least noteworthy, but looking through the thick air of Tyler 401 at his roommate, that threat seemed more or less neutralized. If nothing else, very very chilled.

"Hey, you mind closing the window?"

"Man, you gotta re*lax*. And if I close the window, you think Bill's gonna be relaxed?"

"Well, perhaps not. But shouldn't you be studying for finals?"

"Man, I got plenty to study. The life I'm living. That's worth studying, isn't it?"

"Have you told your professors that? Or you planning to once you write your final essays?"

"Dude. It's just not that important. Listen, the song you need is 'Blue Jay Way'. That's the *next* phase of life, man, and you're there, like, now."

"Isn't that just them singing about not being very long forever? *My* interpretation is that they're talking about the song itself while they sing it."

"That's deep, man. But no, you're wrong. It's about rushing around everywhere. Don't be too long, get here, get there. That's what your twenties'll be like, man. But now you're gonna be there early. Then maybe you'll die early too. Who wants that?"

"Well, my professors probably wouldn't mind."

"My friends have lost their way." David giggled quietly to himself.

"Have you noticed that it's *fucking freezing* in here?"

"Uh, no. Have you?" It was hopeless, and Matt fled for the library.

TWENTY

I t had taken Rita half the afternoon to track down the phone number while Officer Joe Ewing tried to put together the facts of the case. They were few and miles apart. No one was willing to link the kid to drug use or sale. While no one was particularly concerned with defending him, beyond the typical parental urges, no one really seemed that close to him either. The boy didn't have much of a life that he could piece together, and his motives seemed contradictory. And he still wasn't talking to anybody, except to deny everything. Even the public defense lawyer they'd sent him had made no headway beyond acquiring more denials. Here he was investigating what he was sure would be the biggest drug bust in state history and all he had was a raft of know-nothings and now a phone number in Taos, New Mexico.

The phone rang three times prior to "Hello?"

"Uh, yes, this is Officer Joe Ewing with the Philadelphia Police Department in Pennsylvania. I was wondering if a Joaquin Garcia would be present?"

"That's me."

"Excellent. Now Joaquin, so you're advised of your rights, you should know that this is a criminal investigation and the phone is tapped."

"Tapped? Who's listening?"

"Just us, but a tape is being made of this conversation for both of our protections."

"Am I in trouble?"

"No, Joaquin, but a friend of yours is and we were hoping you could answer some questions."

"We?"

"The Department."

"I see. Well, okay. What's this all about?"

"Were you aware of the arrest of Matthew Norton?"

"I think I heard something about it before I left school. Hey, should I have a lawyer on the line?"

Ewing sighed loudly, creating a staticky wind through the wires. "You are technically entitled to one, yes."

"Well I can't exactly get one *now* can I?"

"If you *insist* upon this, we would have to wait until your return to Pennsylvania. In the mean time, you may miss out on an opportunity to help Matthew Norton."

"Well, I'd like to help and all. And I don't go back for almost a month."

"Then you'll cooperate?"

"You sure I'm not in trouble?"

"Should you be in trouble?"

"Of course not."

"Then you have nothing to worry about. Now then, Joaquin, what day is it?"

"What *day*? Don't you have a calendar in your office?"

"It's for the tape, for the phonetap. Humor me."

"Uh, it's the day after Christmas."

"Which is?"

"December 26th."

"What year?"

"2000."

"All right, and no one else is listening in on your end, are they?"

"Uh, no."

"And what's your name?"

"Joaquin, like you knew already."

"For the tap. Your full name, please."

"Joaquin Alberto Garcia Jr."

"Great. Now then Joaquin, how do you know Matthew Norton?"

"He's a friend of mine at school."

"School?"

"Harrison College. He lived next door to me on Tyler 4th."

"Would you say he was your friend?"

"Yeah."

"A good friend?"

"Good enough."

"He's been described as your best friend. Would you say that's accurate?"

"I guess. Not a crime to have friends, right?"

"No. Now then, when did you last see him?"

"The night he didn't come back. A week ago, I guess."

"And what did he not come back from?"

"I don't know."

"You don't?"

"No. I think it was something in Philadelphia. But I have no idea what or where."

"*No* idea?"

"None."

"Whatsoever?"

"Absolutely not."

"What were you doing that night?"

"Sleeping. I had a final the next morning."

"What subject?"

"English."

"And Matt didn't tell you where he was going?"

"No. How many times do I have to answer that question?"

"Just try to be patient. We're trying to help Matt, you understand. Now then, do you know who Matt was going with?"

"No."

"Did you *see* Matt that day?"

"I already told you I did."

"Was there anything unusual about him?"

"Unusual?"

"Was he nervous, apprehensive, unsure? Preparing something big? Anything like that?"

"I don't think so."

"You didn't notice any changes?"

"No. I was focused on my final."

"Right, your math final?"

"No! My English final! Are you even listening to me? Is that why you're taping this?"

"Okay, so you were focused on your final, Matt just up and disappears."

"More or less."

"Were you surprised by this? Did you try to find out where

he'd gone?"

"I was taking a test the next morning."

"After that?"

"I had to catch a plane home."

"Right after your final?"

"The next day."

"What did you do the afternoon of the day after the arrest?"

"Heard about it."

"From whom?"

"Well David said he hadn't come back that night and then Bill said he had been called by police in Philly."

"David, his roommate?"

"Yeah."

"And who is Bill?"

"The R.A."

"Ah. Okay, so what did you do then?"

"I went home."

"You didn't try to contact your best friend?"

"I had a nonrefundable ticket."

"I see. Now then, were you told why Matt was arrested?"

"Yeah. Something about drugs."

"Was Matt involved in drugs?"

"No."

"You're sure about that?"

"Positive."

"Was Matt involved in any criminal activity?"

"I dunno."

"You don't know? Anything? Shoplifting? Trespassing? Underage drinking?"

"He's a college kid. Odds are everybody drinks, right?"

"Okay. Did he drink?"

"Probably."

"You don't know, Joaquin?"

"Okay, he drank. That's not a felony. Nothing major. Nobody busts the frat parties and everybody's underage there."

"The frat parties?"

"Yeah, my roommate is in this frat and we went there once. Everybody's practically in high school."

"Your roommate? What's his name?"

"Oliver."

"Is he a friend of Matt's?"

"I wouldn't say that."

"Would anyone? Would Matt?"

"No."

"You sure?"

"Very."

"Matt didn't get along with many people, did he? His roommate, your roommate. Who else did he hang out with?"

"Well, sometimes my sister."

"*Your* sister?"

"Yeah. The three of us would hang out at her place and then they got kinda close."

"I see. Were they romantically involved?"

"You're talking about my *sis*ter!"

"People date other people's sisters, Joaquin."

"Not Matt. Not *my* sister."

"But they did hang out?"

"C'mon, man, my sister's a *senior*. Matt was a frosh like me."

"They did hang out though? Sometimes without you there?"

"Do you want to talk to *her*?"

"That's a good idea. In due time. Now, to the best of your knowledge, did Matt and your sister hang out together without you?"

"Once in a while."

"I see. Did they do drugs?"

"No!"

"Did they drink?"

"I don't think so."

"And they didn't sleep together?"

"*No!*"

"What *did* they do, Joaquin?"

"Talked about art."

"Excuse me?"

"Art. You've heard of it, right?"

"As in, drawings and paintings? Was Matt an art major?"

"No, but my sister is."

"So they'd sit around all day and have nice little innocent chats about *art*?"

"Yes! Not all day. Look, you can talk to her about all this."

"As I said, I intend to. Does your sister live off campus?"

"Yes."

"Does she go to Philadelphia?"

"No."

"Never?"

"Practically."

"Did she go with Matt to Philadelphia the night he was arrested?"

"No!"

"Why are you so sure?"

"Because I *talked* to her."

"Okay. Could you put her on the line please?"

"Hang on." Ewing could just barely make out the yelling of "*Tohhhhhni*!!" before the phone was cupped by the static-laden grasp of a hand. While Ewing couldn't hear, Joaquin told his sister. "Phone for you. It's some cop in Philadelphia. He's trying to get information about Matt. He thinks you two were sleeping together."

"How does he even *know* who I *am*?"

Joaquin looked away. "I told him."

"Did you say we were sleeping together?"

"Absolutely not! I'm not lying to a cop."

"Really?" She raised her eyebrows.

"Well not about that."

"Here, lemme talk to him." She reached for the phone. "Hello officer?"

"Yes, this is Officer Joe Ewing and I'm here, on this tapped phone, to ask you some questions about Matthew Norton."

"Is that legal?"

"Of course! Oh, you mean the wiretap? With your consent."

"Sure."

"Could you state your name for the tape, please?"

"Antonia Maria Garcia."

"Okay. Now then, how did you know Matthew Norton?"

"He's my brother's friend."

"And your friend?"

"Sure."

"Your *boy*friend?"

"Nope."

"You sure about that?"

"I think I'd be the one to know if that were going on."

"How old are you, Antonia?"

"Toni."

"How old?

"Oh, my *name*'s Toni. My age is twenty-one."

"Twenty-one. Convenient. Did you buy alcohol for Matt and your brother?"

"Nope."

"Did you buy other things for them?"

"Other things?"

"Substances?"

"Nope."

"But they used substances?"

"Not to my knowledge."

"No drugs? No alcohol?"

"Nope."

"Your brother told me there *was* drinking."

"Ah. Well, I didn't know about it."

"I see. Now then, when did you last see Matt?"

"I dunno. A few days before I left."

"How many?"

"I don't remember. I was helping them with their English."

"*Them*?"

"Quino, my brother, and Matt."

"Who is Quino?"

"Oh, that's what I call my brother."

"I... see. So they were in the *same* English class?"

"Sure."

"And they would have had the *same* final exam?"

"Sure."

"At the *same* time?"

"Sure."

"When were you helping them 'study'?"

"A couple days before their test."

"A couple *days*?"

"Sure."

"Not a couple *hours*?"

"Nope. I think they were sleeping then."

"Both of them?"

"Sure. But then, Matt might have missed his final. I don't know when he was arrested."

"You heard about his arrest?"

"Sure. Qui-, my brother told me."

Ewing was about to give up, but then one more thing

189

occurred to him. "Do you know who Katie is?"

"Katie?"

"Yeah."

"Sure."

"Who?"

"Matt's girlfriend. Right? Or maybe his ex. I could never be sure."

"So he told you about her?"

"Sure."

"What'd he say?"

"Stuff. You know how guys are when they're in love. It's real cute. Said I looked like her or something."

"Oh? Was he flirting with you? Trying to impress you?"

"I don't think so. I saw a picture. Looked more like fact, to me."

"She looks like you?"

"Sure."

"You sure he wasn't trying to impress you?"

"Sure."

"What would he do to impress you?"

"I just said he wasn't."

"But if he were. Hypothetically. Anything?"

"Um. He'd probably draw me a picture."

"A picture?"

"Yeah. That's my guess, officer."

"*Did* he ever draw you a picture?"

"Nope."

"I see. Now then, how often do you go to Philadelphia?"

"Almost never."

"I don't suppose you know anyone there?"

"Nope."

"No friends in Philly?"

"Nope."

"People who just graduated? People working there?"

"Nope."

"Ever hear of Elizabeth Fields?"

"Nope."

"You're sure. Elizabeth Fields. Not a friend of yours?"

"Nope."

"You ever see Matt drive an Oldsmobile?"

"Nope. I never saw Matt *drive*."

"Could you put your brother back on, please?"

"Sure. Have a nice day, Joe." She turned to her brother, who'd been sitting in front of her the whole time. "Tag, you're it."

"Again?"

"Sure."

"Hi."

"Let the record show that Joaquin is back. Now then, did you ever see Matt drive?"

"No."

"An Oldsmobile?"

"Nothing. Matt didn't have a car."

"Okay. That's all I have for now. If I call you back at this number, you'll be there?"

"We aren't going to *move*."

"No, I suppose not. Well thank you for your cooperation. We'll be in touch."

"Bye."

"Bye."

TWENTY-ONE

There are some things that people do not have the opportunity to choose in their lives. Among these, one will often be told, are the members of their families. Part and parcel with that are some things which one's family may impart to them. Kernels of wisdom, knowledge, common sense, or perhaps ignorance are often passed from generation to generation in a family, producing instinct instead of thought and creating knee-jerk gut reactions where careful deliberation may have once been.

Oliver Joseph had been told since birth that he should never enter someone's vehicle unless he knew them well and trusted them completely. No exceptions, his parents had said. Oliver suspected that his father had actually whispered this to him through the walls of his mother's womb, for when he first could recall hearing it, it sounded unreasonably familiar and already ingrained. It made immediate sense and even if it didn't, it was pressed into his head so thoroughly that he would need multiple neurosurgeons to remove it. It had become rote, like driving or typing is for many people. His brain was no longer bothered when making the decision of whose vehicles to climb into.

Matt Norton, meanwhile, had been raised to believe that he should never ever snitch on his friends, or upon anyone who could possibly have more power than he did. This possibly lacked the logical backing that Oliver's similarly held conviction had, but was reinforced equally strongly by hours of television, and one personal experience. Nobody liked a snitch, and most people killed a snitch. Being a fall guy was rough, but snitching was a sure-fire ticket to the bottom of the nearest waterway with a pair of weighty sneakers. Besides, he had "told" on a bully in second grade, been rewarded with a recess shove, and seeking sympathy from his father, had received the "nobody likes a snitch" lecture that would remain a theme of the rest of his life. This again was not a decision Matt was prone to consider so much as react with.

There are, however, the remainder of the choices which face people, and almost all of these are actually opportunities for varying levels of exercising free will. Most of one's daily choices are mundane, and indeed the more mundane, the more control one generally has. What clothing to wear on a given day, or what food to eat, or what music to hear, how to walk or talk or get from point A to B. Thousands of choices besiege Americans almost constantly, and they are rarely conscious of their impact. The impact is often miniscule. Sometimes, though, the impact of a seemingly trivial decision is monumental. More often, the impact of a monumental decision is apocalyptic.

When Matt had found Joaquin outside the Sigma Sigma Sigma bathroom door, third in line, and told him it would probably be faster to just come back to the dorm, they both had left fairly confident that they would never again see a man known to them only as "Corndog". Though they had not given it much thought, they were pretty sure that if he *were* to reappear in their self-contained lives, it would not be in the midst of finals week, at 8:19 at night, just before their English 101 test would mark the conclusion of their first semester at college. December 19th proved them both wrong.

They and David were eating pizza in Matt's room, awfully sure that they were about to ace the easiest (and dullest) test of their recent lives, when Oliver and Corndog burst in. "Benowski!" yelled Oliver.

Nonchalantly through some cheese, "Hey Ol."

"Benowski, we're going into town to buy. You wanna come?"

"Town? To buy?"

"Philly. To sc*ore*, y'know."

"Score some *weed*, man, yeah!" added Corndog, complete with excited gestures.

"You don't do this, I take it, at the local Seven-Eleven?" For someone who was becoming a little bit hip, he sure sounded awfully naive.

"No, Dave, that's where we get your mom. Pot's not so cheap. Gotta go to Philly. Corndog here knows this guy--"

"They call him *The Man*," his excitement was just bursting out into the pizza-smelling room.

"Right, 'The Man', and we're gonna do a little deal."

"What," he took a sip of Coke from a liter bottle, "do you need *me* for?"

Oliver's smile fell a little. "Uh, y'know, strength in numbers."

"No thanks. I think I'll stick to the consumption end."

"I consumed your mom," Oliver sighed.

"Dude, we'll get you a *dis*count if you come with us. Buy it from the *source!*" Corndog was really trying.

David pondered this, examining his Coke with one eye closed. "Nawww," he concluded.

All this while, Matt and Joaquin had been ravenously munching after the night's light studying. Joaquin's thoughts could easily be summarized in a somewhat smug realization of how much smarter he and Matt were than the rest of those present in the room. Matt's thoughts were caught by a wilder vein, though, borne of his trepidation at returning home to a Catie in need of impressing. He had tried growing facial hair a week before, and after no one had noticed anything more than a smudge over his lip, he'd been forced to forgo the effort. This had slightly relieved him, since he'd been unsure that Catie would approve of the change, even if it were successful. A real life account of a drug deal, though...

"I'll go!"

Eight eyes turned, or rather *darted*.

"You smoke?" Corndog asked.

"No! But I'll go. I'm *curious*. It'd be fun."

"Matt, are you bonkers?" Joaquin's pizza slice was cheese-down on the floor.

"Your *mom* was fun," Oliver said almost simultaneously, in surprise.

Matt looked uneasily at Joaquin. "We'll be back tonight, right?" he asked the others. "It's what, a three-hour trip?"

"Something like that," Corndog agreed.

"Matt, are you on *crack*? You don't just go to a *drug deal* for *fun!*"

"Look, Joaquin, they need numbers, like they said. I'm doing them a *favor*."

"Your mom did me several favors. Well, bring a jacket. We're late."

Matt grabbed his jean jacket, Oliver rolled his eyes, Corndog chuckled and slapped Oliver on the back. "You know how to find 'em, Mama-Boy," was his parting comment, from Joaquin and David's perspective.

"I'll be back tonight," Matt unknowingly lied.

"You better be," Joaquin admonished when Matt was still in the doorway. When he'd just left, he added, "Moron."

The drive to Philadelphia took them through dark cold woods, the heater blasting from vents across Corndog's BMW. The ride was quite comfortable, and Matt was focused on how he would tell Catie about this upon his return home within the week. Oliver was exchanging jokes and funny stories with his best friend and "brother," secretly trying to keep his mind off of what he was about to do. The purchase order they had was enough to elevate them to small-time dealers themselves. They had to supply the Sigma Sigma Sigma brothers for the coming semester, as well as many subsidiary individuals, such as David Benowski. Corndog claimed to be familiar with Philadelphia, but he claimed to be and do many things that were truly beyond his capability, depending on his mood. Oliver had really not wanted to get anywhere near this, but as a final task for initiation, every pledge had to do an illegal service for the house. They had to demonstrate, beyond doubt, that their loyalty was higher to the fraternity than to the state. It killed him, as he laughed dutifully at Corndog's fittingly corny jokes, to think that, at that moment, some other new Sigmas were at a liquor store trying to buy with a fake.

The plan, as Corndog explained when the lights of Philadelphia became prevalent on the horizon, was to park about five blocks from the meeting place and walk. The meeting place and time had been designated before, in some nondescript back alley. They were almost certain to be late if they followed the plan strictly, but they were under strict orders not to drive the whole way. They were to be looking for a large black vehicle with a guy sitting on its trunk.

"You mean you haven't *met* the guy?"

"Mama-Boy, relax. I've dealt with The Man's operatives before. Tonight we finally get to meet The Man himself. Literally."

"Does anyone else have a bad feeling about this?"

"Well, I'm a little *nerv*ous," Matt admitted, awaking from his hour-long muteness. "But that's natural, right?"

The question went unanswered as Corndog deftly navigated the dark streets. They parked in what looked to Matt like the most threatening neighborhood he'd ever seen. It was like being on a bad episode of *Cops*. They got out silently, mentally reciting the plan to themselves, walking with feigned conviction, following Corndog's lead. There was an alley in every direction, but the ninth one was the right choice, and there it was, like a script fulfilled, a trenchcoated guy atop the trunk of an enormous black car.

"Shit!" he said in a true mix of yelling and whispering. "Where you been? You're real late."

Corndog kept the lead. "Sorry, Man. I mean, The Man. Good to meet you after so long."

"Shut up. Get in the fucking car."

"What?"

"Get in the goddamn car! Now!"

Matt and Oliver had caught up, facing The Man, who was strangely shorter than any of them. Matt saw no reasons, however, for this to justify disobedience. He opened the back right door and sat down, feeling some give under his feet.

Outside, Oliver was taking issue. "Corndog, don't get in there. We don't know this guy. Where'd Matt go?"

"What part of '*get in the fucking goddamn car*' don't you understand?!"

"Well, the get in the car part, mostly. Why do I have to get in the car?" Corndog was standing there, very confused at the whole unfolding reality, not sure that after that long drive, it really was reality. Maybe he was asleep at the wheel?

"That's where I operate. You wanna make a fucking *scene*?"

"Well, no, but--" And then he was blinded, the target of two headlights.

"*Car*!!" The Man screamed. "*Run*!!"

This prompted swift compliance from both Oliver and Corndog, as the former had never been raised by a family of deer to pause in the face of headlights.

Matt had been looking around the expansive car, unconcerned with the argument outside. He heard the yelling of "*Car*!!" and assumed they were getting heated in their disagreement over the vehicle. He was becoming more and more unsure of how Catie would react to this story, but hopefully he'd see some drugs soon, or more money than he could imagine, and what were those headlights? There was almost certainly the telltale set of unlit lights just above the car roof. He should slow down, but he wasn't even driving! The car was stationary. Did the guys know? He opened the door to warn them and was confronted by the wailing of siren and the flashing of colorful lights.

The sound of a car door opening, but not in this car.

"Don't move!"

Matt didn't. Now *here* was something to tell Catie about!

Two officers, guns drawn hesitantly, approached the car. "Put your hands above your head and step out of the car slowly." They kept ducking their heads to peer into the car, not seeing any other heads. Why would the only person be in the back of the car?

Matt followed orders well, almost cheerily, increasingly nervous, and looked up. There was too much light in his face and he shut his eyes.

"This your car, sir?"

"Uh, no." He didn't think of quite how suspect it would be in the back of a car he didn't own, when there was no sign of anyone else around. Where *was* everyone else?

"Whose car is it, sir?"

"The Man's." He really wasn't thinking clearly. The siren was doing the thinking for him.

"Which man?"

"I don't know."

One of the officers, invisible to Matt's clenched face, shined a flashlight through the open door, illuminating several bags of marijuana covering the floor of the car. "You mind if we search the trunk, sir?"

"Uh, well, it's not my trunk."

"You have the keys?"

"No."

The other officer patted him down, searching for both keys and weapons, finding nothing.

"This your stash, sir?"

"Stash?"

"The stuff on the floor."

"I thought there was something on the floor."

"Well, might as well get this over with. What's your name?"

"Do I have to tell you?"

He fished Matt's driver's license out of his back pocket, briefly surprised to find no wallet. "Matthew Norton?"

"Um."

"Matthew Norton, you are under arrest for drug possession and dealing. You have the right to remain silent. Anything you do or say can and will be used against you in a court of law. You have the right to an attorney. If you can not afford one, one will be provided for you. Do you understand these rights?"

Matt quite suddenly understood something else. He was probably not going to make his final exam tomorrow. "But I didn't do anything!"

"*Do you understand these rights?*"

"Yes. I went to government class."

"Well maybe you can defend yourself, sir."

The backup car arrived, having run the plates and bringing lockpicks. The car had been reported as stolen and the trunk contained smaller bags of harder drugs. By the time Matt reached the police station, grand theft auto and several more serious drug possession charges had been added to his arrest. His rights were not similarly increased. He was *not* charged, officially, with one count of poor taste for having stolen a run-down 1986 Oldsmobile.

SECOND SEMESTER
TWENTY-TWO

L ife is not a courtroom drama.

Despite the proliferation of courtroom dramas and their accompanying consciousness in the American media, and thus in the mental scope of Matt Norton, life very rarely ends up being decided in the courtroom. The average person is far more likely to end up in court for jury duty than for the commission of a crime. And quite frequently, those cases which do make it to court spend very little time there. Few trials not involving major celebrities or multiple deaths last more than a week.

While the jury, in theory, does get to decide the outcome of a case, the lawyers and the judge combine to have far more impact than the twelve hand-picked representatives of the societal conscience. They decide, between them, how the facts will be presented, how they will be packaged for sale, and what facts are appropriate for potential presentation and packaging. As a result, any given jury receives the same trustworthy information from courtroom proceedings as it might from a day's worth of thirty-second television commercials, and accordingly tends to bring the same attention-span to both.

Furthermore, very little information is actually revealed in the courtroom itself. While the testimony of witnesses may be news to the jury and random spectators, everyone else involved has full access beforehand through the process of depositions. The facts of any matter are discovered there, for preparation of the application of spin before judge and jury. Then, reverberating from the given spin, the jury decides whether or not the accused owes a debt to society. The size of the debt, however, is again in the hands of the judge.

None of this is to suggest that courtrooms are a haven of collusion or misinformation, but simply that the earnest portrait of the big-hearted American courtroom drama is a myth, or perhaps an American dream. The honest quest for truth and justice and twelve angry men is more frequently trumped by a weighty blindfold. Eventually, we all must wake from our dreams.

Matt Norton, however, was still asleep when his fate was decided. He spent an inordinate amount of his jailed time sleeping, finding prison to be the first place in his life more stiflingly dull than Kansas. Though he had to admit to himself, in bouts of reflection which he had a great deal of time for, that Harrison had not been substantively more exciting than Topeka High. Until the day that he decided to *make* it more exciting, that is. And once the novelty of being incarcerated had worn off (this had lasted at least twelve blazingly exhilarating hours), he was left to consider ongoing tedium. Which was painfully bland without the benefit of a television.

His state-appointed counsel had been able to get Matt placed in a minimum-security facility shortly after his arrest. In this locale, most of the inmates were in for the short-term and, like Matt, had no history of violent behavior that might warrant placement in higher security. The officers on the scene had recommended higher security because of the nature of the crimes, but admitted that the suspect had been remarkably docile during the arrest. Matt's lawyer, a Ms. Schwartz, had made sure to get the transfer to minimum security since, in her lengthy and frustrating communication with Matt, she had been able to discern only one clear fact from him. He feared prison rape.

Be this a product of the media or reality, prison rape has been the primary deterrent against incarceration for a number of years. Widely publicized prison guard indifference to such matters has been cast off as part of making jail an undesirable place to spend one's time. The utterly distasteful nature of the subject has kept it from widespread public scrutiny. It is almost certain that if the People's Republic of China were well known for a high quotient of prison inmates being raped, this would be an international human rights scandal of grand proportion. Nevertheless, people expect human rights violations to be a non-issue in the United States and China executes most of its prisoners before they can worry about rape anyway.

Matt worried about rape, though, since Toni's discussions of the matter had impacted him greatly. She had managed to convince him that no human act was more reprehensible, and without possible justification. It wasn't until the third time he awoke in prison (he wasn't sleeping well to begin with) that he realized this was a threat to himself as he currently stood, and he demanded to see a lawyer immediately. Being just after dawn, one took two hours to arrive and he was almost stupefied by the time that Samantha Schwartz was introduced to him in a meeting room with a table, two chairs, and an armed guard.

"Hi."

"Hello, Matthew," she yawned slightly.

He looked blankly out at her, then was compelled to burst out with "Get me out of here!"

She smiled, a bit wryly. "That *is* the general idea."

"No," he whispered, drawing closer, "I mean *here*."

The wryness faded slowly. "Matthew, I'm afraid you'll have to be clearer. It's kinda early."

"Look around. *Here!*" he insisted.

She sat back, then drew up quickly as he had done. "If this is the beginning of an insanity defense, I can spare you the trouble of using it on *me*. There's this thing, Matthew, called *attorney-client privilege*. Anything you tell me--"

He looked disappointed. "I know, I know. I went to government class." He sighed. "There's also this thing called *rape*."

She looked shocked, fell back against her chair again, turned to make quite sure the guard was there. Got eye contact, just to be absolutely sure. "Is that a threat?"

"No, it's not *you*." The disappointment in the state's ability to appoint *counsel* was ever-increasing.

"You raped somebody else? That's not among your charges, is it?"

He rolled his eyes. At least his stupefaction was fading with the frustration. "No. This. Is. A. Jail. With rapists. I don't want to get raped here."

"Oh. I see."

"Can you help with that?"

201

She shrugged, still uneasy. "Yeah, I think so."

"Nothing is more important than you doing something about that."

"Well, about your defense..."

Matt was staring intently at her, campaigning for eye-contact. "No. First I want you to understand that nothing is more important than getting me somewhere rape-free."

"I said I'll work on it." She shyly met his eyes, then quickly flitted away.

"Good. If I get raped here, it's your fault."

"I don't really think that's--"

"I'll sue you."

"Matthew, this doesn't sound like you're opening up to me. I'm charged to *defend* you. To do that, I'll have to have a *working relationship* with you."

"I'll sue you. That *is* a threat. No rape, and we'll have a working relationship."

"Um."

"Deal?"

"I'll *try*, Matthew. Can we move on to the facts of the case?"

"You're not going to like them." He folded his arms, leaning back in his chair.

"Try me. Now, everything you're about to tell me is protected information. If you're guilty, you can tell me, and I'll still defend you to the utmost and I'm sworn to never tell anyone what you've said. Got it?"

"Yeah."

"So, the best way of me defending you is to first know the truth. Okay?"

"Yeah."

She was brightening, trying to relate to this kid, trying to understand how degrading it would be to be faced with prison rape, hoping she was about to get down to the facts of what looked to be her most important assignment yet. "Okay, first up, did you steal the car?"

"No."

"You sure?"

"Oh yeah. You'll notice they didn't find the keys. I never saw them."

"Hm. How about the drugs? Yours?"

"Nope. The same as the car thief, I suspect."

"I don't suppose you met this guy?"

"Not really, no."

"A little, though?"

He thought for a moment, still nestled with folded arms. "No, not really."

"Okay. Matthew, I can't help but think you're hiding something from me. This privilege from your government class really *is* real."

"I know. Look, this was a really bad mistake."

"You were an innocent bystander?"

"More or less."

"What were you doing in the car?"

He thought for a moment. "Watching a drug deal?"

"You're asking *me*?"

"It's not a crime to *watch* one, is it?"

"Well." She considered this. Why was he acting like she was the *prosecuting* attorney? "If you don't report it, it is."

Matt chuckled humorlessly. "Didn't exactly give me time, did they?"

She looked down. "I suppose not. So you saw the people do this deal?"

"Well, no. The deal wasn't done. They ran off."

"Leaving you in the car?"

"Now you're getting it."

This was getting ridiculous. "And I suppose you were just *curious* about the deal? Just a random bystander, wanting to know a little more about the underworld culture so you could help be a citizen plainclothes cop?"

Matt judged this against his predisposition not to snitch, then weighed the remainder opposite the truth. "Pretty much, yeah."

"Look, kid, I don't think you're taking me seriously as your attorney. *But*, if you want anyone to take *you* seriously, you better come up with a better story than *that*."

"What's the evidence to the contrary?"

"The evidence?"

"Aren't these cases tried on evidence?"

"Well, in theory. But a smoking gun is pretty good evidence. You alone in a stolen vehicle loaded with enough drugs to fund a Colombian revolutionary group is pretty good evidence."

"Okay, okay, but how about *hard* evidence?"

"You mean other than you in possession of a stolen car and

all those drugs?"

"Possession? I didn't have the keys, did I?"

"Well no, but you could've thrown--"

"And *finger*prints?"

"You wore gloves?"

"Which are *where*? And what about friends who could testify that I was in Fifeburg when the car was stolen?"

"Fifeburg?"

"When *was* the car stolen?"

"I don't know, three days ago? Four, maybe."

"Tons of people could put me back at school then. Even people who don't like me."

She raised her eyebrows. This was starting to look plausible. Actually, *nothing* was looking plausible at all, but that nothing was as many parts the evidence against him as the evidence for. "If you're telling the truth, you have to know someone who was there and ran off. You weren't just walking the streets of Philly at night?"

"Look, we can discuss that later. Can you get me out on bail?"

"Bail?"

"Well, that's the easiest way out, right? No forced rape on the free streets."

"Well, what about minimum security?"

"Is there less rape there?"

"Most folks are in and out in months. And non-violent."

"Hm. I think I like the bail odds better."

"I'll try. You got anyone with money to put up?"

"Don't worry about money." He realized, literally for the very first time, that it would be exceedingly difficult to keep this whole debacle from his parents.

As it turned out, Public Defender Schwartz was unable to procure bail for Matt. She had found her case that Matt was not a flight risk rather uncompelling, even to herself. She based it mostly on his being young and docile. It was pointed out that the latter was at gunpoint, and the former was hardly a case *against* runaway likelihood. And if he could steal a car, he could get away, right? She was able to then cut a deal for minimum security, holding sway with the judge that he was non-violent and might be in stir a while, given the building investigation that Philadelphia PD had declared would be necessary. He may be a flight risk, but not from any place with even minimally armed guards. In the face of arms, he was prone to resist very little. Besides, Officer Ewing was on the case, and given his recent statement that this could bust an entire drug ring, the investigation alone would last until New Year's. She left the courthouse confident she'd avoided a frivolous suit from her client, and maybe he'd even owe her something now. Like cooperation.

When dealing with both Ewing and Schwartz, Matt was a model of non-cooperation. In his preliminary questioning, Ewing was flabbergasted by the kid's ability to deny and obfuscate. He admitted to the bare facts of the case as documented by all involved and not a word more. He volunteered for a drug test, which he passed resoundingly, leading him to inform Ewing that he had never even tried drugs, let alone tried to deal them.

"That doesn't explain," noted a brow-furrowed Joe, "what you were doing at a drug deal."

"I already *told* you I was curious."

"Or how you got from Fifeburg to Philly."

"I was *driven*."

"By whom?"

He scratched his head. "I really can't say."

"I suppose you were knocked over the head and blindfolded and woke up in the back of a stolen Oldsmobile!"

"That doesn't sound like curiosity, does it?"

It wasn't that Matt was genetically predisposed to *never consider* the idea of ratting on his friends. He was just generally disinclined towards the idea, given his family and media background. The problem was that he knew entertaining the notion was awfully frivolous. Oliver and Corndog were hardly more responsible for the incident than he was, given that they hadn't actually suc*ceed*ed in purchasing any drugs. Attempted drug possession? That couldn't be a crime on the books. The person responsible for everything went by "The Man" and had the single descriptive feature of trenchcoat possession. Telling everything would get Oliver in trouble, add two counts of hilarity at the mentioning of Corndog and The Man, and bring nothing but discredit to his defense. Best-case scenario, the Sigma Sigma Sigma brothers would be after him, and he could never set foot in Philadelphia again. This was, of course, assuming that Oliver and Corndog admitted their role, which they, having escaped, had no incentive for whatsoever. Not only was snitching a horribly repugnant stance in the first place, but he'd be exposing himself as even more of an idiot than he now appeared.

So he maintained his own one-man version of the truth, to both his lawyer and the investigator. The former was alarmed that she received the same story as the latter, but was starting to realize that Matt's analysis of the evidence against him was remarkably accurate.

As time progressed, thankfully uneventfully in the minimum security prison, and boredom set in, Matt began to imagine himself in the courtroom setting. He had an inkling that they would find witnesses from Topeka and even Harrison, but no matter how he envisioned the unfolding drama, he didn't know what they would have to say against him. He could imagine Joaquin condemning his stupidity ("curiosity", he insisted), but also supporting his lack of experience with drugs and crime in general. Who would speak against him? Perhaps David would outline a string of unsubstantiated accusations, and Matt imagined himself standing and shouting "Lies, your honor! All lies!". But *why* would David lie? There was tension between them in 401, but surely not hatred that would span a criminal court case. No, the only witnesses would be the arresting officers, whose testimony might just override the entirety of his dramatic self-defense, citing his inability to name anyone else connected to the car or the contraband as sufficient reason to lock him away.

Indeed, David had very little idea what his courtroom drama would look like, though these imaginings occupied the bulk of his mental energy through a lonely Christmas and a dreary New Year's. He had avoided his parents, unable to process facing either of them in the face of these surreal criminal proceedings. Apparently, they were also unable to face *him*, for they had failed to make an attempt in that direction through the third day of 2001. Ms. Schwartz had asked if he wanted her to bring them in as character witnesses.

"That's assuming that they witness my character."

"Well don't they?"

"Not for some time now. I don't know if they'd have anything good to say anyway."

"Couldn't they make something up?"

"You're very focused on invention."

"Beats this reality, doesn't it? I'm responsible for defending you, not falling on your sword with you."

"It's not that sharp a sword, is it?"

"I don't know. It seems like a lot of years in one of those rape-prone prisons."

"That's not funny."

"Well, it's possible, Matthew. You've gotta wake up eventually and help me come up with something."

"Don't you think that my parents would have tried to *contact* me by now if they were interested in helping?"

"I was wondering about that. They haven't shown up, have they?"

"I suspect they have work."

"Work?"

"They take it very seriously, you know. It's good money."

"You're their son!"

"Does that make *me* good money?"

She looked pained. "They could at least write you a check for a better lawyer."

"Now who's not helping?"

So Matt went back to his cell and slept while Samantha Schwartz drove to Officer Ewing's office at the Philadelphia Police Department. She ignored Rita's admonition to avoid walking in the office unannounced. The Officer was listening to a tape of his discussion with Catie.

"Hey Joe."

"Sam. Your hands broken? Can't knock anymore?" Ewing demonstrated that his own hands functioned and turned off the tape, just as Catie was commenting on Matt's propensity to buy gifts.

"Whose the tape of? We gonna depose any of these kids?"

Joe shook his head. "I can't recommend any depositions to the D.A.. Other than the arresting officers."

"You're going to take this to trial without a *single* witness who *knows* the kid?"

"Isn't it *your* job to get the ones who know the kid?"

"Isn't it *your* job to bust this enormous drug ring that he's *supposed*ly running?"

Ewing fiddled with paperclips on his desk. "He's afraid of somebody. Somebody bigger than he is."

"Then give him immunity."

"Doesn't keep him safe when he gets out."

"Put him in the Witness Protection Program."

"Would he go?"

"I don't think he likes anyone enough in his current life not to."

"What about this Katie girl?" For illustration, he pushed the play button again, which was a nice change from all the paperclips.

"Who?"

"His girlfriend? Or ex? Or the girl he was obsessed with? Whatever she is."

"Haven't heard about her."

"You sure we're dealing with the same suspect here? It's the only person he's called since the arrest."

"Huh."

"Well, look, even if he'd go into the Program, I don't think he'd testify against anyone. To hear him talk, there's no one to testify *against*. Except his own *curiosity*. What a load of crap."

"I dunno." She looked out the window. "You don't have enough evidence, do you?"

"What?"

"To get a conviction. It's too risky, isn't it?"

It was time for a paperclip fiesta in Deskville. "Two officers of the law saw him alone in a stolen vehicle with thousands of dollars worth of illegal narcotics." He was very focused on enunciating each word.

"And no one else believes he had anything to do with it. Listen, Joe, if I see you get out of a car, that doesn't mean you own it, does it? Or that you own everything *in it*?"

"No, but--"

"And the *back* of a car? That doesn't mean anything, right?"

"Well--"

"I think my client would be amenable to a settlement."

"You'll have to talk to the D.A. about that."

"Absolutely."

"And you'd be getting away with murder."

She turned to leave. Without facing him, "Not murder, Joe. Sitting in a car."

The D.A. was tired, overworked, disappointed in Officer Ewing's failed promise that this drug bust would be his ticket to re-election, and willing to settle. On principle, however, he could not let a case this compelling go completely, lest it be exposed by a political opponent proving him soft on the drug war. Thus far, the case had thankfully escaped any media attention. "Get him to plead guilty," he said, "and we can get him probation and community service."

"No jail time?"

"Does he have anyone else he can testify against?"

"I doubt it."

"Well, the guilty plea's enough."

"What about no-contest?"

"Guilty."

"No-contest?"

"He'll be serving the community *a lot* if he pleads no-contest."

Which he did. So he did.

TWENTY-THREE

I could spend a lot of time here whining about injustice. I don't really want to do that. There's plenty of injustice in the world and I've sure faced my share. Probably well more than my share. What is someone's share, anyway? That's not for me to say.

So I don't want to whine. The entire point of this is not to whine. When I was in jail, I heard a lot of whining. Not as much as when I was in college, say, but a lot. So now I'm out of jail, and out of college, and I'm kind of ready for a time when there's not much whining. So I shouldn't whine if I'm going to do this and I guess that's that.

Seems like every paragraph is getting stuck on a tangent already. That's probably a sign of bad writing. I mean, that's what they told me in school for sure. But they also told me to write in stream-of-consciousness, to follow my heart or my mind and just let go. So I'm trying that too. There's a lot of things I'm trying lately. But this is one of them, and I'm not making much progress, but it feels kinda good to have someone to talk to. They say that if you talk to yourself, you're normal, but if you talk back, you're crazy. I guess writing saves you the trouble of talking back.

Or looking crazy.

So, you probably want to know stuff about me. I'm 18, but I'm going to be 19 real soon. That's not very exciting, is it? I live in Philadelphia, in this nice place my parents bought me. They're not together, but they both bought me this place, I mean they're renting it for me, but it feels bought because I'm not paying. I mean it's not too nice, it's just nice. You know? This sounds

210

awfully conversational for writing. I don't know what I think of that. Here I go getting sidetracked. I could use an editor.

And I keep addressing this mythical audience. Like someone's going to pick up my diary and say "Oh! Here's something to read!" and then not get bored. Well, whoever you are, don't get bored. I promise I'll get somewhere. Even though it's not really a diary because I'm not dating things or timing things or writing down when stuff happens. There'll be today. And maybe today will be today and maybe it's tomorrow and maybe it's ten days from now. I got tired of keeping track of time in jail. There was sleep and awake and they were both boring.

Why is everything so <u>boring</u>? Boring boring boring.

So where was I? Nowhere interesting. The place. It's a nice place, but not too nice. I said that already. Yeah, I think my folks felt bad for me or what I'd gone through. Someone probably told them it was their fault. Dad didn't play enough catch with me so I went and dealt drugs. I <u>didn't</u> deal drugs, but the cops caught me dealing drugs. Someday maybe I'll explain that. For now I'll use the words no contest.

<u>No</u> contest. Remember that.

So because of that I'm on probation and I have all this time to serve my community. Give something back. You know all the cliches. There's supposed to be an accent over that word somewhere, I think. I don't know where though. But it looks kinda wrong, like it would be said <u>clitches</u> or something.

<u>Editorial</u> comment: too many editorial comments.

<u>Editorial</u> comment 2: too many <u>underlines</u>.

But I like underlines. They make my point. And I can't really write sideways. Hell, this is already sideways, so maybe I could try hard to <u>print</u> and that would be italics but I don't care. Underlining gets the point across. You see? Here's my <u>point</u>. I bet you looked hard at that word.

Okay, so I'm not telling you anything about me, but maybe I shouldn't. Maybe you should just figure it out as I go. I feel like I'm on some reality TV show. It's like this is the lens and I'm on, what would it be? The Real World? Like those kids ever do anything meaningful anyway. I mean, community service would be a day for one of them between having sex and whining. What about Survivor? No, it's not that bad. I guess this is the Real World meets Survivor, except I don't have any friends. No enemies and no friends. And no sex. I have this nice place though.

I'm surprised how nice it is. My parents came and picked it out, since I couldn't go back to Topeka with the probation and all. So they came to visit and felt real bad about all the not visiting in jail and the putting me in jail (remember Dad not playing catch?). (I have to watch use of parentheses, because I really like them and then there won't be anything else. It'll just be layers of parentheses and you'll feel more like an archeolagist than a reader. (Wait, is that spelled right? Archaeolagist. Archeoligist. Hm. No spell-check on paper.) Right, so I like history more than english anyway.)

Parent guilt. That's really all I need to say. So I have this kitchen and bathroom, but I have to clean it all myself. And then I go to the shelter and clean shit too. It's a bunch of cleaning, all the time. I clean the shelter in the morning and then I walk across town to the soup kitchen and serve lunch and cook dinner and serve dinner and go home. It's all walking and I've only done a week and I'm real tired. <u>Real</u> <u>tired</u>. I want you to remember that too.

I am not whining. I will <u>not</u> whine.

I just don't know a lot of 18 year old (year-old?) kids who work 10 hours a day. I'm trying to do that because I have so many hours to fill and it's better than doing 8. Or 6. I heard someone did 6. But I'm only on probation for a while, so I guess I could go back to school and do the rest of my service then. I don't know if I have a deadline. I don't know much about this. My defense attorney, Schwartz, she was supposed to tell me more, but I don't really know. I think she was just happy that I didn't have to stay in jail.

Don't get me wrong. I'm happy too. <u>Very</u> <u>happy</u> about that. Man, this is like I have an emotion buzzer. Just read the underlines to see what Matt's <u>really</u> thinking. Real tired. Not. Very happy. All you need to know. It's like cliff notes to my own life.

I just used third person up there. That's a bad sign relative to all that talking-to-myself crap. Oh well. If I was in jail, I'd really be in trouble with that.

But jail is why I'm doing this. That and no friends. I thought my roommate back at school, at Harrison (Christ, you don't know anything about me, do you?), I thought he had no friends. But this is really no friends. Everyone at the shelter and the soup kitchen is either over 80 and bored or in their late 20s and doing time like me. How come no cute high school girl gets assigned 5,000 hours of community service?

Okay, I was at Harrison College. In Fifeburg, PA. And that's David Benowski, my old roommate. I would be there still, but there's the jail and the service and all.

But I like Philadelphia. Really. I mean, the city hasn't been the best to me, but I'm not whining. It's gotten me a no contest trip to probation and 5,000 hours of cooking, cleaning, and serving. Lots of serving. Catie even says she might visit sometime.

Damn. I wasn't going to mention her.

That lasted a long time. Okay, she's, well, an ex. Why lie to paper? It's like lying to air. Air doesn't care. I'll just have to burn this sometime. Catie (it's not Catty, so don't even go there, just imagine a K) is this girl I loved. Really. But she didn't have sex with me and, well, I don't think about much else. Okay, that's not true, but you know what I mean. Okay, I am now resisting the temptation to just rip this page out. It looks so naked there on the page. Oh, I am so clever.

I'm having a hard time not envisioning someone reading this, someone who would sit here and laugh at me and, well, I'm really just seeing David getting ahold of this I think. But he'd interpret it to mean all kinds of crazy shit, like me having the secret to life or the perfect critique of American society and its people or something. That's bonkers. This is just me. And not even me, but my perception of me. It's like David looking at me looking at me. Really, I'm just killing the time that isn't my 10 hours a day. Because I don't have a TV here. And I'm too tired to do 12 a day. So I just sit here and talk to my, okay I'm writing.

We create our own reality. Don't believe me? Talk to someone, anyone, about what's important to them, to their life. Chances are, you'll get a different list than you have for yourself. Everyone's got a different list. So we all have a different life reality. And it just goes on down the list. I had better ideas for this point before, but I lost them. Tune back later.

Why didn't my parents let me get a TV? And would they know? I mean, they don't really give me much money, since they think I'll buy drugs. You should have seen me try to tell them that I don't do drugs. My mom was so upset. She kept talking about how she loved me, but how could I do this to her? How had she gone wrong? But why, said Dad (I hadn't seen them together in years) had I pled no contest (I told you that would come back) if I were innocent. Why didn't I <u>prove</u> my innocence? It's like talking to a brick wall out there sometimes. The finer points of <u>no</u> <u>contest</u> vs. <u>guilty</u> were lost on daddy. I think he even worked something in about no science classes. Maybe I'd learn something about proof, he said.

But what have I got to prove?

I'm not saying that I like this better than college, but I just want to throw out there the idea that this isn't the worst thing that's happened. I mean, there's my roommate, who was probably plotting to kill me anyway, and there's the <u>boredom</u> factor. That's looking pretty universal. But I mean no one here is judging me. That's a nice change. I don't get graded, I just get told what to do. And if I fuck up, I fuck up, and they tell me, but I don't have to pay for it for the rest of my life.

No <u>transcript</u>.

Okay, I'm lying now, not wanting to, but I did. Because I pled no contest (I'm going to try to stop underlining that now) and now I have to have that on my <u>record</u> forever. Or 7 years or something, which might as well be forever. I mean, where will I be at 26? Christ, let me think about 21 first. So yeah I do have a transcript, but at least there's no F's. For Felony. Get it?

I really like the one-line paragraph.

It's <u>dramatic</u>.

I feel like a kid in the candy store of language, but this is really the first time I've been writing. You know what it is? It's all these Civil War journals and shit like that that really gets me going. You know, it's history. I'm just a piece of history. And like history, it's create-your-own-adventure. It's like those books, but not really. <u>That</u>'s my audience. That's who <u>you</u> are, reading this! You're the <u>Future</u>. I am your Past, and you are my Future, and we are linked through Time. I've got chills. This is really cool.

And you probably think I'm lame for writing that. But I don't care. I am your <u>Past</u>, and that's cool.

But I am only one past. I am not all pasts. All pasts would be the real truth, or the perspective, or the grand total or whatever. You can call it reality. But this is my reality, and I create it, or I perceive it and then create <u>this</u>, and that's a reality. This is what historians have to put up with. If the world blows up and all that's left is my copy of this diary, then your whole reality of Earth is this. That's it. You have this shoddy attempt at writing by some dumb criminal kid as your account of Earth. And I can write it and you have to believe it, because nothing gave you a <u>choice</u>, right? It's like I've got a gun to the head of your history books, and I'm about to fire away if you throw this away. That's right, Mr. Anthropologist of the Future. I am talking to <u>you</u>. Listen up. Here is <u>The World</u>.

I should probably tell you something about the world, you say? The whole world?

Okay, it's round and has 6 billion people, which are the going rational creatures. Sentient, that's a good word. We're the sentient ones and there's a lot of us, and this country, the United States of America, is the one I live in. It's good and bad. I've seen the bad lately, with the criminal proceedings and the community service. Community service is what you do when you're bad, and you help the other people in bad shape. It's sort of a cycle. But 80 year-olds sign up for it too, because they're bored. The Bored and the Bad. I could create a TV series.

So I'll be telling you more about the world. But we have cities and small towns, like where I grew up, in Kansas, which is in the corn-growing center of the world, I think. It's really small and boring. I bet you think this is all very boring.

What if you don't know my <u>language</u>?

Then you've probably already thrown this away. That's a lot of futility. Wow. Just think about that, all that time I'm spending now working on this and you've thrown it away. Well, if you're this far, you haven't, but I'm still working my ass off here. Maybe you don't like my language, <u>that</u> kind of language. But I really feel like I'm working my ass off. Oh, I'm young. Give me a break. Get off my case.

I think I keep nudging this line of "talking back to myself". When do I know if I cross it? Will the people at the shelter try to lock me up? Would I retroactively have temporary insanity and get out of probation and service and get a nice long trip to a padded cell? I've always thought that a padded cell sounded more like recreation than anything else. It's like you're so bored in there that there's nothing to do but throw yourself into the wall and see if you bounce. Wee! Here I go, and it's soft, and then you just bounce all day.

I guess they don't put you in a straight jacket then because how can you bounce in a straight jacket? That would be no fun at all. You'd just sit there all day, in a straight jacket, wanting to bounce, not being able to. It's like this Far Side cartoon I saw once where these cows are in a room with a ringing phone and one says to the other that they don't have opposable thumbs. Okay, it's funnier if you see the actual cartoon. But you get the idea. <u>Yearning</u>.

Let's not go down the yearning road just now, okay?

Speaking of roads, I keep passing over this overpass. That looks kinda weird, but it's true. You gotta wonder what kinda people you're passing over. I mean, who are all these folks who commute through Philadelphia? I suppose I could actually bother to look at them. From what I've seen of the traffic, there's never a fast flow underneath. The lunch rush or something. Or maybe that area never runs smoothly. This is an awfully big city.

Without enough room for all its people. That's the end of population that I've really been getting to know. I don't know what good it does to say that I <u>know</u> them, but you know what I mean. Or maybe you don't. I mean this: I've been spending <u>time</u> with them, but this has very little to do with knowing them. I know my own view, my own interpretation, I see them as they get their food or leave the housing in the morning. They're looking for work or looking for drugs or looking for someone to con, and I honestly can't tell you who is who. They all get food, they all get shelter, and we're not paid to judge them, but we help if we can. That's what my supervisors tell me. I just do what they tell me to. Too.

I wonder if old defense attorney (interesting that I can't say D.A., because that's district attorney, which is the opposite, and yet the same, from the same source) Schwartz would ask if this is the beginning of my insanity defense. I <u>do</u> talk an awful lot about schizophrenia and padded walls. Well when hydrophobia sets in, you'll know I'm in trouble. Well <u>you</u> won't, but <u>I</u> will. And maybe I'll let you know.

Rabies is probably about the only disease these people don't have. I don't know if that's really true, but you go by the looks of it and that's what I see. I mean, they tell me "we" don't judge, ("we" the institutional we, like a royal we but not as important) but I'm judging these folks all the time. Everyone I see, everyone I smell, there's got to be something behind them. They all have a story, and most of them are lying, I bet. And some of them aren't. I mean, who am <u>I</u> to tell someone they're lying? These days. So I don't <u>tell</u> anything. I think, though. Sometimes you invent a history for them and come up with a name (if you don't know it) and a history and a family and a crime, or a disease, and you wonder what <u>that</u> smell is or where they picked up the cough from. And it's not all bad, either, sometimes you wonder how someone that pretty got to be that way, but I guess you <u>know</u> don't you?

It's hard to use the first person without the second. And not even when I'm talking to <u>you</u> you. Sometimes when I'm just talking to the world, or to the average person. There is no average person, which makes them such a good listener.

Well listen to this: I looked over the edge of that overpass today and (look, I know I don't intend to differentiate today from today but if it's all present tense, you'll never know, right? Or just barely? I'll leave you to think about that while I go on) I saw the prettiest girl in the world. I kid you not. If you are the anthro man from the future, with only my manuscript to peruse before disregarding this planet, I have salvaged for you the memory of one of the most precious gems. Christ, I find one pretty girl and I go all poetic. But really. I have seen the future and it's a little brighter.

She was, well, a description's just going to undo the justice, right? I mean, right now, whoever you are (and I hope to God you like girls so you have a good description--although it seems that girls, even straight girls, have this funny way of knowing when a girl's pretty even if they don't really want her or anything, which is weird, so maybe you're like that and you don't need to like girls to have a vision) but whoever you are, you've got this idea in your head right now reading of the prettiest girl in the world. <u>For you</u>. And maybe it's not this girl, which just proves your lack of imagination. But for me, I <u>know</u>. I guess I'm lucky. But if I start to tell you about her, it's just going to take away what you think she is, and maybe I like blonde (I do) but you don't and thus you've already lost the prettiest girl image if I start telling you she's blonde. But she is and, well shit, I've fucked up already.

And don't give me this garbage about whoever you like now being prettier. I mean, they are, to you, in a way. But this is another problem of perspective. You see, I've found, and a lot of folks I know agree, that if you <u>like</u> someone enough, I mean if you <u>love</u> them or close to it, they start to become real attractive, even if they aren't. I don't just mean their soul. I mean their <u>body</u> is <u>hot</u>. Get close enough to someone, and you <u>want</u> their body big-time. That's not objective, that's just you. That's interpretation and

217

perspective and pretty soon we've got nothing left. Well I don't want to go there, because then you don't appreciate this girl I saw today. I mean, you can't fall in love at first sight; that's just lust at first sight. There's so many places (like there) where I normally use commas and I should be using semicolons. That English 101 class really got to me, though. It's like I knew how to write going into it and coming out of it I was always second-guessing everything. It didn't do shit except get me to <u>worry</u> about my writing. Can I <u>diagram</u> this sentence? No! But it's a sentence all right, and I used to know it was till that fucking class. Now, later, I can diagram a sentence and I don't even know where to break a paragraph anymore. And I wouldn't be writing any of this meta-shit if it wasn't for that class. Weren't for that class. Wasn't? I don't even know anymore. Clearly.

Okay, so this girl restores my faith in the objective. That was my real point. That wasn't so hard, was it? A new paragraph gets me thinking clearly. Watch:

This girl is the one that anyone would think is most pretty.

Awkward. Yuck. Try again:

This is the prettiest girl in <u>everyone</u>'s opinion.

Well that's not really true; that's not what I mean. I mean there's a certain poetic style there, but I just got done talking about everyone's opinion and how their lover (if they <u>really love</u> them, which I think is rare) is really more pretty to them than anyone else. Or more attractive. You get the picture. Point being, opinions are fallible. But they wouldn't be <u>if</u> they saw this girl. So:

This is the prettiest girl in everyone's objective opinion.

Does this beg the question? I'm not sure. But if I keep talking about it too much longer I'm going to stop thinking about how pretty she is and go to sleep dreaming of sentence structure. That wouldn't be any fun. And don't get any sick thoughts. Or do if you want. I'm not going to talk about that. There's this small chance I have to consider that you actually know me, or maybe you just <u>are</u> me in the future like I said, and then you definitely won't want to remember certain things. Will you? Maybe it's too late. I can't really give you the choice from back here, so I'll have to guess.

Who would I let read this other than me? Than you? Maybe you stole this. Bastard!

I am so easily distracted. Like I was today, on the bridge, the overpass, whatever you want to call it. There's this car, this very green car going underneath on the highway. Not really <u>going</u>. But close enough. It was just crawling along in the traffic, probably coming back from lunch. Not the car's lunch, the girl. That should be clear. Because she sure was.

At the angle she was coming in, I could just barely see her, so I don't think she's too short, but maybe she just sits up or who knows? It's too hard to tell. But she was in the fast lane, which wasn't fast at all. So I'd just gotten to the middle of the pass, and she was there, just left of the divider, and I think I lost my breath. It was like the whole world stopped and made sense for a second. I mean, it didn't stop, it was probably just the traffic, but these things get blown up in your mind afterwards.

So she had curly blonde hair and these eyes that I swear matched the car perfectly, just shining this green. It was like a dark forest green, and I think you could just go wandering in the forest of those eyes. (Give me a break, okay? I know it's lame, but I wanted to drop some poetry on the car immediately. Just take a paper out of my pocket and do something crazily brash and scrawl shit out and drop it on her car. And with my luck it would land on the car of this fat man in his 70s who would read it and start hanging around the overpass because he had nothing better to do. Or if I put my phone number on it... shudder) The rest of her features were perfect. I mean, I know objectification is thought to be important, but I think if I take her apart, it really does undermine her. No, this isn't some of Toni's theory or me talking about the basic dignity of woman, this is really true. Just physically, if you break her apart, she breaks apart. You'll just have to trust me that she's <u>perfect</u>.

Which you're not going to do. But you should, dammit.

Toni? You would ask about her. Toni looks exactly like a browner version of this girl back home that I wasn't going to mention and now I've done it twice. Yeah, Catie. So they looked a lot alike, which I guess is why I really hung out with her at first. But nothing happened. Just a lot of talk. I mean, she had these drawings which were pretty cool. Now <u>there</u>'s someone I would have expected to show up by now. But I haven't really contacted anybody, so hey. I guess I kinda like the idea of being this guy who disappeared from college. I mean, practically nobody knew me when I was there. But now that I'm not, who knows? People must notice I'm gone. The whole hall, for sure, and maybe most of the building. I mean, I'm not saying they <u>miss</u> me, but know me a little more now, right? Know <u>of</u> me. And that's gotta count for something, I figure.

So I'm going to be looking for her everyday. The girl, not Toni. I wouldn't have been able to really do anything with Toni, anyway. She would have talked about rape and respect and I would have felt like shit just for being alive. In some ways. She had that effect, sometimes. But the prettiest girl in the world doesn't. She's just pretty and looks a little bemused to be in all that traffic. What are the odds that she ever sees me? I mean, what are the odds that she's even there again? I don't want to think about this reasonably, I want to hope. I want to hope! Woweeeeeeeeeee!

If I can hope, she'll be there all the time. And it'll always be noon and that means the sun will always be behind me, so even if she sees some person, she'll never see me. But that has its advantages, doesn't it? I mean, think about it. I am <u>not</u> the most attractive guy in the world, not even by the standards of those who really like me. I'm not about to be. So just on looks, she's not going to fall in lust with me. There'd have to be something I could do. Like poetry. What's the accuracy of paper airplanes? I could leave a number or a place to meet or both and then what?

I'd shit myself silly.

I mean, what do you say to the prettiest girl in the world? I don't think "Hello" cuts it. Something much more like "I am honored and graced to breathe the same oxygen that you have access to". Or maybe "I can never live up to living in the same area code that you do". Those types of things are just the beginning. Then you've gotta just keep adding it on. Piling it on. I mean, worship is never enough. I'm sure she gets worshipped all the time. I'm surprised there isn't a little red carpet on the highway. Maybe I could put one there...

Now there's this problem with pretty girls, though, so often. It's something I really was just starting to get the hang of with Toni. Maybe it's good I never went home to Catie, 'cause she had this problem with eating disorders apparently. I mean this is all just me guessing. But I really hope whoever this girl is doesn't have some problem like that. I don't know. It's not that I can't understand, but I just can't really deal. I mean, how could you be with someone who had an eating disorder?

Now I'm not saying I have. But Joaquin told me that Toni did and Catie's a little thinner than Toni, and he seemed to imply that there's no way that Catie didn't. He's never met Catie though. I mean, Toni's confident too and she had one (I guess), so I guess that means Catie could've too. That's just so difficult. I mean I'd feel like I was whipping the girl or something. I mean, with Catie, I was whipped, and I still was till this morning. And it's silly to be done with Catie now, but she hasn't taken much interest, has she? No one really does. But I have to be practical. I'm not in Kansas anymore. She is. This girl's in Philadelphia.

Maybe she was just passing through.

Maybe maybe maybe maybe maybe maybe. I'm going to make myself sick. Then I'll throw up and have an eating disorder of my own.

Okay, here's the real sick thing, you've gotta pay attention to this. Seriously. Want to learn something about this planet? There's these girls who get these disorders. They say they're all fat and shit when they aren't. I mean, they look in the same mirror that I do or you do and see what really is a thin girl. But they don't see. Instead they see this fat person, or this too fat person. I don't understand it really. I mean I understand wanting to be more attractive, but you don't see me taping cardboard muscles on myself, or molding plastic on me or something. Or running till I kill myself. I just can't do it. I'd need surgery and all sorts of shit. But this isn't about me.

So they look thin but they see fat. It's that simple. They abuse food then. It's like frat boys, but the opposite. They don't binge drink, they binge eat. Or never eat. But whatever they do eat, they throw up. Again, I'm just learning about this shit. Joaquin told me all about it back at school. I wanted to talk to Toni about it, but I had a feeling she'd throw me out her window. So they don't retain food. They have food, but they don't use it. They abuse it.

Now I'm working in this soup kitchen, where we take care of the folks who don't have food. They just get what we give them, and sometimes not even that. We do a noonish lunch and a late dinner. And that's a lot of food, but usually folks just come in for one and not the other. It's the one good meal they get. I mean, these folks would starve without us.

So naturally I think this is all pretty twisted irony, right? We've got one side of town intentionally starving, mostly because they see food as a burden, and the other side unintentionally starving, because they don't see food at all. It's a big joy in life.

So I think that's fucked up.

Ready for real fucked up? I started watching it and realized, slowly, that some of the kids are both. I mean we've got folks in the soup kitchen who don't eat half their shit, or who run to the bathroom for the wrong reasons after the meal. There's not many, but if you pay attention to the thin ones, to the real <u>thin</u> ones, the teen girls... It's bad news. You've got kids who abuse the only food they've got. It's like <u>not</u> biting the hand that feeds you. Well, you get the idea. Sometimes being a smartass doesn't quite get the point across.

TWENTY-FOUR

"Hey Matt, how's it going?"

"Oh. All right. Pretty good, actually." He sighed, threw down his backpack, which was very light, in the closet, and went to get an apron. "What am I serving for lunch?"

"You're on the applesauce. A full scoop for every tray. You've done that before, right?"

"Applesauce? Sure. Been here three weeks. We have that once a week, right?"

"Something like that. You'll be working on the line next to Sam, who I don't think you've met."

Matt's supervisor couldn't have known it, but she was wrong about what she'd just said. "Holy shit," was the more honest utterance from Matt's mouth.

"Hi Matt." Sam had always been a kid of few words.

"What are *you* doing *here*?"

"Volunteering. Same as you, I'd guess. You didn't tell me you were in the area."

"Yeah. I'm sorry we lost touch." He was being glared at, so he grabbed a pair of plastic gloves, the applesauce scoop, and went out to the line. Sam was right behind him, and ended up behind the carrots. One per tray, no scooping.

"I'm sorry too." Sam started fingering carrots. "So you're at school in the area? Swarthmore? Haverford?"

"Harrison."

"Isn't that a little, uh, *far*?"

"From here? Yeah." The applesauce was prone to splattering.

223

He was good at it, but not great yet. He swore they put too much water in it anyway.

"So you commute? Or a full day?"

"It's a long story, really. You're going to what, UPenn?"

"Yup. It's local. I have a car. I have time for projects like this. It's fun. You like school?"

"It was okay." He couldn't keep up the act forever, and the past tense had really just slipped out.

"*Was*? I knew you were smart, but you're not *out* already? If you graduated when I left and did it in three years--"

"I was a *soph*omore when you left."

"Well there you go." One of the hungry going through the line mistook this for his tray being ready, as the speakers were facing forward more than each other.

"Thank you," he said, holding his hands out.

"Oh, no, you don't want dessert?"

Matt hadn't been looking at anything other than applesauce. "*What*?"

"Sorry, man, thought you said--"

"'Sokay."

"*What*?!"

"Never mind, Matt, I was helping the guy."

"I'm helping them *too*! Just because you *chose* this and I didn't!"

"What," Sam laughed and dropped a particularly slippery carrot, "you a *crim*inal?"

Matt kept his watering eyes focused on the mottled yellowy milieu before him. It was embarrassment, not tears, but he still feared the moisture mixing with the food. Who would notice? "Well, sorta."

"*Sorta*?"

"It's a really long story. I pled no contest to a bunch of," a big sigh here, "drug charges."

"*You*?!" Apparently you couldn't go home again, but home would follow *you* home upside-down.

"Possession and sale." Another big gulp of air. "I wasn't really guilty, but I guess I wasn't innocent either."

"How does that work?"

"Just trust me here."

"Okay." His pan of carrots was nearing emptiness, and he passed the word on down the line, "Need more carrots." Then to

Matt, "Well, that sucks."

"They'll get you more."

"No, I mean about *you*."

"Oh. Yeah. But hey, you do this for fun."

"Not fun. Because I feel *ob*ligated."

Matt laughed and rubbed his eyes, which irritated them more, but had to be done. "So do I."

Matt looked up for the first time. There were jobs on the line, like carrots or rolls, that could afford one almost constant eye-contact with the clientele. Applesauce, which required an attempt at precise equal distribution in the form of a small scooper, was not such a job. Occasionally, one would have to look up to confirm that someone really didn't want applesauce, so not to waste it, which was really about the only reason they had them go through the line in the first place. That, and to keep some level of contact, so that the served could understand there was human energy and compassion behind the effort, and that the servers could keep the strength and memory of what all the sweat was for.

No one was asking for a tray without applesauce right now, but Matt had secretly started checking, even on the hard jobs, for the presence of the prettiest girl in the world. Virtually no one drove to the soup kitchen, especially not through highway traffic in a decently painted dark green car. And she didn't really exit in time, being in the fast lane when going under the overpass that she'd probably have to be on to get to the kitchen. But it was a fun game to play, to pass the applesaucing time, though he knew that if he actually saw her, he'd probably fall in the pan of sauce, both from shock and to hide.

Every afternoon for a week and a half though, he'd ducked out of the shelter a little earlier and walked a little faster to his overpass, where he would park above the eastbound fast lane and stare. Traffic flow was almost never above what he estimated to be 35 and he always got a pretty good look at the object of his attraction. He found it inspiring, and the dreaming gave him something other than 5,000 hours of community service to anticipate. She had been there so consistently, that it was almost like having a reliable friend. And so much more.

He turned to his arguably less reliable friend. "Do you know a lot of girls at UPenn?"

"A handful." Sam grinned at his carrots. "You looking, huh?"

"Well, sorta. There's one in particular. I don't suppose any of them drive a green car?"

"Green? Hm. I don't know. Alberta drives this really nice white car. So not her. I don't think so. What's her name?"

"I don't know," Matt mumbled.

"Huh?"

"It's just someone I've seen. She's hot." This was so much easier to explain to an audience that really *didn't* talk back.

"Ah, okay. Shot in the dark. She goes to UPenn?"

"Well, she *could*." So, according to his laconic lost friend Sam here, he (Matt) had now become a criminal *and* a stalker. Outstanding.

"Well, a name would help. I'll look for you if you can do that."

"*Really?*" Matt tried to drop the excitement back from his voice, which he was pretty sure had almost cracked. "Thanks."

"Hey, anything for an old friend." Sam was beaming, but in a way that Matt was fairly sure people smiled at the criminally insane or people with an IQ below 25.

"You know, I think you'd know her if you saw her anyway, though. She's really extremely pretty."

"Well, that's cool."

"You gimme some extra applesauce, man?"

Matt looked up to address the request. "Sorry, sir. We're not allowed."

"I won't tell." He smiled a half-toothed grin and coughed roughly.

"No, really. Because then the next person will want more, and pretty soon half of you won't get any sauce."

"Please, man? What if I don't take any carrots?"

"Sir, you're holding up the line. I'm sorry."

TWENTY-FIVE

S o, sometimes life throws you a curve ball. I don't know. I guess I always knew I'd see my friend Sam again, but I was never quite sure <u>when</u>. I was pretty sure it wouldn't be for a while. Sam was this kid I knew in high school and before that, but he moved to Philadelphia. Figures that he'd end up at UPenn. He never was much for taking risks, or having adventures, or saying much of <u>anything</u>. I mean, he was a good friend, but what does that mean when you're that young? Well, that's not a whole lot younger than now, but I guess he might just not have been that great a friend. He was the best of what was there. I guess that doesn't say a lot for Topeka.

But I can't be too hard on the guy, I mean, he was always a good sort. And he was happy to see me, just not to see that in his absence I've become a stalker and a criminal while he's gone on to a good education. I mean, I was always smarter than him, right? That's what he thought. Maybe he just didn't say much. I mean, we didn't show each other report cards or anything like that. Some kids do that, I hear.

A stalker, yeah. I guess that's what I'm becoming. I mean, I don't know what that means, really, but I guess it's just someone who takes an <u>interest</u>. You know, a <u>real</u> interest, one that transcends the typical boredom we all have with each other. I guess I'm a stalker. I mean, Catie would've called me that back in the day, and I'm really going to stop mentioning <u>her</u> at some point. I mean, I have the prettiest girl in the world to mention instead! Who wouldn't pick the latter over the former? Let's be serious about this.

And I've gotten too serious about this girl too quickly. It's not like you can get too serious about someone you don't know, but whatever the limit on that is, I'm getting there real fast. Which gives me something to think about, I suppose. I even told Sam about her a little, just wondering if she's a UPenn kid or something. I guess she'd have to live across town and commute, but people do that. So I hear. I mean, Sam's doing that as far as I can tell. Saves money. And gives him this time to volunteer at my soup kitchen. What are the odds?

But the best lead I have to go on is a green car, or better than that, that she's the prettiest girl in the world. But even though I know that's the objective truth, is Sam going to see it that way? And what are really the odds that she goes to UPenn? All in all, it adds up to not very likely. But I don't have much else to go on. I've thought about trying to look for a license plate, but to do that, I'd have to cross on the other side of the overpass. Which would run a couple of risks. First off, do I <u>know</u> with certainty which car is hers, even from behind? And is it worth sacrificing my afternoon inspiration? I mean, I'm making a big deal out of this already, maybe bigger than it deserves to be, but this sure beats trying to converse with most of my fellow volunteers. Sam is the first person in a while who I've had anything to say to. The old folks and the <u>real</u> criminals just aren't a good match, mostly.

So eventually I'm gonna have to give up one day and go for the plate. At least I've seen her enough now to know that I'm not risking never seeing her again or something crazy. It's like clockwork, so I'm sure she's on some sort of regular commute. Where is she going? To school, most likely. She looks like she's my age. I have to believe that. I'd say 22 tops. And what I'd do with a 22 year-old, I don't know. But I'm hoping it's more like 19. I wonder if she had her first time in the back of that Volvo.

Before you start thinking that I've carried it too far already, I've really taken to thinking about first times and the back of cars. This is a Catie thing, really. You see, I'm a virgin. And it's not like I'm a <u>total</u> loser, I've just had a couple bad breaks. Like the whole arrest and no contest business and all. Anyway, I was pretty sure I was going to end up sleeping with Catie. I mean, I loved her and all (I think). I can't be sure. But the important thing is that she denied me all that because of my <u>car</u>. A Honda Civic. Actually, it was my mom's car, and my dad's was this nice spacious Suburban, but I got unlucky on my last night in Topeka.

To <u>this day</u>, that was my last night in Topeka. Crazy.

Anyway, my dad wouldn't give me the good car so I ended up in this cramped Civic and she saw this cricket. I mean, we had been making out in the grass, and I thought my big chance was coming up, and everything was looking great. We had had sorta an emotional night, lots of crying and some fighting, and I don't think either of us were happy about me leaving. But we were making up and if this damn cricket hadn't started crawling on me, I think everything would've been perfect. But she saw this cricket crawling up my back and she freaked out beyond belief. I was just sitting there, against this chainlink fence, going "What?" and she was screaming and eventually told me she'd seen a <u>cricket</u>. A cricket! But that was enough to get us inside the car.

The car that she would <u>not</u> sleep with me in.

If I sound bitter about all this, it's because I think a car is a pretty lousy reason not to sleep with someone. I mean I hear about those guys that get women just <u>because</u> of their car and nothing else, and I don't know what their sleeping habits are, but they must be better than mine. That's all pretty lousy too. But withholding based on that? I mean, that hit me pretty hard. Who graduates high school without having sex? I mean, I've known some dorks in my time, and I know David sure wasn't having any, but all these other kids must. What else would they be doing with their time? And I can understand Catie being a little young (did I mention that she's 2 years younger? I try not to mention that, I suppose), but she's also a little fast.

I have <u>got</u> to stop talking about that girl.

Re-reading so much of this, I wonder if I sound like I have any intelligence whatsoever. There's a shift in voice, I think, every time I stand up from it and then sit back down again, which sorta defeats the purpose I was aiming at. But even re-reading doesn't help the real stream-of-consciousness project, does it? I mean, who has a stream of consciousness with layered self-awareness? That's like a circle of consciousness. And there's these things that I keep meaning to come back to and I don't. It's like doing the dishes or making my bed, and I keep thinking how much better I'd feel about my place and my life here if I'd just get them done. But then I realize I'd just be doing it for me, and where's the incentive in that? No one ever comes over and maybe I should start inviting random people just so I have someone to <u>tell</u> me to make my bed or clean a dish because <u>I'm</u> not just going to eat off it again. The logical extension of that is that I'm not just going to sleep in the bed, but even I don't hope that way right now.

Catie's probably not coming because her parents probably found out about what happened to me. She was always closer to her parents than I could really figure out. I mean, some people are. And she probably told them the whole thing. Or maybe they heard the message I left; that would've made things real simple. "Hi, I'm in jail." I don't know if that's exactly what I said, but it's gotta be close. It takes a special kind of disoriented to leave a message like that. I'm just that cool.

What is the <u>point</u> of this? Why am I writing? I'm just rambling rambling <u>rambling</u> and no one's ever going to <u>care</u>.

Stop feeling sorry for yourself, dork!

So I walked over the other side today, and I finally found out what I was looking for. It's actually really disappointing. Traffic was even slower than normal, so I was able to see the state and the plate and everything. Yeah, the state. It matters. Illinois.

<u>Illinois</u>.

The plate was at least descriptive. It's like some great force out there (God?) is playing this game with me. I'm half-expecting to see her slap on a bumper sticker with the riddle of the Sphinx on it. What is that riddle anyway? I know the answer is "man", but what's the question? Something about legs. Why that's the Sphinx's riddle when the Sphinx is only about a third of a man, I don't know. It should be "What doesn't roar but is still king of the jungle?"

NTGONE.

It's a designer plate, so that's cool. I was all ready for XTH 093 or something like that, and I was confronted by this really coherent phrase. But it doesn't tell me much. It does tell me that I can't call up DMV here and ask who she is. That I was counting on, with the only possible blockade that she's living with her parents or something. But even then, she drives it enough to be her car. But now I have to call up <u>Illinois</u>?

This <u>does</u> lend more to the theory that she's a student from around here, though. Maybe not UPenn, since Sam (who only comes in on Fridays - how lame is that?) hasn't found anything in his attempts. So she's probably from out of town, but I don't know what she's trying to say. Did she have a close friend with initials N.T.? That would make some sense, except why would she say "gone" if she liked the person? It's more like a celebration of them being gone. Like a bad boyfriend she got rid of. Or some sort of reputation, or who knows? But then I got to thinking that she probably had a 6-letter limit, and with 7, she would have said "NOTGONE". Or "NOTGONE" was already taken.

<u>Who</u>'s not gone?

<u>She</u>'s gone to Pennsylvania! From Illinois, wherever she was there. I guess I could try finding the Illinois DMV, but that would be tough and I'm not sure they'd have much more than her name. Not her address here in Philly, not anything really about her. And more likely, it would be her parents, because they're back in Illinois with her registration.

So I'm still working on this puzzle, but I have a feeling that the day I figure it out, she'll vanish or something like that. It's the way my luck works. Illinois is bad enough luck. I want to ask Sam to do a search of all the folks with initials N.T. at UPenn, but I'm getting more and more of a feeling that that's not her school. I guess N.T. could be gone to UPenn, but he could just as easily be gone to the other end of the earth. Or the grave. Never know.

In other news, there's this homeless guy at the soup kitchen who looks like he's almost old enough to volunteer at the place. He keeps asking me questions about what I want to know. It sounds like the Christian convert gambit, like he's about to ask if I know my soul needs saving or something like that. I don't want to go down that road with anyone. It's bad enough that the shelter is called St. Paul's and they pray before every lights-out, I hear. I'm never there for that, but there's all this Catholic imagery everywhere.

Don't get me wrong, I'm not against religion. I'm just very neutral on the subject. How can I be asked to accept something without proof? And I really object to the way they hold religion like a stick over these poor folks. They say they have good intentions, but it's the carrot of help and the stick of religion. "Here's your shelter and if you don't believe us, there's your eternal fire."

I'm feeling cynical tonight.

So I don't know what I think of religion, but I don't like it when I'm told to. If there's a God out there, why would He force things on people that have free will? But I'm not totally sure about this free will, in which case there's no reason to really have <u>force</u>, because it's all force. Right?

I can hear Toni asking me that if there's a God, who says it's a He? I mean, that's a reasonable question. I guess if you believe in a forceful God, it's gotta be a He. Then again, there's guys like me. I mean, after dating Catie, I'd say force is all with the girls.

If I blocked out all the paragraphs where I mention Catie, or where I'm really thinking about Catie, this would be about four sentences long. All those would be about the prettiest girl in the world, who I have to call NTGONE for now. Ntgone? That looks sorta African. Not Gone. That's such a weird way of referring to someone.

I believe in <u>history</u>. That's a powerful force. History tells us that religion kills. And history tells us that no one ever comes back to tell us what happens next. It's not the past, it's the future. The future is an open question. But most of religion is coercion, from what I can tell. And I have to figure out if this guy is really a force of coercion too. The people, my supervisors, tell me that I have no business talking with the people we're helping, except to make polite conversation. They have professionals who give them verbal help. I just dish up what I can.

Well, I want to talk to this guy and he surely wants to talk to me, but I don't often have much time. And if I set up a time to meet him, is he going to shoot me? Not that I have much to rob, but if I went missing, how long would it take for people to care? This guy, mind you, doesn't look like he could harm anyone. Maybe he's got a disease, but his intent looks awfully nice. Then again, that's how they get you.

But he's asking what I want to <u>know</u>. Not if he can take my soul, or my money, or where to meet him after sundown in a deserted area. So that's worth something. It's like a branch of college, right here. But I have a feeling he's not out to offer the same knowledge. And it's not just that he's singled me out, he asks most of the younger ones. He asked Sam. He just doesn't ask anyone who looks like they're getting older. Most of the supervisors think he's a raving nut. And he probably is. But I'm thinking of telling him that I want to know how to contact pretty girls in green cars from overpasses. Or maybe how to finagle a TV from parents who will only spend money on housing. (Yeah, I bet he'd appreciate that dilemma.) How to get friends? Maybe, just for fun, or to see what he's about, the meaning of life.

It's not like I have anyone else worth talking to.

Except <u>you</u>, of course. Wouldn't want to burn my bridges. Or pages.

I'm feeling a lot more <u>stable</u> these days. It shows, doesn't it? That's good and bad.

TWENTY-SIX

N othing is so dark as the night. When all the lights have faded from the sky, the remaining absence of light is virtually incomprehensible to the human perspective. Stars or the moon provide minimal relief from such daunting darkness, but on especially cloudy nights these sources too are blocked, bathing the entirety of vision in pure obscurity. While this makes movement or comprehension difficult, the avoidance of both in comforting sleep is most enhanced by the invisibility of night.

In cities, however, the unending light of civilization is dimmed by neither night nor clouds. In all hours, there are those who do not seek sleep and others who will always find fear, and these two forces combine to ensure that light always plays a role in urban life. People in search of sleep without the luxury of shelter are left to acclimate themselves to a permanently lit lifestyle.

The quest to avoid light, as well as other more natural elements of an outdoor urban existence, is typically satiated in one of two ways. The acquisition and use of cardboard boxes is one of the more popular and popularized methods of homeless adaptation. The illusion of home is simulated with four square walls and a ceiling, with only the substance and square footage lacking. While the floor is often of cement, in winter months, the use of heated grates as box-flooring provides less escapism, but more likelihood of survival. In both cases, blankets are useful to soften the hard realities of a cardboard residence.

There is a lesser sense of ownership accompanied with the

use of overpasses, but arguably more comfortable and spacious living accommodations can be made there. The space beneath any given overpass is often sloped on both sides of the underpassing road, providing an angled path to a good night's rest and a passable excuse for privacy. Steel beams divide segments of the overpass support structure into room-like sizes, providing walls of steel and a freeway ceiling with the vague sounds of overnight traffic to hum an industrial lullaby to the resident urban outcasts. Blankets are even more useful here, especially without the benefit of heated grating, but the darkness is more authentic and less claustrophobic than when one is packaged within cardboard.

Their reasons for coming here are as varied as the people themselves. Many object to shelters, either in principle or personal experience. Privacy is a valued right for most people, though the Constitution of the United States of America does nothing more than hint at an allusion to such a value. Nevertheless, the shelters are less likely to protect such a right (or privilege, if one prefers) than the overpasses and boxes of any given city. They are also more likely to wreak havoc with those who do not feel themselves to be in need of help. The same people who are willing to cheat or steal their way to relative advancement are often least likely to accept direct charity. Charity is also distinctly trying for those who are raised to believe that giving is of greater moral value than receiving. The conscience-based threat of burdening one's neighbors drives people scowling from buildings to wrap themselves in ratty discarded textiles.

Many cities simply refuse to accept that there are any within their limits whose burdens exceed their means. In such areas, there is often little option for those who do wish to welcome charity. A dearth of shelters and food banks is most frequent in smaller towns where politicians decry their larger counterparts as havens of crime and poverty that would be unthinkable in their own climes. The greatest threat to survival is found here, and the most able of the neglected will often migrate to larger cities more cognizant of their own shortcomings. The least able often perish.

The effect of survival on the mental fabric of any given individual is great. Most become defensive, increasingly aware of the negative capabilities of the human condition, and the propensity of those in threatened situations to become even more threatening. Many lose their grip on reality, often enhanced by a deliberate severance from reality through the habitual use of escapist substances. Others become more steadfastly gripped by reality, building their perception of the world around them through heightened contact with it. For these people, time slows to a pause in which the world can be observed without distraction, and key observations carefully noted without obstruction. This alarming clarity is often mistaken for insanity or disconnection, which yields isolation to the person who, freed of their more earthly trappings, wants nothing more than human contact.

These insightful humans, weary from their travels through manmade landscapes, curl up nightly amongst abandoned cloths, steel and cement, beneath the cars and feet of the more fortunate.

TWENTY-SEVEN

I've been thinking lately about how these people I'm trying to help end up <u>needing</u> help. I mean, honestly, some of them don't need the help per se. Not really. They could do without. It's just a leg up. And some of them <u>are</u> lazy. Some of them are jobless by choice, have homes to go to, and just want a free way of taking care of the necessities while they use money to accommodate drug habits or, far more often, alcoholism. This happens a lot more at the kitchen than at the shelter. The ones that have homes to go to don't spend much time looking for outside places to stay, especially when we check if they have any illicit materials.

But there's a lot of them who are really just in trouble. I'm not saying anyone's been <u>perfect</u> and ended up at our door, but then again, I can't say anyone's been perfect at all. That's a cliche, but it's important to remember. Maybe all this Catholic dogma around me is sinking in, and I'm just trying not to cast stones or whatever. But it's more than that; I'm becoming more forgiving.

Take this guy who keeps asking me about what I want to learn. I've taken to talking to him a little bit. We call him Crazy Billy when we're preparing the food, but he just wants to be called William. So I'm calling him William and asking him what he has to teach. But he insists that it's not him doing any teaching, just the world around us. He says to walk, to listen, to pay more attention. All I'm finding to pay attention to is this girl behind the steering wheel of a green car. I think it's a Volvo, or some other kind of station wagon. There aren't any logos on the car, so I guess she scraped them off or something. Sounds like something a college kid would do.

Here I am, talking (writing?) like I'm more connected to charity organizations I'm forced to give my time to than the college I <u>chose</u>. I guess it's just adapting to my environment.

So William ("Crazy Billy") is telling me to just look around me more. I must say that I was already doing that a lot before he advised me in that direction. You can't really help it. Just walking across the city of Philadelphia, you start to get a sense of the way it breathes, its patterns and rhythms and what makes it tick. It's kinda weird, but not having a car and having to actually <u>go</u> places on foot makes me much more aware. I guess I had the same possibility at Harrison, but there wasn't much going on. There was campus life and there was going down the street to Toni's place. That's about it. And the one night we went to the frat party, and that was just a weird night. I'd say I did notice stuff then too, but nothing like these weeks here in Philadelphia. The city has a whole different way of <u>being</u>.

But I don't have any really great observations. I mean, I notice <u>more</u>, just nothing interesting. It's not as boring as life in Topeka (I drove everywhere there anyway, and that just means noticing red lights and stop signs and other things that stop your progress), but it's still just little things. And the prettiest girl in the world. I wonder what the record is for that phrase appearing in a given piece of writing? It would be better if I had a name to go on, but I'm just left with Ntgone or Not Gone, and I swear I'm going to break down and call the Illinois DMV and set this straight soon.

One thing I've noticed a lot is that there's a lot of <u>bugs</u> in the city. Mostly not flying bugs. Just things like ants. There's anthills all over sidewalks, with their little mounds of tiny grounds of dirt. Tiny little ants, making their little mounds of progress and always rushing wherever they go. It's funny to look at those on the overpass, when I'm waiting for the green station wagon. I get to look at the rushing ants and the cars that wish they were rushing, and everyone's got somewhere to go. <u>I</u> have somewhere to go too, it's not like I've got an ivory tower or anything, but I feel like I'm above them standing on that overpass. Maybe it's just a physical thing. I <u>am</u> over them.

Okay, that's not really original, though. I mean, the first person to compare ants to people probably lived in Egypt and looked down from the first pyramid and noticed an ant on the brick underneath them, which looked about the same size as the buildings in the distance. And they realized what a hurry they were in to finish the pyramid, and what a hurry the ants were in to burrow in the pyramid, and made all sorts of smart conclusions from the comparison. And ever since, people have been making the parallel and thinking themselves intelligent. And one of them, maybe an Egyptian on the hot Sahara, made the observation that there was "nothing new under the sun". And then that became a standard part of the whole picture. Trying to be original is just impossible.

And yet, why do we keep ending up in the same situation? Maybe if we stop <u>trying</u> to be original, we'll actually have change.

Times like this, I wish I was back at school learning more about history. But that's just the history of the big leaders and the famous people, and the ones whose lives were important <u>enough</u>. I'm never going to be important enough to learn about. Unless, of course, as I've talked about earlier, this is the last thing being read from a planet that got wiped out. I've got to wonder <u>how</u> the planet got wiped out in that case. And you can't reach back and tell me. But I could guess. I could imagine all sorts of ways everything would fall apart. It's harder to imagine ways that everything except my meager diary fell apart.

All the people I work around, I work for, I work to help, they all have ways that their lives fall apart. And I know I do too. But what are the odds that everyone is like me? I don't like to think about how much <u>luck</u> is playing a role in everything. The Catholics tell me it's all God's will. I don't know if I believe <u>that</u>, but everything has this bizarre way of making some kind of sense. I mean, I don't want to jump on the "it all works out" bandwagon, but I can't think of many ways that I'd have run into either Sam <u>or</u> the prettiest girl in the world sitting back in Fifeburg and studying the history of famous people. Which is a better situation? I don't know. I have my own place here and I'm not living with David, so that's a plus. And I don't see any people now, except all these very real people with big problems. Is that better? Worse? About the same? I can't really complain, even though I want to and often <u>do</u>.

I never end up coming up with answers. If I could title this attempt at self-direction, it'd end up being something like "Reverse-Jeopardy!". That works on a lot of levels. We've got the fact that I've really got all the questions, but not the answers, which is the opposite format of the game show. Then we've got being in danger, but I'm on the safe side, both not being in jail or homeless or whatever. That's really workable, I think. Maybe I'll start calling this RJ. It makes it seem more like a person, too. Which is useful. Because I don't see people anymore.

Except William.

He's telling me that I should come "hang out" with him sometime. Who hangs out with homeless people? I can't figure out if he's just unlucky and didn't end up caring about money, or lost it all, or if he's one of the wasted, and just gets drunk and stoned and never does anything. So many of these people are lazy, but some of them seem like they've been forced to be lazy. But once you start spinning down, it's really hard to dig yourself out without money. I can't say I'm too far from these folks. Wrong place, wrong time, and it's only because my parents buy me a place that I'm not living in some halfway-house with hookers and dealers. And how do hookers and dealers get to be in their place? They just need money and don't have any. You work with what you've got. If you've got a body, or the will to do something illegal, then you can make that into something.

Everybody's got resources.

Another good title for this thing would just be "Schizophrenia". Because I've got a lot of that too. Sometimes it's hard not to hate these people. I mean, aren't they just taking and taking when I'm giving, and everything's free? In some poor country, I could understand, but this is the land of strong economies and money and we're over Steinbeck's dusty days. There's just some of them that you know are freeloading and there's nothing you can do. But there's ones that aren't too, and families, and people whose parents got them in this situation. I'm learning a lot, with or without William's advice. It's too complex for me to figure out or even deal with. How's anyone ever going to fix this? It's too much to deal with.

I guess what I am doing is just thinking about other people more. I mean, not just wanting them or liking them. There's people that I can't stand at this place, that I clean up after or feed and they're ungrateful, but I'm trying to understand why they are. Like I said, more forgiving. Maybe I can only do this because whenever I explain my real situation, what really happened to me, they just look at me like I offered them a crack pipe. Seriously. It's crazy. I did want to see a drug deal! I did want something to impress Catie with. It was a spur of the moment thing. I wouldn't do it again, even not knowing what I know. But I had to grow up somehow to make Catie want me again, or so I guessed. Who knows what's really in her mind? Or anyone's mind? I'm just trying to look into people's minds, by spilling my own all over these inky pages.

My minds.

Sam told me today that he's thinking about being a Classics major. We had a little discussion about it, which made me feel awfully weird in front of these old folks and these other criminals and all the homeless folks. Something about discussing Greek tragedies makes me feel irrelevant to all the people I was serving spinach to. But it wasn't till I got home and faced the riddle one more time, just about to call information and find out all the Illinois area codes, that I put it together.

aNTiGONE.

I'm just guessing there, and maybe this is me seeing the prettiest girl in the world in everything, but I'm starting to believe that this would make sense. It's the most likely 6-letter combination. ANTGNE is also a good one, maybe a better one, but that could be something like Aunt Gene. Or who knows what. I admit that not starting the sequence with an A makes me wonder if it really is Antigone, but a college kid is just the kind to pick a tragic Greek heroine.

Speaking of heroin, I'm pretty sure that someone at the kitchen was on it today. He was just curled up in the corner shaking and nobody wanted to do anything about it. I was going to tell the supervisors, but they'd just throw him out and I didn't think that was a good idea. If you're going to be in a corner shaking from drugs, you might as well be inside. Or where someone can give you food. Does food help get you over heroin? For someone living on the edge of a ghetto and spending all his time there, helping the ghetto people, I sure don't know shit about this stuff. Which I guess is why I'm thinking about taking up William's offer to "hang out".

Where do the homeless "hang out"? I guess I assume they're like me and bob back and forth between the shelter and the kitchen. And when I'm resting or writing, they look for work, or beg for change, or buy booze. There's a lot of common people that I see all day, both at the shelter and the kitchen. They leave in the morning as I arrive to clean the shelter and I see them at both lunch and dinner down the road. I wonder if anyone else is in the habit of seeing Antigone?

Can I call her that now? She seems like she'd be into Greek stuff. Maybe she's Greek? She's always wearing these beads around her neck and arms. Is that a Greek thing? I don't know shit about the Greeks either. I don't know shit about a lot of shit.

I like "Antigone" more than "Not Gone". That's for sure. It has an elegant ring to it.

So I think I'm going to go spend some time with William. This could be a very bad idea. But I don't really have much to lose right now. Most of my future plans include hoping that one of my friends eventually shows up here while I dream about contacting this girl somehow. There's got to be a way. But I spend way less of my time thinking about ways of contacting her than the type of contact. I'll leave the rest to your own imagination.

TWENTY-EIGHT

A coffee house. A table. A cup of coffee opposite a can of orange soda. A grizzled old man opposite a nineteen-year-old boy.

"Nice place," William observed.

"Not bad," Matt concurred.

"Come here often?"

"Never before." He paused. "I don't really *hang out* much."

"Thought that's all kids your age were supposed to do." He coughed loudly, spat into a napkin, and replaced the saliva with his coffee.

"Along with our drugs?" he asked, lips moving just above the lip of the soda can.

William laughed long and quiet. "Don't have to be young to do that. Just stupid."

"So you don't?"

"One of the biggest signs of intelligence," he hung on this, draining the rest of his coffee, "is the ability to admit one's own stupidity."

Fingering the pop-top of the can carefully, confusedly, "I'm not sure that answers--"

"Interpret freely," he interrupted. "Now then, what do you want to learn today?"

"Well," Matt's head tilted, eyes finding the dark sky and accompanying bulbs of contrast. "I was wondering where you live."

"Ah no," he smiled, "no specifics." His visual focus joined Matt's outside the large picture windows of the coffee house.

243

"What do you think *you* would say to me if *I* asked that question? I, a homeless person, one of your disadvantaged not-to-be-trusteds. You can help 'em but don't let 'em have a look at your keys and feel for your wallet every half-minute! Don't wear a watch and make sure that you *ask* all the questions without giving answers! And leave your change in the dish at home unless you plan to throw it, second hand, to the liquor store on the corner. Right?"

"Well, um."

"Maybe *I* have a home. Maybe *I* have a place to hide from all the people throwing help at me." He was pointing a dirty finger at Matt. "I can't lock the door, no, but maybe that makes it all the more important that I don't give out the address! And maybe you don't want to steal my blankets or my shopping cart, but maybe you *do*. Maybe you'll tell the shelters about me so I have to live at the whim of a social worker trying to pad her resume!"

"I uh."

"I asked if there's anything you want to *learn*. Not anything you want to dig up from my interred bones." Matt was studying the veneer on the wood table, wondering whether the dreadful finger had finally descended. "What does a guy have to do to get a refill around here?"

Matt looked up, scanning the edges of the interior. "I think you go over there."

"No waitress?"

"See that sign that says 'Refill Station'?"

The man sighed and utilized a three-step process to rise from his chair. "Thought you said you don't come here."

Matt returned to the veneer. "Don't. Just, these places are all the same."

As William waddled to the Refill Station, Matt had to wonder what he *did* want to learn. Weren't teachers supposed to just share their knowledge, indiscriminately of student interest? Who had ever heard of a class without topic or direction until the *students* spoke up? You have a math professor, and you don't ask him what happened *in* 1550, you ask him if x *equals* 1550. A homeless teacher? You ask him about living on the 1550 block of Main Street *without* a home.

He'd blocked the only discussion that seemed relevant.

William returned, coughing and settling upon sitting down. After a brief time, studied by Matt, "You were at college? Before your... incident."

"Harrison College."

"You study anything?"

"History. Or that was the plan."

William blinked. "No wonder you want *facts*." The coffee burned his tongue and he bolted back from it, spilling some liquid on the veneered table.

Matt made no effort to clean it up. "I dunno. History's as much interpretation as fact. Probably more so. War of 1812: biggest battle that was fought was after the war had actually ended. The mail took a few days to get from Europe to New Orleans. Many died because they didn't have the facts. That's interpretation making history."

"Or just not enough facts." He picked up the cup, making a second attempt at consumption.

"But what do we know about the Battle of New Orleans? Latitude? Longitude? No, we know what firsthand perspectives were on the field. We know what people said of those who died and lived and what wording they used. Who's reliable? Who knows? That's interpretation."

William shook his head ambiguously, and set the cup down, leaving a small ring of coffee outside the larger collected pool. "Ah, the luxury of writing."

"Well without writing there's no history! Writing *creates* history, really."

William sighed deeply. "Not a fan of oral history, I see. Not a believer in the illiterate. I'm surprised you'll even be seen with me."

"Well with oral history, you're just getting the latest interpretation. It's not *old* history, just today's look at something old."

If William had glasses, he would have taken them off and rubbed the bridge of his nose. He probably needed glasses, but had never really bothered to find out, or take action on what would be found. As it was he just blinked again. "Well I guess you don't want to learn."

"Try me."

He looked up hazily. "Fine. I'll tell you about my days as a supermarket manager."

"I thought you said you couldn't read." A last swig of orange soda, and the can rattled upon finding the table again.

"Do you want to hear the story or not?"

Matt sat back in his chair for assent, William slurped some coffee and began. "Like I was saying, I used to manage a supermarket. Nothing fancy, just a little twelve-aisle job with some fresh vegetables on Monday and a long meat fridge in the back with fish on Friday.

"I was in charge of everything for the market. I hired, I fired, I bought, and I sold. With any luck, I sold. If I didn't sell, the head offices would get bitchy, and if they got bitchy enough, I'd be looking for another market." Matt just kept nodding at the right moments. It felt a little like a parental lecture, but he knew that interrupting with so much as a *sure* would prompt possible derailment of the narrative.

"One day, I guess it was a Friday, we get our shipment of fish in. We get it this Friday, but I guess it was meant to come in the Friday before, or maybe a *lot* of Fridays before. Anyway, it's *bad*. Real bad. So this customer opens the fridge and wham, drops the fish on the floor. She sorta moans around a little and then she throws up." Matt really wanted to say something, but he just raised his eyebrows.

"She throws up, right there all over the linoleum. Right on top of the dropped fish. So we've got vomit and bad fish all over the floor. Well nobody wants to clean it up, but some customer comes to me and complains. Actually they tell the sweeper that something should be done, but he just tells the restock boy. And the restock boy tells the fish department guy because, after all, it is in the fish department. And the fish department guy tells the meat girl, because *he*'s only there once a week, and what authority does he have? Well the meat girl comes back and tells one of the checkers, because she's busy dealing with a shipment. And the checker on that aisle tells the checker on the aisle next to her. And she tells her bag boy. And the bag boy goes to the check-out supervisor, and he finally brings the complaint to me."

This sounded to Matt like more than twelve aisles worth of market employees, but he had never really *examined* the number of employees at a market, had he?

"Well, I finally just tell the customer that I'll be happy to have the sweeper clean it up, and would she like some free fish? She tells me not from *this* establishment, and walks out. So I go find the sweeper and tell him that this really is part of his job description to clean it up. So, begrudgingly he does, and I watch him start. Then I go back to my office. But meanwhile, the kid goes and throws up just as he finishes the job. He got the fish out of the way, but he hadn't really gotten the stench of vomit out of his face, so he just upchucks everywhere.

"Then, it becomes more than he can deal with, so he doesn't tell anybody and checks out and goes home. It's about five minutes before another customer comes up and *she* complains to the restock boy, who's putting some better fish in the fridge. The restock boy looks at it, gets a little frustrated, but he goes to the fish guy, and the fish guy yells at the meat girl for not telling anyone about the vomit problem. The meat girl gets upset and say it must be the checker's fault, goes to the checker, who relays it to the other checker, who goes to the bag boy, who comes back to the check-out supervisor, who angrily comes to me. So I go looking for the sweeper so I can chew him out. But I can't find the kid. So I find the restock boy in front of the fish fridge and can't help but notice that the pattern of the vomit looks a little different. Holding my nose, I tell the kid it's his new job to clean up.

"So he does it. But he's only halfway through the job, the weakling, when he adds to it himself. Two big hurls, and now the mess covers about twice as many tiles. Well he goes to the fish guy and says he's too sick to stay, so he bolts without even clocking out. He almost bowls over this customer who's going for the fish, and is a little concerned. And that customer looks behind the kid, and he sees that half the back part of the store is covered with vomit. So he gets a little worried, looks around to see if anyone's on their way with a mop, and then goes up to the fish guy. He's not there to ask about fish, he wants to know if anyone's going to clean up the mess. The fish guy yells at him and says there were two people on the job, but he looks over and sees that it still isn't clean. So he turns his anger at the meat girl, who just isn't making progress through her new shipment. She gets pissed and screams at the checker that the mess is still there. This checker thinks it's hysterical and she has a good laugh with the other checker, which the bag boy overhears and runs off to the check-out supervisor one more time. By this time the check-out supervisor is ready to kick the boy, pretty sure that this is a bad game of telephone. Why would the same message keep coming in? But he comes to me and tells me all this. So I go to the back of the store again, where I'm thinking about camping out, and can't find half my employees.

"So I look at the fish guy and tell him that this *is* his department, so maybe he can take care of this problem. He looks at me long and hard to see if I'm serious, but I am getting *very* serious about this problem, so he hops to it, and he's already looking a little queasy when I leave. I mean, I've finally got trained professionals on it instead of part-time minors. So when another customer walks through the deserted and vomit-covered area, actually stepping in it before she notices, she can't find anyone to tell but the meat girl. She has to ring the bell four times before the meat girl comes out, looks down, looks around, and comes to the front of the store, asking what the *fuck* is going on? The checkers look at each other and the bag boy looks to the office door of the check-out supervisor, who shrugs and knocks on my door. I go back to the meat girl and ask her if she thinks she can handle this problem. And she says sure, since *no one else* can.

"This is a pretty good thing to tell me at this point, so I go back to my office and am practically counting the minutes till someone else knocks on my door. There's only about two customers left in the store, and Friday is usually a big day, but one of them comes up to the check-out counter and says very politely that the meat girl, who he knows pretty well, was just running in the parking lot with what looked like *throw-up* all over apron. So they don't even head back there till I come out of my office again and tell one of them to, or how about this, why don't they work together on it and the bag boy and the check-out supervisor can work together checking people out. Hell, *I'll* come out and be the new check-out supervisor, and there should really be a meeting about this on Monday. But the checkers go back and see half the store covered in vomit, but there's two of them and they get the second mop from the back room. They really just end up swilling the vomit around on the floor before they add to it. The smell is almost wafting up to the front of the store when we hear the emergency exit alarm go off, because they've just set it off by running out the back door.

"Once we shut off the alarm and get the customers back inside, one of them tells the bag boy that he's pretty sure he smells something bad coming from the meat fridge area, and he doesn't want to get any closer. So he goes back there and does quite well cleaning up about two-thirds of it, but when he goes back to the slop bucket and sees *that* filled with the vomit of past cleaners, he fills it the rest of the way himself. He at least has the courtesy of coming up to the supervisor and me to tell us that it's hopeless and we might as well close. Well neither of us will stand for that, and so the supervisor, one of these real no-nonsense guys, says he's never thrown up in his life, so he'll take care of it. I stay behind to check people out. He comes back, dry heaving and spitting, and telling me to close the store. So I do, and he goes home, and I'm alone in this dark store. I figure if I don't *see* the stuff, I can take care of it. So I take a new bucket from one of the aisles, and a new mop from the next shelf over, and address the problem.

"I manage to clean it all up. Every last bit. So finally that problem is behind me. And I'm all proud of myself for taking care of something that wrecked the store. I remember why *I'm* the manager, and next time I'll just take care of this shit my*self.*

"So I'm locking up, double-checking everything, and just as I'm leaving, I throw up all over the automatic door sensor part of the floor.

"I've never thrown up so much in my life. I heave and heave, and there's so much weight from my past meals on this sensor that the damn thing won't *close.* And I'm still queasy, and adding a little to it as I try to get the doors closed again. I didn't know I had *ever* eaten that much. And I'm just hurling and hurling, so I say *fuck it* and leave."

Matt waited for a while, utterly disgusted, surprised by William's intense verbosity, and not sure if the story was over. If it was *ever* over. "So?"

"So," he replied conclusively.

"Did you keep the job?"

William coughed and tipped his empty coffee cup. "You don't see a nametag on me, do you?"

"Excuse me?" said a girl with a nametag, just slightly older than Matt. "We're clearing some tables out for the poetry slam."

Matt got up. "Poetry *slam*?" William inquired.

"Yes, sir, it's uh, every week. We have poets come in and read their poetry for prizes. It's open mic, actually, so if you want to take a *dif*ferent seat..."

William coughed in the girl's face. "Should be leaving anyway," he told Matt. Matt nodded and they made for the glass doors.

On the street, William smiled cryptically at a lightpost. "They had to tear the place down."

"What place?"

"The market. Tore it down. All three bulldozer drivers threw up into the rubble before they were done."

TWENTY-NINE

A lright, so Crazy Billy might be one of the ones that <u>needs</u> help. <u>Mental</u> help.

I hate to go back to calling him that and all, but he isn't leaving me a lot of choice. We met up at this coffee house, actually we went there together after dinner at the kitchen. We had this discussion and he told me this story that was almost entirely about <u>barf</u>. And a past I don't think he really had. Now, I've got a pretty strong stomach, but <u>barf</u>? He was going on about the oral tradition of history, but I didn't know he meant that so literally.

I've been digging around for metaphors, but it reminds me too much of English 101. Which reminds me that Joaquin is finally coming down to visit me next weekend. Damn mentioning time again, but I kinda have to. I'm <u>anticipating</u>, and that's something that someone in my position doesn't get to do very often.

I didn't even find out where William lives! (Sorry - jumping around) But I didn't. It upsets me. How am I supposed to relate to the homeless if they don't even tell me where, well, they <u>don't</u> have their homes! This leaves me very little to go on. Not that I want really to know where William lives, but it'd be useful. Does that make sense? Doubtful, huh?

Alright, the point is just that I want to really <u>see</u> what these people are putting up with. How bad is it? Maybe that's what William wanted me to learn, but he sure doesn't make it easy if it is. More likely, he's just another crazy bastard with problems and smells and maybe even diseases. But he can weave a good story. Okay, not a good story, but a good weaving. It's like a really

251

perfectly done tapestry, but the picture <u>on</u> the tapestry is disaster. The fabric's nice and the colors sparkle, and the weaving is immaculate, but the result is undone by the image. I mean, he's got this kinda poetic style that surprises you coming out of a half-dead body. But at the same time, he is just talking about barf.

Isn't he?

So I'm looking forward to seeing my friend Joaquin. Joaquin told me not to go to Philadelphia and I was pretty sure that meant he'd <u>never</u> come to Philadelphia after what happened. But hey, it's reunion days around here! Woohoo! So my friend will come see this place my parents bought and maybe he can even sneak in a TV. Nobody's watching, right? I've even thought about getting a job somewhere around here, but I really don't have time. I can work when I pay my debt to the state. Till then I'll work off debt.

Some people have credit card debts, right? Or other things that aren't really doing something <u>wrong</u> so much as kinda fucking up. I mean, they aren't <u>bad</u>, they're just dumb. Not dumb, really, just, you know, didn't think ahead. Like me. I'm not the only one. So they work hard for nothing. Some of them must end up getting meals from me. <u>Those</u> are the ones that earn it. Right? I mean, what if they were tricked into having debts? Somebody scammed 'em? Then they weren't stupid, they just <u>trusted</u>. Are you going to tell me to call people who trust the bad people?

Or what if you end up in a gang because of that? Or doing crack? Or pointing a gun or something? Then you're just in the wrong place at the wrong time, maybe with real wrong people. But that doesn't make you wrong. That makes you human.

And so by that standard, I'm pretty lucky to be on the outside, just working. Not in prison, not getting raped, not having all sorts of terrible things happen. Appreciation. That's what I need. Some good old <u>appreciation</u>.

I'm going to list the things I appreciate. This'll be good.

1) Not being raped.
2) Not being in jail.
3) Having a home.
4) Joaquin (coming to visit).
5) The prettiest girl in the world.
6) Anticipation (daily and long-term).
7) Not being sick.

Okay, so it doesn't look like much just there, but it's good for me to go through. So Thanksgiving isn't for another eight months or something (more time references, bad me), but at least I can be appreciative. Because that's what all this work has really done for me. I now see that I don't have it so bad. I was bored, but bored is just another word for not fucked-up. Being comfortable is boring. But it's also <u>comfortable</u>!

Now I'm bored, but it's different kind of bored. It's more appreciative bored. Which is about the same, but now I have this work to do and things to look forward to. And the prettiest girl in the world, who has been looking a little sad of late. Maybe it's just the glint in the sun or something, but I swear she's not doing too well.

Maybe she's just bored? Or running out of things to anticipate? I could give her something to anticipate...

Christ, I'm sounding like <u>Oliver</u> now. Oliver! Talk about someone I never want to see again...

It's kinda fun for me to sit around and think about the prettiest girl in the world (henceforth, just for fun, Antigone) and wonder what she's really like or what she does. Just make stuff up, try it out, see where it goes. Very few of these roads really lead to me meeting her, but then I get thinking about destiny and shit. That makes me happy, I guess, but again, what does the prettiest girl in the world say to <u>me</u>? She must know how she looks. Why would she be sad? How could she <u>ever</u> be sad?

So there's fate and there's making things happen. Is me ending up here fate? I've talked about this before (I really come back to very few topics, I guess), but I made this happen. And it was fate. Or neither. I don't know. Clearly, I haven't figured <u>that</u> out.

But how can I make things happen with Antigone? Can't just throw something down in a paper airplane. I almost tried jumping up and down the other day, but that's nothing. It's not like she ever ever ever sees me. Not one sighting. She's always so focused on the road. Or on singing along. She sings sometimes. Almost enough to make me call up David and tell him to tell me about some tunes. Can he lip-read? Does he know all the music? Please God tell me that Antigone isn't listening to Magical Mystery Tour.

<u>Almost</u>.

Antigone just <u>sounds</u> like someone out of my league, doesn't it? Antigone and <u>Matt</u>? Antigone belongs with someone like Claudius or at the very least Alexander. Something regal. I'm just

Matt. Who wants that?

But I see her and see her and I can't stop thinking about her. It's like that other Greek thing. By Homer. I could start calling the girl Helen. Gets the same point across. But that never made sense to me. <u>Helen</u> is the name that your 99-year-old great aunt's dog has. That's not a beautiful name. Helen's just clunky. I mean, Helen Hunt has her moments, but you never think of her as <u>Helen</u>. Maybe it's the hell thing. Antigone's different.

So now I get back into this love stuff and I start wondering how I know if I'm in love. This isn't something I'm great about. I remember one of the few decent conversations I had with David about all this, and he said something about graffiti. Antigone looks more like the kind of kid to <u>clean</u> <u>it</u> <u>up</u> than to be flattered. But you never know, I guess.

Christ, I'm just a one-track stuck record.

At least it <u>isn't</u> Magical Mystery Tour. Sometimes I'll be falling asleep and tired as hell from the day at work and trying to think about Antigone and all I can do is hear some song from that goddam CD. So many of those songs are so repetitive. I mean, if it's "Baby You're a Rich Man" or something, forget sleep. It should be like counting sheep, but that never really worked for me. It's more like counting seconds, realizing each second that you've stayed up for another one. The more you get caught up on time, the more it's <u>there</u>. And then it starts to own you. That's not what I'm here for.

But maybe it already owns me. I've got to be at work at a time, then to the overpass at a time, then to work again, and it all starts over. I have my weekends, but there's nothing to do but write in this thing. And go to the library. I've started doing that, because there's no TV and nothing in my house but the little food I get on my parent's allowance. It's like they know that if I think I can eat okay, I'll go get a TV and this will send me back to drugs. Or I'll get <u>drugs</u>! I swear, you make one wrong turn...

So, yeah, the library. There's stuff to do there. Maybe I'll look up Antigone, see if I can find any clues. Like if the guy she marries is named Matt.

Look, I don't get many jokes in here, okay? I'm trying. Can't be a smartass when you're working all day for people who never get a break in life. They'll go crazy on you, or pull out religion and the hypocrites, or something like that. Or the worst, the little kids or something, or the mothers, they'll just tear up and kinda turn their head away and you know you've done it then. So I have to keep it here, and I'm way out of practice.

The mothers. Those are the people I feel bad for. I mean, I know <u>everybody</u> feels bad for mothers, but it's like how do you show a kid the ropes when you've got no ropes to hang on to? The kid screams cuz it's hungry and then the mom joins in. That's not a way to live. I mean, I'm not saying I was raised in the model environment. But you don't grow up thinking that food is something great. You grow up thinking the latest computer is something great. And then, when you don't have that, and you see what people who don't have food do, you're just like well shit. How'd that happen? How'd I get what I got and they got nothing?

Fate or making it happen? I can tell you this, the kids didn't make <u>anything</u> happen.

We just cry.

THIRTY

They shook hands on the steps of Matt's apartment building.

"Good to see you. When'd you get the car?"

"Toni got it at semester. When I told her I wanted to see you, she let me have it for the weekend." Matt immediately tried not to be bitter at her only sending her *car*.

"How's she doing?"

"Fine. Needs the car for art shows. And after graduation. Early present from the parents."

Matt nodded reflectively. "Thought you might come in by bus or something."

"Would've brought *Corndog*'s car before doing that." Matt was unamused. "Kidd*ing*. This place have an inside?"

"Not much of one. But sure." They went upstairs, and it was striking to be with Joaquin, and to hear the footsteps on stairs, and to remember. "So how's school?"

"Same's always." Joaquin looked up the stairs. "I mean, we miss you. But nothing else's changed."

They reached the second-highest floor and Matt pushed his unlocked door open. "Like I said, it's not much."

"Roommate?"

"Nope."

"Then it's a whole lot." Joaquin grinned. "Maybe you aren't the *total* moron I thought you were."

"Gee thanks."

"Seriously. You saw me on your way out the door." Joaquin rubbed his chin. "Thought I was never going to see you again."

Matt sighed.

"Moron," he was only half-joking.

The phone rang. Joaquin started at this rebuttal to his insult.

"Who the hell is calling *me*?" Matt looked around. "*You're* already *here*!"

"Parents?"

The phone rang. "They never call. Except to bug me once a month to make sure I haven't been evicted."

"You gonna get it?"

He picked it up. "Hello?"

"Good afternoon, sir, how are you today?"

Sir? "Fine, who is this?"

"Well, this is Brett from Working Without Wires. I'm calling to tell you about a very special offer from your friends here at Working Without Wires."

"Um."

"We've actually tried calling you earlier, but you must work nights. We don't often call people on the weekends, but we've made a special exception for you."

"Uh, okay."

"Do you have a cell phone, sir?"

"Uh, well, I'm kinda working without *cash*."

"That's okay! Working Without Wires is perfectly willing to work with a number of credit plans."

"Okay, by 'cash' I mean anything that could possibly be mistaken for money."

"Well--"

"I don't think I'm interested. Good bye." He hung up. "Figures the only call I get would be from a damn telemarketer!"

"You shoulda hung up earlier. Sounded like he had you going for a minute."

Matt shook his head, then said "Problem with telemarketers," Joaquin shrugged, "they need to *sell* things. That means moolah that I don't have."

"Nothing they could sell you?"

Matt took no time to think. "A TV. If it was less than ten bucks."

"Huh." An awkward silence, from the pure untenability of spending as many months without seeing each other as they had known each other in the first place. "So what do you do for fun around here?"

257

"Fun?"

"Well you're not in jail."

This *did* take time to think. "Well the *most* fun is going down to the overpass." He looked out the window, as though he could just see the green Volvo in the distance. "But it's Saturday."

"What?"

"It's Saturday. So she won't be there."

"*She?*"

"Ah, right. See, I've been writing a bit in this diary and I talk about her all the time. Since I don't really *talk* to people, I guess I just..." he ran out of words and scratched the back of his neck, returning to the window.

"Hm, that might be a good read."

"That's *too bad*." He did a quick look around the room to make sure he hadn't left it out in a glaringly obvious place. "Anyway, it's the prettiest girl in the world. That's the she."

"How can you say something like that?"

"Because it's true." The words and tone were definitive, rock-solid.

Another pause. "So she hangs out at this, *overpass*? On weekdays?"

"She drives under. Lunch rush. Traffic's always slow, so you can get a good look. She's just beautiful, that's all. Worth getting that look."

"You do this a lot, huh?"

"Every day." He looked down from the window. "'Cept the weekend."

"She's never there?"

"Wellll," looking up again, "I've never *check*ed."

"You *are* a moron, aren't you?"

"But it's past noon. And who has seven days of school?"

"How do you know she's driving to school?"

"Wellll..."

"C'mon, I've got my car out front."

"We'll walk. No place to park it on the overpass." He looked around for his jean jacket. "Besides, I walk there every day."

The route to the overpass led them past the shelter, which was cleaned by someone else on weekends. Someone who wasn't on probation and had a job during the week and only a few hours left to fill. Matt had never seen the person, but he figured they were guilty of whatever crime they'd been charged with. Maybe that was an unreasonable expectation.

"That's one of my jobs," he pointed.

"Whatchya do there?"

"Cleanup. They kick everyone out in the mornings so I can pick up their shit."

Joaquin looked across the run-down neighborhood. "Sounds like you really respect these people."

"It's hard to know," Matt was defensive, "*who* to respect."

"Sounds like college."

"How so?"

"Oh, y'know," Joaquin laughed lightly, then covered it with a clearing of his throat. "Just is. This the overpass?"

"No, it's the drawbridge. For the moat."

"Well I didn't know if it was, y'know, *the* overpass."

Matt nodded and surveyed the fast-moving traffic. "Couldn't see her anyway. At these speeds."

Nevertheless, they wandered over to the center of the overpass and stared down. Matt folded his hands and carefully examined the distance for glints of green. Shielding his eyes, Joaquin joined him in the westward search, then ducked his head to stare straight down. A while passed.

"I feel," Joaquin began. Then, "I feel like we should have fishing poles or something."

That's it! "Fishing poles!" Matt exclaimed, amazed at his lack of prior forethought.

Joaquin mistook the response for incredulity. "Yeah, y'know. Like those guys on real bridges. They stand up there all day and try to haul in the only fish that have survived some urban river. And I mean, this ain't a river, but it kinda *feels* like it, huh?"

But what's the *bait*? Matt sounded distant, "Yeah, I know. I get it."

"What'd you catch here, I wonder?"

Matt was awed, "The prettiest girl in the world."

"Ah yes," Joaquin chuckled "how could I forget?" Then, unable to resist, "She, uh, into worms these days? Or you gotta use flies for her?"

Matt turned on his friend. "What do *you* think?"

"Me?"

"Poems? Prose?" Eyes blazing back to the carstream, "A card?"

Joaquin shook his head, and muttered "A Hallmark Highway

259

moment," which broke the spell a bit.

Matt, just dulled, "Okay. Not a card."

"What're you looking for? Her jumping ship from her car and being pulled up to your waiting arms?"

The idea was captivating, but "No, just, well, *con*tact." He watched a semi truck pass under the overpass, mildly surprised (in the back of his mind) that it made it under. It seemed he could walk out onto it from where he stood. "I guess a phone number would help."

"You do something like that and she'll be curious enough to call." Joaquin pondered the filth around him which, once noted, suddenly piled up in all directions. What looked dark was dirt. "Or too scared to."

"Gotta show her that I'm, well, not a stalker."

It took a minute before Joaquin started laughing. Once he got going, though, it took a while to stop. Upon stopping, "But that's exactly what you *are*!"

Matt went from downtrodden to offended. "Not so. I may look from afar, but I stay planted where I am." He felt the rant building, like the plaintive courtroom appeal he was never able to deliver. "I *have* to be on this overpass every day! No way to get from job to job otherwise. Not my fault if I stop to smell the *ro*ses. Do I follow her home? No! Do I try to acquire a car, or taxi, or hitch a ride with a trucker, in order to follow her? No! Have I found any information about her? No! Even though I have her license plate, have I used this to track down a phone number or address? *No*!!"

"You have her plate?"

Matt shrugged. "Yeah. N-T-G-O-N-E. Illin*ois*."

"Antigone?"

"*May*be. Hey, how'd you get that so fast?"

"*You* said it."

Matt mouthed the letters to himself, nodding at the distinctive sound. Then he saw a blue Volvo out of the corner of his eye and almost fell over the cement and into the highway. Catching his breath, he was unsure whether he was more nervous over thinking that he might have seen her car or the slim risk of falling over the edge.

"You okay?"

"Thought I saw her."

"Do me a favor and don't jump on her car dire*ct*ly, 'kay?"

"You got it."

Some more time faded, with more flowing cars and the slow progress of the sun into their eyes.

"You ever go down to their level?"

"Whaddya mean?"

"*Under.*"

"How?"

"Well, there's an onramp, right? Just follow that."

"Into the road?"

"There should be a shoulder."

Matt shrugged and started hiking in that direction, toward the soup kitchen. There wasn't much room to walk down the onramp, but the traffic was as thin as it was speedy. Once on the highway shoulder, Joaquin wandered under the onramp, urging Matt to follow him to the overpass' underside. Once there, both were taken aback by the presence of other pedestrians.

They walked to the center of the cold darkness of the underpass and scanned the ramp-shaped structure which led all the way up to a steel-beamed ceiling. Most of the people around them (there were three or perhaps four, mostly pacing or sitting) were sullen and gave them a wide berth. Matt looked to the road, realized that the view of the cars was infinitely poorer than from above and then jumped a foot at the sound of a familiar voice.

"So, couldn't keep away, huh?" The voice was increasing in volume, and he turned to face it. "I guess there's no secrets from America's youth. Found me. Happy?"

"Hi William."

"Who's this kid?"

Joaquin was keeping out of this. "Um, this is my friend Joaquin, from school. My old school. And, uh, Joaquin, this is William. He's one of my, well, uh, he goes to the kitchen." Getting a disappointed look from the old man he added, "And we hung out, once..." He trailed off to the unsettling sound of whirring cars behind him.

Joaquin shook William's grimy hand slowly, regretting the polite decision as it was in progress. "Nicetomeetyou," he mumbled.

"And you too. So Matt here put you up to this? Had me trailed or something?"

"Uh, no, actually it was my idea to come down here."

"We didn't know you were here!" Matt added.

"Just a lucky guess?" William seemed skeptical, but examined the roadway, the shadowy structure of the highway, and slowly nodded. "Well, it's pretty obvious, really. Lots of us live here. Cold in summer, warm in winter. Hidden. Until now."

"Mmm" wandered out of both the younger guys' mouths.

"Hey," he turned brightly to Joaquin, "you want to hear about my days as a supermarket manager?"

Matt thumped Joaquin in the back, not very subtly. "Uh, well, we were just passing through. Really should go."

"You just *got* here!"

"True. But, uh, Joaquin has to go home." The spoken-for nodded dumbly.

"Well, suit yourself. But come back sometime. You bother to *find* me, you may as well be my *guest*."

"Sure thing." They were already walking away, the opposite way from whence they came. Slowly, turning around to face the overpass once out of earshot, "He's crazy. They call him Crazy Billy back at the kitchen."

"Seemed nice enough to me. A little, *dirty*." Joaquin shrugged. "But given the *con*text."

Joaquin had not turned with Matt, but was now prompted to. "How would you get up there?"

"Up *there*?"

"To write something."

Joaquin examined the overpass carefully, first the exit signs on the far right side, then the blankness of cement just beneath where they'd been standing. "You mean graffiti?"

"Well, yeah."

"I'd probably just lean over and write upside-down."

"Someone once told me that love was graffiti on an overpass." Matt was trying hard to forget that it was *David* who'd said this, in a strange fit of rationality.

"Was that person by any chance," Joaquin looked down to attempt eye-contact with his friend, "in the spray-paint business?"

THIRTY-ONE

I am a man with a plan.

Through a series of discoveries and careful planning, I have crafted a plan. A plan. The very idea shakes me to my core.

I know I'm talking all dramatically, and this is probably of no real consequence, but it feels like consequence right now. Consequential. That's how I feel. And I have the direction that only a plan can give somebody. It's like having a new lease on life.

Incidentally, Joaquin almost became the first reader of this. Imagine! That would not have been great. I mean, if anyone actually close to me reads this, I'm going to be in trouble. Aren't I? I speak the way I feel about people in this. And I keep seeing this as talking instead of writing. I can't help it. There's no one to talk to. But Joaquin was here to talk to for a while, and I ended up losing sight of the difference between him and you. Not really, but you know what I mean. It was like you've been the target audience, so I kept having to fill him in on things. Not everything. But things.

But he had a great idea that I didn't give him. Fishing poles.

I can hear all the jokes now. Nice catch. Gone fishing. Get it? Gone finishing. Not gone fishing. Though I guess it really is Antigone. If you say it out loud, it sounds an awful lot like Antigone. So there you are. Lots of jokes. Reeling her in. But that's exactly the plan.

The plan.

I was going on about appreciation and anticipation, but now

263

it's all accelerated. It's gotten to the point where I act now or spend the rest of my life wondering what-if. What if I had taken action? I have enough regrets in this lifetime already. I'm tired of regretting things. Action is the key to getting around regrets. And if there's <u>anything</u> to <u>act</u> on, it's the prettiest girl in the world.

Put it this way, it <u>better</u> be Antigone. Because that's going to be immortalized in stone. Or cement, I guess. Close enough.

The only conversation I can remember really making sense with David was about love and writing someone's name on an overpass. Writing a name so the heart just dips into either end of the names. The fringes of each name being consumed by the heart. David and I disagreed (<u>surprise!</u>) about where the heart should be, but he was wrong. It should just take up the last part of the first name and the first part of the last name. So I'll have a T and an A swimming in the heart, with the names on both sides.

If she's not Antigone, it's not going to be good.

But if she is, then she'll see the graffiti as art, a permanent art on the overpass she passes five days a week. What could be more <u>romantic</u> than that? She won't know me, necessarily, unless she's somehow seen me all along. But I'd know, wouldn't I?

So then I'll be there, with a fishing pole, ready to hand down my phone number. And maybe a poem. I should try to write the poem. Something catchy. Something, maybe, about admiration from afar. <u>Secrets</u> <u>no</u> <u>longer</u>. That's a line I like. It's so hard to write a poem without sounding cliche.

But at least I'm getting in my writing practice. Right?

Stream-of-consciousness has got to help with poems. I hope.

So a fishing pole, thank you Joaquin, is the answer. Maybe she'll come back and drive through. Or maybe I can dangle the line as she passes under, the first time she sees it. It can't all miss her attention. There's a way to make this work. I'll find it.

Will she be mine? Who knows? But I must admit that even the prettiest girl in the world doesn't see her name on a highway all the time. I had to borrow money from Joaquin to buy a pole and three colors of spray paint. All the colors have got to help the message get across. This is going to be <u>perfect</u>.

And perfect is the only way I don't spend the rest of my life asking myself what-if. The only way I can move on, one way or the other. Which I need right now.

The sacrifice of not buying a TV with Joaquin's money was huge. You don't even know. But why spend the rest of my life admiring women on TV when I could've had the best one with spray paint and a fishing pole?

I even thought about getting the paint, but not the pole, and just tacking on my phone number to the graffiti. It wasn't until I talked to William (who won't leave me alone now that I found out where he lives, which is under the overpass!) about it and he pointed out that the cops wouldn't take too kindly to my claim of responsibility. I didn't even realize for a long while that this is a crime! I mean, it's called graffiti, which I don't like calling it, but that's what it is. But now that I think about it, that's my probation on top of everything. That would be a problem. So as artistic and immortal as I may see it, it's really just another crime I don't want tacked on my record.

Actually, it's not even another crime. It's the first crime. So I guess I'm due to get away with some crimes at this point right? It's in the name of love, anyway. Hell.

Besides, the last thing I need is more lousy telemarketers calling me. First phone call ever not from Joaquin or my parents, and it's some damn cell phone company. I don't understand how they just call everybody. I mean, they should do some background check. Don't tell me they don't have the information. Someone who lives where I do doesn't have the cash for a cell phone.

Unless they're a drug dealer.

A real drug dealer.

What if this all works out? Maybe you're Antigone reading this! Holy shit. That would be the coolest thing ever. Think about it. A romantic approach. But if this works out, do I burn this thing immediately? Probably. It's nothing but insecurity and crap. Insecurity walks out the door the day that Antigone walks in. I mean, just being in her presence without her ignoring me would be enough. And after doing something this gutsy, I've gotta be doing better, right?

So maybe I keep this for amusement. I mean, Antigone, I love you. I'm about to write it for the whole world to see. How can you think this much about someone before you meet and not love them? I'm out of other possibilities. And if you're reading this, I certainly love you! So there you have it. Just see this as an early testimony to what I've always known. And maybe you've known it too. A soulmate, out there from the beginning. And all this had to happen just to make that work.

William hasn't given me a religion speech, but I get this

265

feeling it's in him. If it is, I bet anything he'd be happy to see what I just wrote. Wow. It's like I'm believing all of it too. What's Antigone's stand on religion?

What's Antigone's stand on my looks? Why do I have to keep coming back to that?

It's funny too, because if I didn't have all this to think about, I might just be taking a second look at this friend of Sam's who has been coming in. I don't really know what her deal is, but she goes to UPenn with Sam and is our age and all. She's really cute, but doesn't have a whole lot to say.

What if Antigone doesn't have a whole lot to say?

You see all this what-if I have to get rid of?

If Antigone doesn't have much to say, then it's this country. I was thinking that the other day. What about all this comfort? It's the same here as school and Kansas. Not exactly, but remarkably close to being exactly. I know that didn't make any sense, but do you see? It's the comfort thing. The comfort and the boredom. They're so similar. And I thought it was Kansas. If you grew up in Topeka, you'd think so too.

But maybe it's not. Maybe it's America. I can't believe it's the world, because everything I see today is like a whole society in other countries. That's what history tells us. America's consolidated the money better than anyone. It's great for us, at least, but has it made us a nation of the bored? The quietly damned. Waiting for the excitement of starvation and crime and graffiti on an overpass.

So Antigone might be boring. And I'd marry her anyway. I know that. Because look at her! But then I'd have to burn this (look at what I just wrote!) and maybe we'd both move to another country.

If we had any money. I need to get back to school.

The future brings enough worries to keep me from being bored.

Christ, I don't know. I don't know. At all. Any of it. But I stay up nights now, thinking about this poem. And the pole and the paint. The cans are in my kitchen, waiting. There's green and red and blue. I thought it had to be colorful. And we need the green because of her car. And we need the blue to stand out. I think the letters of her name will be green, and mine blue, and the heart red. And I have to outline the heart. And I have this bad feeling that none of this will come out anything like I want it to because I'll be so rushed as I commit a crime. I'm trying to feel out William for keeping watch because he lives under that overpass.

He lives under that overpass! I was going to talk about this, but it's just such a surprise. And it seems so much less than the other things lately. When Joaquin was over (I'm giving up on my time resistance, sorta), we ran into him looking for Antigone. We were looking for her, not him. Yeah. So we saw this whole colony of homeless under the overpass. Unreal. I guess they don't like the shelter, but they stay close just in case. Or close to the kitchen. But under an overpass! It's like everything coming together. I can't imagine living there.

I thought they all lived in boxes or the shelter. It's insane.

So maybe William and a friend of his (does he have friends? Sounds weird to say roommate) can keep watch at first while I do what I do. It's gotta be the middle of the night. And a weekend, because otherwise I'll lose a day or two of work. Then I'll come back later with the pole and the poem. Or at least the number. No one can spray paint in broad daylight.

And, yeah, it's risky. But what's love without risk?

God, I'm nervous just writing about it. Just thinking about it. But there's nothing else to think about. Sam's friend Alberta doesn't even look good to me anymore. There's just one in my vision. And seeing her today, knowing that she doesn't know but she's about to just made me go crazy. I wanted to yell, to jump, to do something to say "Hey soulmate! Over here!"

But she just drove along in her beads and her tie dye T-shirt like she was born thirty years too late.

Hell, even if she likes Magical Mystery Tour, I can handle it. I'm starting to see something in the Fool on the Hill, maybe. It's all this religion around me, just hovering, I feel like it's waiting. Things make too much sense to me. It's all coming together. I don't know if I see the point in destiny, but hey, if it works like this, I guess I'll take it. Christ. Literally.

No wonder David thinks religion is what you find at first. I'm not going all crazy religious, but there seems to be order. I'll leave it at that. And I really see myself as a fool on the overpass. I mean, I'm not Jesus. Christ. But really, I feel like I'm on the verge of something here. I'm about to crack life wide open. And so what if I'm on probation? That's just a record. I can go anywhere.

I sit with my paint and my pole and I try to write the poem. I started reading <u>Antigone</u> (the play) for inspiration, but it's really not in the direction I want to go. I mean, there's not much romantic to go on. It's almost anti-romantic. I just don't know.

At least I have a phone number. And a pole. And paint. It's coming.

MATT (heart) ANTIGONE.

I could play it safe and write NTGONE, but that's not romantic.

Every day, I'm there, thinking. Maybe she'll just look up, just once, just to see what's coming.

THIRTY-TWO

M att on turkey. He passes the tray to Sam, on mashed potatoes. He sends it to Alberta, on gravy.

"Thanksgiving in March," Sam commented. "I guess these people have to be thankful year round."

This resonated with Matt. "Less you have, more important that you appreciate, right?"

"Wow," said Alberta, a little absently.

"I would think," Sam paused, almost missing a scoop of potatoes, "it should work the other way."

"Huh," Alberta contributed, pouring gravy over a roll as well.

"It *should*, maybe," Matt agreed, "but it doesn't."

The clatter of trays. The smile of the homeless. A hello from William for the lineup. A wink specifically for the man behind the turkey.

"Hey, it's Friday night tonight," Sam observed after a while.

"Yup," Alberta concurred.

"It's always Friday when you're here," Matt still wondered at how much less Sam did than he. Understandably, but still. It just didn't seem like they *really* worked together, somehow.

"True."

"So?"

"Well, you keep saying you'll come hang out with us, Matt. And I thought tomorrow night would be great. I know you work tonight. But tomorrow, we could go over to Starbucks."

"You just mentioned *Starbucks* in this place?" Matt found this clearly incongruent.

"Well, y'see, uh, Alberta's *friend*,"

"My *girl*friend!"

Matt raised his eyebrows. "Right, her girlfriend, works there. And has to work Saturdays. So I thought we could all go hang out. It'd be fun. You could see a different side of Philly. Maybe even hit a party back at UPenn." Matt pondered the words, observing the turkey's texture carefully. "Whaddya say?"

Then the ton of bricks hit him. Or the cement, perhaps. "Oh. Can't."

"Huh?"

"Sorry. I actually have something else to do."

"Something *else*?"

"Yeah, it's really important."

"Is this about that *girl*?"

"Uh, no. It's just important."

Alberta and Sam sighed, giving up. "Okay," Sam added resignedly, "it's your life."

THIRTY-THREE

I have to keep my resolve. Must maintain resolve. Life will try to get in the way. But I will persist.

Time stops tonight. Time is relevant again, but then never again.

The relevant time is the day and a half between now and then. The paint and the pole.

Good thing this is a bad neighborhood, or it'd be gone in that time.

Now is relevant. And thirty-six hours that will almost kill me.

But I must keep my resolve.

<u>Resolve</u>.

Wish me luck!

THIRTY-FOUR

A ntigone was no more fond of Monday mornings than anyone else she knew. But with her new routine, and the weeks stretching out like overblown years, she felt that every Monday morning required her to feel frantically at her wrist for a pulse. The faint reflective beat always surprised her a little. A jump start for the day.

It was the *dreading* Monday that was worse than Monday. Her morning was really an early afternoon, but she was still getting up with Betsy's cacophonous air-raid alarm. And Mondays were terrible, because Betsy was always mooning about the end of her weekend and how blissful Sunday had been. And now even Sunday bliss was fading in the dulling light of her relationship with that vacuous college girl. Antigone had taken a part-time job on Sundays just to be out of the house when Alberta was over. They'd get together every Saturday, stay in, sleep late, wake up, and start fighting. And their fights were endlessly inane, punctuated by backhanded compliments that Antigone felt she could see right through.

Where was *her* vacuous but hot college kid to play around with?

But she didn't want that. More than that, she still wanted Martin Arthur Tucker. They were becoming friends, and Antigone earnestly didn't know whether to push the friendship more so that they could become *close*, or keep away from the friendship so they wouldn't get *too close*. The specter of too close was looming, she knew, and it drove her nuts as she dreaded the Monday morning to come. And her lousy job, which was actually *waitressing* on Sunday afternoon and night. She could barely bear the thought of it.

To think, she thought, that she had taken this job to minimize dread. And now it was piling up on her. She checked the scenery. The familiar traffic, familiar overpasses, and--

What had she just seen?

That couldn't be. It came, like a vision from one of her pages and pages of carefully saved scrap paper. Thousands of potential customers had gotten just a little less attention because Antigone shared a heart with MAT. And all would have been so right with the world.

Surely her mind, from so much strain and boredom, and use of scrap paper had *imprinted* it on the overpass!

But no, those *colors*! Blue and red and *green*!

And the *order*!

The order!

MAT loves ANTIGONE. She was sure of it. With a big heart in the middle to signify the love.

Should she go back and check? "No, no, no!" Her eyes were barely on the road. "I have to take action *now*! Even if I made it all up, it's a *sign*! God has sent me a sign. This is all the karma. This is everything. Breathe, Antigone, breathe. I can't believe it, but I *can't* check. No way." She fumbled for her cell phone, a free perk of her job and the incredible sales to go with it. Rick never called this one.

The number had been on speed-dial for months. The rings were eternity, passing in the beat of her pulse which no longer required monitoring.

"Hello?"

"Martin? Oh, Martin, I'm so glad you're there!"

"Is this, uh, Antigone?"

"Yes, Martin! Yes it is!"

"Well hi. What's up?"

"What's up? What's *up*?! Martin, we've become awfully close lately, haven't we?"

"I suppose. I mean, you've been very good for the company."

"The *company*? Martin, this has nothing to do with that damn company! Just listen to me for a minute, Martin. I believe, I've always believed, that somewhere out there, waiting for me, is a match for my soul. A true soulmate. Someone who *knows* me.

Storey Clayton

Who *understands*. Who I barely have to talk to because they see me. I've spoken to this person, whenever I talk to myself, I'm talking to them. I pray every day for this person. I hope all the time. And Martin, I just saw something, something that has shown me the *way*." *I'm not making sense*, she knew, but who can *blame* me at this point? "Martin, let's have dinner tonight. I want to see you. *See* you."

"Uh." There was a long dead pause. "Don't you work on Sundays now? I thought you said some--"

"No! Just quit. Because of this feeling. It's the most important thing in my life right now that you have dinner with me." And that, she knew, was probably the *dumbest* thing that she'd ever said in her life. But this was a *sign*! "Please, Martin, even if I'm just exaggerating, *please* have dinner with me."

Another suffocating staticky pause. "Is this a date?" The voice sounded neither hopeful nor dreading. It was even-keel.

"If you want it to be."

Antigone was beginning to hate silence more than anything in her life. "Why don't we meet at that Italian place by work."

"I'll be waiting for you."

"What time?"

"I said I'll be *waiting*." And she hung up. There was no more dealing with the silence.

To fill her own silence that consumed the car inside-out, she began talking to herself. Her attention was scattered, her mind going numb and her lungs hyperventilating. "Okay, okay, just breathe. This is going to be the best day ever. Don't call work. Just no-show. It's okay. God dammit, you better be right about this one. This better work. But it's perfect. He wrote that, the bastard, he wrote it, or had a friend do it, and he's just playing hard-to-get. Or God wrote it for me, somehow. I don't know how, but it's meant for me and it's going to happen. There's a chance. Oh Buddha, just give me a chance. That's all I want. That's all I…"

The sentence was never completed. She looked up, holding on the "I" syllable as she hit the brakes. She was in time. But the car behind her was not. It rammed into her, throwing her car into the stopped double-trailer truck in front of her. She went through the windshield and was killed almost instantly.

The driver behind her, still talking into his cell phone, which had been knocked out of his hand by the airbag, saw none of what happened. He did vaguely wonder why the brake-light ahead that he'd been watching had not lit up.

The truck driver got out of his truck, walked behind it slowly, saw the remains of the Volvo and its driver, and threw up on the roadway.

THIRTY-FIVE

I haven't written for almost a week now, because every time I try, I start crying. There's reactions I could've expected to this, but her disappearing was not one of them.

I'll start over.

She disappeared.

<u>Gone</u>.

It's like some sort of sick joke on me that I take action just one day too late. It's the earliest I could've, but every day I'm out there with my pole, there's no green Volvo. I was late to the kitchen three days in a row because I waited an extra half-hour for the prettiest girl in the world. Maybe she went back to Illinois. Maybe it's her school's spring break. I can still hold out hope. But I think the graffiti cleanup crew will be coming any day to take away my work of romantic artistic genius and I'll be alone.

Christ, what have I done?

Whatever it was, it was a day too late. She was there on Friday. And Monday, gone.

Time matters again. How painfully time matters again.

I even wrote this poem, though I can't even look at the words without crying now. I never cry. Now I'm a leaky faucet of life. I can't face the words I've written in the past, can't face my history, can't face any of it. Everything was in place to make this work, but it falls apart. Just one day.

One day.

The what-ifs are consuming me raw.

<u>WHAT IF</u>?

Maybe just another job. Or just another place. Or back home

for good. I can't know.

I hope wherever she is, she's happy.

I am out of things to say. There's nothing left to say. Everything I could talk about comes back to her. Everything. I am bad luck incarnate. I have lost the prettiest girl in the world.

Alberta has disappeared, too. Sam says she's distraught about breaking up with her girlfriend. Her girlfriend was a psycho, she says. At least Sam knows where Alberta is.

I don't know where Antigone is. Where'd she go?

I give up.

This is not comfortable.

This is not boring.

I don't want to remember.

I don't want history.

I need to replace all that spray paint with whitewash, leaving it all behind, cleaning it all up.

Give me amnesia or give me death.

THIRTY-SIX

I t was a warm June in Philadelphia, a relief after one of the harsher winters of recent years. The city was celebrating its basketball franchise's first trip to the NBA Finals in many years. Denizens had united behind the small victories, claiming a moral success amidst the weight of being crushed by the country's newest sports juggernaut.

People dined on open-air patios downtown, dropping generous helpings of change into panhandler's cups. Stale cardboard boxes, soaked and redried over grates throughout winter, could finally be discarded. Hope was renewed in the hearts of many of the poorer quarters, inspired by prosperity in the city, and word of a tax-cut that might lead to increased donations to charity organizations. They tried not to focus on the corresponding possibility of cutbacks on the government-sponsored charities.

Matthew Norton and a guy that no one knew by any name other than Crazy Billy walked down one of these streets, approaching the downtown. Dusk was settling. The skyline, from its base, seemed powerful and triumphant in the face of the light's recession.

Stepping out of the shadows, an old acquaintance of Crazy Billy's, whom he didn't remember, approached the two. He vaguely overheard their conversation about food, and then the weather, and then food again. It was unimportant. He wasn't interrupting anything.

"Hey, guys. Um, you like to, well, *party?*"

"What's that?" asked William.

"You know, *par*ty?" He put two fingers to his lips and

sucked in air. "I can hook you up."

"Well now," William sounded neither interested nor disinterested.

Matt shrugged, stared straight into the stranger's eyes, and sighed. Tilting his head towards the sunset, he admitted "Never tried the stuff."

Printed in the United States
1254200002B/89